CHASING LIBERTY

THERESA LINDEN

PRAISE FOR CHASING LIBERTY

"… a futuristic look at what our culture might become if we keep on the same trajectory as we are presently heading. As in the books, 1984 and Brave New World, where the authors pointed to an extreme version of the worst elements in society, the danger is real, even if only in part. Such authors speak to us through fiction and remind us of an important truth about ourselves. In this case, humanity needs families to be fully human."

~Ann Frailey, author of *Last of Her Kind*

"Theresa Linden's prose is beautiful. This story is suitable for younger readers, perhaps age sixteen and up. Such books are needed these days, because Liberty's dilemma may end up becoming reality if Americans do not change course."

~Amazon review

"… my heart was in my throat. If you like dystopian, you'll love this book, but be forewarned it ends on a cliffhanger so you'll want to read the next one. I love how family and faith are so pivotal in this story and how horrible life becomes without them."

~Amazon review

"This is just a fantastic read from the first page until the last."

~Amazon review

"It is a must read as this book takes you further in what happens to a society that is government run than the book Agenda 21 by Harriet Parke and Glenn Beck."

~Joe Goldner, co-host at The Truth Is Out There-Voice of the People Radio Show!

BOOKS BY THERESA LINDEN

CHASING LIBERTY TRILOGY

Chasing Liberty

Testing Liberty

Fight for Liberty

WEST BROTHERS SERIES

Roland West, Loner

Life-Changing Love

Battle for His Soul

Standing Strong

NEW ADULT FICTION

Anyone But Him

SHORT STORIES

"Bound to Find Freedom"

"A Symbol of Hope"

"Made for Love" (in the anthology *Image and Likeness: Literary Reflections on the Theology of the Body*)

"Full Reversal" (in the anthology *Image and Likeness: Literary Reflections on the Theology of the Body*)

"The Portrait of the Fire Starters" (in the anthology *Secrets: Visible and Invisible*)

CHASING LIBERTY

www.theresalinden.com
Print ISBN-13: 978-0-9968168-0-9
eBook ISBN: 978-0-9968168-1-6
First Edition: Linden Publishing, September 2015
Second Edition: Silver Fire Publishing, June 27, 2018

Cover: Theresa Linden
Editor: Katrina Haritos

DEDICATION

To my family, friends, and every faith-filled American.

1

"Your name?" The psychiatric technician, a shorthaired redhead in her thirties, glanced at the wall where a series of green LEDs showed the recorder and other devices in working order. She sat across from me at a square table in a dimly-lit, pale gray room the size of a closet, the blandness of it all a precursor to my future.

"You know my name." All emotion had left me days ago, and my tone reflected it.

The technician smiled, her eyes narrowing with a look that showed she hadn't expected my cooperation. Leaning towards me, she grabbed my hand with unnecessary force and dragged it over the ID implant reader in the center of the table.

I winced. They had said it wouldn't hurt a bit to reinstall the implant.

My information flashed on a small screen next to the reader. "For the record, I am interviewing Liberty 554 dash 062466 dash 84 of Aldonia." As the technician spoke, she faced the wall with the LEDs, though the microphones in the room would no doubt pick up the slightest whisper. Every word we uttered would end up transcribed by a voice-activated writing program.

I dragged my arm back to my side of the table. *My name is Liberty.* The numbers stood for the breeder facility in which I was born, the date of my birth, and my place in the total number of births for that year. One hundred twenty-seven live births per year were permitted in that particular facility. It was a precise number, determined by teams of scientists and environmentalist who had in mind the amount of resources available for quality of life, the needs of the people, and the amount of damage that the earth would inevitably sustain from our existence.

It has been this way for generations. We were a society that cared for the earth, balancing resource consumption with replacement initiatives, unavoidable pollution with clean-environment efforts. Before this time, people had been the earth's worst enemies.

"Why do you think you are here, Liberty?" The woman blinked her overly made-up eyes.

Ours was a responsible society. All contributed and all were cared for. I don't know why I had always found myself so dissatisfied.

The woman reached into the bag at her feet and brought out a notebook, a box of pencils, and my pocketknife. She slid them across the table.

I chuckled under my breath. The items belonged to me. They must've found my hiding place.

"You will use these for your first stage of re-education. You will write your story, explaining everything that happened to you from the day you first came across these." She tapped the notebook. "You will include the reasons for your behaviors, the things that motivated you."

I met her gaze.

She smiled with a sincerity that reminded me of my favorite preschool nanny. "This is not a punishment. It is a form of therapy, a way of cleansing, purging destructive ideas from your mind. A team of Re-Ed specialists and I will help you move through the stages of re-education. They may at times seem difficult, even unbearable, but our methods are very successful. We will help you to re-evaluate your past choices and ideologies."

Her eyebrows and forehead wrinkled. She stretched her arms across the table as if she thought I might take her hands. "We will help you be satisfied with life in our society."

I was glad she didn't say *happy*. I may complete their program and re-enter society, but I would not be happy. I believed what she said, though, that their methods were effective. We'd all seen people returned to society after Re-Ed. I couldn't compare them to their past selves. They relocated graduates to distant cities to avoid renewing harmful relationships. Re-educated people tended to have distant, unemotional gazes. Their smiles lacked sincerity and they moved through life at a relaxed pace that surpassed the typical citizen's leisurely pace. Few dared ask what happened in Re-Ed. Graduates never spoke of it. I would find out soon enough. This first stage seemed harmless.

I slid the box of pencils closer.

She nodded and withdrew her arms. "Write everything you remember, retelling in chronological order all that happened to you, beginning with the incident of the bunker."

I tapped a pencil from the box, one of the few pencils that I had previously sharpened. I remembered how my hands ached as I taught myself to write. I looked at her and sort of laughed. "Writing my story will take more paper and pencils than this."

"Yes." She stared as if trying to read my mind.

I glanced under the table. The bag at her feet may have held more supplies, but I couldn't tell. I looked at her again. "I'm quite proficient on a keypad."

"Yes, we know."

"You really expect me to write this by hand? You're using a voice activated writing program." Dropping the pencil, I jerked a thumb at the wall with the panel and the green LEDs.

"It was pencil and paper that set you down the wrong path, Liberty. Pencil and paper will redeem you."

Biting back a sarcastic reply, I crossed my arms and slouched down in the chair. I would accept this willingly because of the promises they had made me. I would need to leave out a few details so as not to put others in jeopardy, but I would do this because many that I cared about would be given a chance. They would not be forced into re-education programs. They would be permitted to join our communities in good faith, allowed to prove that they can adjust to life under the Regimen Custodia Terra without intervention.

The Regimen would probably need to adjust the number of births permitted at breeding facilities for a few years. They would generate a workable formula. It was just a matter of calculations. I hoped they would not separate the families. I couldn't imagine how devastating that would be, especially for the children. They did not permit me to know the details of their integration. They only gave me a promise. I hoped they would keep their word.

I picked up the pencil again. "You'll keep your word, won't you?"

2

I brought my shovel down hard. Metal rang against metal with a hollow sound that carried in the hot summer night over this grassy plain between the outskirts of Aldonia and the impassable boundaries. The sound echoed in my mind, like a warning or a wake-up call. An unfamiliar feeling sparked within me and every hair on my body stood at attention.

The feeling . . . *Secrets made known. Cages bursting open. Walls coming down. Chains broken. Light piercing the darkness. Waters and sky, pure and endless.*

Before I could lift my shovel again, the presence within me, the one I think of as *My Friend*, made Himself known. My eyelids flickered. I shut them as I tried to attend him. *My Friend* did not communicate in words, so it took effort to understand Him. Often, it took days. Sometimes understanding would come when I was not seeking it, when I least expected it. His message, this time, came easily. It was connected to the feeling.

There would be something special, even life changing, about this discovery.

I had come out here with the others reluctantly, expecting to regret my decision. But now I was glad. And the feeling inside me, I now realized, was hope.

Tatum stopped digging and climbed out of a hole two meters from mine. She squatted by the hole I had made and stared at the crumbling ground through wide-eyes. "What'd you hit?"

"Something big." I stood on the slope of a meter-deep hole, loose dirt all around and trickling into my boots. The spark that struck out when my shovel first hit metal now kindled into flame with the conviction that there had been and could be again another way of life than the one in which I presently found myself trapped. "Let's keep digging," I said.

"Could there be a mineral deposit out here?" Tatum picked up her shovel and jumped back into the hole she had started. When we had first come out here, Finley, the leader of our expedition, used a metal detector to show us where to start digging. Tatum should hit metal soon.

"Or maybe a tank from the wars we learned about in History?" she said. "Or some kind of old machine or a hidden treasure?"

I laughed. "I don't know. Keep digging."

As I cleared more dirt, my shovel scraping metal, the others quieted their loud, obnoxious conversation and turned to look at us. The four of them, Finley, Sid, Darin, and Silver, sat on the ground around Finley's industrial flashlight, shadows and blue light playing on their faces, Silver's wild hair looking almost metallic. They had all wanted to come out here, couldn't stop boasting about how brave they were and how wicked it would be to sneak out to these grounds. Once we got here, their tone changed. Darin had brought a cooler and as he cracked it open, their curiosity and sense of adventure fizzled, just like that. So Tatum and I had taken up the shovels. I didn't care. I liked physical work.

"Told you, Liberty." Finley jumped up, passed his bottle to Sid and came over. He looked from me to Tatum to Silver and the guys, shadows filling the deep creases on either side of his big grin. "Told you there was something out here." Still grinning, as he usually was, he reached for my shovel.

I yanked it back, giving him a cold glare. "I finish what I start."

He smirked as if some lewd thought had come into his mind. He knew that lewd talk and insinuations really got my goat, and he must've really wanted the shovel, because then his expression turned to one of innocent pleading. He even frowned. "Come on. Just let me have it for a minute."

I relinquished the shovel with an air of authority and climbed out of the hole. We had only started digging twenty minutes ago, but I had worked up a good sweat, so I aired out the front of my shirt to cool myself.

Sid had his eyes all over me while he downed whatever Finley had been drinking. "If you knew something was out here," he said to Finley, "why didn't you guys dig it up?"

"No way, man." Finley scraped the shovel against the underground metal structure. Then he stopped and said, half-laughing, "We'd done enough work for one day. Some of those guys on my team are lazy."

"Some of them, huh? Not you?" Sid tossed the empty bottle over his shoulder. He and Silver got up at the same time. He wiped at the seat of his pants while she flexed her arm muscles. Darin grabbed another bottle and rested one arm on the cooler.

"Hey, I'm not lazy." As if to prove his point, Finley set himself to digging while he spoke. "I brought you dudes out here, didn't I? Besides, we had a big mess to clean up today. Motorcycle hit an old storage shed and flipped over the fence." He gave a nod to indicate the damaged chain-length fence we had climbed over to get here. "Junk went everywhere. Took forever to clean it all up. Boss made us scan the whole area with a metal detector. Don't know what he thinks. Nobody going to step on scrap out here."

I had three reasons for not wanting to come here with these guys. First one: Sid. He had an attraction to me that bordered on obsessive.

Second reason: I shared little in common with these guys. Tatum was my roommate, though not by choice, and Finley her boyfriend. The others were their friends. I didn't like their destructive forms of entertainment or their contented attitudes. I was not content.

My third reason: The stretch of land inside the seven-meter high, electric Boundary Fence was off limits, though the law was not strictly enforced. If a ball or something happened to fly out here, one could retrieve it. But no one wanted to get caught hanging out here. The thought of the consequence was always in mind.

I finally agreed to go with them because I liked the idea of doing something behind the Regimen's back. Plus, Finley had assured us we wouldn't get caught.

"So you guys realized something was out here and just went home for the day?" Sid sounded as though he couldn't believe it, but we all knew the work ethics of the Environmental Stewardship Units. They didn't like to overexert themselves.

"Hey . . ." Finley stopped digging and leaned on the handle of the shovel, a crooked smile on his face. "That cleanup took a long time. To start digging, we would've had to go for equipment, mark off the area, get more help . . . It takes a while to get started. So we submitted a Work Order instead."

Sid laughed. "A Work Order? Now you have to get Regimen permission to dig?" He came up to me, looking me over in a way that made my skin crawl.

Unlike most girls my age, almost twenty, I intentionally dressed in plain, even ugly clothing. Today I had on an oversized shirt, tan workpants, and a work belt full of tools. I wore my hair pulled back and never wore makeup. Not wanting the attention of others, I did nothing to attract it. Sid must've had an imagination, though, or he considered me a challenge.

After giving Sid a harsh glare, I turned my attention to Finley.

Finley shrugged and thrust the shovel into the ground. "Could take months to get through the proper channels. Could be months before the ESU gets back out here." He glanced at Sid. "That's why I thought *we* could check it out. Maybe there's something interesting underground. Whatever we find, we can take. No one will even know."

Silver crushed out a cigarette and sauntered to the hole Tatum was digging. There she stood, head cocked to one side and hands on her hips, towering over skinny, little Tatum down in the hole. Tatum stopped digging and peeked up. Silver stuck out her hand. Tatum, a girl who seemed to feel the need to please everyone, climbed out of the hole and gave up her shovel. Silver jumped in.

Tatum brushed dirt off her arms and came to stand by me. "Do you hear that?"

At this hour of night, in this part of the city, crickets and an occasional bark of a dog or the sound of someone shouting made the only sounds. So the whir of distant sirens caught my attention immediately. While still some distance away, they were coming closer.

My heartbeat quickened. I nodded and scanned the area. If they came for us, where could we hide?

With the awkward movements of a drunk, Darin got to his feet and tossed the bottle he had been holding. "Hey, we should, like, get out of here." Facing the outskirts of Aldonia, swaying a little, he peered into the night.

Floodlights on a warehouse shone like eyes over the shadowy shed and other structures by the chain-length fence. Hundreds of moving points of light, cars and scooters on a freeway, looking like a ribbon of fireflies, glowed in the distance. A deep orange glow from city lights in the densely populated areas colored the night sky at the horizon.

"Don't worry," Finley said, still shoveling. "They're not coming for us. I got us here unnoticed. I'm sure of it. I told you, I know which surveillance cameras work and which are down. That's our job."

"Don't you replace them?" Though he was talking to Finley, Sid still stared at me. He must have thought my coming along tonight was a good sign for him.

"Sure, but it takes time." Finley grinned. "Last place a camera would've caught us was the strip of nightclubs we passed through. I'm sure about the route we took. It was a carefully orchestrated route. Why do you think we went down so many crazy streets and alleys, zigzagging our way here? You can trust me."

"I don't trust you," Sid said. "Besides, they can easily check the location of any one of us." He tapped the flexi-phone on his wrist and then glanced at my belt. Most people wore their phones on their wrists, the way they were designed to be worn. I wore mine on my belt, but I always had it with me. We all did. You had to. They did a Roll Call at least once day. Your phone had to be within so many meters of your ID implant. If it wasn't, they put you on a list. Get on the list too many days in a row and you'd have problems, consequences. Nobody wanted those consequences.

Darin staggered toward the chain-length fence, weaving around clumps of grass as if he thought they would trip him up. But when Silver's shovel hit metal he stopped.

My heart leaped. We were getting closer to discovery.

With a look of satisfaction in her eyes, Silver scraped the shovel against the metal, cleaning away dirt. Then she stooped and brushed it with her hands. "Sounds hollow, like a bunker."

"A bunker? Like a bomb shelter?" Tatum said. "I remember learning about those in school, when we studied the time of wars. I wonder how big a bunker is. We could dig all night and not find the way in." She turned to me, her heavily made-up eyes having a cat-like appearance in the moonlight.

"Let's find out." I went to where the guys and Silver had been sitting in the grass. Finley's metal detector lay beside the flashlight that cast a beam of light on the two diggers. I snatched it up, turned it on, and swept the search head over the ground as I walked back toward the others. Two meters from the diggers, the detector started beeping and the display on the control box flashed a code that I didn't understand. I moved away from the diggers, heading toward the great Boundary Fence barely visible in the dark. After going about a dozen meters, the beeping ceased. I stopped.

Silver and Finley continued digging, but the other three watched me.

"I'd say it's about fifteen by three meters," I shouted as I started back to them. "You guys are digging near the end. If the door's not there, maybe it's at the other end, or in the middle."

Silver and Finley stopped digging at the same time. They exchanged a glance and climbed out of the holes that they had widened considerably in their short time at it.

"Where's the middle?" Silver had a threatening tone to her voice, as if she blamed me for her wasted effort. She walked up to me, coming to stand too close, and glared down her wide nose at me. Silver worked at one of the health facilities in Aldonia as a personal trainer, but she used the equipment more than she helped others to use it, as her exaggerated muscular physique proved.

Glad to move away from her, I went to where I figured the halfway point was. "Here. The middle is here." I spoke with confidence, though I couldn't be sure. If the door wasn't here, Silver would probably take it out on me. She had a problem controlling her temper.

Silver came to the point I indicated, and I backed out of the way. "We'll try the middle first," she said. With a two-handed grasp, she brought the shovel up and stabbed the ground as if she were slaying a mythical dragon. Her hair flew about her face and the muscles of her arms rippled as she attacked the earth. Finley dug too, but not with the same vigor, though I gathered he worked harder than usual.

Tatum, Sid, and I stood back and watched. As the sirens grew louder, Darin stood spellbound, facing Aldonia. Once they quieted, he staggered to the flashlight and then came to stand by us with the flashlight and his cooler in hand. Within a few minutes, the diggers hit metal. Less than an hour later, they had a hole two meters square and a meter or so deep.

I dived in and helped, brushing dirt from the structure with my hands. Before long, we had it all cleared off.

A hatch door. It was about one square meter of solid steel with a single long handle breaking up its smooth surface.

"Let's do it." Finley flung his shovel and grabbed the handle. He tugged but the door didn't budge.

Silver shoved him aside and gave it a try, her triceps rippling at the effort. It still didn't budge. She straightened up.

"It's locked," Finley said.

"Obviously," Silver said through gritted teeth.

I laughed. The tension that these people generated killed me.

Cussing, Silver climbed out of the hole and snatched the flashlight from Darin. Darin had been lying on his tummy and peeking over the edge, shining the light for us while we worked. He mumbled a protest as she stomped off, but he wouldn't have wanted her to hear it. Silver could eat him alive if she wanted to.

"Now what?" Tatum said.

I ran my fingers over the hatch door and found a little metal plate. The plate swung aside revealing a keyhole. "Anybody know how to pick a lock?"

Sid slid into the hole and squatted beside me. I thought he was checking me out again, the way his eyes roved over me, but then he said, "What've you got on that belt?"

"Not a lock pick," I said. "Just ordinary tools."

"Got a small screwdriver?"

I gave him the only screwdriver I had, but we could both see it was too big.

As he handed it back, someone above shouted, "Charge!" in a wild voice. Darin glanced over his shoulder and shouted, "Look out!" before scooting away from the hole.

I dove to the far side of the hole, rolling up onto my feet. Sid and Finley backed into the dirt wall.

Silver flew into the hole, holding something overhead. With one fluid motion and a loud grunt, she brought it down onto the hatch door with a bang.

We all stood there, stunned, gawking at her. But she had done it. She broke the lock upon impact, with a big stone.

She gave a self-satisfied grin and yanked open the hatch door. "Get the flashlight," she hollered as she descended into darkness. The woman, apparently, had no fear.

~~~

We followed Silver down a rung ladder into the darkness of the bomb shelter, Finley first. As I climbed down, Finley shouted, "Put that out! Are you crazy?"

Silver stood about four meters away, the flame of a lighter flickering in front of her face, Finley dashing for her. He had the flashlight, anyway, so we didn't need her little flame.

"What if there are explosive fumes down here?" He snatched the lit cigarette from her and crushed it under his boot.

She grabbed him by the shirt and slammed him against a big metal cabinet. "Pushing your luck, boy." She ripped the flashlight from his hand and shined it around. "If there were fumes, we would've blown up already. I flicked my lighter as I came down."

Tatum stood by the ladder, rubbing her arms and staring up at the open hatch. "Where's Darin? Isn't he coming down?"

Sid shook his head. "He's afraid of enclosed places. Finley has him filling in the holes you girls made."

The bunker went back about six or seven meters on either side of the ladder. Silver and Finley went to one side, Sid the other. He motioned for me to follow.

"I didn't know Darin was claustrophobic," I said.
~~~

"Darin has a lot of problems. Sees a shrink every month. Takes a lot of medications. Not everybody's perfect . . ." Sid looked me up and down. ". . . like you."

I didn't justify the comment with a response. I sure wasn't perfect. Granted, Regimen representatives thought I had the ideal physical constitution and intellect for my future vocation, but they found grave fault in my personality and ideals.

Silver investigated the other side of the bunker, moving slowly, the beam from the flashlight causing shadows to stretch and shift around us. Three bunk beds lined the walls on this side, the lower halves stuffed with big pillows and looking like couches. The upper beds bulged with clear plastic cubes of blankets and linen. Several square, flat light fixtures hung from the ceiling. Maybe they worked. Maybe I could find a—

"Is that why you always turn me down?" Sid stood behind me, speaking over my shoulder.

I jumped inside but pretended I saw something I needed to check out. I did in fact see something, now that I had lunged forward. It looked like a switch there on the back wall.

Sid followed me. "I'm not good enough for you?" He spoke low, his voice deep and smooth.

Reaching the far wall, I swept my hand across the switch. There came a click and a humming sound, then a flicker of light and —light! From one end of the bunker to the other, we had light.

Everyone let out a gasp of delight.

Industrial carpet covered the floor. Finley had the far end of it lifted up. He said something to Tatum, who then took hold of it while he squatted. Silver lifted the lid of a storage bench and started talking to herself, sounding pleased.

Sid still stared at me, his expression sullen.

"Don't you think this is cool? Doesn't it make you wonder whose it was? How old it is? What is was used for?" *What significance did the bunker hold for me?*

I tried to step around him, wanting to explore the other half with everyone else, but he blocked me. I met his gaze. "Look, Sid, don't take it personal. I'm just not interested in getting with anyone. It's not you.

You're a nice enough guy." I had to concentrate on keeping a sincere expression. In my estimation, he wasn't a nice guy. In fact, I had always felt he had something evil deep inside. He was selfish, for sure, but so was almost everyone I knew. I guess I was selfish, too. It's the way we were all raised. *If you want something, take it. If it feels good, do it.*

"I'm not hot enough for you?" He moved in and took my hand, gazing at me through lustful eyes. "I could make you happy."

I backed up, wrestling my hand free. Sid had appeal, in his own way. As a roofer, he had developed a tone, muscular body and deep caramel skin. Wavy black hair and thick brows accentuated his stormy blue eyes. While a hand taller than me, he reminded me of a teenager because of his round face and inability to grow more than a hint of stubble on his chin and upper lip.

Sid leaned toward me, his eyes on my mouth.

Something on the other side of the bunker made a hard click sound. I shoved Sid back and moved past him. "Come on. Let's see what's over there."

Several tall metal cabinets lined one wall, an odd stove and cupboards lined the other. Silver hovered over the open storage bench, a long brown rifle in her hands. "Check this out," she said as I approached. "Ever see anything like it?"

It was nothing like the black military-grade rifles with the scopes and accessories that the Regimen's Unity Troopers carried.

"It's so primitive." Silver brought the butt of the rifle up to her shoulder and peered down the barrel.

"You look natural with a rifle," I said.

She gave me a nod and a satisfied grin. "I've always wanted to work for the Unity Troopers."

"I've always wanted to be a mechanic." I put a hand to my work belt.

She gave a nod and returned her attention to the stockpile of weapons in the storage bench.

"People should be able to choose what they want to do," I said. "It's not right that the Regimen tells us."

While wrapping her fingers around the grip of a pistol, Silver gave me a sideways glance. "You'd better watch yourself. Don't want to get caught talking like that."

No one seemed to have a problem with breaking laws, all sorts of laws, but everyone worried about what you said. Disgusted, I shook my head and walked to the farthest end of the bunker, to where Finley had been.

Tatum crouched by an open panel in the floor. The carpet was folded back and Finley's voice came from somewhere below. Tatum glanced as I approached.

"What's down there?" I said.

"Looks like big drums of water and stuff," Tatum said.

"Power generator and purification systems," Finley said, straightening up. His headed popped out of the hole in the floor. Then he climbed out. "Some first-aid stuff, too, bandages and medications. It's really old. I'm sure none of it is good."

Sid stood before an open metal cabinet, shoving things into his pants pockets.

I picked a cabinet and lifted the latch.

Cans of food in neat little rows filled the shelves. Beans, potatoes, carrots, fruit, hash . . . lots of hash. This was someone's emergency food stash. How many people could live off this food and for how long? Whose bunker was this, and what had become of them? Tatum was probably right: this was a bunker from the time of the wars. It was a time, we were told, when every man was for himself. This bunker would have been built for an individual or several people so they could hide from the chaos of the warring world, or from the government. It saddened me to realize they never got the chance.

Something purple on the bottom shelf caught my eye. Someone had stuffed a big bag on top of the cans. I pulled the bag out. It was a backpack. It took some effort to unzip it, but I found cool things inside: a purple brush, a box of multi-colored beads, a tiny flag with red stripes and white stars on a blue square, a picture in a frame, a notebook, and a box of pencils.

I recognized the notebook and pencils because we had learned about them in school. I had seen pictures of them on a computer, but I had never seen the real things. The pages of the notebook were a bit crinkled and yellowed. Someone had drawn on the inside cover of the notebook, a childish picture of a little girl in a dress and a big hat. The name *Emily* had been scrawled under the picture in big, sloppy letters. I ran my finger along the strangely-shaped letters. Emily, whoever she was, probably wrote this herself. She had written it with a pencil.

"Let me have that." Silver stood over me, a hand reaching down, a gun at her side.

"What?" I couldn't imagine her wanting anything I had before me.

"The backpack." She stooped, swiping it up as she answered me. She turned it upside down and let its contents crash to the industrial carpet on the floor. "I'm taking guns."

"Aren't you worried you'll get caught?" I knew she wasn't. I only said it because it amazed me how easily people broke laws, yet they wouldn't dare utter a word contrary to Regimen views.

Tatum came over to me, her eyes on Silver who stooped over the storage bench stuffing pistols into the purple backpack. "She can't take those out of here."

"Watch me." Silver didn't even glance. She just kept sorting through guns, examining pistols, grabbing cartridges . . .

"Citizens aren't allowed to have guns," Tatum whispered, her cat eyes open wide.

I shrugged. "Silver's not your ordinary citizen." I went to the next cabinet and found plastic dishes, big boxes of plastic bags, a fire extinguisher, and pans.

The distant whir of a siren sounded through the open hatch door. I kept looking through things, expecting Darin to peek his head down into the hole and warn us. Minutes passed, the siren grew louder, and he still hadn't shown. Maybe he had taken off. He never seemed like one to take a risk for others.

I took the box of pencils, the framed picture, and the notebook. "I'm out of here," I said, loud enough for everyone to hear. It was getting late, anyways.

"Those sirens aren't for us," Finley said. He and Sid were stuffing tools into a black leather bag. "I told you that the route I took—"

"I don't care." The box of pencils fit nicely in my tool belt, but I had to shove the notebook into my waistband, and I'd just have to carry the picture. "We'll have to get back by curfew. If we leave now, we'll have just enough time."

"Wait for us." Finley shoved one last item into the bag and slung the strap over his shoulder. "You don't want to get spotted on the surveillance cameras. We'll have to go back the way we came."

3

I left for work early so I could take an alternate route down streets and alleys that Finley had shown us last night, streets without working cameras. I had no reason for doing this, except that it gave me a feeling of freedom to think that the Regimen couldn't watch me even if they wanted to. Of course, I did have my phone . . . and the ID implant . . . They could track me. If they wanted to, they could send Unity Troopers—

I adjusted my purse strap, took a deep breath, and let it out slowly. They couldn't watch me. That was enough for the moment.

Older apartments rose up around me in this city of concrete, glass, and metal, towering brick structures with balconies and barred, ground-floor windows. A shirtless man on a fourth-floor balcony eyed me as I passed. Broken glass crunched under my feet. A few bicycles raced by. Clouds drifted overhead, aimlessly following the laws of nature, gloriously unaffected by the laws of man.

What had life been like at the time the bunker was built? It had six beds, probably for six specific people. Who were they? What fear prompted them to build it? Why hadn't they used it?

Movement a stones-throw away, between the corner of the apartment building I just passed and one of the few remaining inner-city trees, caught my eye.

I turned my head but before I could think, the whirr of a motor scooter sounded behind me. Close. Too close.

I spun around and jumped back.

The scooter hopped onto the sidewalk, coming closer, the driver laughing. Heading for me—

Heart in my throat, I dove and landed on my shoulder on the hard ground.

By the time I rolled to a squatting position, the scooter had gone. It turned down an alley between shops across the street.

I got to my feet, heart thumping wildly, and made a quick scan of my surroundings. The man on the fourth floor had gone inside. Nothing moved by the corner of the building. The only people outside, that I saw, were too far to notice the incident, or too bored to care.

I hated this feeling, that I was being followed, though it wasn't a new one. The many ways in which the Regimen monitored us probably gave others besides me a certain level of paranoia. I often found myself glancing over my shoulder with nothing more than an impression of danger. Sometimes I passed through areas I knew to have high crime levels just to give myself a reason for feeling this way.

My purse had fallen, so I swiped it up, glad that the kid on the motor scooter hadn't wanted it. He would've been disappointed. I carried nothing of value to anyone but myself. No new 3D game, no candy, no illegal drugs.

Slinging the strap over my shoulder, I continued on my way.

I wanted to bring the notebook and pencils to Abby, but I couldn't stuff them into my uniform. Abby liked to talk about her childhood, when no one else was near us, when her flexi-phone was a good distance away, and when not sitting under the eye of a camera. Pencil and paper might have been before her time, but she would appreciate them.

I turned off the residential street and came to a row of shops and bars with bricks peeking from behind missing slats of dusty siding. Teens rested against storefronts, looking like they had no purpose in life. I took an alley that looked familiar, no longer sure if it was one Finley had taken us down. Two men stood in an open doorway. A few bicycles leaned against a brick wall.

Stepping from the shade of the alley, I came to a sunny street of buses and scooters. Pedestrians crowded the sidewalks. A line of people stood outside the Betterment Office. The smiling face of the president, painted on the side of a three-story clothing manufacturer building, watched me join the crowd. All the security cameras worked on this street, Finley had said.

I neared the Senior Living and Recreation Center but had to squint to see it. The high glass wall of its façade reflected sunlight, blinding all who dared look at it.

As I stepped through the doors of the center, my nerves calmed and I exhaled. A group of people stood in a circle at the far end of the lobby, their voices carrying. I couldn't make out faces, but I recognized the high-pitched voice of my boss.

Colorful abstracts on huge canvases hung on the walls that separated the sunny lobby from the activity rooms. I always found myself gazing up at them, finding in the vibrant reds and blues a way to transition my dissatisfied, negative attitude into one of joy. I didn't want to share my gloomy disposition with the elderly. Everyone here had struggled through a life of service to the Regimen. They had faced their share of troubles and suffering. They'd survived to at least age seventy-five, the age of retirement. They deserved a kind word or a smile, at the least, from the workers in this place. The Regimen Custodia Terra promised a place of rest and relaxation to everyone at the end of their service.

"Liberty."

A smile came to my face as if by impulse as I spun to face the old man who called my name — Richter. Dressed in a sleek charcoal-gray suit and hat, blue eyes bulging from under wild gray brows on his mocha-colored face, and with a smile that stirred my heart, he walked toward me in the sunlight that streamed in through the wall of glass.

I hugged him and took a deep breath, relaxing even more. "Hi, old man."

He transferred his cane to his left hand and grabbed my hand with his right, turning me toward the tall doors of Activity Room B. "How's my Liberty?"

I linked my arm with his as we strolled. "As happy as the Regimen allows." I chuckled though I knew he wouldn't respond; his blue eyes held a distant look. "What're you doing out here? Waiting for someone?"

"Me? No." His brows and mustache lifted and fell as he spoke. "Just getting some exercise. Got to keep healthy, you know."

I smiled, but I knew all right. It broke my heart when someone got sick and had to go to the RCT Hospital. Too many never came back.

"Something I ate last night not sitting right today. Thought maybe I could walk it off."

"Maybe you need a shot of whiskey to settle your stomach."

He chuckled. "Maybe I do. Not allowed. Doctor says it's no good for me." He lifted the hand with the cane as if he thought the ID chip under his skin was visible. The unspoken message being that he couldn't get alcohol legally. No bartender or liquor store salesperson would scan his chip and approve such a purchase.

I held open the door for him.

He nodded as he passed. "Don't you work too hard, now, Liberty. Pace yourself like those other kids do. Ain't a one of them work near as hard as you."

"I like to keep busy. Besides, serving you guys isn't work to me."

He chuckled and kissed my cheek. "You are one fine girl, Liberty. This world doesn't deserve you. One fine girl." He transferred his cane back to his right hand as he walked away.

Richter headed for the table of his friends. The tables had video games built into them. To activate them, one simply had to touch a screen. But these men preferred old-fashioned, hands-on games like chess, dice, cards, and other games of chance. A newcomer stood, hands on hips, watching the men play.

I weaved through the seating arrangement, three couches and four rockers around a coffee table, mouthing, "Hello," to the women sitting there, the early birds. No one had brought them coffee or tea yet.

Abby sat alone at one of the round tables on the other side of the room, a coffee mug in her hands, her eyes holding a distant, somewhat mournful gaze. Her friends wouldn't be here for another hour. She typically woke earlier than the others, took a stroll around the building, and made herself tea.

She didn't seem to notice me as I pulled out the chair across from her.

"Good morning, Abby." I couldn't help but smile when I was with her, though she never smiled back. Over the past four years of my service here, she had grown on me more than anyone else had. When I went home for the day, I honestly missed her.

Abby straightened up, blinked, and then focused on me. "Oh, are you here already?" The blue-green of her eyes matched the color of her abstract-patterned shirt. She glanced at the digital clock on the wall, its big glowing letters showing that I was a few minutes early. "I'm always glad to see you, then I know those bums will soon be leaving." She snorted and threw a sideways glance at the three guys, the housekeeping crew, loitering in the doorway of the kitchen.

One of them, Nyeb, brought a cigarette up to his mouth. Catching my glance, he sneered as if challenging me to report him for violating the rules. Smoking was forbidden in most places, public or private. The other two boys turned to peer at me, but their gazes snapped to the clock and they started peeling off their gray work-coats.

I returned my attention to Abby, slung my purse onto the table, and reached inside. "I have something for you."

"I wondered why you had a purse, and such a big one." She pushed her empty coffee mug aside and rubbed her fingers together as if they had something on them.

After glancing to each side, I pulled out the notebook and pack of pencils. I slid them across the table to her.

She gave me a funny look. "Where did you find these?"

I thought it best not to answer that question. "Have you ever used things like this, I mean to write, you know, when you were little?"

"How old do you think I am?" Her mouth tightened, wrinkles forming all around it.

"Well, I don't know. I thought maybe when you were a little girl . . ."

She ran her hand down the smooth cover of the notebook and then opened it. Her eyes twinkled when she saw the childish picture inside. "I may have. Can't say I remember. Only used computers in Primary and Secondary. Perhaps before I was admitted to the children's facility . . ." She lifted the notebook to her nose and inhaled. I had smelled it too, last night. It had a musty scent.

"I thought you might like to have it." I shoved the box of pencils to her. "And these."

She picked up the box and opened the lid. "They're not sharpened. What am I going to do with those?" She slid the pencils and notebook back to me. "Even if I could remember how, I can't write with these old hands." She massaged her right hand then glanced over her shoulder before saying, "They keep tingling, falling asleep on me."

"Maybe you should get that checked out."

Her eyes shot to mine. She shook her head and her forehead flinched. She never wanted to see a doctor. "I'll go when they demand I go," she always said.

"Well, it could be something little. Something medicine can cure."

The look in her eyes showed she worried about the alternative. She gave another shake of her head and returned her gaze to the notebook. "Besides, you're young. You should use it. Write something secret." She actually smiled . . . a crooked, sneaky smile.

I laughed and slid the items back into my purse. Maybe I would try my hand at writing. No one would know what I wrote, unless I showed someone. That could prove liberating.

"Speaking of doctors," she said, "don't you have an appointment?"

"That's tomorrow." I made a face. I hated how often I had to check in, just because of my vocation.

"Has Vocational gotten back to you? About your request?"

Frowning, I shook my head. My stomach tensed whenever the subject came up. If I didn't find a way to control myself, my temper would spike and I'd start ranting.

"I'll get you more tea." I snatched her mug and pushed out my chair.

My thoughts soured as I headed for the kitchen. I had submitted form after form to the RCT Vocational Department, trying to get my vocation changed before it was too late, before I turned twenty. They denied me every time, but I couldn't give up. I loved fixing things and working with my hands. A few projects in Aldonia's East Secondary School had gotten me started. Once I turned sixteen and entered the working world, my love for hands-on, mechanical work blossomed. It took forever to get something around the apartment fixed, so I learned to do it myself. Neighbors had come to rely on me for help, too. My reputation spread through the area, presenting me with opportunities to exchange my handy services for goods that I wouldn't have been able to get through ordinary channels: work boots, tools, and my work belt among them.

The Regimen, however, had long ago decided my fate. Once I turned twenty, my vocation would begin and life as I knew it would end. I would live at and be unable to leave my vocational facility. I wouldn't be able to see Abby or any of my friends for the next five to ten years. Some girls envied me. I would live a life of luxury in a modern, well-maintained facility that overlooked the Fully-Protected Nature Preserves, chefs and massage therapists at my beckoning, entertainment according to my wishes.

Still . . . I did not want to be a breeder.

~~~

Heat up, already! While trying to block out the music, laughter, and loud voices of Tatum, Finley, Silver, and Sid in the living room, I stirred the soup that I had dumped into the last clean pan. I wanted to fix my dinner and take it to my room, where I would have some privacy and I could try my hand at writing. I had hung out at the Senior Recreation Center well after my shift ended, wanting to spend time with Abby before my dreaded vocation began. As the day drew near, my heart ached at the thought of not seeing her and many of the other seniors at the center. I felt more like myself around them than around anyone else.

When I left the center I had to stop at the Commissary and get my rations for the week. They had few fresh vegetables—something about crop damage on the other side of the continent—so they gave me canned foods this time. My big purse came in handy carrying it home.

"Well, no one would help me." Finley's voice was too loud to ignore. "I had to fill those holes all by myself."

"You lie." Sid's voice was soft, but I could tell he faced me as he spoke. "I helped."

I set the soupspoon down and took an apple to the sink.

"Hey, I was busy dragging Darin's dead weight around," Silver said. Then something went thud and someone grunted.

I forced myself not to look. If I did, they would include me in the conversation. I just wanted to get to my room.
~~~

They couldn't stop talking about last night. When we had climbed out of the bomb shelter, searchlights from a police car were sweeping the neighborhood. We couldn't see Darin anywhere. The holes Tatum and I had made hadn't been filled, though Finley had told Darin to do it. Sid found Darin hugging a shovel and passed out in one of the holes. We just wanted to scram, but Finley insisted we cover our tracks. No one maintained the stretch of land out there. Weeds, wild bushes, and clumps of tall grass grew sporadically, but if anyone were to look they might notice the holes. They might wonder about them.

Silver would not let Finley throw dirt on the bunker door. They fought about it, physically. She won. We ended up dragging branches and boards over to hide it. All the while, the Unity Troopers kept searching for someone. We worked as fast as we could, hoping they wouldn't come any nearer to us, hoping they wouldn't see us. They didn't. But by the time we finished, it was near curfew and we had to run to get back in time. The whole gang stayed the night, Finley in Tatum's room, Silver on the couch, Sid and Darin on blankets that were still on the living room floor.

I dried my hands on the kitchen towel, stirred the stew once more, picked up the apple, and reached for a knife. When I turned to the counter, I jumped. The knife bounced off the counter and tumbled to the floor.

Sid stood at the entrance to the kitchenette, leaning one shoulder against the wall, the dim overhead light throwing shadows on his tan, sulky face. "Is that scooter yours?"

I glanced at the knife on the floor and then at the scooter. "Mine? No. It's a neighbor's. I'm repairing it."

It was an older model, a grey and white Vespa with graffiti on the body. A few days ago, I parked it in the living room, between the couch and the door, a rather inconvenient location. I nearly knocked it over every time I came home, but I had nowhere else to put it. Tatum hadn't complained this time. She simply asked whose it was. I told her I'd have it out of here in no time. It only had clogged jets and a damaged vacuum line. I should've been working on it now.

"I see you walking everywhere. Never take the trolley, do you? Why don't you get your own ride?"

"Why don't you have one?" I leaned forward, about to stoop for the knife, but he leaned too, so I backed off.

He grinned and then squatted. "I will soon. I have connections." He straightened and handed me the knife, making sure our fingers touched as I took it. "I can get a deal for you."

"No thanks. I'll save and get one when I get out." I rinsed the knife and grabbed the apple.

"You gonna let me have some of that? Smells good."

"What'd you trade your food for?" I smirked and, with unnecessary force, chopped the apple in half.

Glaring, he pivoted on his shoulder and pushed off the wall. He must've taken my comment as an invitation to draw nearer. I regretted saying anything.

"I'll pay you back. Share with me tonight, and I'll make you dinner tomorrow."

"No, thanks." I didn't make eye contact, but I could feel his eyes drilling holes through me. Moving like an assembly worker, I snatched bowls from an overhead cupboard, slapped the apple slices into one, shut the stove off, and dumped the stew into another. After tossing the pan into the sink, I turned around.

Sid blocked my way. "I think Silver likes you." He sounded jealous.

"What?" I glanced into the other room.

Silver had Finley down on his knees. She squatted behind him, one arm wrapped around his neck. He wavered between his typical grinning expression and a bug-eyed look of panic while he clawed at her arm. Tatum wrapped her little hands around Silver's other meaty arm, trying to break it up.

"You like girls, is that what it is?" Sid's lower lip stuck out in a pouty way.

"No, I don't like girls." They had pounded it into us in school. Experiment with your sexuality. Be open, uninhibited, free. Long ago mores dictated sexual orientation and preferences. Certain things were not acceptable. People lived in fear and oppression if their attractions did not receive social favor. Those days have ended. *If it feels good, do it. If you want it, take it.*

It irritated them to no end that I didn't want it and wouldn't take it, and that I wouldn't experiment with my sexuality. It repulsed me to see how self-indulgently many behaved. I had questions and opinions about the natural order of things. They didn't want to hear it. Of course, once they had slated me for the vocation of breeder, their tone and dictates changed. I was among the few unsterilized, so I had to be careful.

"Then what is it?" Sid said. "You'll be off to that baby-maker facility in less than two weeks. Time's running out. Don't you want to see what it's like to get high? They'll never know." He stepped closer and whispered, "Don't you want to see what it's like to be with a guy?"

I slipped past him and set the bowl of apples on my arm so I could open my bedroom door, which was right next to the kitchenette.

He got the door for me and followed me into my bedroom.

I scooted between the wall and my bed, set the bowls on the nightstand and turned around. "Sorry, Sid, you'll have to get me out of your mind. We're not getting together."

"What about when you get out?"

"No."

He glanced at the ceiling and huffed. "You like guys, don't you?"

I took his arm and turned him to face the door. "You know, Sid, actually, I consider myself to be asexual." I shoved him through the doorway.

"Asexual? What's that?" he said as I closed the door in his face.

Voices traveled through the thin walls, and the room wasn't much bigger than my bed, but I was glad to be alone. I tasted the stew, dragged my purse from under the bed, and got out the picture, notebook and a sharp pencil. With a pocketknife, I had whittled nice, sharp points on three pencils as I strolled to the Commissary, all the while considering how I might make a pencil sharpener. During the day, at the Senior Center, I found myself writing on tabletops with my finger, trying to figure out how to form letters.

I grew increasingly excited about having a way to express my thoughts without the worry of getting caught. I could write words without having them tagged and evaluated by the Counter Terrorist Teams or the Citizen Safety Station, without getting on a list or getting counseling. I lost the few friends I had from high school because of messages we sent each other, because of ideas.

Cradling the bowl of stew, I scooted back on the bed and sat cross-legged. I set the framed picture from the bunker on my lap. A man and a woman stood next to a shed or building, three little children and a baby on the grass in front of them. The children came up no higher than the man's chest and appeared to range from ages four to ten or eleven.

That didn't make sense. If the picture had been taken at a primary residence, the older children wouldn't be there. If it had been taken at a secondary residence, the younger children wouldn't be there. Why wasn't the baby in a breeder facility? Babies remained in breeder facilities until age five. Then they transitioned to a primary residence.

I sipped a spoonful of the stew. Maybe the people in the picture didn't live in typical residences. Though we learned nothing of it at school, I had the impression that separate housing facilities for different age groups hadn't always been the norm. Who knew what life was like back when this picture was taken . . . back when these people lived?

My gaze rested on the girl in the picture. When I focused, I realized the girl had a name on her shirt: Emily.

The spoon slipped from my hand. Goosebumps came out on my arms.

There were six people in this picture. Six beds in the bomb shelter. It was *their* bomb shelter. I had the notebook that once belonged to the little girl in the picture. They were a *family*. Abby had mentioned *families* before. I would have to ask her about them again.

After finishing the stew and eating the rest of the apple, I slid to the floor and leaned against the bed. I closed my eyes and tried to focus on *My Friend.* There was something special in the discovery of the bunker. I had yet to understand it. Would He shed some light? I felt His presence but no inspiration, no warning, no clues. I would have to work on this puzzle alone for now.

I picked up the pencil and spent a few minutes scratching letters on the inside cover of the notebook, along the bottom edge. Then I tried to organize my thoughts. What should I write about? I hadn't much paper, and I didn't want to waste it. I would just write my thoughts, thoughts forbidden to express.

Finally, I put pencil to paper.

Every day, the walls close in a little more. The air in my apartment reeks of cigarettes, alcohol, and body odor. The music and voices are often so loud they push the thoughts from my head. I want to scream. And run. But there is nowhere to run to. Walls are everywhere.

I dare not speak my mind most of the time. My thoughts and ideas are hate-filled, a threat to society, I am told. Generations ago, others thought like me, generations ago when poverty, inequality, and hate destroyed our world. So I keep my thoughts to myself, but sometimes it makes me want to explode. If not for my one Friend, I would explode. I cannot be who I am because I do not agree with THEM. They, and all who go along with them, claim to have the answers to all life's questions. No one can think for himself, take his own risks, decide his own future. Whether I succeed or fail, I want the freedom to choose.

Finding paper and pencils in the bomb shelter, I hadn't known what release this would provide me. I feel like a mute given her voice. It feels good to put words to paper, to write. This is a new experience for me.

We are taught the keyboard in Primary. We learn letters by sight, sound, and by their location on the keyboard, so I can type almost as fast as I can form a sentence in my mind. It is turning out to be a challenge to write a sentence by hand. Writing by hand is awkward. For when I think of letters, of words, my fingers know which ones are needed and which way on the keyboard they must go. I don't think about my fingers at all as I type words and sentences and ideas. Though I am continually aware of the words I write and the message of my writing.

Now I must think of every aspect of writing, every word, every letter. How do I hold the pencil? How do I form the letter h, *the letter* g? *There is no spell-checker automatically cleaning up my mistakes, no grammar check to suggest a stronger sentence, no database to verify my facts and offer corrections.*

I have always been at the top of my class in school and better than my peers when it comes to typing. Most of the young adults I know have a primary-school ability on the keyboard. They have become dependent on speech-activated programs, creating messages and documents without lifting a finger. Many consider keyboarding an unnecessary skill now days. The voice-activated programs rarely misspell, correct grammar, and are even linked to vast databases that check facts instantly. We don't need to know much to create a college-level document.

There is software being developed that can create messages from thoughts. What then? Is that the future? Will we lose our ability to articulate, to speak, when our voices are no longer needed for communication? Will our thoughts, then, be monitored? Rebellious thoughts tagged, re-education enforced as it is now for messages that don't mesh with the government's ways? Hate crime? Can we lose the freedom of thought as we have the freedom of speech?

What had we lost when we lost our ability to write by hand? Our attention to detail, to nuances of line and pattern? Or have we transcended the burdensome requirements of primitive forms of communication? Could one ever have formed words by hand as quickly as one could keyboard them? Speak them? Think them? Surely not. Does speed of communication lead to intelligence of communication?

Writing by hand is private. No one knows of these words but me.

My bedroom door flew open and someone fell into my room laughing.

I dropped the pencil and shoved the notebook under the bed while turning to see who had invaded my shred of privacy. *Finley.* I would have to think of somewhere secret to keep my notebook.

4

Doctor Supero meant to reread the report he had begun to make, but his image reflecting in the sleek computer monitor caught his attention. His eyes with their pale violet irises ringed in black stared back at him. Sage, his last assistant, couldn't focus on her duties when in the same room as him. She found him attractive. What could he do about it? Women liked his eyes. They were striking.

He forced himself to focus on the patient file, to glance at the old man's holographic image rotating above the desktop, to reread the report. He did not enjoy this part of his job, though he understood the need for it. How should he word his professional recommendation? *The patient will have low quality of life even with the treatment that . . .*

Dr. Supero slammed his fist on the glassy surface of the computer desktop, causing his image on the connected monitor to jiggle. "Why should it come as any surprise to a seventy-five-year-old man—"

His words appeared in the report the instant he spoke them. He cursed the computer, leaned back, and breathed. He had to do this. Society depended upon people making tough choices. "Computer, erase that last line."

The words vanished.

He cleared his throat. "Should the patient receive the treatment previously detailed, the expected lifespan would not significantly—"

The door to his office slid open.

He swiveled his chair to face the door.

Ivy, the new, young, seemingly efficient but presently annoying assistant, sauntered into the room. She wore her green-streaked blonde hair in a bun today, not loose around her shoulders as she had worn it all week. Her shimmering eye make-up and gaudy white necklace accented her tight gray dress. Horridly bulky shoes shattered the otherwise enticing look.

Ivy never smiled, not that he'd noticed. She worked hard, whenever he was looking, but her ivy-green eyes seemed to hold contempt whenever she looked at him. Maybe she'd heard rumors about the last assistant.

Guilt tugged at his heart. It wasn't his fault.

She stopped a meter from him and glanced at her pocket-computer. "I received a file addressed to you, but I can't open it."

He stared in disbelief. Aldonians received their vocations based on their abilities. Putting on the nicest smile he could manage, he replied, "Ivy . . ." Her name came through clenched teeth. He relaxed his jaw. "You're my assistant. You came highly recommended, and you've proven to be quite capable so far." His grin turned into a grimace. "A file? You can't open a simple—"

"It's a locked file." Her green eyes flickered. "I'll need your personal password, or I'll have to forward it to your personal mailbox."

Teeth gritted, jaw set, he took a quick breath. He did not have time to pour through all the junk sent to his *personal* mailbox. He had been very clear in the interview. That was one of her duties as his—

"It's from the Department of Pathology."

His blood pressure plummeted. Stars filled his vision. The muscles in his face went limp. The Department of Pathology? The results of his biopsy? His hand shot to his head involuntarily. He smoothed his hair to give meaning to the reflexive movement.

"Good. Send it to my computer. That is fine." He spun his chair to face his work again, trying to look as unconcerned as possible, despite the pounding of his heart in his throat.

"Do you want your 9:15 shown to an exam room?"

His gaze drifted to his reflection in the monitor. Perhaps he should shave the beard. It, too, drew attention. He trimmed it to resemble a starburst, a black starburst with points stretching along his jaw and on either side of his mouth. One under his bottom lip. He had first grown it a dozen years ago to give himself an air of maturity, of authority. He needed it no longer. He had risen to the position of Head Physician of the entire facility. He sat on several boards. The Governor of Aldonia's own staff often consulted him.

"Doctor Supero? Your 9:15?"

He glanced at her over his shoulder, glanced at her hard green eyes. "My 9:15?"

"Liberty 554-062466-84 of Aldonia." Ivy hadn't even glanced at the computer pad. Her memory was remarkable.

"Yes, of course." *Liberty* . . . The name sounded familiar. Why couldn't he connect a face? He seemed forgetful as of late. Or was it his imagination? His hand twitched, but he resisted the temptation to reach for his head.

As Ivy sauntered from his office, he switched the screen on the monitor to show the view of the facility's waiting area.

Chairs lined both sides of the long hallway they had converted into a waiting area. A communication station stood at the very end. It almost seemed like an afterthought, building a waiting area onto this portion of the huge medical facility. Technology came first, patients second.

Videos played on overhead monitors spaced every three meters, the ones that still worked. Few of the two-dozen patients seemed to notice them, their attention instead on their flexi-phones as they played addictive 3D games or compulsively sent senseless messages to friends.

Supero glanced from woman to woman, looking for a familiar face. He almost passed over the girl in the workpants and oversized button-front shirt. Slouched in the chair, arms folded across her chest, looking at neither monitors nor phone, she had rebel written all over her.

A bad taste came to his mouth. "Oh, yes. Liberty of Aldonia." How could he forget? She was a most negative and unlikeable girl.

Her file popped up on the corner of his monitor. He scanned it. . . . *slated to be a breeder, comes to the facility in ten days* . . . Red flags marked her formative years. Yes, he remembered her. She had excellent physical and intellectual composition, but her attitude and outlook bordered on political dissidence.

~~~

After examining the two women and the man who had appointments before Liberty's, Dr. Supero stepped into her examination room.
~~~

The examination bed was empty.

He backed up to check the room number. P15. Yes, this was the right room.

A girl peeked then stepped out from behind the door. She wore street clothes rather than an examination gown. "Looking for me?" She put a hand on her hip and gazed at him through pale green, perfectly shaped but expressionless eyes. In ten days, she would turn twenty, but her make-up free face and the way she wore her plain brown hair tucked behind her ears cut at least two years from her appearance.

"Shouldn't you be in a gown? And sitting on the examination table?" Dr. Supero glanced at his pocket-computer in order to hide his annoyance.

"I was . . ." She sauntered to the exam table, shrugging her button-front shirt from her shoulders. She wore the gown underneath. ". . . for the past hour. I almost gave up on you."

When she began to remove her pants, he turned away as a courtesy. "My apologies. We get very busy around here, as you must know." He opened Liberty's file on his pocket-computer.

Ivy had sent the file from *Pathology* to his personal mailbox immediately after their conversation an hour ago. She was terribly efficient. Why couldn't he get himself to open the file? Most cysts in the brain turned out to be benign, noncancerous. He really shouldn't worry himself. He should just open it. But no, now was not the time. As soon as he finished with this girl, *yes*, then he would read the diagnosis.

He focused on Liberty's file. "I see you have kept all your past appointments. Today's blood work looks good. All systems normal. No drugs, no venereal diseases, eating well . . . Good, very good." Hearing her hop onto the examination bed, he turned to face her. "It appears you have been following the prescribed diet. Have you obtained non-registered foods?"

She shrugged. "Not really."

"I always discourage the eating of non-registered foods. The FDA cannot ensure the safety, quality, or nutritional value of foods outside their supervised channels." It disgusted him to consider it, but a large racket had developed. People traded food for illegal drugs, favors, and *wanted* but not *necessary* supplies. Most of the food in the illegal system had probably passed FDA inspections and had been assigned to someone legitimately before it got traded. But some food was actually homegrown or came from unknown sources. Why would a person risk it? Who could doubt that the human race leaned toward self-destruction?

With a few touches to the computer screen, and holding the pocket-computer near her chest, he picked up her heartbeat. "In ten days you enter the Breeder Facility. Getting excited?" He gave her the same smile he gave all the girls lucky enough to have this vocation. The girls always beamed back at him, excitement radiating from their pores, the honor and privilege not being lost on them.

Liberty huffed and averted her gaze, her lip curling up on one side. She stopped tugging her gown to cover her knees and folded her arms across her chest. Aside from the scowl she now had for him, she had no facial disharmonies or abnormalities. Her features—a symmetrical, oval-shaped face, wide cheekbones, full lips, glowing skin—could engage one in reflective contemplation. But that scowl . . .

"I gather this privileged vocation does not appeal to you?" he said.

"No, I'd rather be a mechanic. In fact, I—"

"A mechanic?" He snorted. "Mechanical processes are automated. Do you see yourself finding satisfaction overseeing machines?" He touched the screen on the pocket-computer to dim the overhead lights and then to get a beam of light for the examination of her pupils.

"No. But I can fix things. I do it all the time. Beats waiting around for the Regimen's mechanical technicians. Half the people in my apartment building turn to me when they have a problem anyway."

"And how do they pay you?" He swung the beam across one eye. Both of her pupils constricted and dilated appropriately. "Not in non-registered foods, I hope."

A smile flickered on her lips.

He tapped her chin, indicating with a nod for her to tilt her head back. "The vocation of breeder affords luxuries you have yet to experience." He flashed the light in her nostrils and throat. *Healthy. Perfect.* "You should consider yourself lucky. Any girl would jump at the chance."

With a touch of the computer screen, the lights brightened. He tapped the head of the bed.

"Not me." She lay back. "I filled out a Vocation Change Request."

"Another?" He slipped a hand under her gown and pushed on the cold, smooth flesh of her abdomen. "I reviewed your file. What is this, your fifth, sixth request? They do not grant such requests often. You are probably the first breeder to make such a request." Finding nothing abnormal, he motioned for her to sit up. "Do you not realize the pleasure and comfort that will be yours for the next several years? The facility overlooks the Fully-Protected Nature Preserves. The living quarters are luxurious with four times the space you have now. Chefs and massage therapist will serve you. Entertainment according to your wishes."

"Why should breeders, government officials, high level military, and top physicians have luxuries that the common people can never hope to obtain? No matter how hard a person works, they'll be stuck in—"

"You should be thankful for the way of life under the Regimen. We have no poverty, no hunger, no homeless, no inequality. No one is forgotten in our society. You studied History. Certainly you realize the great chasm that existed between the rich and the poor in generations past."

"How is that any different today? Compare your residence to mine. I live with an assigned roommate. My bedroom is so small I can barely get around my bed. The furniture I am permitted to use—"

"Those with greater responsibility ought to have a bit more comfort. *We* must see to the welfare of all."

"Ha!" Liberty slid off the examination bed and went to her clothes on the floor in the corner of the room. "People should be able to choose what they want to do with their lives, instead of being told by the Regimen. I don't want to be a breeder. It's a violation of my dignity." She shoved her foot into a leg of her pants.

"A violation?" To see her dressing before he had finished the exam made his jaw twitch.

"Yes, a violation. And it's unnatural." She pulled her arms out of the sleeves of the exam gown and turned toward the wall. "I can't imagine what it would be like for natural reproduction to occur. You guys go deep into your laboratories and—"

"Imagine this!" A vein in his forehead throbbed. "Imagine babies born with debilitating conditions, the names of which you may have heard in school but are not likely to remember. Babies born addicted to drugs, their brains damaged in the womb. Babies born unwanted and in poverty." He found himself approaching her, thought he should stop, but reached for her arm instead.

Her eyes widened as he spun her to face him. She fumbled with the buttons of her shirt.

"Every baby born in our time is planned and needed. They will be cared for, taught, and have a specific duty to perform, their unique contribution to society. There are no birth defects, no intellectually or physically deficient members in our society. You have no idea what burdens had been placed on others because of natural reproduction."

Her mouth twitched as though she wrestled to keep from cussing him out. Her gaze flitted back and forth from one of his eyes to the other.

Feeling the tension in his jaw and seeing a white dot fly before him like a gnat, he took a deep breath. He released his grip on her arm and smiled, consciously trying to look sincere. "Liberty, put aside your selfishness. Be thankful for the system we have today. People need limits in order to be happy. The Regimen Custodia Terra provides that to the benefit of all. There is no risk of overpopulating or destroying the earth. There is no poverty. All are cared for from cradle to grave."

She stooped for her boots and straightened up, saying, "We have no freedom."

He held her gaze for a moment, forcing himself to bite back a rude reply. "Good day." He left the room at a brisk pace. He could not control everything, but he could control this. Her warped ideology must not infect others. She needed—

Ivy strutted from an examination room down the hall. She gave him a glance and turned toward the assistant's station.

"Ivy, come to me." He motioned her over with a jerk of his hand. "I need you to schedule an appointment for that girl, Liberty. Schedule her for a full psychiatric evaluation."

With her expression unfazed, bored even, she reached into a side pocket of her tight gray dress and pulled out her pocket-computer.

"The appointment needs to be now, today."

Her eyeballs shifted under shimmering eyelids as she gazed at the computer screen. "Today? Not possible."

"Make it as soon as possible." He glanced over his shoulder to see Liberty tramping from the exam room. The girl threw him a cold glance on her way past. He stared until she turned a corner then said to Ivy, "The Breeder Selection Committee may see her as an indispensable asset. I do not. I think she is a candidate for re-education."

~~~

I couldn't get Dr. Supero's freaky image out of my mind. His black pointy beard, the conceited look in his pale eyes, the cocky grin as he spoke . . . The things he said . . . He annoyed me so much that angry thoughts filled my mind as I stormed through the halls of the medical facility, turning down one hall and then another, without regard for direction. I wanted to scribble in my notebook just to reign in the thoughts, to organize my ideas, to bring clarity to what bothered me so much about what he said. If only I had connections with my friends from Secondary Residence, I could have an ally, someone to talk to, a way to release my frustrations. Since Secondary, I had yet to come across anyone willing to argue openly against the Regimen's ways. I felt so alone.

My Friend caused a faint stirring in my heart. Did it offend Him that I felt alone? I believed, now, that He had always been with me, though He made Himself known to me on the day of my First Transition.

On my fifth birthday, I sat on my bed, hugging my few possessions, waiting for my escort. Although I had experienced many others leaving our residence on their fifth birthdays, I couldn't understand why I had to go. Did my nannies no longer want me? Had I done something wrong? I had been told many times how things would be, how I was growing up and getting ready for Aldonia's East Primary Residence, but I couldn't imagine life without my dear nannies and all the babies we played with. There would be no babies in my new residence. Tears streamed down my cheeks. I thought my heart would burst. At that moment, *My Friend* made Himself known. He came like a wave, a warm blanket that enveloped and
~~~

soothed my aching heart. He spoke no words but gave the distinct impression that I was not and never would be alone, that He would always be with me.

It comforted me to know of His presence, but today I longed for someone of flesh and blood with whom to share my feelings.

Snapping my attention back to my surroundings, it occurred to me that I hadn't passed anyone as I strode down this hall and the last. I should've found more traffic, not less, as I neared the big glass doors of the exit. Perhaps *My Friend* had stirred my heart to warn me, rather than comfort me. I had taken a wrong turn and was now lost.

I slowed my pace. Narrow hallways, abstract paintings, and dim lights characterized all I had ever seen of this facility, but these halls had no decorations. Aldonia's Breeder Facility was connected to the medical facility, though I had never seen it. Could I stumble across it before my time?

My stomach flipped.

No. The thought was unreasonable. From what I had heard, the facility wouldn't be so plain or so lacking in security. No one would be able to simply stumble across it. No one would be able to come and go at will from that place.

A shuffling sound came from around the next corner.

I slowed. Taking silent steps, I crept to the corner and peeked.

A man in a gray uniform stooped in a dark open doorway across the hallway. He grunted and then muttered. A moment later, he straightened and turned with a stack of plastic crates in his arms. He glanced.

I gasped but resisted the urge to step back. I wasn't doing anything wrong. I was only lost.

Without another glance, he proceeded down the hallway. The door of the room he came from slid shut, revealing the word LAUNDRY on it.

I exhaled and then followed the worker. At the end of the hall, he pushed open a door, letting in a burst of sunlight that shrunk as the door closed.

I pushed open the same door. Sunlight blinded me for an instant but a welcome floral-scented breeze tickled my face. A delivery truck at the end of a long driveway spluttered to life and rolled away. I had come out on the far side of the facility, a side used by workers and for deliveries, a side closer to the Nature Preserves. From here, I could actually glimpse the stretch of grass and the high fence of the boundaries. Lush green trees rose up behind the fence, fluffy white clouds above them. My heart stirred.

I took a deep breath, wanting to enjoy the floral scent again, and then gagged. Diesel fumes from the truck filled the air. I had hoped the floral-scent had come from the Nature Preserves, but it probably came from the laundry detergent the worker had just delivered.

I turned away and, not wanting to look suspicious, jogged toward the more-traveled sidewalks.

What did the deep woods smell like? How would it feel to walk among acres of trees and wild plants? Would I ever know? They say the Breeder Facility has balconies that overlook the woods. A privileged few have even visited a secluded vacation facility outside the boundaries.

People converged on the wide walkway leading to the main doors of the medical facility. Despite the humidity and the fierceness of the afternoon sun, they all moved at a casual pace. A single figure stood motionless, facing me it seemed. By the time I gave him a second glance, he had blended into the crowd.

I alternated between jogging and walking as I cut across the expanse of concrete that lay between the towering facility and the somewhat less imposing RCT business offices. Soon, I stepped into the shade of the office buildings. I weaved around more and more pedestrians. My walk home would take me down busy streets, past a strip of warehouses, and finally through vacant alleyways. I would see concrete, brick, and glass, passing no more than half a dozen trees.

Trees. To walk among the trees. I sighed, gazing at a patch of blue sky visible between buildings. Would I ever experience that? The discovery at the bunker had led me to believe in something more than this. Perhaps that *something more* could be found outside the boundaries, in the Nature Preserves. How could one ever hope to leave the boundaries? Even transferring from city to city was difficult, occurring only when the needs of the Regimen required it. To think of leaving was senseless.

I rubbed my right hand. The ID implant in my palm would always give the Regimen a way to find me. We had to keep our Regimen-issued flexi-phones near at all times because several times a day, our phones read our ID implants and sent our locations back to the Citizen Safety Station. Roll Call. If one happened to lose his phone, CSS team members would track him down. Flyover drones could read ID chips in those cases. Had anyone ever escaped? Did drones do sweeps outside the boundaries?

I left the crowd and strolled past a strip of warehouses. Workers stood in a group outside one unit. Others loitered in open garage doorways. Delivery trucks, motor scooters, and a trolley passed by. Before long, I turned down a shady alley, glad to walk alone. Four bicycles leaned against one wall. The backdoor to the RCT Commissary was propped open, music and voices traveling through it. Someone had recently painted a mural of our continent's president between doors. At the end of this alley I cut over to another one, a quiet, narrow one.

Halfway down this alley, goose bumps came out on my arms.

I glanced over my shoulder. Stacks of wooden crates stood on one side, a dumpster on the other. I saw no one and nothing unusual. Still, I picked up my pace. A sense of urgency overcame me. I hadn't had a day off work since my last physical, and I wanted to get back to my apartment and enjoy it. Tatum would be at work, so I'd have the place to myself today. I had saved aside dried figs and nuts, payment for fixing a neighbor's ceiling fan. And I couldn't wait to write down my thoughts. The things Doctor Supero had—

A warning hit me like a slap in the face. Then someone from behind grabbed my arm.

I spun around and jerked my arm free.

"Hey, Liberty." Sid stood so close I could smell his cologne and see the desire in his stormy blue eyes. He stuffed the thumb of one hand into the front pocket of his pants. His other hand he held behind his back.

I backed away. How and why had he snuck up on me? "What're you doing here?"

He smiled, sauntering to me, and took my arm again. "I was gonna ask you that? Shouldn't you be at the old folks' center?"

I pulled my arm from his grasp. "No, I-I had an appointment." I shouldn't have answered him. He would know I had the rest of the day free. He would try to spend time with me. "I have to go." I turned away and took a step.

He darted ahead and blocked me, still keeping one hand behind his back. "What's your hurry? You don't need to be anywhere. Neither do I. Why don't we hang out?"

I shook my head. "I have things to do." I tried to step around him.

He sidestepped, chuckling. "No, you don't. You're all mine today." He gave a crooked grin. "We're gonna hang out. I know you just had your last checkup before you get locked away in that baby-making place. So no one's gonna care what you do tonight. No one's gonna know. You always complain about having to do what the government wants, now you can do something they don't want you to do."

I shook my head, glaring. How did he know about my appointment? How would he know I take this way home? Had he followed me?

"Why not? Afraid of getting caught?"

"I'm not afraid. I told you, I don't like you that way. There's never going to be *you and me*."

"You're gonna give me a chance. You'll see. You won't want to leave me." He touched my cheek and leaned to kiss me.

I turned my face and grabbed the arm he held at his side, meaning to shove him out of the way.

He brought his hand up, something long and thin in his grasp. A knife? A needle?

My breath caught in my throat. Before really getting a look at whatever he held, I turned and bolted.

A figure shot out from a dark doorway.

I smacked face first into a hard, unyielding body. Hands latched onto my shoulders and shoved me back but didn't let go.

I looked up and my stomach sank.

Silver stared down, her silvery eyes locked on me, her hair like a great metallic mane around her tan face. The muscles in her arms bulged and rippled.

I thrust my arms up and out, smacking against Silver's arms but not lessening her grip in the least.

Silver laughed and flipped me to face Sid, locking my arms behind my back.

"Don't hurt her, now, Silver," Sid said. "That'll ruin her experience. Just let me give her this." He sauntered toward me, an injection needle in his hand.

My heart pounded against my ribs. What was in the needle? I jerked and struggled to twist free of Silver's vise-grip. "No! Don't!"

"Don't worry, I won't hurt you." Sid spoke calmly. He brought the needle up, put his thumb to the plunger, and squirted a few drops in the air.

My breaths came short and hard. I jerked and twisted, tried to drop down, tried to slam back.

Sid inched closer.

I thrust my foot behind me, cracking it against Silver's calf.

Silver chuckled and tightened her grip. "Relax, girl."

Sid chuckled. "Yeah, relax." His grin turned into a frown as he jabbed the needle into my upper arm.

A pinch, a rush of heat. I stopped struggling.

Sid's eyes snapped to mine.

"What did you give me?" Anger and helplessness brought tears to my eyes.

Sid touched my cheek, wiping a tear. "You'll wake up in an hour. And then you'll—"

A shadow then a figure came from above us. The figure dropped onto Sid, a mottled gray cape billowing out around it. Silver released me and lunged for the caped figure.

I staggered back, taking slow steps away from the three of them. My strength was fading. My face tingled.

The caped figure flung Sid into Silver. Silver's face contorted, and rage flashed in her eyes. She shoved Sid aside. Sid fell to his knees.

The caped figure spun around and leaped, bringing up one leg and then the other. A boot cracked Silver's face. Silver flinched at the impact but bounced back, fists ready.

She swung. He dodged.

He swung. She blocked.

I backed against a crate. My knees grew weak, and I slid to the ground. Who was the stranger? He wore a hood and shiny black shades. Was he a Regimen agent? One of the Unity Troopers?

Sid got to his feet and joined the fight, ramming his shoulder into the caped figure. Silver wrapped her arms around the stranger from behind, her arms like a steel trap.

My stomach turned. I leaned my head against a crate. Whoever it was, I couldn't bear to see him defeated by those two. What could I do to help? I couldn't even stand. It took all my strength to keep from tipping over.

The figure thrust himself backward into Silver, who held him by the arms, and kicked Sid with such force that Sid crashed into the crates near me. With another swift move, the figure slammed Silver into the wall and got free. He spun to face her.

The two of them fought, lunging, swinging, twisting, and kicking, his mottled cape flapping and billowing out around them. Sunlight reflected off the stranger's shades. His movements had grace and precision. Silver had strength and rage, her mane like bolts of electricity whipping around her face.

My head grew light. My strength faded more. I put a hand out, knowing I was about to go down. I toppled over, thankful that I had been sitting. The ground felt like cotton against my cheek.

Sid, less than a meter away, had gotten up on all fours. He looked at me and then pulled himself up with the crates. Before he stood straight, Silver's body crashed into him. Crates clattered onto them and the ground. Silver popped back up and lunged for the stranger. Sid rolled onto his stomach, his face to me. Blood trickled from his forehead, and he had a swollen eye.

Out of my peripheral vision, I glimpsed the swift movements of the other two. Muffled grunts and blows sounded above me. My eyes felt heavy, too lazy to move. I gazed at Sid. He gazed at me. Both of us lay on the ground, less than a meter away.

The fighters moved in slow motion now, like a strange choreographed dance. They made no sound. Silence.

Sleep called to me. I blinked, my eyelids heavy and slow. I let sleep come.

5

A moth fluttered by a pale light. It was either huge or very close to my eyes, I couldn't decide. The wings separated from the body and lowered. Its legs moved in a way that reminded me of human arms. It turned.

"Are you awake?" The voice had a deep timbre.

I dragged in a breath of air and blinked. My head ached. Every muscle in my body felt heavy, especially those of one wrist.

The man—not a moth—edged toward me, his shadowy figure getting clearer as I blinked.

Eyes on the stranger, I rolled onto my side and tried to push myself up. Something covered my body, holding me down. I groped and clawed but hadn't the strength to get it off. It enveloped me like a cocoon, rough and scratchy, unfamiliar. My heart raced. I tugged at it. I wanted it off.

"You're okay." The man stopped a meter away. "You probably feel a little strange but—"

I looked to see what held me down and gasped. I had a bulky, black device on one wrist. I tore at it.

"Hey!" The man dropped to his knees by my side. He reached for my arms, hesitated, and then grabbed them.

At his touch, warmth radiated deep into my arms. I twisted away, digging, scratching at the thick band on the underside of the device. I drew blood but instead of pain it gave a pleasant sensation.

"Stop! You don't want to do that." Leaning over me, he grappled for my arms, my wrists . . .

His body heat made my head spin. Wrestling him, hair in my face, heartbeat racing, tugging, prying at the device, I thought I might lose consciousness. I wanted the device off before I passed out.

"Hey, stop." He had me by the wrists. "You're okay. No one's going to hurt you, Liberty."

I stopped fighting. *How did he know my name?*

In our wrestling match, I had managed to sit up. The cocoon was only a rough blanket. The moth was a dark-haired man in his twenties, kneeling beside me. I sat on a low mattress on the floor of a big, dimly lit area, voices and strange noises echoing around me. My farsighted vision hadn't returned, so I couldn't gauge the size of the room. Blue and white lights flickered at some distance off to my right. My body felt heavier than usual. And my head— What was wrong with me?

The man released my wrists, took a breath and smiled. He sat on his haunches. "I didn't think you'd wake this soon. How do you feel?"

I rubbed my arm. The impression of his touch lingered. "Who are you? Where am I? What's this?" I lifted my wrist to indicate the device.

He smiled again, glancing away. Something about him struck me as strange, but I couldn't place it. His eyes?

He twirled a finger as he said, "You're here for your safety." He tapped the black device on my wrist. "You're wearing that for ours."

"For yours?" The device had no markings or features other than a tiny hole on one side. The band fit snug and . . . Oh. It had a keypad. "I want this off."

"We'll take it off when you leave. You need it to wear it down here or they could pick up your implant. It bounces the reading, makes it seem—"

"They? The Citizen Safety Station? They can track me by my phone." They didn't always do it, but I'd heard they could. If one was considered a possible threat to society, they listened through the phone.

"You don't have your phone. It . . . broke."

I groped my work belt. My phone wasn't there.

"And how did it break? Are you going to tell her?" A black-haired woman in gray camouflage clothes walked past us, smirking. She held a computer pad. She *did not* have a black box on her wrist. Nor did he, for that matter.

He glared at her and turned back to me with guilty eyes. "You can't bring flexi-phones down here. You can report it lost or stolen. They'll give you a new one."

"Why don't you have a black box?" I said. "Why doesn't she?"

"Some of us do." He nodded to my right.

I looked.

Monitors, three high and nine across, hung on two walls on the far side of the room. They displayed various live city scenes: sidewalks and streets, common areas and storefronts. One screen and then another flipped to a different view. I imagined this place resembled Citizen Safety Station, where they monitored feeds from security cameras throughout Aldonia. Where was I?

About a dozen people sat or stood at a disorderly arrangement of control stations, computers, and other equipment under the monitors. One man had the whitest hair I ever saw and more wrinkles than I thought possible. The black-haired girl went up to the old man and showed him something on her computer pad. Two guys and one girl did have black devices on their wrists. Why didn't the others?

"She needs to lie down." An older woman came up behind me. "Why is she up?" The woman squatted and took my wrist, the one without the device. Her touch brought warmth, soothing and deep. She flashed a smile, her dark eyes conveying kindness, before glancing at her wristwatch.

"I don't know," the young man said. "She just woke up. I think the antidote worked. She doesn't seem, uh . . ." He blushed and stood up.

"What happened to me?" I said to the woman, wanting to trust her. I couldn't take my eyes off her hair. She wore a ponytail and white strands ran all through the chestnut brown, especially along the sides, though she had a young face. She couldn't be over forty. No one turned gray at that age.

"You were drugged." She let go of my wrist and touched my forehead. "I gave you the antidote. You should still be sleeping. It works better that way. How do you feel?"

"Heavy. My body feels heavy. What was I drugged with?"

The woman and young man exchanged a glance. Then he cleared his throat, stuffed his hands in his pants pockets, and turned away. The woman said, "The street name is *Thrill.* It causes a brief period of unconsciousness. Once awake, it negates a person's natural inhibitions and enhances tactile sensations, making physical contact with others more pleasurable. The effects last for hours."

The blood drained from my face knowing why Sid had given it to me.

"Don't worry." She patted my hand. "I gave you an antidote. That's why your body feels heavy. And you probably have a headache." She stood up. "And you should be sleeping right now. Cover up. Try to rest. Sleep should come easy."

I pulled the blanket around my chest. My heartbeat had slowed and my eyelids wanted to close. "I have a few questions first, like, *where am I* and *how did I get here* and *why*—"

"Help her. She needs to rest." The woman spoke over me, to the man, and then walked off.

He squatted again and reached for my arm, but then drew his hand back. "Take it easy, Liberty. All you need to know is you're safe here. You can trust us. I-I can't tell you—"

A low alarm sounded. Red lights flashed above the monitors. The man at my side jumped up. Everyone spoke at once, one voice louder than the others. "Unity Troopers are in pursuit of a candidate." The teen that spoke stood at a control panel directly under the monitors. He turned to face the others. "They want him for Re-Ed."

"His time is now!" The old white-haired man spoke with authority. "Who will extract him?"

"I will." The man near me dashed to the wall where I had first seen him. He put shiny black shades on and swung a mottled gray cape over his shoulders.

Was he the one who saved me? My head grew light . . . numb. I lay back, keeping my eyes on the commotion.

The alarm had ceased but the red lights continued to flash, giving everyone and everything a pulsing reddish shine. The black-haired woman in the camouflage and two men in similar clothes joined the first man.

Each put on dark shades and a mottled gray cape, a row of moths against a pale light. The teen at the control panel shouted street names and other things that got lost in my mind. The old man said something about a tunnel. Something like, "Take tunnel seven." The team flitted away, out of view.

Voices and footfalls . . . The flapping of wings . . . Sliding sounds . . . The hum of a huge vacuum . . . Muffled speech.

My eyes closed.

Moths flapping by a dim light . . .

~~~

Secrets made known. Cages bursting open. Walls coming down. Chains broken. Light piercing the darkness. Waters and sky, pure and endless.

I rammed a shovel into the ground. Metal rang against metal with a hollow sound that echoed in the room . . . echoed in my mind like a wake-up call.

"Liberty, time to get up. Liberty . . ."

I gasped and sat bolt upright.

Monitors flickered and mumbling voices sounded to my right. The woman with the graying ponytail squatted beside me, her hand on my arm. Where was the man I first saw? The commotion . . . I remembered now. He had left with a few others to rescue someone. This place was now calm as a secondary classroom.

"It's time to go." She helped me up. "You'll need to wear these." She slid sunglasses over my eyes.

Everything went black. "They're too dark." I reached to take them off.

She latched onto my arm, preventing me from removing them. "They're meant to be dark. You can't know where you are." She tugged me forward. "I'll lead you home."

I faltered along after her, clinging to her hand. "Who are you guys? Are you with the Regimen? Why can't I know where I am?"

"It's a matter of safety." She changed direction and slowed down.

My hand brushed a doorway we passed through. The door slid shut behind me, cutting off the hums, chatter and quiet beeps of the monitoring station. The dark glasses allowed me to see no more than
~~~

shadowy, incoherent shapes. It was much darker this side of the door. Where were we?

Trusting myself to her, or to anyone, went against my grain. My feet tingled. A shiver ran through me. With each step, I expected to smack into something. I sensed that *My Friend* wanted me to trust, but anxiety and fear took turns with my mind all the same.

I trusted myself. When I worked with my hands, with tools, engines, and mechanical parts, I knew what to expect. Physical principles and the properties of materials never let me down. Who could ever rely on a person with equal confidence? People made decisions based on emotion, whims, and self-interest. What did these people do? What did they want?

As the woman led me, I counted my steps, determined to keep track of the number and any changes of direction we should make. Her stride had me jogging to keep up, at times. I soon lost count of my steps. Our footfalls echoed. Water dripped in the distance. A layer of sweat developed between our clasped hands, though the temperature had dropped since we left the station.

These people had saved me from Sid, and for that I was glad. But why were they so secretive? They knew my name. Had I mumbled it in my sleep? Maybe they scanned my ID implant before affixing the black box to my hand. How did they know of my trouble with Sid and Silver? Had they seen me on one of their monitors? What did they know about me?

"Keep up," she said. "There's a tunnel kart ahead."

I got the impression we traveled through a long underground tunnel though we often passed stretches of blackness on one side or the other, cool breezes and distant sounds coming from them. She stopped in a particularly dark area.

"Here." She placed my hand on a cold metal bar, told me to step up, and guided me onto a bench seat. She climbed in beside me. A second later, she had the engine cranked to life but it coughed and sputtered.

I was jerked back as we set off. The cool, rushing air felt good on my face and neck, but it smelled foul at times. The engine continued to run rough. "You need new spark plugs," I said.

She laughed. The cart slowed and we turned. "New spark plugs. I know. Parts and supplies aren't always easy for us to obtain." She sped up.

"Because of all the forms the RCT requires?" I remembered what Finley said about the wait the Environmental Stewardship Unit could expect in order to get the Regimen's permission to dig.

She laughed again. "No, not because of forms."

Liking the sound of her laugh, I smiled. I wanted to take off the glasses and see her eyes. There was something unusual about her eyes and the eyes of the man. "The guy I first saw, was he the one who saved me?"

"Yes. But he shouldn't have gone in alone. Besides, it's not your time yet."

"My time? What does that mean? Who are you?"

She sighed, loud enough to hear over the rough motor. "I wish I could tell you. You'll probably know soon enough. Many lives are at stake, so we have to be sure we can trust you."

"How will you know if you can trust me? And what do you mean, I'll know soon enough?"

The cart jerked to a stop. The engine silenced. "Slide out this way." She took my arm.

We walked a few meters and then stopped. She let go of my hand. Something chest-high made a sliding sound. An illuminated keypad became visible even through my shades. She stepped in front of me, blocking my view with her body, while she punched keys. A heavy, metallic sliding sound followed.

"Come on." She grabbed my arm and tugged me forward. "Be careful."

A few steps later, she guided my hands to a rail on a wall. The stale, hushed air and the surrounding blackness made me think we stood in a small room. "Can I take the glasses off?"

"A moment."

A quiet tapping, the heavy, metallic sliding—a door, I guessed— the creak of a distant gear . . .

The floor tilted and the room lifted, leaving my stomach behind. We were on an elevator. I clung to the rail, willing my heart to settle, until the elevator jerked to a stop.

The heavy door slid open to a silent room. Sweet smoke lingered in the air. Dim light showed from a distant doorway. The woman led me to the light, to a room with pleasant conversations and the clanking of dishes. Did anyone see us? No one said anything. We moved from room to room, voices, shuffling, and other sounds of life in many.

We stopped in a dark, quiet area.

"Here we go." She lifted my hand, the one with the black device. After a moment of fidgeting, she removed the device from my wrist. "You can take off the glasses."

Finally! As I ripped them from my eyes, the woman pushed open a door. Sunlight blinded me. A hand landed on my shoulder.

"Please keep what you know secret. The safety of others depends upon it." The woman shoved me through the door.

Blinking as my eyes adjusted, I took in my surroundings.

The backs of shops towered over me, their names familiar though I hadn't been to this side of the mall before. The mall?

I turned to face her. "Who are you? Are you with the Regimen?"

The door was closing fast. "We are the Mosheh." The slamming of the door punctuated her statement.

The Mosheh? What did that mean?

~~~

Lying motionless on my bed, I concentrated on taking deep and slow breaths, my belly rising and falling. *Waves rolling in and out. Clouds drifting in a clear sky. Silence--*

A clank and a thud sounded on the ceiling for the third time, noise from the unit above ours.

I huffed and sat up. The pillows needed adjusting anyway.

As soon as I had come through the door of my apartment, I snagged throw pillows from the couch and took them to my bedroom. My mind had gone numb on the walk home from the mall, but I knew I had much to consider. I wanted the help of *My Friend.* I washed up in the bathroom, got an apple and a glass of water from the kitchen, and returned to my
~~~

room. I was alone in the apartment, but I closed my door anyway. After taking a swig of water and adjusting the mountain of pillows, I lay down. For almost an hour, I lay still.

My Friend remained silent. Maybe I hadn't tried hard enough.

My stomach churned, so I took a bite of the apple and another swig of water. I hadn't eaten since breakfast and it was past dinnertime, but I didn't want to eat too much in case the feeling wasn't hunger. Who knew what side effects the drug and antidote had? I hated throwing up.

After adjusting the pillows, I sunk into them. My muscles relaxed. I let my mind go blank, making myself open to the slightest inspiration. My focus drifted back and forth from my mind to my heart, the places where He lived.

Dr. Supero's lavender eyes invaded my mind. His cocky grin. His pointy beard.

My jaw tensed. He'd spoken with such arrogance. How could anyone tolerate him? He thought society was better off with the Regimen controlling every—

No. Get out of my mind. Clouds drifting in a blue sky. Waves rolling in—

How did Sid know I had an appointment? His sudden appearance, his attack . . . It all seemed planned, as if he knew when I'd be walking home and the route I would take. I hadn't told anyone about my doctor appointment, except for Abby and Tatum. Tatum had told me to enjoy having the apartment to myself afterward. She knew how I liked my privacy. She even said she and Finley would hang out at his place after work. Had she told Sid? Would she betray me like that?

My thoughts soured. Why should betrayal shock me? People couldn't be trusted.

I sighed, closed my eyes, and breathed deep.

After talking with Dr. Supero, I had wanted to write in my notebook. I wouldn't write about him or the things he said. I'd write about . . . What had the woman said? They were the Mosheh. Every organization sprung from or was regulated by the Regimen Custodia Terra, but *they* didn't seem to be. The dark-haired man had said the black box on my wrist bounced my signal to prevent the Citizen Safety Station from knowing my location. The Citizen Safety Station had no idea about these people, the Mosheh.

What a strange name. What did they do? Their monitors showed live feeds from around Aldonia. What were they looking for? They extracted someone slated for Re-Ed. Did they look for people the Regimen came after and save them? The woman said I would know soon. Did the Mosheh watch me? Why me? They had called the person they went to rescue a candidate. Was I a candidate? They needed to be sure they could trust me . . . with what? Could I trust them?

The eyes of my rescuer appeared in my mind, warming me interiorly. What made them so different from everyone else's eyes? The dim lighting had prevented me from studying them, but his eyes had drawn me all the same. They conveyed something. Safety? Serenity? In contrast to the eyes of most men I knew, they held a childlike innocence and purity. The woman with the ponytail had a similar look. These people were different—

A clank and heavy footfalls sounded on the ceiling.

I opened my eyes. Sometimes the walls and ceilings seemed so thin I half expected someone or something to come through them. I sat up and took a bite of the apple.

What did the Mosheh do with people they rescued? Maybe they were bad, using people for purposes even the Regimen forbade. But they did save me. Could I trust them?

"Talk to me," I said aloud, frustration in my voice, my heartbeat quickening. "Tell me what to do. You made yourself known at the bunker. There was something special, life-changing about that discovery, you said. I don't get it. Why didn't you warn me about Sid?"

Even as I asked, I knew *My Friend* had tried to warn me. He tried to warn me from the moment I left Dr. Supero's office, but I was busy fuming over things the doctor said. Then He tried to communicate peace when I walked blind through the tunnels with the woman. Did that mean He wanted me to trust *her* or to trust Him, *My Friend*?

"I do trust you," I shouted. "Why won't you speak to me?"

A wave of love washed over me, taking my breath. I closed my eyes, still sitting but losing awareness of my body. An impression came to me.

Dying of thirst, I clutched a glass of water but didn't drink. Next, I came to an open door but didn't go through. Then, I found myself at the foot of a tall staircase but didn't climb.

The communication ended.

I understood. I took a deep breath and opened my eyes. I understood, but I didn't like it. He wanted me to wait, to relax, to be patient. Wait for what?

I got up from the bed and went to the closet. Writing out my thoughts had helped me before. I'd try it again.

Tatum and I shared the walk-in closet between our bedrooms. I yanked open the door. Her bedroom door was open, her room dark. A scraping sound came from her room.

My heart skipped a beat. Tatum wouldn't be here. She was going to Finley's. Darin wouldn't come around without Silver. Silver and Sid wouldn't come over now, not after the beating they took from the Mosheh guy. Would they?

I grabbed the doorknob to the closet door on Tatum's side. Light flashed in the living room, visible through her open bedroom doorway. I peered into the dimly lit room and then exhaled. It was only light, reflecting off the chrome on the neighbor's motorbike. I should've been working on that bike. *Later.* I closed the closet door and hit the light switch.

Tatum's side of the closet had empty hangers, wads of clothes on a few shelves, and piles of clothing on the floor. She loved fashion but had no instinct for neatness. I had considerably less outfits, all of them folded or hanging. My toolboxes lined one wall, each of them organized and fairly clean.

I kicked a pile of clothes from the middle of the closet floor and grabbed the handle of a tool chest. After sliding the chest to the middle of the floor, I stepped on it and reached for the ceiling. Neither Tatum nor I had more things than we could store in our rooms or in the closet, so we never bothered with the upper storage. Until now.

I tugged the storage door open and reached inside. My fingers landed on the notebook. It was right where I had left it.

Sitting on the floor and leaning against the bed, sharpened pencils at my side and the notebook on my lap, I was ready. I decided to write about today's experience. Maybe the details would come together and make sense later, the way inspirations from *My Friend* often did.

I wrote the first thing that came to mind.

Mosheh. What did the name mean? What did any name mean? Liberty 554-062466-84 of Aldonia. A computer program had generated my name, randomly. The numbers following it had meaning, impersonal meaning. Data for reference. Abby had two names before her numbers. Abby Rosier. Her second name reminded me of roses. She said people once named the babies. Someone named her. I thought she meant the girls in the Breeder Facility. But she shook her head and sadness entered her eyes.

We studied novels in school, stories meant to show us the imperfections of past societies, stories of war, slavery, inequality, destruction of the earth, and racism. "Gone with the Wind," "Red Badge of Courage," "Huckleberry Finn." In almost every novel, the characters had double names and no numbers.

I always liked the Adventures of Huckleberry Finn. He had a cruel nanny in the Breeder Facility, Nanny Pap, and couldn't wait to transition to Primary Residence. But a couple years later, Nanny Pap transferred there, too. So one night, he escaped and hooked up with Nanny Watson's slave. The message of the story, our teachers made clear: before the Regimen Custodia Terra came to power, people lived by fear and prejudice, thinking only of themselves and not the environment. I got something different from the story: Their reckless adventures on the river and in nature appealed to me. The rebellious nature of Huckleberry and the way he didn't fit in with the others spoke to me.

I brought out the picture from the bunker. I smiled, gazing at it, not knowing why a picture would make me so happy. The woman in the picture was either smiling or laughing, but her eyes were on the baby. The man's gaze was on the woman. Two of the older children looked at each other as if they had been talking, but Emily looked at me—at the camera, that is. Did Emily have a double name? Did numbers follow her name? If these people were a family, would they have a common last name, the way I share a last name with everyone born in Aldonia? I couldn't relate to the concept of a family, though it seemed natural. Lions, buffalo, and primates lived in family groups.

I scribbled in the notebook: families . . . names . . . Mosheh. Then I tossed the pencil and leaned back against the bed. How long would it take for the Mosheh to trust me? Did they plan to rescue me? Did they know I had to move to the high-security Breeder Facility in a week? Rescue would be impossible from there.

I had too many questions and too little time. I couldn't wait. I had to try to find them.

6

The next morning I walked to work under a dull, overcast sky, my pace increasing as thoughts tangled in my mind. I needed to know more about the Mosheh. The people seemed strangely kind and levelheaded, sincere in a way unfamiliar to me. I needed to find them. I would have to use caution to avoid drawing attention to myself or exposing them. "Keep what you know secret," the woman had said. "We have to be sure we can trust you." If they trusted me, could they save me from my Regimen-imposed fate? If so, any rash behavior on my part could blow it for me. I had to stick to my routine. Had Abby ever heard of them? Was there a way I could ask her without breaking their confidence?

By the time I reached the Senior Living and Recreation Center, my heart pounded a healthy beat and a cool sweat covered me, the result of the high humidity and my fast pace. As I stepped into the controlled temperature of the glass lobby, a shiver ran through me, refreshing me and renewing my determination. I would get through my workday and find the Mosheh. While I worked, I would talk to Abby. Questions I could ask her started forming in my mind. I could be discreet. I just had to make sure to avoid cameras when speaking with her.

I pushed open the tall doors to Activity Room B. Rough music with a heavy beat came from the kitchen area. A solitary woman sat in one of the rocking chairs in the seating arrangement, her attention on a news show blaring on the wall screen. On the opposite side of the room, two men played a game of chess. The newest man to the center watched them. I expected a bigger group on that side of the room. And Abby . . . Where was Abby? Her table was empty.

I glanced at the digital clock on the wall. I was early but not that early. Where was everyone?

The kitchen door swung open and Nyeb peeked out, a puff of smoke with him. His gaze swept the room, paused on me, and shot to the clock. He withdrew and the door swung shut.

The smoking, the loud music . . . Those creeps had no respect.

I took a deep breath and stomped to the kitchen. I smacked the door open with the palm of my hand.

The three guys on the third-shift housekeeping crew, all huddled in the middle of the smoky kitchen, snapped their faces to me. None of them held a cigarette, but one of them had a computer pad. He pressed it against his chest and gave me a funny look.

"Man, Liberty, what's your deal?" Nyeb said, sauntering toward me, his lanky arms swaying at his sides.

"What's my deal?" I tried to equal his arrogant expression. "There's no smoking in this place. And you can't play your music here. Show some respect for these people."

He smirked and glanced over his shoulder at the other two. They snickered. One threw me a rude look.

"You gonna tell on us?" Nyeb looked amused rather than worried.

I wanted to report them. But it would mean filling out a form and waiting. By the time an official got to my complaint, I wouldn't remember the details and they'd belittle the violation. "What good would it do?"

He flicked my shoulder and winked. "We're out-a here anyway. You can have these people. Show them all the respect you want."

One of the other two stooped by a closet and stood up with a backpack. The music went off, and he started unbuttoning his gray uniform shirt.

Nyeb went to the one with the computer pad and leaned an arm on his shoulder. "Did you get my bet in there?"

I turned to make my exit and put a palm to the swing door.

"Yeah. My bet's on frowning Abby."

I stopped and spun around. "Abby? What are you betting about?" I dashed for the guy with the computer.

Nyeb jumped in my way, blocking me with his long arms. "Mind your business, girl. Your shift doesn't bet."

Eyes on me, the boy with the computer pad squatted and stuffed his computer into a backpack. What did he know about Abby? Where was she? Where was everyone?

I stepped to the side, wanting to get around Nyeb.

Nyeb blocked me and shook his head.

If I could get around Nyeb, I could easily snatch the backpack from that kid. He always backed away when confronted. Could I convince Nyeb that I wanted in on the bet? I had never gotten along with the third-shift housekeeping crew. With the exception of Nyeb, I didn't even know their names. A cold war had existed between third and first since before I began working here. My attempts to befriend them, they took as acts of war. I introduced myself. They gave me fake names. I asked how their shift went. They left buckets of filthy water just inside the kitchen door. And so on.

I folded my arms and forced myself to smile. "So what are you guys betting on?"

Nyeb smirked. "None of your business."

My jaw twitched. "Where's Abby?"

"How should I know?"

We stared at each other for another hot second. Then one of the others said, "Time to go," and the three of them pushed past me and blew through the doors.

What did they know about Abby?

Most of the first shift workers came in late. Today I'd start work late. I sprinted to the back door of the activity room and down the hall, heading for the elevator.

Several doors came off this long hallway, doors leading to conference rooms, an exercise room, the dining room, stairs, offices . . . and at the far end, the extra wide door, called by many the *Door of Death.* That door only opened for emergencies, when a person went to the hospital on a gurney.

The retired folks lived in the apartments upstairs. I had only visited her apartment once, but I knew Abby lived on the third floor, room number 310.

I hit the button to call the elevator. The button flashed red. Did that mean the elevator was in use?

Abby's image came to mind, her serious expression, her turquoise eyes, her trembling hands . . . How long has she had this symptom? What could it mean? Did she have other symptoms? She wouldn't have told me. She never complained about her health. *Please, don't be sick, Abby.*

I hit the button again. It flashed red. Next to the button was a black box with a small screen. Words scrolled across the screen. "Scan ID to activate elevator . . ."

Of course, they would have security. They wouldn't let just anyone up to the seniors' rooms. I put my palm to the reader. I worked in recreation. Would I be allowed up?

The button turned green and the elevator doors slid open.

I darted into the elevator. Bouncing on my toes, I waited for the elevator doors to close, waited to reach the third floor, waited for the doors to open. As they crept open, I squeezed through and dashed down the hall.

Room 318, 316, 314 . . .

I slowed. My heart throbbed in my ears.

The door to Abby's room hung open wide.

I held my breath as I neared, dread creeping into my mind.

Hushed voices came from her room. A white-haired woman stood just inside the doorway. An old man sat on the end of the bed, one hand resting on a cane, his face to the corner of the room. He nodded and mumbled something.

I stepped inside the room. A wave of nausea hit me. Where was Abby? This was her room, wasn't it?

All heads turned to me. Seven or eight people crowded the little bedroom, all standing, except for the man on the bed. The white-haired woman smiled at me, though sorrow colored her expression. She stepped to the side and there, on a high-backed chair in the corner of the room, sat Abby.

I exhaled and dashed to her side. Relief flooded me. Fighting back tears and the urge to smile, I dropped to my knees and grabbed her hands.

She pulled one hand free and patted my cheek. The other hand clutched something. "You heard about Richter?"

I gasped. I hadn't thought— "Richter? What happened?"

"They took him in the night."

"Is he . . ." I couldn't get myself to say 'dead.'

"We don't know," said the old man on the bed. *Samuel.* That was his name. He was one of Richter's best buddies. They played games together in the mornings. "He'd been complaining about his stomach past few days. Indigestion, he said. Don't know what happened in the night. Maybe a heart attack or a stroke." He shook his head. "He called for help. They came and got him. I saw them come. Quite efficient, they are." His gaze went to the double call buttons on his wristband. All of the residents wore them. They could press one button for staff assistance, the other for an emergency.

"He could recover," said a petite old woman I didn't recognize. "It could be something little." Smiling but red-eyed, she cast a pleading look at a few of the others in the room. When no one responded, she pressed her lips together and dropped her gaze. Everyone knew the slim chances the elderly had of returning from the hospital.

Abby made a deep and chilling sigh. She pushed my hand from hers and caressed the object in her hand. She seemed to want to keep the object hidden, but one hand began to tremble. The object reflected light. With a quick movement, she grasped her trembling hand. She had two things to conceal now: her trembling hand and a watch with a shiny face and a thick leather band.

A man's watch. Richter's watch, I supposed. Abby had little hope in his return.

I kissed Abby's cheek and stood up.

A digital photo frame hung on the wall above her, scrolling through pictures of Abby. Residents received the frame as a gift from the facility on their eightieth birthdays.

I couldn't take my eyes off it. I had never known Abby before I worked here.

The photos displayed as a slide show, pausing for a second on each. Most were of Abby, taken here at the Senior Recreation Center. A few showed her younger, in her working years. She had silky brown hair, striking blue-green eyes, and the same serious expression. Richter was in a few of the pictures taken here, playing cards with her, eating dinner with her, posing at one of the dances . . . They rarely spoke on my shift, so I hadn't realized the depth of their friendship.

I gave a little gasp when I saw the next picture.

Abby was smiling. Her face glowed. It seemed to be a candid shot taken in the garden behind the facility. Abby and Richter sat together on a bench, talking.

What happened to make Abby lose her smile?

~~~

Two men flanked the entrance to Recreation Room B, their dark, armored figures out of place among the slow-moving elderly and the sheepish staff. Dressed in scaled armor from their necks to their groins, various weapons and tools hanging from their belts, they stood tall and silent, like sentinels on guard. The white stripe down their pant legs showed them to be external officers of Citizen Safety rather than Unity Troopers.

As I stepped through the doorway off the hallway, their eyes locked on me. In an instant, they towered over me. "Liberty 554-062466-84 of Aldonia?" one of them said, his face expressionless. The other had the hint of a sarcastic smile.

"I, uh . . ." I gulped. Paranoia suggested they came for me because of my tardiness. But, *no*, I had reached the center early. I just hadn't started working. Besides, everyone else came late all the time. Citizen Safety had never once shown up for them.

"That's me: Liberty 554-062466-84 of Aldonia." I turned to the nearest table, purposely putting my back to them, and started straightening chairs.

"What happened to your Regimen-issued flexi-phone?" the stone-faced one asked. He pulled out a computer pad, ready to note my response.

They would've noticed I didn't have it when they did Roll Call last night. Several times a day, at random intervals, the Citizen Safety Station did a citywide scan. One's phone had to be within reading range of one's ID implant so it could read the signal and relay the data to CSS. They
~~~

didn't care so much where a person was; they just wanted to know. They recorded each person's location and tracked patterns.

"I don't know what happened to it. I lost it." I straightened the last chair at the table and considered retreating to the kitchen. The Citizen Safety, like the Unity Troopers, was an arm of the Regimen, a far-reaching and invasive arm, working for and reporting everything to them. Individual officers may have meant well, but they irritated me nonetheless.

I forced myself to make eye contact and tried to conceal my annoyance. "Someone attacked me in an alley."

"Attacked you?" Stone-face said, an eyebrow twitching. "Did you report the incident?"

"No, I got away. I'm fine." I held the back of a chair, standing with the table between us.

The two exchanged glances. The one with the hint of a smile nodded to the other. They both turned to me.

"When you lose your flexi-phone," Stone-face said, "you need to report it immediately. It's a violation of RCT—"

"I know. I was going to report it. This morning."

"I see this is the first time for you, losing your flexi-phone." Stone-face glanced at his computer. "Take care it doesn't happen again."

"At least not for another year." The smirking one handed me a new flexi-phone. "All your contacts and favorites are on here. You're ready to go."

I watched them leave, amazed that they had come so soon with my new phone. They must've had a drone flying over my apartment last night. What if I hadn't been there? Would they have scoured the city for me? As long as I had the ID implant, they could find me. How could I ever avoid my dreaded fate?

My boss came over, smiling. "They take good care of us, don't they?"

I huffed. "You didn't find that a bit invasive? I lost my phone last night. They're here first thing in the morning. I didn't even report it missing."

"Efficient, I'd say. They must be the most efficient branch of government."

"Most invasive. Do they watch us in the bathroom?" I stomped to the kitchen to make tea for the two women in the sitting area.

She followed me. "What if we didn't have them? They keep us safe."

I pushed open the swing door and went to a cupboard. "Safe? I was attacked in an alley last night."

"The tea's already made." She took the pot from the burner and filled two cups. "If you'd gone missing, they'd have found you."

"They don't keep track of us to keep us safe. They want to control us." I put the steaming cups and two plates of cookies on a tray.

"You're just upset because soon you'll be leaving all your friends. It's only for a few years. You can come and see us when—"

I pushed open the door with my hip. "I don't want to be a breeder."

Everyone had stopped talking. I felt their gazes and the eyes of the security cameras.

"Each of us has a part to play, our unique contribution for the good of all. We need each other. One person can't do everything. The government keeps it all organized. Can you imagine if you had to do it all by yourself? It'd be impossible . . ."

Her words made me bristle. Instead of continuing with this argument I'd never win, I imagined myself surrounded by trees, a warm, flower-scented breeze blowing through my hair, my notebook on my lap. No cameras, no phone, no ID implant, no Regimen. The image comforted me and helped me get through the day, though a day had never crawled like this before.

Abby had her meals brought to her room, so I hadn't seen her again today. For the first time I could remember, I left work exactly on time.

Towering cumulus clouds in moody shades of gray filled the sky, hiding all but a trace of blue. One round cloud hung low and resembled a fist on its way to strike the earth. People packed the solar-powered trolley that ran down the main streets. It would have to run on electric today. Bikes hurried past me. Very few people walked.

I started jogging opposite the direction I normally took to get home. My destination: the mall.

Few people would go to the mall today. Would that work for or against me? I didn't know which cameras worked behind the mall, which sections to avoid. If Citizen Safety was looking, I'd stand out. They might wonder about my business. But I couldn't just go home and do nothing. I had to find out if the Mosheh could help me. My days were numbered.

Turning onto a street full of motor scooters and cars, the mall became visible in the distance. The traffic slowed and then stopped. I assumed they stopped for a traffic light, but then a few cars honked and a middle-aged black man on a scooter shouted, "What's the holdup? Get a move on!" just as I approached.

Our eyes met and he nodded. "Don't want to get caught out in this." He turned a hand up and glanced at the sky. "You better get yourself to a trolley."

"Thanks." I smiled and kept walking.

His dark skin and gracious gesture reminded me of Richter. A twinge of pain struck my soul. When people his age went to the hospital, they didn't often come back. No one would even have the chance to say goodbye.

I jogged again, the humid air making my cheeks cold and damp, the speed an outlet for my frustration.

Sirens blared in the distance and then silenced.

Our society boasted of eradicating diseases and debilitating conditions, of keeping the earth clean and safe, but they could do nothing to help people past a certain age. Abby's tremor could be something simple to fix, but she wouldn't dare complain about it. Seniors who wanted to live kept those things to themselves.

I stopped to cross the road. Traffic moved in one direction only. I cut between cars, checked for traffic in the moving lane, and took a step.

A siren blared in my ears. A burst of wind hit my face.

I jumped back, slamming into one of the stationary cars.

Three black cars sped past, going the wrong way, lights flashing, sirens blaring. *Unity Troopers.* They turned down the next road. Who were they after? Would the Mosheh come?

Regaining composure, I darted across the street, after them.

They turned again, down a narrow road between a fuel station and a scooter dealer. The sirens stopped. Orange and blue lights flashed on the backsides of low buildings farther down the road.

My lungs protested but I pushed myself, running faster and faster to catch up.

Heavily armed Unity Troopers in shiny black helmets swarmed the area, shouting to one another. "He went down the alley." "No, down there." "I have a visual." "He's gone." "Move, move, move!"

Not wanting them to see me, I slowed my pace and kept to the walls as I neared one of the Unity Troopers' area cars.

An officer came from out of nowhere, sprinting at an unnaturally fast pace, headed for the area car.

I flung myself into a crack between buildings and peeked out.

The officer had a metallic exoskeleton on his legs. He wore bulky boots and had— what I guessed to be— a power pack on his back. I'd heard that a few Unity Troopers had special devices to increase their strength and speed. I'd never seen them before.

Movement on the top of a building opposite me caught my attention. Someone crawled on the roof. One . . . maybe two people. Was it a Unity Trooper or the one they hunted?

The speedy officer opened the door to the area car and reached inside. He straightened up, talking into a hands-free phone, a small object and a crime-scene bag in his hands. "Don't know what it is? Haven't seen one before." He held the object up, but I couldn't see it well. "Shaped like a small gun but not like any weapon I've ever seen . . . Yeah, one of them dropped it as I rushed him. Don't know who they were. Probably the same weirdoes we've encountered before. There were three of them . . . No, we lost him . . ." The officer dropped the bag into the car and headed back to the fray.

Unity Troopers continued searching and shouting, but their pace had slowed. Some of them gathered in a group, gesturing with their arms as they exchanged information.

I smiled and even felt a sense of relief for whoever just evaded capture by the Unity Troopers. If the Mosheh had just rescued someone—

Movement on the roof drew my gaze again.

A man in a mottled gray cape squatted on the edge of the rooftop. He lifted his dark shades.

I gasped. It was the man who had saved me. Had he come to talk to me? I took a step forward.

He was too far away for me to make out his expression, but the way he jerked his arm, motioning for me to go the way I had come, told me he didn't like seeing me here. He slinked back and disappeared.

I did as he wanted and took off. A sprinkle of rain started but stopped as I reached the fuel station. I slowed my pace and looked back.

If the Mosheh had rescued someone, they would probably take him to that elevator in the mall and to the underground facility. Did the Mosheh guy really expect me to just turn around and run on home? I didn't want to go home. I wanted to talk to them. If I hurried . . .

I put up my hood and headed for the mall.

Two streets later, the mall once again in sight, someone called my name.

I walked the length of an abandoned brick building, tennis courts with cracked asphalt and drooping nets to my right, old apartments beyond that. Not a soul in sight.

"Over here." The voice came from overgrown boxwood shrubs near the corner of the building.

A few steps later, I saw him, the dark-haired man who had saved me. He leaned against the wall with arms folded and one foot propped up behind him. He wore his hood up but held his shades in his hand. "Give me your Regimen phone." He pushed off the wall and reached a hand out while remaining hidden behind the foliage.

"No. I just got it. It's a new one. They said—"

Head down, he stepped out of the branches and snatched the phone from my belt.

"Hey." I grabbed his wrist.

He twisted free. "We'll leave it here." He dropped my phone into the shrub. "Come with me." Concealing his eyes with dark shades, he darted around the corner. Did he think someone watched? Was a security camera nearby?

After a glance to both sides and a quick scan of the area, I followed him. I rounded the corner, coming to a row of boarded-up shops. An awning hung over windows and doors of the block-long strip of abandoned shops. A field lay across the street, separating this area from the outskirts of the mall. Where had he gone?

Upon a second inspection, I realized the door to the first shop hung open a crack. I ran to it and slipped inside, into darkness.

The guy snatched my hand.

"Hey!" I tried to jerk free.

"Stop." With one smooth motion, he secured something to my wrist and released my hand. Another one of those ID signal bouncers, I guessed.

"If you want to talk to me . . ." He took a few steps back and folded his arms. ". . . you'll have to wear that. You don't want me to get caught, do you?"

Dull gray light streamed in through gaps between and above the boards covering the windows. The shop, no bigger than my apartment, had been gutted — loose floor tiles, broken glass, and darkness were all that remained.

The man moved into a beam of light. At first, he had the hint of a smile. Then his expression turned hard. "I told you to go home."

I laughed. "Who are you to tell me anything?" I regretted my rudeness at once. I wanted his help.

He sneered and took a step toward me, jabbing his finger in the air as he spoke. "Don't draw attention to us. You'll ruin our work."

"I need to know what you guys do."

He turned away, shaking his head. "You need to be patient. You'll know soon enough."

"How soon? Do you know I go into the Breeder Facility in nine days?" My face grew hot. Other girls envied my vocation. I felt shame.

"We know."

"What happened to the guy the Unity Troopers hunted? Did you rescue him?"

He hesitated, glanced. "Yeah."

"Where is he now?"

No answer. A glance. A twitch of his jaw. "He's safe."

I took a deep breath and gritted my teeth. Why couldn't he give me specifics? Why the game? "What will you do with him? Where will he go?" I struggled to sound calm.

Jaw tight, he shook his head.

I pushed my hood back and turned away from him, laughing, an edge to my laugh. "Wow, I mean, you took my phone. Gave me this." I twisted to face him and jerked my hand up to indicate the black box. "There's nobody here." I flung my arms out. "Why can't you talk to me? Tell me what you guys do."

Motionless under a muted beam of light, he looked at me.

I paced the floor by the boarded up windows. "If you can't tell me anything, why should I trust you? I've never met a guy I could trust. What makes you so different? Maybe you kidnap people and use them in a far worse way than the Regimen would. The Regimen doesn't know about the Mosheh, does it?" I turned to see him, to gauge his response.

Silent as a shadow, he had come up behind me. Another step and we would've bumped.

I gave a little gasp, not because of how close he now stood but because of his eyes. Light fell on them. They glittered like gemstones. They were . . . brown. Brown as fertile soil. Deep as the untouched forest. I had never seen brown eyes.

He stepped back. "My name is . . . Dedrick."

"Dedrick," I repeated mindlessly.

"For those who are not satisfied in this society, there is another way. Your leaders know nothing of it. They cannot know, or the other way would not be possible. Your rulers are very controlling." He gave a little smile. The tension between us lifted.

I smiled back. "Yeah." It wasn't the most intelligent reply, but it was all I could give. Could I believe him? His eyes conveyed something pure and honest.

"Not everyone is a candidate for rescue. We can do nothing to jeopardize others." He pressed his lips together as if to stop himself from saying more. "Be patient. Don't go looking. Your time will come."

We appraised one another in silence for a moment. Then he stepped to my side and lifted my hand by the black box on my wrist. His eyes went to mine. "We do not offer an easier way."

"Is there freedom?"

"Yes. There is freedom and much responsibility." He pressed buttons on the mini keypad on the black box. "But there is no going back."

~~~

Rain sprinkled my face as I stepped from under the awning of a shop. I jogged to the side of the building and to the overgrown shrub, to where Dedrick had tossed my flexi-phone. The full foliage made the bush a good hiding place.

I pushed big wet arms of the shrub aside, water splashing my face and neck, and peered through the foliage at the tangle of black branches inside. It took a minute for me to recognize my phone. It was lodged on its side in the lower half of the bush, resembling a branch from my perspective. I reached into the bush. Branches pushed my sleeve up and scraped my arm. I couldn't see where I reached, so I groped around until I felt something thin and smooth.

Got it. I shook the water from my arm, secured the phone to my belt, and took a deep breath. Dedrick had better be for real.

The quickest way home would take me through a dangerous section of town, but the rain and black clouds made me decide to risk it. If I alternated between running and walking, I might get home before it poured.

I adjusted my hood and sprinted.

Halfway home, in an alley I would never go down on a sunny day, my lungs forced me to walk. Dumpsters overflowing with refuse lined one side of the alley. Graffiti covered both walls and even parts of the cracked blacktop. Boards covered one of the doors I passed, a back entrance to a bar. I kept alert, glancing behind every now and then, peering through the rain to make out shadows in the distance.

Though I saw no one, an impression formed in my mind. I wasn't alone.
~~~

A few steps later, I glimpsed a person sitting on the ground between the dumpsters ahead. He leaned against the wall, hugging himself, his face to a smelly dumpster and his hood up.

I averted my gaze and walked faster. Maybe he wouldn't notice me. Druggies hung out here. People lost their lives in these alleys. Keeping my head down and clinging to the opposite wall, I walked past the person. My heart still pounded from the last sprint, but I thought I had the strength to run again. I should start running. What if the person—

My Friend stirred my conscience. A wall of self-reproach stopped me in my tracks and wouldn't let me go on. What if the kid was hurt? What if he needed help? In this rain, I would probably be the only one to pass by.

With a breath for courage, I turned around.

The kid hadn't moved at all. He wasn't dead, was he?

I walked right up and stared at him, looking for a sign of life.

The kid shivered.

"Hey," I shouted. "Are you okay?"

No answer.

I kicked his shoe. The sole was worn and peeling off. "Hey, you should get home. It's going to pour. Do you need some help?"

His head jerked, and he turned to me.

"Darin?" I gasped and dropped to his side, one knee splashing in a puddle. I checked for signs of injury. As cold as my hands were, his jacket felt like ice.

He gawked at me and shivered again.

"What are you doing out here? Come on, let's get you home." I forced his arm up and over my shoulders. With my arm around his back, I lugged him to his feet.

He staggered to one side, dragging me with him. We crashed into the dumpster.

A waft of putrid air gagged me. Something cold and sticky brushed my face, something hanging from the dumpster. I wanted to drop Darin and run, let the rain wash me clean.

I tightened my arms around him. "Come on, Darin. Stand up."

He shifted his weight to me and rested his head against mine.

"That's good. Now let's walk." I took a few steps, clutching his wet jacket, sprinkles in my eyes, moving awkwardly under his weight. "Do you think you can jog a little? It's going to pour soon."

He twisted his face to mine. Water dripped from his nose. "Liberty?" He sounded like he only just realized who helped him.

"Yeah, it's me." We staggered forward. Would we even make it to the end of the alley? "I was kind of shocked to find you out here. You're really stoned, aren't you?"

He nodded. "My boyfriend took off."

"Not much of a friend then."

He gave a lazy sort of chuckle.

By the time we made it to the end of the alley, his legs worked better. He reminded me of a newborn foal, from the videos I'd seen, when it struggles to take its first steps and then staggers along awkwardly, keeping close the breeder horse.

The rain began to pour. Arm in arm, hoods blown back, rain pelting our faces, we ran and ran. I felt stuck in a never-ending nightmare as I clung to him, bore his weight, and ran. He couldn't tell me how to get to his place, so I took him to my apartment.

Once we stepped inside, he collapsed, face first, onto the carpet. His arm landed on the tools by the scooter I had been working on, but otherwise he looked comfortable.

I closed the door and took off my dripping jacket. "I'll get you some dry clothes."

"Dry clothes," he mumbled.

I turned on the lights. The muffled sound of the rain outside, the yellow light inside, the blankets on the floor and the couch, even the stale, warm air combined for a comforting effect. The nightmare had ended. We were safe.

I flung my jacket over the door to the shower stall and unbuttoned my soaked shirt on the way to my bedroom. After changing in the closet, into dry clothes, I grabbed a second pair of jeans, a towel, and one of my work shirts. I tossed them onto the bed and went to retrieve Darin.

He still lay face down on the floor.

"Come on, Darin. I got you some dry clothes." I squatted by him and pushed his shoulder.

He rolled onto his back and squinted at me. "Why you so nice to me, Liberty?"

I chuckled and tugged him up by the arms. "I don't know, Darin. Somebody's got to be. Can't leave you lying by a dumpster in the rain, can I?" I helped him to my room, sat him on the bed, and unzipped his jacket.

"My boyfriend left me. Took my stuff." Once the jacket was off, he slouched, leaning to one side.

"Don't you have any real friends?" I grabbed his shirt collar at the back of his neck. His shirt stuck to his body, squeaking against his wet skin as I peeled it off him. I rubbed his hair with the towel, jogging a vague memory from my childhood. *The smell of chlorine. Sun in my eyes. A smiling, dark-haired woman helping me towel off after swimming.*

Darin shivered and goose bumps appeared on his skin. He hugged himself. "No, I've got nobody." He looked at me out of the top of his eyes. "Do you?"

I shoved his arm into a sleeve. I had my friends at the Senior Living and Recreation Center. No one my own age. But I also had *My Friend.* I couldn't have made it through life without Him.

After buttoning the shirt, I helped Darin out of his wet pants. The musty odor, frayed hems, and worn knees tempted me to throw them away, but I draped them over a toolbox in the closet.

He managed to get the dry jeans on one leg, up to his shin. Then he just sat there, slouching, staring at me through droopy eyes. "Ever feel like you're alone in the world, don't belong anywhere or to anyone, nobody cares about you?"

"Let me help you." I crouched and stuffed his other foot into the other leg of the jeans. "Sometimes I feel that way. Is that how you feel?"

"I hated leaving my first home, you know, the breeder facility, going to Primary," he said, speaking slowly. "My nanny was real good to me. I remember her."

"Up you go." I helped him stand, pulled up and fastened his pants.

"Why you so nice to me, Liberty?" He fell back with abandon, his limbs flopping onto my bed.

I worked the blanket on my bed down, helped him get under it, and fixed the pillow under his head. "You can stay here tonight. Are you hungry?"

He shook his head. "Just high."

I sat on the floor and rested my chin and arms on the bed so I could look into his glazed eyes. "Are you thirsty?"

He smiled and gave a little headshake.

"Just high?" I smiled back. After a moment of staring at each other, I said, "I wish you wouldn't do drugs. You're going to hurt yourself. Like tonight. Staying out in the rain all night, you could catch pneumonia. You ever think about rehab?"

"Rehab?" He coughed, shivered, and pulled the blanket tight. "Why? So I can get back on my feet, contribute to society?" His eyes closed. "Know what I'm supposed to do? My unique contribution?"

"No, you never told me."

"I'm supposed to be a butcher." He chuckled. "A butcher. Kill cows and cut up their bloody flesh. They sent me to Ehrlich, farm town east of here." He took a deep breath and continued talking with his eyes closed. "I couldn't do it. They showed me my duties. Showed me the cows." He chuckled. "I saw cows before, primary school field trip. I like their eyes. Their eyes are brown. And sad. I know we don't get it much, but I won't eat beef anymore."

Dedrick's brown eyes flashed in my mind. "Have you ever seen brown eyes on a person before?"

He laughed and looked at me. "People don't have brown eyes. Only animals do." His grin faded. "They look sad, the cows. Reminded me of me. I couldn't kill them, cut up their flesh, their blood on my hands." He rolled onto his back. "The only thing they could get me to do is sharpen knives. But then this happened." He slid his arm out from under the blanket and pushed the sleeve up, revealing a thick scar on the underside of his forearm.

"I bet that hurt."

"They said I did it on purpose, wanted to kill myself."

"Did you?"

He shrugged. "They sent me to Re-Ed," he whispered as if fearing to speak the words aloud.

Re-Education. What happened to a person in Re-Education? I wanted to know, but I didn't dare ask. No one ever talked about it. I'd never known anyone to admit having gone there.

"Sent me to shrinks, too. I get disability. Don't have to work. Did you know that?"

I nodded. Deep sorrow welled up inside me. My heart, moved by *My Friend*, ached for him. How alone he must've felt. What suffering he must've endured.

"It doesn't matter." He swallowed hard. "Nothing I do matters."

I grabbed Darin's arm and pressed my hand to his scar. "That's not true. You matter."

"I don't contribute. I'm a drag on society."

"There's more to life than work, more than contributing to society."

He snickered. "Yeah? Tell me about that."

I couldn't. I didn't have words for it. I only knew it in my heart. It seemed to me that thinking, caring, choosing, dreaming, being — the things that made us distinct from animals — made us more than just parts of a whole. We, each of one of us, were important for ourselves. *My Friend* had taught me this without words, over the years.

My Friend spoke again, intensifying my compassion and my grief over Darin's loneliness. Emptiness and longing filled my heart, physically causing a sharp pain. He cared deeply about Darin. Maybe if Darin knew how to listen, he'd hear *My Friend* speaking in his own heart. He would know His importance.

"Do you ever hear a voice inside?"

Darin didn't answer. His breaths came slow and regular.

"Do you ever get an impression or hear a voice counseling you to do or not do something?" I traced the scar with my finger. "Sometimes He's silent when I wish He'd speak. I don't always sense Him with me. But I believe He is. He's with you, too. You're not alone, Darin. You have a friend. He's with you all the time. All you have to do is listen." I rested my head on the bed and stroked his arm. "You're loved, Darin. You're important."

Two hours later, I had finished making and eating dinner. I left a bowl of chicken noodle soup and a glass of water on the nightstand for Darin, for when he awoke. Then I sat on the floor and leaned against the bed to write in the notebook. I had come to rely on writing out my feelings, keeping a sort of diary, knowing that no one but I would read these words. It seemed important, almost vital, to have some means to express myself. I wrote about today, about Abby and Richter and the care of the elderly, about the Citizen Safety officers, the Unity Troopers, Darin and Dedrick.

Would I see Dedrick again? Was he for real? Or was he only a kid who had never grown up and who found a way to live out the video games of his youth. Maybe the Mosheh was nothing more than a group of people doing the same thing. It was only a game, a risky game, a game the Regimen wouldn't like. People lied and manipulated others every day. Why should I think these people were any different?

If he did come for me, should I trust him? I knew nothing of where he would take me or what would happen to me. I would be taking my chances. What if they didn't come for me in time? I had only a few days—

The door to the apartment flung open with a bang. Loud voices, laughter, and hooting followed.

I held my breath, listening, wondering if it was only Finley and Tatum.

"Man, that was like taking a shower," Finley said and laughed.

"With our clothes on."

My stomach dropped at the sound of Silver's voice.

"Is she here?" Sid said that.

My breath caught in my throat. He probably noticed my closed bedroom door.

I stuffed the notebook and pencil between the mattresses. I shouldn't have anything to worry about. Sid wouldn't bother me with Finley around. Finley never tolerated guys being aggressive with girls.

The instant I got to my feet, my bedroom door flew open.

Sid stood in the doorway, glaring at me through one good and one black eye. He leaned against the doorframe, touched his bottom lip, and checked his finger. He had a purple bruise on the side of his chin, near his mouth.

"What do you want?" I put my hands on my hips and glared back.

"Won't your boyfriend be mad?" He nodded at Darin asleep in my bed.

"I don't have a boyfriend."

"Someone did this to me." He lifted his wet t-shirt, exposing a well-muscled but bruised and bandaged abdomen. "And this . . ." He curled his arm, flexing his bicep, turning it to display a big purple bruise.

"And this." Silver came up behind Sid and peered at me. Her hair, matted to her forehead in wet, grayish spikes, drew attention to the big gash on her nose. "That freak busted my nose." She pushed past Sid and took a few steps into my room. Her gaze shifted to Darin and she stopped. "What's he doing here? Something wrong with him?"

"No," I said. "He was out in the rain. I brought him here."

"Is he high?" Silver grinned and her silvery eyes shifted, her gaze turning to me.

I shrugged. She knew Darin well enough. She didn't need me to tell her anything.

"So what's his name?" Sid said. "Your boyfriend. How come we never seen him before?"

"Yeah, and why the costume?" Silver said. "What's he afraid of?"

"I don't know. I never saw him before either. I'm just glad he was there to save me from the two of you."

Sid glanced over his shoulder as if checking to see if Tatum and Finley listened. Then he swaggered up close to me and said in a low voice, "I'll find out who he is. I know you know him. Or he knows you. He told me to stop following you. Maybe he wants you—"

My phone buzzed. Someone sent me a message.

"Maybe that's him." Sid reached for the phone on my belt.

I backed up, smacking into the wall, and snatched the phone first. I brought it up to read the message that scrolled across the curved screen.

Silver ripped it from my hand. She read the message to herself and laughed. "You have a mandatory appointment with Dr. Bailey, DPM." She smirked at me. "What's a DPM?"

"Isn't that a psychiatrist?" Sid said to Silver.

She shrugged, tossed my phone to the floor, and stared down her broken nose at me. Her lip curled up on one side. She stepped closer.

"I-I don't know. I guess it's a psychiatrist." I wanted to retreat but my back was already to the wall.

Silver gave me a long hard stare. "It's not wise to make an enemy of me."

7

I got to work early without seeing or hearing anything out of the ordinary along the way—to my disappointment.

Patience. Dedrick said I needed patience. I spent the past two days trying to practice patience, sticking to my regular routine, going to work early, stopping at the commissary on the way home, and all the while keeping my eyes and ears open for the Mosheh. In the evenings, I worked on my neighbor's scooter, finally finishing it. I'd return it to him today. For now, I had to work on getting through another workday. I had begun to count down my days. In two days, I would have a psychiatric evaluation. In seven, my fate would be sealed.

I stepped into the recreation room.

Not a sound came from the kitchen. A solitary woman sat on a recliner, watching a show on the huge wall screen. Two men played a video game at one of the tables. A man and a woman came into the room at the same moment I did, through the opposite doorway.

I expected to see more seniors, but I was early. Maybe Abby would come down today. She'd been spending her days alone in her room and I missed her.

"Good morning," I said to the woman in the recliner, on my way to the kitchen. My flexi-phone buzzed as I pushed open the kitchen doors.

No one was in the kitchen. The third-shift kids always hung out in the kitchen at the end of their shift. Where were they? They left the chairs askew, cleaners on the table, dirty dishes on the counter and—

I did a double-take at the sink.

Murky brown water filled it to the top.

I flipped the switch to the garbage disposal. The unit hummed but didn't spin. The dirty water kept me from seeing the problem, but I wasn't quite ready to stick my hand in it. I never minded dirt and grease on my hands and arms when working on motors. I could see what I worked on. No surprises. Nothing lurked beneath the surface.

Where were those guys?

I stomped from the kitchen, snatching my phone from my belt to check the message. At the press of a button, words scrolled across the screen: *The RCT Vocational Department wishes to inform you about the status of your Vocation Change Request. Your request has been denied. If you believe you have received this message in error or need further assistance, you may contact the RCT Vocational . . .*

I whipped my flexi-phone at the wall and swore.

The old woman on the couch looked at me with questioning eyes.

I approached her, forcing the anger from my expression. "Have you seen the cleaning crew?"

"Cleaning crew?"

"The guys from third shift? They usually hang out in the kitchen about this time."

"Oh." She pointed to the door that led to the Senior Living. "They're cleaning out a room. Richter's room."

Her words pierced my heart. We hadn't heard anything about Richter since he left that night. Had he—

I bolted for the door to the Senior Living.

"Your phone," the woman shouted.

I dashed down the hall and to the elevators, waved my hand over the ID implant reader, and squeezed into the elevator. As the elevator rose, a cheerful message from the Senior Living and Recreation Center president played. "You are invited to participate in our summer evening activities. On Wednesdays we have . . ."

The overly cheerful voice grated on my nerves. I started bouncing on my toes.

"Be still."

My Friend communicated this message with such force it seemed like He spoke audibly.

I breathed deep and shook my arms, but I couldn't stop bouncing on my toes. "I'll try," I said, lacking interior commitment. I couldn't stand the thought of Nyeb and the other guys touching Richter's things.

The elevator lurched to a stop. The doors parted. I slipped out and dashed down the hall.

Richter's room was a few doors down from Abby's. A big platform cart, holding three plastic boxes, sat outside the open door. One of the cleaning crew, the guy who had the computer pad the other day, came out of the room and stooped over the boxes. He dug something out of a box and went back into the room shouting, "The old dodo left us a whole box of cigars."

Dodo? They called Mr. Richter a dodo? I clenched my fists as I ran.

A strange sensation swept through me, a warning from *My Friend.*

I forced myself to walk and took a deep breath. I needed self-control. The third shift guys, while extremely rude and insensitive, were only doing their job.

"He should've smoked them himself," Nyeb said.

"Maybe he was saving them."

"When you're his age, you shouldn't save anything. Smoke 'em if you got 'em."

They all laughed. Musty-scented smoke came from the room.

"I knew he didn't have long." Nyeb sounded boastful. "That's why I bet on him . . ."

Bet on him? On when he'd die?

The warning flashed through me again, but I numbed myself to it and stomped down the hall, leaving the warning in my wake. *My Friend* would not like what I was about to do.

" . . . I even told him he didn't have long."

"Did not."

I stepped into the doorway.

None of them looked my way. The shy one leaned against the bathroom doorframe with his foot propped up on the opposite side. Nyeb stood with one hand on his hip, his back to me. The other guy had his face in the bathroom cabinet. They each held a lit cigar.

"I did too." Nyeb snickered. "Day before they took him out of here, he puked all over the bathroom. I had to clean it up. So I told him, I said, 'Your days are numbered, old man.' He thought I said something else, I guess, because he told me, 'Thank you.'"

They all laughed.

Stars filled my vision. I lunged at Nyeb and rammed my shoulder into his back.

He grunted and stumbled forward, dropping the cigar. He spun to face me.

I slammed my palms against his chest. "You guys are evil. You shouldn't work here."

"Man, Liberty, what's your problem?" Nyeb regained his balance and grabbed my arms.

I broke his grip with an outward jerk of my arms and shoved him against the wall. "I can't believe you bet on when people will die." I pressed my forearm against his neck, pinning him. "What kind of sick, twisted . . ."

Nyeb pried at my fingers, grimacing with anger and amusement. The sheepish guy slipped past us, headed for the door. The other kid came around behind me. In an instant, he hooked his arms around mine. "Easy does it, wild thing." He pulled me off Nyeb.

With a backward thrust, my elbow cracked ribs. The kid behind me doubled over. I slugged Nyeb across the chin. Nyeb swung back, but I ducked.

"Liberty!"

Nyeb and I froze. I turned to see who'd called me with such a stern voice.

Abby stood in the doorway, arms akimbo, mouth a thin line. Her expression softened when she spoke again. "Would you mind escorting me downstairs? I think I'd like to have tea in the recreation room."

I could picture my fist removing the smug grin from Nyeb's face. I wanted my anger to teach him the importance of these people. Each of them deserved respect. A man had died.

Abby stared. She nodded and reached out her hand. "Come with me, Liberty."

I took a breath and unclenched my fists. I threw Nyeb a dirty look over my shoulder as I went to Abby.

He sneered.

Still trying to regulate my breathing, I took Abby's arm and we strolled down the hall. "You want to go down, huh? I'm glad. I've missed you."

She walked slowly but steadily. "I've missed you, too." We stopped at the elevator, and she brought a hand up to the implant reader. "It's been hard for me. Tears have been my bread. Richter. So sudden." She shuffled into the elevator.

"I know. Me too. When did he . . ."

"I don't know. No one could tell me."

Neither of us spoke as the elevator descended and we walked, arm in arm, to the recreation room.

I helped her into her chair. "I'll get you some tea."

Abby captured my hand. "Wait. Sit down."

I took the chair next to her.

"Talk to me first." She lessened her grip, now resting her hand on mine. "Tell me what's wrong. I've never seen you explode like that."

"You mean besides Richter being gone and not coming back?" I couldn't tell her about third shift's bets on who would die next. I couldn't tell her about the Mosheh and my waning hope.

She squeezed my hand. "I think you're upset because this is your last week here. Don't be afraid of your vocation."

"My vocation." I huffed and slumped back in the chair. "I got the answer to my Vocation Change Request."

She patted my hand and nodded. "I know. You were denied again."

I glared at the nearest camera, the one over the door to the Senior Living.

"I know why they selected you." Abby leaned forward, rubbing my hand, the hint of a smile on her lips. "You're healthy and strong. You're beautiful. You're intelligent. You have something many young people lack . . . compassion."

I pulled my hand from hers and shifted in the chair. "They don't care about that. They want my eggs and my body."

"You'll be a nanny to the babies, too. All those little ones, they'll need a girl with compassion."

Unable to give a response she'd like and not wanting to break her rare, pleasant mood, I simply shook my head.

"It's a very nice facility, I hear. Nicer than your apartment now, I would imagine. You'll get away from your wild roommate and her troublesome friends." Amusement flickered in her eyes. "I've never met a girl who wouldn't trade everything for the vocation of Breeder, before you, that is."

"I don't care how nice it is, how big my room will be, how many chefs and massage therapists I'll have at my call, how it overlooks the Fully-Protected Nature Preserves. I'll feel trapped. And used."

"You'll be bringing new life into our world. That's an awesome vocation."

"It's unnatural, the way they do it."

"Unnatural? You should feel lucky that you have all your parts, your God-given — I mean, the things that make you distinctly female." She raised her brows and nodded. "They sterilize girls your age."

I chuckled. "I guess. But it really is unnatural, isn't it?" I leaned toward her, resting my arms on the table and taking her hands. "How was it in the past?" I peered into her eyes, hoping to read an answer. "There wasn't always a Breeder Facility. What do you know about families?"

She twitched and then glanced at the camera over the door. The hint of a smile faded as she leaned back. "Watch what you say."

"You just said something about God."

She shook her head. "It's an expression."

"Is it?" A close friend of mine in Secondary, Sarkin, believed in God, an all-powerful, uncreated Creator. He said logic brought him to the belief. But he spoke too much about it and they took him away, to Re-Education, we assumed. We never saw him again.

"We are all one family. We rely on each other. We need each other. Each has his own role to play, his or her own unique contribution to society . . ."

My ears closed. My heart went numb. I watched her placid expression as she carried on, promoting the ways of the Regimen, a smile in her eyes.

I remained without comment until she ran out of praises for the Regimen. Then I went to the kitchen to fix her tea.

Pushing open the kitchen doors, laying eyes on the mess and the clogged sink, I sighed. I had forgotten about it. I crawled under the sink and pushed the reset button on the underside of the disposal. Then I got up and flipped the switch. The disposal hummed but wouldn't turn.

I went to the closet for tools.

Why had Abby spoken that way? She sounded like Dr. Supero and the other Regimen lovers. Had an RCT counselor spoken to her? Changed her? I hadn't seen her since they took Richter. Had she done something rash that brought a counselor in to speak with her?

Back under the sink, I stuck an Allen wrench in the socket on the underside of the unit and twisted. It did nothing to free the blades. I went to the meager toolbox and snatched a big screwdriver.

Would Abby have told them about the things I've said? What had I said to her? What specifically had I said lately? Anything that would call for a psychiatric evaluation? I wasn't looking forward to that.

I leaned over the sink, shoved the screwdriver into the disposal and moved it around, hoping to clean the flywheel. It bumped against junk and more junk. What strange things had third shift dropped into the disposal?

A flip of the switch made the unit hum, but that was all.

I tossed the screwdriver to the floor. Of course, it wouldn't be a simple fix. I'd have to remove the whole disposal. The other first shift girls always came to work late, so the seniors would have no one to call on until I finished.

I laid towels and a bucket under the plumbing and crawled under the sink with a pipe wrench to remove the J trap.

The psychological evaluation might only be routine. Could a person fail the evaluation? What then? Would they want me at the Breeder Facility? Could this be a way out?

Darin came to mind. He couldn't fulfill his vocation, make his contribution to society, so they gave him counseling and medication. I didn't want that either. I wanted—

The slip joint nut gave way. The J trap shifted and dirty water burst forth, spraying me.

I dropped wrench and shielded my face with one arm, lifted the bucket to catch the water with the other. A few minutes later, I had the disposal out and on the table. As dirty as the job was, I found satisfaction in working with my hands on a task I could accomplish. I had every confidence I'd get the thing working.

With the slightest hesitation, I scooped food from the unit with my bare hands and dumped it into an empty bucket. I cleaned the impeller arms with my fingers, discovering something lodged under one of them. A paring knife helped me pry it free.

It was a little gear. For a watch? Why would anyone put a watch in a garbage disposal?

My breath caught in my throat when the answer popped into my mind. I thrust my hands into the bucket and dug through food. A leather watchband, more parts . . .

My hands trembled. Richter's watch. They had taken it from Abby and destroyed it.

~~~

"I know who you are . . . Dr. Supero." Chief Varden spit the name out.

Dr. Supero withdrew his outstretched hand. Who did Varden think he was?

Standing arms akimbo, biceps bulging from under his black t-shirt, Chief Varden faced an array of wall monitors in the Central Surveillance Control Room. He glanced at Dr. Supero over his shoulder, a sneer on his strong-jawed, freckled face. "You're the head physician at Aldonia Hospital. You're on the Aldonia Medical Board Committee, the RCT Medical Board Committee, and the Regimen-only-knows what other committees. You sit in on every board meeting that concerns Regimen budget or finance, finagling greater funds for your worthless projects."

Varden took a step closer, his steel-gray eyes narrowing into slits. "Weeding freckled skin from the gene pool, creating new designer eye colors, hairless legs . . ." His gaze flitted back and forth from one of Dr. Supero's eyes to the other, his face screwing up. "What are those? Purple eyes?"
~~~

Dr. Supero winced to see a man of Chief Varden's stature displaying such vulgar jealousy. "The projects for which I serve as advocate greatly increase quality of life, longevity, and can even help *you* at the Citizen Safety Station by reducing crime. Germline modification not only allows the engineering of physical and intellectual traits — we are learning to identify and manipulate personality traits. Wouldn't it make your job easier if rebellious personalities were not passed on to future generations?"

"What about arrogance? Can you weed out that?" Varden, still with arms akimbo, turned away and stomped to the nearest worker.

The worker, a wiry boy in his twenties, straightened up in his padded, ergonomic chair and gave Varden a wary glance. "What? Did I miss something?"

He was one of the twenty or so workers in the room who had the exciting job of staring at monitors and eavesdropping on conversations of individuals flagged as potential threats by the surveillance computer program. How to get Liberty flagged and on that list?

"You look like you're sleeping over here." Varden leaned on the worker's station, making the worker lean out of the way, and scrolled through a few screens. "Need a stimulant from the good doctor to stay awake?" He gave Dr. Supero a sideways glance.

Dr. Supero stepped over. "I'm here to inform you about a citizen you need to monitor."

Chief Varden huffed. "Oh yeah? Why do I *need* to do that? My commands come from higher up, and my leads come from our own computer system and extensive databases. We can competently identify and track every possible threat to society. We have this game under control—"

"Listen to me." Dr. Supero spoke with command and lifted his chin. If only he wasn't several inches shorter than the chief. "Her name is Liberty 554-062466-84 of Aldonia. And if you are not presently observing her, consider her a new threat."

"According to who? We have our hands full. Because of you, we have less money in our budget. CSS is the single most important branch of the Regimen. The stability of our society depends upon us. Unity Troopers depend upon us so they can keep our city safe from domestic violence. The governor, even the continental president, depends upon us to warn them of potential threats. You depend upon us. We are the watchers that keep Aldonia safe. But because of you, we have surveillance equipment, cameras, and other systems in need of repairs and no funds to do it. We have to waste time generating studies and reports so we can choose which sections of Aldonia warrant immediate repairs of surveillance equipment and which can wait. Because of you and your pet projects getting more than your share of funds—"

"Chief Varden!" Supero spoke through gritted teeth. A white gnat weaved through his vision. "You are sadly mistaken if you think that the CSS is the most important branch of Regimen. The medical advancements that come from our facility affect generations to come, exceeding in importance anything that CSS handles from day to day."

"Yet, here you are . . ." Varden ginned. ". . . begging for my assistance."

"Begging? I do not beg!"

A few workers spun their heads to look at him.

Perhaps he spoke too loudly. He could not allow Varden's arrogance to become a hurdle to his goal. If Varden would not help him, he had only the girl's psychiatric evaluation left. Supero took a breath and relaxed his jaw. Perhaps flattery . . . "Am I mistaken in thinking that you care about the quality of life for future generations?"

"I have a job to do. Lives depend upon me *now*." Varden walked away, to the far side of the room. He snatched a computer pad from a workstation.

"Liberty is an anarchist."

Varden's attention snapped to Supero. "An anarchist?"

"That is what I said. Check her files. In Secondary, she—"

"Secondary?" Varden snickered. "How old is this anarchist?"

"Age does not matter. She's slated to be a breeder in a week. She has ideas that threaten the stability of our reproductive program. If her ideas infect others at the Breeder Facility, what will happen to Aldonia? The reproduction rate is very precise, very important for maintaining balance in our society and with the earth. We cannot allow—"

"Spare me the lecture." Chief Varden shoved a dark-eyed girl from her station and took her seat. The girl folded her arms and watched through heavy-lidded, sumptuous eyes as Varden manipulated data on the smooth surface of the data entry pad. "Liberty 554 . . . What did you say?"

Dr. Supero gave him the numbers.

The instant Varden input the data, Liberty's holographic image popped up on one side of the workstation and began slowly turning in a circle. Her file appeared on the station monitor, and a wall monitor flipped to a live feed of the Senior Living and Recreation Center. A few of the elderly stood in a group, others sat at two circular tables, and others lounged on furniture and watched a televised program or dozed. Where was—

Liberty burst through a set of double doors. She linked arms with an old man and escorted him across the room.

"Do you have records of her phone conversations?" Supero said.

"Sure. We have everyone's phone conversations." Varden bounced in the ergonomic chair. "They're in a database. A program examines every one of them. Certain words and phrases bring up red flags. If she'd been flagged, we'd have examined it already."

"I want someone to go over her phone conversations."

"Well, that's just too bad. I haven't the manpower. If she had said anything—"

"That's not good enough. Designate someone to—" He set his sights on the girl with the sultry eyes. "Her. She can do it."

The girl stuck out her bottom lip, glared at him, and readjusted her folded arms.

"You overstep your boundaries, Doctor."

Supero's mouth twitched. "Give me a week. That's all I ask. I need a thorough investigation of this girl before she comes in and destroys what we have worked so hard to accomplish. The ideas of an anarchist, when spoken aloud, become a poison to us all."

"Are we back in primary school? Drop the lessons." Varden moved his hands across the data pad and a second wall monitor showed the Senior Recreation Center. "This was yesterday." He continued to move his hands, manipulating a search in the database. "I'll set a program to search the video database and pull up any segments with her in it. We can get a list of her friends and contacts, shopping patterns, walking routes, records of her purchases—legal ones anyway. We'll go back a week and see what we find."

Images flashed on the station monitor, each one shrinking to a thumb-sized square and lining up on the screen. Varden leaned back and clasped his hands behind his head. He grinned at Supero. "So, you think she's planning something?"

"Does an anarchist plan anything? I think she's a danger and—"

His flexi-phone played his personal ringtone, too loudly. He had specifically told Ivy to hold his calls unless . . . "Excuse me, Chief Varden, I need to take this."

Dr. Supero smoothed his hair. It was too soon, really, to think that the Medical Care Evaluation Panel had arrived at a decision. These things took time. Cancer. The thought that a cancerous cyst grew inside his head made his skin crawl. It was such a contradiction. He devoted himself to healing others and increasing quality of life. Yet he, the physician responsible for submitting professional recommendations to the MCEP for expensive or risky procedures, had had to write one for himself. He'd never considered the agony a patient experienced waiting for the panel's decision, until now.

Supero stepped into the hallway and answered the call.

"Dr. Supero?" Ivy's holographic image hovered above the flexi-phone on his wrist. She tossed her dark-green-streaked blonde bangs from her long-lashed eyes and took something— gum? — from her mouth. Was she flirting with him? She seemed more pleasant as of late.

"I'm on important business," he said. "What do you want?"

"You said for me to notify you immediately if anything changed with Liberty."

Supero clenched his fist, causing her holographic image to jiggle. "Yes? What is the change?"

"Her psychiatric evaluation has been rescheduled." Ivy spoke with indifference.

"Rescheduled? It is already too close to her entry date. It can't be rescheduled."

"Well, it is."

"Why?"

"How should I know?" Ivy tucked her hair behind her ear and cocked her head to one side. "I do know that your old assistant works for the psychiatrist."

Supero's eyes nearly popped from their sockets. "Sage? Sage?"

"Yes, Dr. Supero, Sage."

"Why that, that—"

The door to the surveillance room slid open before Supero could wrap his mouth around a crude enough word. The sultry-eyed girl stood in the doorway, one hand on her hip, the other she held up to examine her nails. "Chief wants to see you. There's some footage."

Supero followed her through the room, back to Varden.

Varden nodded at the monitor. "This happened two days ago."

The video showed a flurry of Unity Troopers, guns drawn, searching an alley. The orange and blue lights of their automobiles flashed, reflecting off their black helmets, giving color to the gray scene on this overcast day. A trooper with a metallic exoskeleton on his legs approached an area car. He held something small in his hands.

"What is this? Where is Liberty?"

"There." Varden pointed at the lower corner of the monitor.

A figure stood between buildings, almost hidden in the shadows.

"I don't understand. What is going on?"

"Unity Troopers were after a guy we'd been following for months. We finally got permission to bring him in for Re-Ed. He's one of those *Everyone Deserves a Vote* whiners." Varden grimaced at Supero. "I guess he's not satisfied letting only the smart and powerful run our world. Wants everyone, even the idiots on the street, to have a vote."

"There are no idiots on the street. We learned to identify that gene decades ago."

"Whatever."

"Does Liberty know him?"

"Don't think so. No records of phone communication. A video search of her and this guy together brings up nothing." He hunched over the workstation again. "It's probably nothing. She must've seen the Unity

Troopers and got curious. She has a pattern of taking alternate routes wherever she goes. Hardly goes the same way twice. Even seems to know how to avoid working security cameras sometimes. I attribute that to her friend Finley. He works for the Environmental Stewardship Unit. They replace or repair surveillance equipment according to our directives, when they get around to it."

The video continued to play, looping to the beginning of the feed. Liberty jogged into view and darted into the shadows. The Unity Troopers scurried like rats through the alley, no prisoner in hand.

"What happened to the kid? Did they catch him?"

"Um . . ." Varden shifted in his seat. "No, he, uh . . ." He looked directly into Dr. Supero's eyes. "There's a group of kids that we only have a glimpse of on video. They got him first."

"A group of kids?" Supero sounded shocked, though he wasn't. The Unity Troopers weren't the most efficient arm of the RCT.

"Yeah. We don't know who they are. We call them the Anarchists. They interfere with our work, on occasion. Kidnap people. They wear black shades and capes so we can't ID them. All our recognition software needs is a face or eyes. Even a body structure would help."

"Their implants?"

"No, I don't think they have any."

"What? Everyone has an implant."

"Well, if they do, we can't read them. Maybe they have a way of confusing the signal."

The video continued to play. Liberty looked up. She seemed to look directly at the surveillance camera. Her expression went from shock to annoyance.

"What is she looking at?" Supero leaned in. No, not *what*. "*Who* is she looking at?"

8

My Friend abandoned me. I walked alone, the sun warming my back, the cool air clearing my mind, people all around. I should've been jogging. If I ran, I might get to the Psychiatric Center in time, but I couldn't get myself to care. So what if I arrived late for my appointment?

Four loud teens, probably fresh out of Secondary, rode skateboards in the parking lot I had to cross. One of them had purple hair worn straight up in a style that resembled a flame. They turned their heads and gawked as six scooters rumbled up to them. A boy on a scooter shouted something. Some of them laughed.

"I think it's a girl," one of the kids said, probably referring to me.

I kept my gaze on the horizon and my gait steady. I had never felt so alone. Abby hadn't recovered from her uncharacteristic pro-Regimen frame of mind. *My Friend* had remained silent for days. Maybe He never existed. In the fear and loneliness of my childhood, as I waited to transfer from my nursery to my primary residence, perhaps I created Him. I needed someone by my side, close to me, ever present . . . so my imagination brought Him into existence, and I heard His voice and felt His inspirations whenever I needed someone.

Reality had a numbing effect. We were all alone on this journey of life. The decisions I had to make, I had to make on my own. I had no special friend on my side to counsel me, no one to strengthen me in weakness, direct me in confusion, encourage me, or comfort me.

Once through the parking lot, I turned down a quiet street that intersected Tenth Street at the next block. At my pace, it would take twenty minutes or so to reach the opposite end of Tenth Street and the Psychiatric Center. I'd be ten minutes late for my appointment, the appointment that would determine my fate.

I stopped on the corner of Tenth Street. People walked past me. Ants crawled in a line at my feet. A foul odor wafted from a nearby trash receptacle.

I stood at a crossroads not knowing which way to go. Should I give the psychiatrists the answers they wanted to hear? If I did, I'd enter the Breeder Facility and begin my vocation as breeder in just two days. I hated to lie. Why should I have to? Why couldn't I have beliefs and ideas contrary to the philosophy of the Regimen? What if I told the truth about my opinions and my distraught mental state? Would they send me to Re-Education? Is that what happened to Darin, what changed him and stripped him of all hope and joy?

After taking a deep breath, I forced myself to walk on.

Would the Mosheh rescue me before my entry date? Time was running out. The Breeder Facility had tight security. The rescue I witnessed and my own rescue from Sid and Silver took place in less-traveled places, in alleys with no security. The Mosheh had access to security feeds from cameras throughout Aldonia. They also seemed to know the intentions of the Unity Troopers. They had costumes and ways of traveling that did not draw attention. Could they break into a high-security facility and get me out? Seemed unlikely.

Maybe I wasn't high on their list of candidates for rescue. Did they trust me?

I slowed my pace and tension gathered in my brow. Did they know my appointment had been changed? Maybe they planned to rescue me on my original appointment date.

My legs moved like lead. My mind reeled. I slowed more, staggering a bit. A girl behind me called me a name and passed me up.

Had I missed my chance? I scanned my surroundings, salmon-colored single-story professional buildings on one side and older brick two-stories on the other. Scooters and cars drove down the street, most going the same direction as I. People. People everywhere . . . strolling the sidewalks, standing in groups, crossing the street . . . all under the watchful eyes of the Regimen.

Was the Mosheh watching me now? Would they risk a rescue on such a busy street?

No. I had to do something.

I turned around and dashed.

"Hey, watch it!" The man I smacked into sneered.

"Sorry." I pushed past him and jogged back the way I came. The Mosheh had known when the Unity Troopers wanted a man for re-education. They knew exactly when to step in. Skipping my appointment would draw the attention of the Citizen Safety Station, wouldn't it? If I got Citizen Safety or Unity Troopers after me, the Mosheh would know it.

I couldn't remember details about the rescue they planned while I had recovered in their underground facility, but I had nearly witnessed a guy being rescued. It took place in one of the alleys on the back way from my apartment to the mall.

Heart racing, I reached the parking lot with the teens. The time? Five minutes past my appointment. How long before the Psychiatric Center wondered about me?

As I crossed the parking lot, I slowed to catch my breath.

Sirens sounded in the distance. They couldn't be for me. Not yet.

I needed to reach the alleys behind the mall. Jogging again, adrenaline coursing through my veins, I went down one street and then another. Getting closer. Running now.

The sirens grew louder. The fuel station and scooter dealer came into view. The image of the Unity Troopers hunting that man flashed in my mind. How close had they come to catching him? But they didn't catch him. The Mosheh saved him.

My heart leaped. The Mosheh would save me. They would be able to rescue me in an alley back here.

When I reached the alley, I stopped running and leaned over to catch my breath.

Sirens blared behind and before me. Blue and orange lights flashed on the far side of the alley.

Had the authorities come for me so soon? My mouth went dry. My heart got stuck in my throat.

Still struggling to catch my breath, I spun in a circle, glancing from rooftop to rooftop. No one. No sign of Dedrick or the Mosheh. *Don't panic. They'll come.*

Blue and orange lights flashed on every side, drawing nearer. A black Unity Troop area car sped into the alley, headed toward me.

I bolted for the next alley, a ten-meter dash. I hadn't seen the guy the Mosheh had rescued. He must've been down an alley. Where, exactly, had the rescue taken place? Several alleys cut across this one. It must've been down one of them.

I skidded into the alley. Dirt, doors, trash receptacles, a waist-high crate. No sign of the Mosheh. The sirens hurt my ears. I ran for a door.

A vehicle screeched to a halt at the end of this alley, kicking dirt up into a cloud. Car doors flung open. Men shouted commands.

The doorknob I tried wouldn't turn. I bolted to the next door. The Mosheh would've heard the order given to the Unity Troopers. They would've known that I was about to be picked up. What if they didn't come? What would the authorities do with me? Would they send me to Re-Ed? For simply skipping an appointment?

A towering black monstrosity stepped through the dirt cloud, a trooper in black-scaled armor with a robotic exoskeleton on his legs and a gun at the ready. His visor turned toward me and he spoke. "Liberty 554-062466-84 of Aldonia." His voice rumbled through a loudspeaker in his helmet. "Do not resist."

My breath caught in my throat. My hand slipped from the doorknob. I stumbled back, crashing into a crate. Rough wood scraped my arm.

I turned and dashed.

Thuds and whirs sounded behind me as the robotic legs propelled the trooper forward.

I raced for the end of the alley, my lungs screaming.

Blue and orange flashing lights appeared before me. A sleek Unity Trooper motorcycle sped into the alley. The rider jumped off.

I skidded to a stop and peered at rooftops. *No one, no one.* My heart beat furiously and sank to my feet.

Behind me, the towering monstrosity advanced by slow, loud steps. The motorcycle trooper stood before me.

I shrunk back.

Hands latched onto my shoulders from behind. The robo-trooper spun me to face him. "Come with me." He shoved me forward.

Not wanting him to push me again, I did as he commanded. "Where are you taking me?"

"Seems you're wanted at the Psych Center." His voice rumbled through the helmet but it carried a hint of amusement. Could he be one of the Mosheh?

"Am I the first person to skip an appointment?" I wanted him to lift his helmet. "They send Unity Troopers after me? Why not a phone call?"

Two other troopers met us at the area car. One of them identified me, checking my implant. The other shoved me into the backseat. They strolled away while speaking to their control center about their successful capture. Unity Troopers, definitely Unity Troopers.

My body and my heart ached. I slumped down in the seat, hugging myself. Dedrick had betrayed me, abandoned me. Why hadn't the Mosheh come for me? Did they not trust me? Maybe they lied to me and never intended to rescue me. What could they offer anyway? A life underground? A life of hiding?

It was foolish to think I could resist the Regimen. I was foolish to try. They did take care of everyone, had it all figured out, all things considered. Every member of society had their own unique contribution based on their individual talents and abilities. My intelligence and physical make-up made me ideal for my vocation. *Breeder*. Why should I shun the vocation? I should've been flattered.

I sat up, smoothed my hair, and took a deep breath.

The driver glanced at me through the rearview mirror. We were almost to Tenth Street.

My vocation would only waste a few years. Then I could do what I wanted, to a degree. I could become a mechanic. I could visit the Senior Center and Abby.

I took a deep breath and gazed out the window.

We turned down Tenth Street. Sunlight reflected on windows on the west side of the street, keeping me from looking that way. On the east side of the street, one building rose up taller than the others, a better kept, bone-white, block-long building with a strip of black windows on each of the ten stories. The Psychiatric Center for Evaluation and Rehab.

~~~

Dr. Supero paced the floor of the empty conference room the CSS had allowed him to use. Every few seconds he glanced up at the wall monitor. Chief Varden said he would stream the live feed of Liberty's interview at the Psychiatric Center.

Supero glanced at his watch. They'd had the girl in custody ten minutes ago. What took them so long to begin the interview? Perhaps she had not gone willingly. Perhaps she had tried to fight. Or perhaps the incompetency of the CSS—

An image popped onto the screen.

Dr. Supero darted to the center of the room, for optimal viewing, and then froze with his eyes glued to the monitor.

Liberty sat alone, slumped back in a chair, arms folded and head down. The door slid open and Sage, the new assistant at the Psychiatric Center, swayed into the room. She wore a loose-fitting, short white dress that drew attention to her thighs. Her cropped ginger and copper hair glowed gorgeously under the ambient lighting. Liberty shifted in her seat as Sage sat cattycorner her at the table. Sage crossed her legs and put a finger to her ear, probably adjusting the earpiece through which she would hear the psychiatrist's comments and questions. Liberty stared.

Sage glanced directly at the main camera and gave a nod. She gave the hint of a smile to Liberty and said, "My name is Sage. I will be conducting your interview. May I have your full name?" Sage's lips moved seductively as she spoke.

Dr. Supero's body stirred at the feelings she brought back. He inhaled, imagining he could smell her balmy scent, feel her smooth skin . . . She had meant more to him than he had understood. Something deeper than the physical. With a sharp exhale he forced the thoughts from his mind.

"What?" Liberty glared. "You guys set the appointment. You don't know who I am?"

"Your full name, please."

Liberty huffed and averted her gaze.
~~~

"Very well." Sage reached, gracefulness cast aside, for Liberty's wrist.

Liberty drew back. Sage latched onto her arm and dragged her hand over the ID scanner in the center of the table.

Dr. Supero smiled and glanced over his shoulder to share his joy with . . . Oh that was right; he had the room to himself.

Sage fit this job better than she had fit the job as his assistant. She had always been efficient at drawing emotion from others. Yes, victory was at hand. The team of psychiatrists would see the girl's belligerence and recognize the detrimental effect it would have on the other breeders. They would have no choice but to recommend her for re-education and a new vocation.

"Who are *you*?" Liberty glared and rubbed her arm where Sage had grabbed it. "I don't want to talk to you. Are you even a psychiatrist? You're awfully young."

Sage glared into the camera. She took a breath through her mouth. As she returned her attention to Liberty, her look softened. "Let's begin with life after your formative years. Since transitioning from Secondary, you've shared an apartment with another girl. How would you describe your relationship with your roommate of three years?"

Liberty shrugged. "We get along. I mean, it's not like I chose my roommate." Her eyes and voice hardened. "Some group with the Regimen did that, just like they pick everything we—" She shut her mouth. Her expression turned placid. She dipped her head forward, ran a hand through loose strands of hair, and lifted her head. "I'm sorry. This is hard for me."

"I'm sorry?" Dr. Supero shook his head. An apology?

Sage placed a hand on the table as if she meant to take Liberty's hand but changed her mind. "I understand."

"It's just . . . this is such a big deal to me. And I can't say I'm happy about my vocation. I know most girls would be, but I—"

"It's okay. You don't have to be like everyone else. Let's just start at the beginning. Your roommate."

Liberty nodded and then . . . smiled like a docile little girl. "Her name is Tatum, and we get along well. She's kind of vulnerable, if you ask me, and easy going. She needs people. She always has people around her, friends over . . . And our apartment's so small. I guess that kind of gets my goat. I like my privacy. I like quiet sometimes. But . . ." She shook her head and shrugged again, her demeanor uncharacteristically meek. "I try not to let it bother me too much. I mean, I'm flexible."

"You . . . flexible!" Dr. Supero stamped a foot and glanced over his shoulder at the empty conference room. "You are the exact opposite of flexible. You are unreasonable and obstinate. What game are you playing?"

"You say Tatum has many friends," Sage said. "What about you? Tell me about your friends."

Liberty slumped back in the chair and folded her arms. Her gaze drifted. She took a deep breath. "I guess I'm closest to the seniors at the center. I really like those old folks. They're honest. Most of them are calm and collected. They let troubles roll off them. They have stories to tell." Liberty smiled. Her eyes held a distant look. "I could hang with them all day."

"How would you describe yourself?"

"Describe myself?" A sneer distorted her face.

Dr. Supero relaxed. He smiled. "That's more like it. Ask the right questions and she won't be capable of this meek, cooperative façade. Her fuse is short, her patience thin."

"I'm perfect in every way," Liberty said. "Isn't that why they want me for a breeder? I mean of all the girls in Aldonia . . ." She sat upright then leaned over the table, her green eyes black with hostility. ". . . couldn't they find someone more suitable than me? Anyone?"

Dr. Supero chuckled and bounced on the balls of his feet. "We'll find someone all right, my dear. Continue to display your malignant attitude. You'll be slated for re-education before your appointment ends."

"Would you describe yourself as outgoing or more of a loner?" Sage appeared unfazed by Liberty's irritation. "Are you easily angered? Patient? How do challenges and troubles affect you?"

Liberty slouched back in the chair. "I don't know. I like to be alone, to take long walks down streets I've never been down before. But I'm not a complete loner." A sincere, disarming smile spread across her face. "I like to be with people, too. I like to help people. More than anything, though, I like to work, to set my mind to a task and accomplish it."

Sage nodded and glanced at the camera. Her long-lashes and dark eye make-up accentuated her perfect almond-shaped eyes. With a flicker of her eyes, she could communicate her thoughts.

Gorgeous. The girl was gorgeous and knew it. Pity he hadn't been able to see her in the silk negligee he'd given her. He could only imagine how delicious she looked waiting for him in the rarely-used conference room that had become their secret meeting place. Who knew committee members would pay a surprise visit that day? And that they would be shown to that exact conference room? It must've been quite a surprise for everyone, seeing the head physician's assistant dressed like that.

His heart twisted. Of course, he had to deny knowing she would be there . . . to deny the intimate, sometimes inappropriate, relationship that they indulged even in the facility. He could not fall with her. People depended upon him. He was too important.

His hand shot to his head, to where the tumor grew, the *cancerous* tumor. He shuddered. Certainly, he was too important for the Medical Care Evaluation Panel to deny the surgery he needed. While costly, the surgery had a high success rate. If successful, his quality of life would not be affected. Why should the MCEP have the power to determine a man's fate?

"Do you have an intimate friend, a boyfriend or a girlfriend?"

Dr. Supero snapped his attention back to the interview.

After asking the question, Sage smiled like a teenage girl.

Liberty's smile mirrored Sage's. "No. I-I guess I haven't wanted one. I've had other things on my mind, and I'm not ready for a relationship."

"What's been on your mind?"

"I don't know. Lots of things."

"Your vocation?"

Liberty's jaw twitched. She nodded.

"Good," Dr. Supero said aloud. "Get to the root of her discontent."

"How do you think you'll like being pregnant? Caring for babies?" Her tone dripped with concern.

Liberty shrugged. No sneer. No vein popping from her forehead. Didn't the question bother her?

After a moment, Sage said, "Do you have any memories from your early years at the Breeder Facility?"

"Memories? I was a baby."

"You stay until you turn five. Some people have memories or at least impressions."

"Hmmm." Her eyes held a distant gaze. She snapped out of it. "I guess . . . my last day . . . I remember not wanting to leave."

Sage smiled and leaned in, comforting, encouraging. "See? It's not so bad there."

"I know." Liberty blinked and shook her head. "It's not that I think it'll be bad. In fact, I know I'll have more luxuries than I've ever dreamed of. And I'm sure the people are nice. I suppose I'll get used to . . ."

"No!" Dr. Supero shook a fist at the monitor. "You're playing a game. You don't belong in the Breeder Facility with your eggs being used for the next generation, your attitude poisoning young minds. You are a detriment to society!"

An unwelcome memory slithered into his mind. Supero, an inquisitive ten-year-old, had a question during the embryology lesson in Biology.

"If a blastocyst needs a sperm from a man and an egg from a woman, why are embryos only made in laboratories? Why aren't they made everywhere?"

His teacher, a mature man with a goatee, had berated him in front of the class. "You may think, little Supero . . ."

Supero, daily mocked for his small stature, had shrunk down in his seat. His classmates roared with laughter.

". . . that you are smarter than everyone else. I assure you, you are not. The best minds have generated the methods we use today, methods that are vital to a healthy society. Imagine, for a moment, the result of your sperm fertilizing an egg, your sperm being used for the next generation. Our society would be afflicted with little men with big egos, a detriment to our society. No, this must be a completely controlled process."

The laughter intensified.

Seized with impotent anger and burning at the humiliation, Supero had vowed to surpass his teacher's knowledge of embryology and genetics, to become the expert to which everyone would turn, to control the production of the next generation.

Dr. Supero spun around, snatched a landline phone from a table, and connected to the office of the psychiatric team.

"This is Dr. Mills," came a nasally voice.

"Are you directing this girl's interview?" He didn't make sense. He should've introduced himself. He should've mentioned Liberty's name. He should've kept his voice down.

"Who is this? How did you get this number? We are in the middle of conducting an—"

"This is Dr. Supero," he said through clenched teeth. "I ordered this interview."

"Oh." A pause. "Forgive me. Yes, Doctor?"

"You are going about this interview in the wrong way. Have you thought to ask why she came to the Psychiatric Center in a Unity Trooper's car? Why she wanted to skip the appointment altogether? Was she hoping to escape? What are her feelings about the Regimen?"

Liberty smiled and dipped her head, laughing about something. Her eyes sparkled with feigned innocence.

Dr. Supero no longer listened to what she said. They had lost control of the interview.

"Very well, Dr. Supero," the woman with the nasally-voice said. "I will instruct the interviewer. Give us a moment . . ."

Supero slammed the phone receiver down and turned his back to the monitor. It pained him to hear Liberty's smooth voice as she blathered on about babies. She was good. She knew how to manipulate. As long as the questions didn't concern sensitive areas—

"I'm sorry to change the subject," Sage said.

Supero spun to face the monitor.

"I need to ask, how did you feel about coming today? About this appointment?"

Liberty's mouth fell open. "Oh. You mean because I tried to skip it?"

Sage nodded.

"Yes." Dr. Supero stepped closer to the monitor.

The door to the conference room opened, letting in the hum and muffled voices of the Citizen Safety Station. A girl with a familiar voice said, "Dr. Supero."

The girl would have to wait. Supero kept his eyes on the monitor. He would not miss this. This was the moment. Liberty would break. She wouldn't be able to lie without it showing.

Liberty cradled her head in her hands.

"What's the matter, girl?" Supero said, relishing the moment. "Did you forget how to speak?"

"What?" said the girl behind him, sounding annoyed. "You're wanted in the central surveillance room."

"One moment." He glanced.

The dark-eyed girl he had seen during his first visit to Chief Varden leaned in the doorway. "Whatever." She turned away while saying, "Chief Varden has something to show you." The door started to close. "It's about that girl . . ."

"That girl?" He spoke as the door latched. The dark-eyed girl was gone. "Liberty?"

"I guess . . ."

At the sound of Liberty's voice, he jerked his head to face the monitor.

"I was afraid. I mean . . . This is such a big step. Such a big change, but . . ."

He caught each word as if she spoke in slow motion.

" . . . I'm ready to do my service for the good of all. I feel peace . . ." She smiled. Her eyes sparkled. ". . . a feeling I haven't had in a long time."

"No!" Dr. Supero found himself gripping the back of a chair. His head grew light. Hands trembling, he lifted the chair and flung it at the monitor.

The door to the conference room flew open.

"Do you make me wait?" Chief Varden stood in the doorway, arms akimbo and muscles twitching. He glanced at the overturned chair and the jiggling monitor. "Use your own office for your tantrums. Get out here. Now." He stormed away, down the hall.

Liberty's saccharine voice echoed in Dr. Supero's mind. She spoke. She laughed. She spoke again. She lied with such ease.

Without another glance at the girl on the monitor, he left the room.

~~~

"We found this." Chief Varden leaned on the back console of a monitoring station, hovering over the young man stationed there. He spun a finger at the station controls. "Roll it."

"What? Uh . . ." The young man shifted in his seat, glancing from Varden to Supero then reached for the controls. "Uh, okay."

A video played on one of the six monitors at his station. Orange and blue lights from a Unity Trooper's area car flashed in an alley. Unity Troopers ran in every direction. Liberty peeked from behind a wall. He had seen this footage the day he came to elicit the help of CSS in monitoring Liberty.

Supero shot a glare at Varden's strong-jawed, freckled face. "You called me for this? Have you nothing new?"

Varden's jaw twitched. "Shut up and watch." He tapped the young man's shoulder. "Zoom in. Show our good doctor what we found."

The young man's hands danced over the controls. The view zoomed in on the windshield of a black Unity Trooper's area car. An image showed on the shiny windshield. An image of a person?

Dr. Supero gasped and leaned in for a better look. "Is that a face? It's blurry. What use is it? Can't you enhance the image?"

Varden whacked the worker's arm again and mumbled a command.

"I'm on it." With his gaze fixed on the monitor, the young man worked the controls with both hands.

The image grew clearer, the image of a man squatting on a rooftop. He wore a mottled cape and black shades. He must've been one of the anarchists Varden had mentioned, the ones who kidnap people and get away with it.

The anarchist lifted his shades, revealing a young face and dark hair. He mouthed something to someone below him, to someone on the ground . . . to Liberty?

"What is he saying?" Supero said.
~~~

"Not sure," Varden said. "Maybe he's just swearing. It's the look on his face and . . . See?"

The man on the roof sneered and jabbed a finger in the air, pointing to one side. Then he backed out of camera range.

"Is that it?" Supero said to the young man at the station. "Is there more?"

The man shook his head while expanding the view on the screen to show Liberty. Liberty's face had been tilted to the stranger. As she turned away and made ready to run off, the man froze the image.

Supero turned to Varden. "What do you know about him? Is he one of the anarchists?"

"I'd say he is. But that's all we found of this kid. Our recognition software can't find a valid match for his face."

"No valid match?" If her interview hadn't ended, he could pose the question to her through Sage: Who was the man on the rooftop?

"But we did find this." Varden pulled something from a back pocket and tossed it onto the operator's console.

Dr. Supero picked it up. Made of a lightweight gray plastic material, it resembled a simple handgun with a barrel, handle, and trigger, but the muzzle was extremely thin.

"It's not a weapon. It's an ID implant remover. We found the missing kid's implant in it, the kid the Unity Troopers were sent to pick up that day."

"What? How is that possible? Implants explode if tampered with. The kid would've lost his hand."

"Not with that instrument. We think it suppresses the destruction mechanism. Don't ask me how it works." Varden snatched the implant remover from Supero and shoved it in a back pocket. "We found fingerprints on it, but they don't match anyone in our databases. We checked the Universal Database, too, not just Aldonia's."

"But every man, woman, and child is in the database," Supero said.

"Apparently not. Or the database has been tampered with, files removed." His gaze drifted and he shook his head. "I think we're on to something. There have been a number of citizens who have simply disappeared. Every one of them is known for holding ideas hostile to our society. When they dropped off the grid, we thought they committed suicide, making their ID implants useless. Now I'm not so sure."

He locked eyes with Supero. "I think they're out there. And I'm gonna find them."

"What is the connection to Liberty? You've been monitoring her. Has she communicated with anyone strange, anyone else not in a database?"

Varden shook his head. He lifted a hand to the monitor displaying Liberty's frozen image. "We're on it. If there's a connection, we'll find it. We're working on isolating facial images of people not readily identifiable by our software. I'll keep you posted."

"Do that." He started to leave but turned back. "I want that image sent to the Psychiatric Center, the one of the man on the roof." Forcing himself to walk when he wanted to run, he returned to the conference room. He grabbed the phone and glanced at the wall monitor while waiting for one of the psychiatrists to answer his call.

Sage smiled and stuck out her hand. "Thank you for your time. I've enjoyed speaking with . . ."

"What? No, girl, you aren't done yet," Supero said just as the woman with the nasally voice got on the line. Dr. Mills, wasn't it?

"Excuse me?" the psychiatrist said. "And who is this?"

"Sage has another question. You are not to let Liberty leave." The words flew from his mouth. He should have identified himself. No time.

Sage and Liberty stood up and shook hands, smiling.

"Stop her from leaving," Supero shouted into the phone. "This is Dr. Supero, and I have one last question for Liberty. Do not let her leave."

"Very well," Dr. Mills said. "What is your question?"

An instant later, Sage touched her ear and glanced into the camera.

Liberty stepped to the door. It wouldn't open without Sage's clearance.

"Liberty, there's just one more thing." Sage smiled and pivoted to face the girl. "I've been given one last question."

"Oh?"

The video feed of the reflection in the window of the Unity Trooper's area car appeared on a screen on the wall. The man on the roof lifted his shades.

Liberty gasped.

Sage repeated the question Dr. Supero gave to the psychiatrist. "Who is the man on the roof?"

"I-I don't know." She kept her eyes glued to the image.

"He seems to be communicating with you. How do you know him?"

"I-I don't . . ." Liberty turned her doe eyes to Sage. "He wanted me to leave the area, I guess. I was watching the Unity Troopers. They were searching for someone, I think. I-I don't know the guy."

"He seems to recognize you."

Liberty pressed her lips together and then said, "He saved me once. I was attacked in an alley, and he came to my rescue."

"Was this the day that happened?"

"No." She returned her gaze to the image and spoke in a whisper. "I don't know why he was there that day. I tell you I don't really know him. He's a stranger. I don't know what his game is. I'm sure I'll never see him again. I'm nothing to him."

~~~

The door to Dr. Supero's office slid open.

Dr. Supero jumped to close the window of the video he had been watching on his computer, but he closed the report he was supposed to be working on instead. Liberty's interview continued to play with the view zoomed in on Sage. He fumbled to close the video then turned to face whoever had entered his office.

Ivy stood behind him, head cocked to one side, chewing gum with her mouth open. "Did you enjoy watching your old assistant interview that girl?"

Dr. Supero stood, grinning and looking Ivy over.

She wore her hair off to one side, the green and blonde wisps nearly covering one thickly made-up eye. The strand of faux emeralds around her neck drew attention to the view allowed by her low-cut top. She wore a white miniskirt that clung to her curves and . . . hideous green boots. What was the deal with her taste in footwear?
~~~

Looking her in the eye, he smirked. "Is my new assistant jealous of my old one?" He stepped closer and risked touching her, rubbing her arm.

She sighed and glanced at the ceiling, still chewing like a cow with its cud. "The psychiatrist's evaluation for Liberty." She shoved her computer pad at him. "You said you wanted it right away."

He snatched the computer and turned his back to her. He scrolled past the long heading, skimmed the letter, and jumped to the last paragraph.

While Liberty has strong opinions about many things, including her future, we feel confident in approving her for the vocation of Breeder. Many women find pregnancy an emotional journey, but she has proven her ability to channel her emotions. She understands the value of the service she will provide to society, and she is willing to do her part. She will make a good companion to the other breeders and a worthy infant caretaker.

"A good companion! A worthy infant caretaker!" Supero whipped the computer pad to the floor and let out a stream of curses.

9

Abby and I sat on the bench nearest the solitary tree in the strip of freshly cut grass behind the Senior Center. A warm breeze rustled the leaves of the tree, making shadows sway and creating a somber song.

The tarnished silver medal in my hand reflected the sunlight, but I couldn't make out the image on it. It resembled a bush growing by a column. I flipped the medal over and studied the other picture, a profile of a woman's head. She had a strange comb or a wing in her hair. Both pictures had letters surrounding them, too worn to read. I fancied that the letters around the woman spelled my name.

I lifted the medal by the chain and smiled at Abby. "I love it. Thank you." I decided not to ask how she got it, though I really wanted to know. Abby didn't like to answer those kinds of questions, and I wanted today to be perfect. I may never see her again. If I did, it wouldn't be for several years.

A tear threatened to leave my eye, so I laughed and pulled Abby into a big hug. "I'll wear it always. It'll remind me of you."

Abby hugged me back but only for a second. She pushed away and brushed the front of her turquoise-colored shirt. "Get ahold of yourself, Liberty. Neither of us is dying. You're just going away for a while." Her blue-green eyes sparkled in the sunlight and she almost seemed to smile.

I made an effort to file this image of her in my mind. I even wanted to hold onto the scent of herbal tea that always seemed to accompany her. Unfortunately, the breeze took that detail away, replacing it with a grassy smell.

After taking a long break and walking Abby back inside, I left the senior center. It was early for me, but I wanted to avoid crying. I had given and received too many hugs and well-wishes from the seniors, my friends.

The walk home tempered my emotions. I took roads less traveled and focused on details: paint peeling from a wall to reveal parts of a mural, a blade of grass peeking from a crack in a pavement, a wrapper skidding along a sidewalk from a gust of wind . . . These everyday experiences would all cease once I entered the facility. Tomorrow.

As I turned down my street, the sight of my apartment building elicited a strange feeling of nostalgia. I had only superficial relationships with the people there. Maybe a part of me wished they had meant more to me, and I to them. Chances were I'd be sent to the opposite side of Aldonia when my time at the Breeder Facility ended, so I'd never see these people again. Did any of them care?

I pushed that thought from my mind. In one day, I would set off on a new adventure. That was the attitude I needed to have. If I fell into self-pity, *My Friend* would probably make Himself known again . . . the way He first had when I feared making my transition to Primary. I knew now that I had created Him as a means to cope. I was too old for Him now. I could handle this without Him. I would be okay. Tonight, I would take my neighbor Brand his scooter, pack my few belongings, and maybe write my thoughts in the notebook one last time. Tomorrow I would set off on the adventure . . . alone.

I opened my apartment door to darkness and the odor of cigarettes. Tatum and Finley didn't smoke so they must've had a friend over recently. Probably Silver.

I tapped the light switch.

Voices rang out with the show of light. "Surprise!"

I gasped and shrunk back.

A roomful of people stared at me. Most of them smiled, some clapped, and more than a few lifted glasses. One even waved at me.

With the eagerness of a child, Tatum grabbed my wrist and yanked me into the middle of the crowded living room. "We're all going to miss you, so we decided to throw you a party."

"Wow, really?"

Bouncy music started playing. People gathered into little groups. Voices grew loud. A light show, projecting from a flexi-phone, lit up part of the ceiling.

"Hey, you did a great job on my scooter." Brand stepped up to me, a big smile on his tan face and a drink in his hand. "I already took it around the block." He motioned with his cup. "Works great. I'll be glad to stop riding the trolley. That thing's crowded."

"Forget your scooter." Lindsey, a neighbor from down the hall, pushed him aside. "What're we going to do without you?" Her blonde bangs hung to her eyes and moved with each blink. "I don't know how many times you fixed those old pipes in my apartment. You know how long it'll take to have the Regimen workers get out here?"

Meeka, Lindsey's next-door neighbor and part-time girlfriend, gave Lindsey a shove. "We have a manager. You only have to call on the manager."

"You ever try that? Takes him longer than a Regimen janitorial team."

Now everyone had something to say about that, each one struggling to be heard over the other and over the bouncy music.

Someone grabbed my arm and tugged me from the chaos.

"Come see," said Darin, clinging to my arm. He led me to the dinner table. "What do you think?" He beamed a smile.

Plates of food covered the table: nuts, dried fruits, cookies, candies, even chocolates and other hard to obtain food items.

"Wow," I said. "I'm glad I got my tools put away last night. I had 'em all over the table."

Darin's smile fell. "Is that all you have to say? Don't you know this stuff is hard to come by?"

I laughed and draped my arm over his shoulders. "I know. It looks great. I'm just wondering where it all came from."

Darin blushed. "Maybe you shouldn't ask." He picked up a dried fig and brought it to my mouth. "Just enjoy it. You'll probably get to eat like this every day in that facility, but I wanted your party to be special."

I opened my mouth for the fig then kissed Darin on the cheek. "Thanks," I mumbled with a full mouth. My heart warmed at his kindness. Then I thought about Dr. Supero's warning about eating non-registered foods, and I laughed.

Darin laughed too. "Try this." He picked up a caramel-colored hard candy.

"No, try this." Sid squeezed between Darin and me and stuck a cup in my face. "It's punch."

I stepped back and shook my head. "Not thirsty."

Sid lowered the cup and dropped his gaze. "I know you don't trust me. And I don't blame you." He swallowed, his Adam's apple bobbing. "I, uh, I'm sorry for what I did. I shouldn't have done it, trying to force you . . . I thought once you saw what it was like, you know, with me—"

"It's okay, Sid. Forget about it." Avoiding eye contact, I pushed past Sid and chatting neighbors and got to the kitchen. Three pitchers I had never seen before sat between dirty cups and dishes on the countertop. I opened a cupboard, found it empty and closed it. I turned.

"Really, man." Sid stood behind me, a sulky look on his face and two cups in his hands. He offered one to me. "I promise it's safe. Everyone else is drinking it. It's just punch. It's not even spiked with booze."

I smiled and accepted it. "Thanks. I am thirsty. That fig Darin gave me got stuck halfway down my throat."

Laughter came from the group by the couch. With the punch in hand, I joined them.

"You're not going to miss us at all," a neighbor lady said when she saw me. "I hear they treat you girls like the queens of fables."

"You mean like the higher-ups in the RCT," I said and everyone laughed.

For the next two hours, I listened to neighbors share what they knew about the vocation of breeder, about the luxuries I would receive, about the food, the clothing. No one mentioned the actual duties of the job: donating my eggs, carrying a new life inside me, and caring for babies.

"Well, curfew is in less than an hour. I'm gonna get going." Lindsey gave me a hug. "Take care of yourself. I'll think of you whenever my pipes leak."

"Thanks." I smiled and walked her to the door.

Before long, everyone who didn't plan to stay the night gave me a final word and handshake or a hug. All that remained were Tatum, Finley, Darin, Silver, and Sid.

I sat in one of the two armchairs and studied the little group.

"I wonder who my new roommate will be." Tatum sighed and leaned against Finley's arm stretched along the back of the couch.

Finley kissed the top of her head and ran his fingers through her bangs.

Tatum turned her heavily made-up cat eyes to me and opened them wide. "Are you getting excited?"

"Excited?" I shook my head and reached for my cup while trying to consider if that was the word for it. Part of me felt defeated and another part scared, but I was a little excited too. At least I was trying to work up that feeling. I probably should've been excited. Of course, Sage, the woman who did my Psychiatric evaluation, said I didn't have to think or feel like everyone else.

I brought my cup to my lips before realizing it was empty. "Do you remember anything of the Breeder Facility, from when you were little?" I blurted out the question without thinking, and everyone looked at me in momentary silence.

Sid got up off the floor and took my cup.

"I was asked that question in my psychiatric evaluation. The girl said sometimes people remember or have impressions."

Silver smirked and leaned back in an armchair. Darin, who sat cross-legged on the floor, lowered his head. Finley and Tatum exchanged a long look.

"I sort of do." Tatum said. "I remember being sad when I had to leave. All my transitions have been hard. I had close friends at each place. I hated leaving them. I cried and cried. Leaving Secondary was the worst. I miss my friends. I don't see any of them around here." She stuck out her bottom lip and faced Finley.

Finley kissed her. "But that's how we met." He looked at me, grinning. "My unit had the boring job of cleaning up vandalism outside an old secondary school. It wasn't Tatum's school, but there she was sitting on a bench, staring off in my direction. At first, I thought she was checking me out, but then I realized she was bummed and staring at the school. So I came over on my lunch break to cheer her up." He looked into Tatum's eyes and smiled. "We've been together ever since."

Sid returned with a cup of punch and set it before me on the coffee table. He sat down next to Darin on the floor.

"Do you remember anything from your childhood?" I said to Finley.

He shrugged. "Not really. I still see a few kids from Secondary. They live around here. And I remember Primary. But I don't remember jazz from my breeder facility."

"I do." Darin gazed at the carpet and swayed a bit, probably from having had too much to drink. "I remember a lot." He gave me a sorrowful glance but returned his gaze to the carpet as he spoke. "I can tell you every detail about my nanny. Her hair . . . soft brown curls that shined like copper in the sunlight. She'd use them to tickle my face sometimes. Soft pink lips kissing me and saying sweet things . . . singing. Her voice like rain on a windless night. Even with all the babies around, I was her favorite. She was mine. Until the last day." His eyelids flickered. He took a deep breath and made eye contact with me, his expression turning to stone. "She wouldn't see me at all that day. I couldn't understand that. I couldn't understand having to leave, having to leave her."

I struggled to hold his gaze, fighting back tears and wishing I had something to say to him, some word of comfort. After all these years, he still hadn't healed from that first transition. Who was I to talk? I had created my own personal *Friend* and hadn't grown out of him until now.

"I remember transitioning to Secondary," Silver said. "I couldn't wait to fly from that hellhole."

Finley let out a sharp laugh. He was probably as relieved as I was for the change in tone. "Hellhole? I've got great memories from Primary."

"Not me. Everyone made fun of my hair." She paused. "It was really wild then."

We all laughed. Her hair stood up in big silver tufts and hung in twisted, unruly strands down her back. Could it really have been wilder?

Silver grimaced, not really looking at any of us. She sat in a reclined position in the armchair, legs spread, feet firmly planted on the floor, arms draped over the sides, forming and releasing a fist to the beat of the music.

"I can't imagine anyone making fun of you. What about in Secondary?" Finley said. "Anyone pick on you in Secondary?"

"In Secondary? Ha! I did the bullying in Secondary. But kids picking on me . . . That's not why I wanted out of Primary. I had this teacher. He . . ." Her eyes narrowed to slits. She formed and held a fist. "Apparently, my crazy hair appealed to him."

"What do you mean?" As soon as the words left her mouth, Tatum gasped as if the ugly reason just occurred to her.

"I mean he did things to me. Things a man has no right doing to a little girl." Her gaze went to each of us as if challenging us to doubt her.

"What a pig," I said when her eyes came to me.

"I'm sorry," Tatum whispered.

Finley shook his head and said, "Yeah. That sucks."

Silver leaned forward and rested her forearms on her thighs, still making and releasing a fist. "Don't feel sorry for me. It formed me. I'm tough. I've been a fighter ever since." She stood, cracked her knuckles and flexed one arm, her gaze going to her bicep. "I could've been a different person. I could've been meek and wimpy." She looked down her nose at Sid who sat on the floor, on the opposite side of the coffee table.

Sid snickered. "Without steroids you'd be a different person."

Silver made a rude gesture. "You're lucky I don't feel like busting on you." She took a few swaggering steps toward him. "So what about you? Don't you have anything to say about your transitions?"

Sid's gaze went to me. "I'm trying to get on the building maintenance team that serves the Breeder Facility."

Silver threw her head back and laughed. "Don't you ever give up?"

I wanted to laugh, too, but I felt sorry for him and didn't want him to get his hopes up. "The RCT doesn't approve vocation changes often."

"It won't be a change of vocation. That's what I do. I'm not just a roofer. So the Breeder Facility would only be a change of location."

"Give it up, already." Silver grabbed Sid by the arms and yanked him to his feet.

Darin scrambled out of the way, squeezing in between Tatum and the arm of the couch.

Sid backed away from Silver, his expression placid though he had to suspect what she had in mind.

Silver lunged and wrapped her arms around Sid's chest. He made a move to block with his knee but too late. She brought him down.

Tatum, Finley, Darin, and I laughed. Silver's idea of a good time was wrestling a guy to the ground.

Watching Sid and Silver wrestle on the floor, laughing with the others, an emotional song playing in the background, joy welled up inside me. My head grew light. I looked into Tatum's eyes, Darin's eyes, Finley. Maybe these were my friends after all.

~~~

A high-pitched, angry, muffled voice traveled through the walls of our apartment. Every morning, the girls next door fought over the bathroom, over clothes, over who knew what. Half the time I knew exactly what they said, due to the miserably thin walls. But I was usually up and on my way out the door by the time they got started.

Up!

I bolted upright and glanced around the room.

My clothes. I hadn't packed a thing last night.

My flexi-phone lay on the nightstand. I snatched it and checked the alarm, remembering at once that I hadn't set it. We'd stayed up late talking. It wasn't until Darin had fallen asleep on the floor that I went to my room. I put one of my pillows under his head, covered him with a blanket, and called it a night. I flung myself onto my bed and fell asleep to the sound of the others talking in the living room.

I threw back the covers and swung my legs off the bed. One leg got tangled in the sheet, making me fall to my knees on the floor. My head ached at the impact. As I reached for my head, it occurred to me that I had a terribly dry mouth. Sid must've put alcohol in my drinks after all. I'd thought the punch had a funny taste but I enjoyed it, and he hadn't made any moves on me anyway.

Since I was already on the floor, I reached under the bed for my black canvas bag. I needed to get my few belongings packed before my ride—arranged by the Breeder Facility staff—arrived.

I groped under the bed until I found the bag. As I dragged it out, my hand brushed the notebook.

The notebook!
~~~

I yanked the bag and the notebook out, tossed the bag onto the bed, and pulled myself up, notebook and box of pencils in hand. Where could I possibly store them? It wouldn't bode well if they fell into the wrong hands, if they fell into *any* hands. I had to hide them.

The nightstand? No. The bed? Between the mattresses? No. The next occupant might want to flip the mattress.

I dashed to the closet. No one used the overhead storage compartment in the closet. I could leave it there. I would just need to push it back far enough. Even if someone found it, they wouldn't know it was mine.

I flung open the closet door and it banged against the wall. I gasped. *Shoot.* I hoped no one heard.

Once in the closet, I turned on the light and dragged one of my toolboxes to the middle of the floor. What was I going to do with my tools? I couldn't bring them. By Regimen standards, I shouldn't even have them. How would I explain obtaining the bulk of them? The Regimen didn't like citizens to trade services for goods. They said it wore on the efficiency of the system.

"What are you doing?"

My heart leaped into my throat. I spun around and shoved the notebook up the back of my shirt.

Silver leaned against the doorframe of the closet door, arms folded, eyelids heavy, and a scowl on her face.

"Oh, I . . ." I glanced at the toolboxes. "I've got to leave soon and I've got these tools. I don't know what to do with them. I sure can't bring them."

She glanced at the toolboxes. "You want them back when you get out?"

I chuckled. "You make it sound like I'm serving time."

"Isn't that how it's gonna feel to you?" She stepped into the closet, forcing me to step back, and stooped by the toolbox in the middle of the floor. She flipped the latches and threw back the lid.

"I guess it is going to feel like that and, yeah, I really want my tools back. I want to do my time and get on with my life, doing what I want to do."

Silver hadn't taken her eyes off the tools since she opened the box. She studied a micrometer, put it back, and pushed a few tools around. "Nice. This is a nice set."

"Yeah. I worked hard for it." I did, I really did, and I wanted them back when I got out.

Silver stood and looked me up and down as if assessing me. "I'll take 'em."

I nodded but couldn't help frowning.

She punched my shoulder and grinned. "Don't worry, Liberty. You'll get 'em back." She grabbed one toolbox with her left hand, the other with her right, and took them away.

I watched until even her shadow had gone. The boxes clanked in the living room. Silence.

Trying to be quiet, I closed the closet door. It made the softest click.

I looked up. *Shoot.* The overhead storage door was just out of reach. Now what could I stand on? Tatum had a chest at the foot of her bed. Maybe I could use that, but I sure didn't want to wake her. She'd want to help me get ready and follow me around.

I shut off the closet light and cracked open the door to her room. Muted morning light streamed in through the ripped sheet she used as a curtain. She and Finley lay sprawled on the bed, each with a limb dangling over the side as if they had dragged themselves to bed last night.

Careful to avoid stepping on clothes and other stuff on her floor, I crept across the room. A pile of clothes sat on the chest. Making no sound, I lifted them and set them on the floor. My heart beat hard. What would happen if I got caught? If someone discovered I had written in a notebook? Did it matter? Would I be reported? Sent to Re-Education? No. Who would care? But still . . .

The chest was lighter than I expected but so big I could no longer watch my step. I clutched its metal side-handles and shuffled through whatever lay in my way, reaching the closet before counting four loud beats of my heart. I placed it on the floor under the storage door, closed the door to her bedroom, and turned on the light.

After a deep breath, I took the notebook and the box of pencils from under my shirt and stepped onto the chest. The overhead door moved easily but made a scraping sound.

I lifted my contraband into the dark overhead storage space and slid it back as far as I could. Standing now on my toes, I pushed it back even farther. There was no light in the storage space so the chances anyone would—

The closet door on Tatum's side opened.

I dropped my hands to my sides and jumped off the chest.

"What are you doing?" A sleepy-eyed Tatum leaned against the edge of the door. Her gaze went directly to the black square in the ceiling. "Do you have things up there?"

"What?" My heart thumped in my ears. "No, I . . ." I stepped back up on the chest, slid the storage door shut, and hopped down. "I just wanted to check." I tried to sound casual. "You know, I've been here so long. I just couldn't remember."

Her gaze flitted from me to the closed storage door and back to me.

I had to change the subject. "So I'm leaving my tools with Silver. She said she'd take care of them." I scooted the chest into the empty space on the floor where my toolboxes had been.

"Oh."

"Said she'd let me have them when I got out, I mean, got back, you know, when I get back from serving my time, or uh . . ."

Tatum scratched her head. "Yeah. So your ride's outside. Are you ready?"

I gasped. "Outside? Now? Are you sure?" I yanked my clothes, hangers and all, from the closet and dashed back into my room.

Tatum followed me. "Yeah, I'm sure. Something woke me up, and the first thing I thought of was your ride. I'm sure they'll be knocking at the door any—"

Banging sounded on the front door.

My eyes went wide.

Tatum smiled. "Want me to help?"

10

I stood gaping at the surreal environment and at the other girls. I totally didn't belong here. I should've taken a moment, made the driver wait, and changed out of the oversized, blue-gray button-front shirt and the baggy jeans that I'd worn yesterday and then slept in.

Young women, girls really, in flowing gowns lounged everywhere, in plush rocking chairs and couches around a movie screen, at little glass dining tables on the opposite side of the room, and even on throw pillows on the thickly carpeted floor. Two girls glanced at me, but the others paid no attention.

The room was as big as the basketball court at Secondary. Classical music came from the dining side, the sounds of a movie from the other. A few men and women in short brown tunics weaved around the room, stopping at one girl or another. Some carried trays of food or drinks. One held a computer pad.

Dim yellowish lights showed from behind the glass wall that ran the length of the room. On the other side of the wall, shadowy figures stooped over tables and moved in slow rhythmic motions.

"Massage therapy," my guide said, catching the direction of my gaze. "Toward the end of your pregnancy, you'll really want to take advantage of that."

"Oh." My mouth went dry. I didn't belong here. How could I ever fit in? I should've let the psychiatric evaluation go in a different direction. I should've ranted about my feelings for the Regimen. I might've gotten sentenced to Re-Education. How bad could it be?

My guide, Lee, a heavily-adorned thirty-something woman in a black one-piece pants suit, chuckled. "What's the matter? You look pale."

I forced myself to smile. "No, I-I'm fine. It's just all so foreign to me." I ran my fingers through my hair and they got stuck. Couldn't I have found time to fix myself this morning? I *so* didn't belong here.

She nodded, smiling. "You'll notice there are no babies in the lounge. This is where our girls go to get away from it all and just relax." She took my arm. "Come. I'll show you the rest. I think you'll like seeing the children and babies."

We pushed through a gauze curtain and left the room through a sliding door. Arms linked, we clomped along the shiny floor of a long, curvy hallway. Ceiling-high windows rose up on one side, and an occasional door on the other. A floral scent lingered in the cool air.

The glass exterior wall provided a view of the Nature Preserves, reminding me of the glass wall of the Senior Center. The extravagant artwork and marble floors in the foyer gave outsiders the impression the center provided class, comfort, and quality. Advertisements reinforced the idea. Insiders alone knew the humble provisions and décor beyond the façade. The view of the Preserves, while captivating, only reminded me that I could never set foot in them. I couldn't even enjoy the scent of the woods through the glass.

Lee stopped at a door marked "Nursery" and released my arm. She brought her hand to the scanner but looked at me, wide-eyed, before using it. "Ready?" She must have thought I was like the other girls, thrilled to be here, anxious to get a hold of a baby and live a life of leisure.

"Sure." I forced myself to smile.

She waved her hand over the scanner and the door opened, a baby's screech greeting us. She stepped into a colorful, noisy room and nodded for me to follow. A few steps later, she turned around.

I stood in the hall, finding my body unwilling to enter the room. "I-I think I'd like to see my bedroom." I glanced either way down the hallway. "Where are our rooms? I'm kind of tired."

"This way first, my dear." She motioned me in. "We need to close the door."

I took a deep breath and stepped into a room of pastels and cribs, of young women, many with rounded bellies, and babies in diapers and little white shirts. Everything in the room was in motion. Girls with babies in their arms swayed back and forth in padded rocking chairs. Other girls sat or lay on the floor, offering toys to grasping, rolling, crawling babies.

In the corner of the room, next to a window, a girl with messy hair and sweat on her brow held a tiny pink baby to her breast. An older woman leaned over her, talking and gesturing. The girl, frustration in her eyes, shook her head. The woman stooped and adjusted the baby.

"Here you go," said a girl to my right.

I turned toward her and found a baby being thrust at me. My hands shot up to catch it. "What are you doing?" I held it under the arms. One of its legs kicked. It stared into my eyes through huge black pupils surrounded by sky blue, appearing wise beyond its years, wiser than any of us. Its head bobbed forward.

"You can't hold her like that," the girl said, a smirk on her face.

"I don't want to hold her. Here." I moved toward the girl, holding the baby out to her.

The girl turned away and strutted off, leaving through a door on the far side of the room.

"Hold her like this," Lee said. My guide took the baby before I turned to face her. She grabbed my wrist and moved my arm into position. "Cradle the baby in your arms. And you have to support its head. But don't worry; you'll learn all about baby care."

The baby's big round head had a thin layer of fine blonde hair. Its arms and fingers moved without purpose. It seemed so fragile and I so clumsy. What if I dropped it?

I readjusted the little thing in my clammy arms, my fingers squishing its chubby body. Was this really to be my life for the next few years? Caring for all these babies? My stomach growing big with new life within? A moment in the lounge, my only escape?

Gears, wires, grease, and tools. These things made sense to me. These things I could count on and manipulate to some predictable, positive outcome. I could easily lose myself in a project. But babies?

"I-I really need to lie down."

"Topaz," Lee said, and a girl with shoulder-length golden hair approached us. "Take the baby. It'll be naptime soon. You can have a turn in the lounge."

Topaz made no effort to take the baby. She looked me over through sulky golden eyes. "Is this the girl taking my room?"

"Now, Topaz." Lee took the baby from me and placed it in Topaz's arms. "You have a nice room."

"Not as nice as it was." Topaz didn't even glance at the baby she held.

Lee pushed my shoulder, turning me toward the door. "We'll take a quick peek at other areas and then you can rest before the tests."

"Tests?"

She waved her hand over the scanner and led me from the room. "Once the babies begin toddling around, they move to a fun room with little climbing toys and educational toys. They're exposed to computers right away, so they can get familiar with them at an early age. You'd be surprised—"

"What did you mean about tests?" They would harvest my eggs and use them to develop embryos. I wasn't ready for that. What kind of a procedure was it, anyway? Did it hurt? Were those the tests she meant?

My guide stayed a step ahead as we clomped down the bright hallway. "You'd be surprised how much their little minds can grasp. Some advance quicker than others. I suppose it's all in the genes." She glanced at me over her shoulder. "I understand that you have quite a high IQ. Your eggs should make some fine babies." She stopped and jerked her head to the side as if recalling something.

I caught up to her. "My eggs? Are they going to harvest my eggs today? What did you mean—?"

She resumed her quick pace. "But only the doctors will know which embryos, which babies are generated from your eggs. It's better that way. Some girls have a tendency to get possessive. I'm sure you can understand."

I grabbed her arm and spun her to face me. "You're not answering my question. What tests will I go for today?"

Her eyes narrowed for an instant. She glanced at my hand on her arm.

I released her. "I just want to know. Are they harvesting my eggs today?"

"It doesn't happen all at once. There are several steps to the process. Don't worry. It won't hurt."

~~~

My scalp tingled. I turned full circle, slowly, half-expecting to find someone with me in this huge room. Maybe there were cameras. I had the feeling I was being watched.

Lee had left me alone to marvel at my new bedroom, a room bigger than Tatum's and my room combined. Space and tranquil colors surrounded me. Fancy wall lamps cast yellowish light on cherrywood furniture, things I had seen on a computer or as projected images but never in real life: a nine-drawer dresser with a mirror, an armoire, a vanity table. A huge pastel painting in the Impressionist style hung over a massive bed. The bed had piles of pillows and a spread in natural beiges and whites, apple green and coral pink. Silky curtains fluttered in a breeze.

Curtains? They hung on either side of sliding glass doors. Could it be?

I darted across the room and slid open a screen door.

The woods! My fourth-floor balcony overlooked the very edge of the Nature Preserves. A stretch of grass and the high electric fence of the boundaries, alone, separated me from graceful branches laden with lime green leaves, evergreens with soft fronds, and dark trunks reaching into a canopy of leaves.

A warm breeze rolled off the treetops and brought a green, woodsy scent to me. I closed my eyes and inhaled the air deep into my lungs, savoring the scent. My muscles relaxed. No, I never expected this moment.

For the first time since I set foot in this facility, I felt lucky to be here. If I couldn't stroll through the deep forests, at least I could peer into them, smell them, and imagine myself there. I would've never had this opportunity with any occupation other than this one. Perhaps the vocation of breeder wasn't so bad—

Something in the room clicked.

I spun around.

The curtains shuddered but no other movement caught my eye.
~~~

I stepped inside and scraped the screen door closed behind me. "Hello? Is someone here?" Taking soft steps on plush carpet, I headed toward the tall sliding doors of the closet. Where else could someone hide? Why would someone hide?

Out of the corner of my eye, I glimpsed movement.

A mirror. My reflection in a mirror on the wall. I chuckled and wanted to relax, but I *had* heard a noise so I continued toward the closet. Once there, I stopped, listened, and put my finger to the edge of the door, ready to slide it open.

Laughter came from behind me, across the room.

I turned.

The golden haired girl, Topaz, leaned a shoulder against the armoire and laughed, her hands to her abdomen.

My face heated. My jaw tensed. "What're you doing in my room? How'd you get in?"

She pushed off the armoire and dropped her hands to her side. "This was my room before it was yours. The ID reader accepted me." She sauntered toward me, her gown shifting and revealing a rounded belly. Stopping centimeters from me, she folded her arms across her chest and glared.

Though I hated when people stood so close, I refused to back up. "So why isn't this your room now?"

She smirked and walked to the glass balcony door. "They move you when you get to be seven months pregnant, say they need to keep a closer eye on you, make sure the pregnancy goes well." She ran her fingers up and down the curtain. "All those things they told you before you came here, all the rumors you heard . . . not true. It's just to make everyone think it's so wonderful in here."

"It looks just like the rumors to me. Girls lounging around, servants at the ready, massage when you want it."

She chuckled, her golden eyes glancing at me. "Yeah, you still get that stuff." She paused. "And more, guys or girls even, just not the servants. You see the servants all the time, so it causes problems among the breeders if someone gets involved, you know, jealousies."

I could imagine. "So what's your room like?"

"Nothing compared to this. Some girls are two to a room, in rooms half the size." She gazed outside.

I came up to her and stood shoulder to shoulder. "Have you ever been out there, in the Nature Preserves?"

"Of course not. Wild animals live out there. What do you think the boundary fences are for?"

"To keep us safe?" It was my turn to smirk. "That's not what the fences are for."

Her eyelids fluttered as if she had to process my remark. "It is. And those are protected areas. Don't you know why?"

"Who doesn't?" We studied to the point of nausea the way earlier generations nearly destroyed the earth by digging great mines, stripping millions of hectares of natural tropical forests, and depleting natural resources. How they polluted the air with vast amounts of carbon dioxide and by burning fossil fuels that created ground-level pollutants and greenhouse gases. How they overflowed the landfills with non-reusable resources. How they had caused an ever-growing list of endangered animals, many of which have been brought to extinction. How they didn't care. Overpopulation was largely to blame. Too many selfish, greedy people. Lucky for us, the Regimen stepped in, or so we were taught. Population numbers are now closely monitored and kept at safe levels. We generate less waste and pollutants, maintaining that critical balance. The forests and wildlife are now free from the terrorism of people.

"But wouldn't you like to be out there anyway," I said, ". . . explore the woods?"

"No. You should've been a scientist. Scientists have stations out there." She strolled to the bed, sat on it, and ran her hands along the spread. "So did you get the tour?"

I nodded. After the nursery, Lee had shown me the toddler area where children climbed through mazes and forts, fought, and cried. In the older kids' area, four- and five-year-olds fought and played. That room had been quieter because of all the little computer stations. The tour had been something of a shock. "Lee never told me what duty I'd be doing. Are you always in the nursery?"

"For now. I spent two months with the toddlers and another two with the older children. I'm supposed to be learning all about babies now. Once this one's out . . ." She rubbed her belly. " . . . I'll nurse babies for three months."

"You'll nurse your baby?"

She lowered her brows and shook her head. "Don't let them hear you call it that. It's not your baby. It's *a* baby, a citizen. They don't even let you know which one is yours. It's important that everyone share in the care of each one. You can't pick favorites." Her golden eyes turned hard.

"Doesn't seem natural."

"Of course it does. It takes a village to raise a child." She repeated the mantra taught in Primary and Secondary.

The moment Topaz leaned back on the bed, the door clicked and slid open.

Lee and a woman in a short gray dress stood in the doorway. Lee glared at Topaz before smiling at me. "I hope you're rested. It's time for your tests." She motioned toward the other woman in the doorway. "The doctor's assistant will escort you to the patient room."

"But I . . ." I shrunk back. I couldn't do this. It wasn't right. "Can't I talk to someone first?"

"Now, Liberty." Her calm expression contrasted with her quick pace as she entered the room. She patted my upper arm and then gripped it. "Please go with the assistant. You have nothing to worry about." She dragged me to the door.

"No. Wait." I yanked my arm free. My hand curled into a fist. They would listen to me. I had questions I wanted answered. I was no one's puppet. I would not be forced—

Peace struck me like a punch in the face and flowed into every cell of my body. Clarity came to me. *My Friend* spoke. "I am here. Do not be afraid."

11

"Have you ever considered a traditional stiletto, or even pumps?" Dr. Supero leaned back in a swivel chair and rubbed his star-shaped beard as he took Ivy in from head to toe.

Ivy sat, with legs crossed, at the monitoring station nearest him. The dark green top, or miniskirt—or whatever—complimented her figure, her sumptuous eyes, and the green streaks in her blonde hair. Supero appreciated the slinky orange tights, but those shoes . . . with fur up past her ankles, high black heels, and shiny black toes . . . they resembled calf hooves. What girl would want shoes that make one think of a cow? And considering her excessive gum-chewing habit . . .

She turned from the monitor and glanced at her shoes. "You don't like these?" She straightened out a leg.

His gaze traveled the length of it. "Like them? No. You have the most hideous taste in footwear."

She shrugged and blew a bubble. "I like them." She tilted her head back and gazed at the ceiling, exposing her long, slender neck.

If they were alone, he'd like to—

Dr. Supero sat up and took a sharp breath. "Are you keeping an eye on the patient?"

Ivy huffed and rolled her eyes. "She's being escorted to the examination room. Then she'll have to wait for the doctor. You know how long that can take. I hear the wait here is worse than patients waiting on you."

"Waiting on— I am the head physician of the entire facility. And I sit on several boards. I have many duties. If a patient waits on me, it's for a good reason."

"I'm not doubting that. I'm just saying. Nothing will be happening to your patient for quite a while. Unless you want to watch her change into the exam gown." Her tone and expression hadn't a trace of insincerity.

Dr. Supero bit back a sarcastic reply. "Just keep an eye on her."

"I don't know why you're so interested in this girl, why you transferred to the Breeder Facility and dragged me here with you. What's she to you? And why make *me* transfer? There are plenty of assistants here."

Supero smirked at Ivy's uninhibited display of jealousy. "She is nothing to me. She is a danger to society. But you, you are an excellent assistant, your memory exceptional, your attention to detail . . . No, I would not have another."

Ivy gave him a contemplative glance. Was she flattered? "So what are we looking for? What do you think she's going to do?"

~~~

I trembled and rubbed my arms as I followed the doctor's assistant down one hall and then another. The peace that I had experienced a moment ago had vanished. I didn't need *My Friend*. I needed to grow up. I could do this. Every girl here had gone through these tests. They wouldn't kill me. I just didn't know what to expect, and surprise never sat well with me.

We got onto an elevator and off two floors later. The assistant walked ahead of me, the sides of her caramel-colored hair flapping with each step. Near the end of a hallway, she slowed and glanced from her computer pad to the room number.

I hoped we were on the wrong floor or at the wrong room, or anywhere that would delay the tests. I never cared for getting a physical but the thought of this one scared me. How long would it take? How many doctors would I have to see? What would they do to me? I couldn't get myself to ask the questions aloud, but I didn't think she'd answer anyway.

"In here." The assistant waved her palm over an ID reader and stepped to the door as it slid open. She stood in the middle of a gray room, next to an examination bed, and looked at me with an expressionless face. "You'll need to undress and put on the gown."
~~~

I approached the bed, my eyes glued to the folded sickly-green gown. "I have to take off everything?" A shudder ran through me.

"Everything." She left the room and the door slid shut behind her.

The overhead strip lighting gave the room and everything in it a soft, hazy appearance. Gray cabinets with a long countertop and a sink lined one wall of the room. Various monitors, equipment on wheels, and a rolling bed with a bare plastic mattress stood in the shadows on the opposite side of the room, behind the examination bed. The cameras hanging in the corners and the long dark window in the back wall shattered any hope for privacy.

With my back to the window and glancing from camera to camera, I undressed and stuck my arms in the gown. Goose bumps covered my body. My hands trembled as I tied one of two ties in the back. The tie around the waist was so long I brought it to the front. As I crossed the ties over, the door to the examination room slid open.

My heart leaped and pounded in my throat. I fumbled with the ties, trying to make a bow.

Two people in gray lab coats came into the room, a brunette with her eyes on a computer pad and a man with blue-tipped, spiky blond hair and blue-tinted glasses. He looked in my direction while he spoke into the phone on his wrist. Once the door slid shut, the woman stepped toward the cluttered side of the room.

The man grabbed her arm, stopping her. "They say you have it." He spoke low. "They gave it to you."

"I told you I don't have it." The woman tucked her hair behind her ear. Her hair resembled mine, same color and length. She yanked her arm from his grasp and strode to the side of the room with the equipment.

"Well, what am I supposed to do?" the man said. His face swiveled to me and back to her, his blue-tinted glasses reflecting the overhead strip lights.

"Improvise." The woman lowered the side rail of the rolling bed and kicked the wheel locks.

The man bit his lip and turned from her to me. He couldn't possibly be the doctor.

"Do it," the woman spit.

The man sprinted to the other side of the rolling bed and, muttering, searched through the equipment stored behind it.

The woman reached under her coat and pulled out something made of shiny white plastic. "We have seconds before security cameras switch on." She cast a glance at one of the cameras while she unfolded the plastic and spread it out on the rolling bed.

"Is that a . . . body bag?" I said as the woman pulled the zipper that ran down the side of the long bag.

The man dashed back from the shadows, shoving a device into his lab coat pocket. Two coils dangled from it. He glanced as he passed me on his way to the sink. Still muttering, he yanked open cabinets and drawers, rifled through them, and took a few things. He turned around with the device humming and gauze, tweezers, and a scalpel in hand.

"You think that'll work?" the woman said.

"It has to." His tone did not convey confidence. "It'll disable the anti-tamper feature." He came toward me, the badge on his shirt catching my attention. *Crematory?*

I shivered. "What are you going to do to me? Who are you?" I backed away, glancing at my pile of clothes on the bed. This was not right. They were not here to perform tests. I needed to flee.

"You have to trust me." The man stood between the door and me. He lifted his hands in a gesture of peace, but he still held the scalpel.

"Trust you? Who are you? W-what are you going to do to me?" I stepped to the side.

He mirrored my step.

The woman rolled the bed to me. "Hurry and do it," she said to him. She stepped around the bed, grabbed my arm, and snatched the flexi-phone from my wrist.

"Hey." I jerked my arm free just as the man grabbed my other arm.

"It's me, Dedrick," he whispered. He let me go and lifted his tinted glasses, flashing a smile before lowering them again.

"Dedrick?" *Of course.* Why hadn't I recognized his voice or what I could see of his face? The blue tipped hair threw me off.

"This is gonna hurt. Sorry." He slapped a slippery paddle onto my palm and another onto the back of my hand.

A bolt of electricity ripped through my hand. My arm jerked. Pain shot from my hand to my forearm. Hard pinpricks covered my arm and one side of my body. Even my scalp tingled. I couldn't speak for a moment, so I couldn't protest.

He let the defibrillator fall to the floor, snatched my wrist, and slit my palm before I realized his intention. With one motion, he dropped the blade and grabbed the tweezers.

My entire arm had gone numb. I felt nothing, but I saw blood.

He slapped something into the woman's waiting hand, my ID implant I guessed, and pressed gauze to my bleeding palm. The woman undid the top buttons of her lab coat. Without warning, the two of them lifted me onto the open body bag on the bed and flipped the bag closed.

"What are you doing? Are you rescuing me?" I tried to sit up.

Someone pushed my head down. "Shhh," one of them said. The bed began to move. Someone zipped the bag.

I clutched the gauze to my sore palm and shivered in the cold plastic bag. Muted light came through the thin plastic and took up the color of the gown, making everything inside a sickly green. The smell of the plastic gagged me.

Dedrick and the woman whispered to each other as they rolled the bed through the doorway, down a hall, and around a corner. She whispered more than he did, as if she was asking questions and he answering. One of them unzipped the bag a bit and stuffed a blanket . . . no, a gray lab coat into the bag.

I pulled the coat over my chest. Where were they taking me? Escape didn't seem possible in this high-security facility. What if we all got caught?

"Be still," Dedrick said.

~~~

Ivy held a computer notepad or something to her chest as she strolled into the security station of the Breeder Facility. Chairs swiveled and all eyes turned to her as she swaggered past monitoring stations, her heels clomping along the floor of the long room.

She stopped in front of Dr. Supero and thrust the notepad at his chest. "That's all Chief Varden had. But he insisted you have it at once."
~~~

He grinned and gave her the once-over. "Take the bovine shoes off. I'd rather you go barefoot."

"Ha." With an air of conceit, she returned to her seat at the nearest monitoring station.

Supero glanced at the object she had given him. "We really must establish a dress code around here. In fact, I think—" His attention snapped back to the object. It was not a computer notepad. It was made of cardboard and paper. A twenty-first century notebook? People stopped using those natural-resource-consuming items decades ago.

He flipped it open. Sloppy, hand-written words filled the pages. A childish picture of a girl and the name 'Emily' was scrawled on the inside cover. He flipped a few pages. Someone had written in over half of the notebook.

"Who is Emily? Why did Chief Varden give this to me?"

"CSS got a phone call from a girl, Liberty's roommate."

"Liberty's roommate?" Supero began to read the writing.

Every day, the walls close in a little more. The air in my apartment reeks of cigarettes, alcohol, and body odor. The music and voices are often so loud they push the thoughts from my head. I want to scream. And run. But there's nowhere to run to. Walls are everywhere. I dare not speak my mind most of the time. My thoughts and ideas are hate-filled, a threat to society, I am told . . .

"The roommate caught Liberty trying to hide this before she left. She called it in this morning."

"Liberty wrote this?" Dr. Supero skimmed the writing, the wonderfully rebellious writing. His heart fluttered with delight. This was just what he needed. He jumped to his feet. "I need only show this to the psychiatrists. She will go directly to Re-Education. There will be no doubt as to her ideology, her destructive potential." He licked his lips. "I will call . . . no, I will deliver this myself." He glanced at the monitor. "Keep an eye on—"

The monitor showed an empty examination room.

"Where is the girl?"

Ivy faced the monitor and straightened up. "I don't know. She was there a minute ago."

Clutching the notebook with one hand, Supero shoved Ivy aside and flipped through the alternate camera views of the examination room.

The room was empty. Empty.

"Where has she gone?" Pressure built in his head. "She could not have left the room. She has no clearance to open doors to examination rooms. Someone would've had to let her out."

"I didn't see it. She was there a second ago."

"You weren't watching." His eyes bugged. He couldn't help but sneer. "Call Chief Varden," he shouted.

Ivy spoke into her wrist phone.

"Now!" Supero shouted louder.

~~~

Shortly after someone had stuffed the lab coat into the body bag with me, Dedrick whispered, "See ya below," and I no longer heard the woman's voice. Dedrick muttered something every now and then.

I remained silent as death.

My back ached from the role I played, the role of a corpse, so I shifted my weight ever so slightly. A dead body shouldn't move. I hadn't heard any other voices, so we passed no one or no one who cared, but security cameras saw everything. If this was my rescue, I didn't want to get caught.

Dedrick pushed the bed faster now.

My feet tingled. When would this ride end? We had gone down corridor after corridor, turned several corners, and taken two elevators. Where was he taking me? Should I trust him?

A moment later, the bed jerked to a stop and my body slid forward.

"Oh, sorry," Dedrick said.

A door clicked and slid. The bed rolled a short distance. The door slid again.

"Okay, we don't have much time." He ripped the zipper open and flung the plastic bag off me.

Goose bumps spread on my skin. "Time for what?" I started to push myself up.

He grabbed my trembling arms and yanked me upright and off the bed. "Fold the body bag. We'll have to get rid of it."
~~~

When my feet touched the cold floor, my legs wobbled. I threw my hands out to catch myself.

He had started to turn away but spun back. "Oh, hey," he said and grabbed me again. "You okay?"

I looked at my own reflection in his blue-tinted glasses. It was hard to read a guy without seeing his eyes. "I'm fine. Just cold."

He smiled. "You'll be warm soon enough." He darted to a steel wall and pressed buttons on a control panel. "Maybe too warm. But only for a moment. You'll have to trust me on this one."

"Did you bring my clothes?" I rubbed my arms.

"Uh, no. I didn't think about that." He glanced. "Fold the body bag." He put his palm on one of three small waist-high doors in the steel wall.

I took the lab coat from the bag and put it on. "Where are we?"

The room had three white walls and the steel one with the little doors. But it had no furnishings except for—

I gasped.

Behind my bed, lay another white body bag on a steel table. It appeared to have a body in it.

"W-w-what's that?"

"Huh?" He came up beside me and grabbed the empty body bag. He glanced at the body as he wadded the empty bag. "Oh that, uh . . . This is the crematory. I need to take care of that body after I send you through. It's necessary for—"

"What?" I backed away from him. "Who are you guys? Is this my rescue? You're going to euthanize me? Is that what you guys do? You take people that don't fit in this world and you euthanize them? You work for the Regimen, don't you?"

His mouth had dropped open as I spoke. He shook his head. "No. No, it's not like that."

Something on the steel wall clicked and beeped. He dashed for the control panel, touched a button, and one of the doors slid open. "Jump back on the bed and let me get you through."

Dancing golden light from a distant flame shone through the open hole in the steel wall.

"No. Do you think I'm crazy? I'm not going in there."

He came toward me.

I backed up. A wave of peace began in my chest, but I couldn't accept it. "No!"

Dedrick grabbed the bed and yanked it to the open door. "You've got to trust me." He glanced at his watch and at a camera hanging from the ceiling. "We've got seconds before the camera comes on and they see us. We'll be caught. Others will be in danger." He ripped the glasses from his face, revealing crinkled brows and brown eyes wide with anxiety . . . eyes that I almost trusted. "Seconds!"

With a strange inner assurance, I jumped onto the bed and scooted, feet first, through the door and into a narrow, metal shaft. I gagged at the faint odor of burnt flesh. My head bumped the ceiling when I tried to sit, so I stretched out on a track of steel plates.

"Lay flat and still and don't be afra . . ." The door slid shut.

Orange and golden light flickered on metallic walls. A motor sounded and the floor began to move. Heat reached my toes.

My heart pounded and I shuddered. I was about to die. Why had I trusted him? Why had *My Friend* made Himself known? I guess I needed Him and made Him come. I had hoped for a way out of my vocation and couldn't bear knowing that I had none. Though I considered myself a fighter, somewhere inside, I had chosen death. My life as a slave to the Regimen was about to end. I lost the battle. I gained nothing. Only death could bring freedom.

A burst of hot air shot to my face.

I shut my eyes. My head grew light and started spinning. The creeping floor shifted, sunk . . . deposited me onto a smooth, sloping surface. Black walls curved around me. I slid, whooshed into darkness, faster, faster . . . I couldn't breathe. My stomach dropped. My heart seemed to stop beating. I flew.

Was I dead?

~~~

"Her signal— What just happened to it?" Dr. Supero clutched the back of Chief Varden's chair and peered over Varden's head at an array of monitors.
~~~

"I don't know." Chief Varden flipped to various camera views of the facility. Two by two, Citizen Safety officers jogged down halls, busted into rooms, and charged down stairs. "Why don't you take a seat?"

"Why did her signal zip across the map like that? Have you lost her?"

"No. She's one girl. We're on it. And Unity Troopers are on the way."

"Where is she? Is that her signal?" Supero thrust his arm out and pointed to a flashing red dot outside the floor plan on the monitor.

Varden slapped Supero's arm away from his face. "Yes. It reads as if she's outside the facility. And I think I know what happened." He shouted into his wrist phone, "Get men outside. I'll send the location to you."

"Impossible. How could she get outside? The security of this facility is superior—"

"It's very possible. The signal zipped across the map because she slid down a garbage chute." He manipulated the map to show a three-dimensional view of the entire facility. Several tubes ran diagonally from the tenth floor to ground level.

"Those are garbage chutes?" He had never considered how refuse left the facility. Or that a person might be warped enough to crawl into one, for any reason.

"Some. Some are laundry. But she was right here, so she took this one." He pointed to a tube that came out on the east end of the facility, near the Citizens' Medical Offices.

"If she has access to a change of clothing, she can blend in. Have we no cameras outside? Flip to the image."

Varden grinned. "Relax, Doctor. We've got it under control. You'll have this girl of yours in custody. She'll be in Re-Education before your purple eyes can return to their sockets."

~~~

Light overcame the darkness. My flight slowed. I slid from the tube and dropped onto a thick mattress . . . alive.

"Right on time," a woman said. She threw a blanket over my shoulders and yanked me to my feet. "Watch your step."

I blinked as my eyes adjusted to the light. Voices and commotion came from across the room. People stood around a cluster of monitors
~~~

and computer stations. I clung to the woman's arm as I stepped off the mattress and onto a cold cement floor.

"Come with me. You can get dressed, and then we'll treat that hand before it gets infected."

"Oh, do you have my clothes?" I felt stupid for asking. How could they have my clothes? I left them in the examination room somewhere far above this place. Where was I?

"They're yours now." She smiled.

I did a double take. It was the woman with the white strands in her chestnut brown hair, the woman who led me from their secret facility the day Dedrick saved me from Sid. She was one of the Mosheh.

"You'll have to start over. You are no longer a citizen of the Regimen Custodia Terra. You're free."

"Free?"

"It'll take some getting used to. And you still have a bit of a journey but, yes, you're free." She led me through a doorway that had a sheet for a door, to a dimly lit room with a cot, a table, a stained toilet, and a sink. A lamp in the corner cast our shadows on the dingy walls. She gestured toward a pile of folded clothes on the foot of the bed. "Those should fit you. Clean up and come out when you're ready. I won't be far. Oh, by the way, my name is Miriam."

~~~

Dr. Supero burst through the doors of the facility, gasping to catch his breath, squinting at the natural sunlight. He had never run so fast and so far in his life. Where was the girl? Did they have her?

Citizen Safety officers and Unity Troopers meandered through the crowd that had been detained directly outside. Chief Varden leaned into a black Unity Trooper area car at the curb, waving a muscular arm and shouting orders. If he had Liberty in custody, he would not be so irate.

Dr. Supero shoved a woman out of his way and stomped through the crowd. He grabbed Chief Varden by the arm and yanked, but the Chief barely budged.

Chief Varden straightened up and turned around with gritted teeth and fire in his eyes.

"So where is she?" Dr. Supero said.
~~~

Chief Varden's jaw twitched. "She's not here. We can't find her."

"You can't find her?"

"That's what I said."

"No. You said I'd have her. She'd be in Re-Education before I knew it. That, Chief Varden, is what you said." Spit flew from his mouth as he spoke. "Where is she?" He flung a hand out and cast a glance at the crowd. "How can a girl in a green hospital gown sail from a garbage chute, crawl out of a dumpster, and simply get away? Aren't you tracking her ID implant?"

"You, Dr. Supero, are out of line." Varden's arm shot from his side, his finger pointing to the facility. "Go back to your office and let me do my job. We'll find her. I guarantee it."

Supero considered remaining there, involving himself in the search, but Varden's eyes flashed flames. So he contented himself with saying, "You'd better."

~~~

"That ought-a do it." The old man tending my wound placed a final strip of tape over a square gauze pad and shut off the LED light on his hat. The cut on my hand required only two thin adhesive skin closures. "The removal of sub-dermal implants typically leaves a miniscule opening, requires nothing more than a little bandage. Didn't Dedrick use the implant removal device, handheld thingy, looks a little like a gun?"

"The *what*? He shocked me with a defibrillator and cut me with a scalpel." Ever since the old man hobbled up to me, I couldn't stop staring at his face. He had two big scars on his wrinkled skin, one under his eye and the other on his forehead.

"A defibrillator? A scalpel?" The man chuckled, deep lines forming around his eyes. He put a hand on my shoulder as he stood up. "In that case, I guess Dedrick's not too bad with a scalpel." With a smile on his face and a black medical bag in his hands, he shuffled away.

I sat in the shadows, alone now, on a crate amidst several crates stacked on one wall of the Mosheh's underground base. Across the room, about thirty people—from teenagers to elderly—milled around a set-up of computers and surveillance equipment. An array of monitors, a few speakers, and dark light bulbs hung on two walls in the work area. Clusters
~~~

of wires dangled from the high ceiling and ran down poles and cement walls. The few ceiling lights lit up only the work area, leaving the rest of the base in semidarkness.

My gaze traveled back to the tube that had brought me to freedom. Three tubes projected from the ceiling in the corner, coming out beside three freestanding glass booths. The booths reminded me of the old-fashioned phone booths we learned about in school, except these had meter-wide tubes sticking out the top and running to the ceiling.

Laughter came from one of the two wide, dark halls on either end the base. A bouncing spot of light showed and then a group of four, two women and two men, headed my way.

The shorter of the two women walked ahead of the group, advancing from the darkness. "Liberty, how are you?" It was Miriam.

Glad to see her, I stood up. "I'm confused."

She laughed and dragged a crate to the ones on which the doctor and I had been sitting. "There are two people I'd like you to meet. You'll be traveling together."

The other woman and the two men joined us, engrossed in conversation. They wore clothing similar to what Miriam had given me, dark shirts and camouflage pants and jackets.

The younger of the men slid a backpack off his shoulder and strolled up to me. He had a clean, round face, the face of a teenager. "This'll be yours to carry on the journey."

I took it from him and, underestimating the weight, dropped it on the floor. "What's in it? Journey to where?"

He grabbed a crate from Miriam and dragged it to a spot across from mine. "It's stuff you'll need. It's a bit heavy, but I try to keep the weight even in each of them."

Miriam continued to pull and arrange crates until she had two rows of three. She took a lantern from one of the crates and set it in the middle of the arrangement. Everyone except for the teen sat on the crates. The other man kept babbling to the other woman. She nodded every now and then, her expression serious, almost sad.

"So where's the journey to?" I said to the teen.

He smiled and waved his brows. "You'll see. She'll tell you all about it." He nodded at Miriam, stuffed his hands in his jacket pockets, and strolled away.

Miriam sat across from me. "Our last pilgrim is Liberty of Aldonia." The man stopped talking. He and the woman greeted me with nods. "Liberty is mechanically inclined, a hard worker and, despite her upbringing, has high moral standards."

The other two chuckled. My face warmed.

"Much to her dismay," Miriam said, "Liberty was slated to be a breeder. In fact, she was rescued from the Breeder Facility, which is no easy task."

"I'll say," the man said. He had an unshaven chin and tousled red hair, strands of which reflected light from the lantern. "Their databases are impenetrable."

"Not exactly," Miriam said and turned to me. "This is Bot, also from Aldonia. He's a specialist in computer systems and database storage and retrieval."

"I worked for the Regimen." Bot's brows lowered over his intense blue eyes. He had the experimental mottled blue that I had seen a few times before. "That is, until I stumbled across old, buried files and got caught. The government we know today, the all-efficient, all-wise Regimen Custodia Terra, is not the only workable, just, and intelligent form of government, as they would have you believe. In fact, on this continent of ours, there was once a government of the people, by the people, for the people. Everyone had a say in it. Everyone had a vote, not just the elite. I just can't say enough about how unfair our system is today. Only the wealthy and highly educated get to vote so, as they say, only the very best rule. Well, I'll tell you—"

"Excuse me, Bot," Miriam said. "You will have days to explain your philosophy on government. Allow me to continue with the introductions."

Bot's mouth hung open as if a word got stuck on its way out. He shut it and nodded. "By all means."

"When Bot uncovered these files and didn't report it, the Regimen considered him a threat. I suppose they might have responded differently, had he not been so vocal." Miriam glanced at Bot.

Smirking, Bot shrugged and shook his head. "Hey, I kept it to myself for a long time. I wasn't even sure it was true. Weeks, months, I read every hidden file I could retrieve. But then it burned me up." The look in his mottled blue eyes intensified. "I couldn't keep my mouth shut. I wanted to know how other people felt, how they would feel if they knew the way things once were. There wasn't always one world government. People agreed with me, liked what I had to say. Oh, not those in Regimen jobs, but the others, the ordinary folk. The way the Regimen runs things . . . It just isn't fair. The right to vote shouldn't be limited to a few. The right to . . ." He caught Miriam's glaring eyes, shut his mouth, and cleared his throat.

"I'm sure you're all aware that the Regimen does not tolerate the spreading of ideas that aren't in harmony with their own philosophy. Bot got on their watch-list and, so, on ours. When they slated him for re-education, we stepped in." Her gaze went to the other woman. "And this is Jessen from Kingsley."

Jessen leaned forward and twisted her arms together, sticking them between her lanky legs, an impish grin replacing the scowl. "Hi." She had a head of short spiral curls and spikes, with one curl hanging on her forehead. "I'm just a student."

"Jessen was studying to be a genetic scientist, top of her class, scheduled to work in Reproductive Technology, improving the processes for in vitro fertilization and gene modification. She became interested in the natural process of human reproduction—"

"Obsessed." Jessen raised her hand, the impish grin back on her face. "I'll admit it: I was obsessed with the natural process. And maybe I shouldn't have done it, but I had a tubal litigation reversal in order to get pregnant the natural way."

"You're kidding," Bot said with a scowl.

Jessen pulled back her jacket and rubbed her rounded belly.

Bot's mouth dropped open. "I've never seen a pregnant woman. I mean, I know there're plenty of them at the Breeder Facility. But I . . ."

Jessen laughed.

"I've seen plenty," I said. It startled me at first, too, seeing bellies so round on thin girls.

"I bet you have," Bot said.

Miriam cleared her throat and regained the attention. "Jessen's pregnancy was reported. The Regimen wasted no time scheduling an abortion and questioning her to determine the need for re-education. So the Mosheh rescued her."

"Where did your rescue take place?" I couldn't imagine her, in her condition, riding the slide I rode.

"I was walking." The impish grin faded. "You ever get really depressed and take a long walk?"

"All the time."

"I didn't even know where I was going or what street I was on. I knew I wouldn't be home by curfew, but I just couldn't turn back. They were going to kill this life in me and send me for re-education."

"We took her when . . ." Dedrick stepped into our little group, lugging a backpack twice the size of ours. He sat on the crate next to mine and put the bag between his legs. ". . . she walked into an alley we have access to, one without working cameras. Jessen's was an easy extraction." He looked at each of us, his gaze resting on me a moment longer.

"Not like mine, huh?" I made an obvious glance at his hair, still blue-streaked and blond, though without the spikes.

He combed his fingers through his hair. "No, I mean not like Bot's. You were there. Day you chased the Unity Troopers to an alley. Day I told you to scram."

My face burned. I wanted to give a sarcastic reply, but my mind drew a blank. I should say something about his hair.

"That was his rescue." Dedrick nodded at Bot. Bot nodded back.

"I suppose everyone here knows Dedrick?" Miriam said, and we all mumbled our assent. "Good. Then I'll tell you a bit about our group. We are the Mosheh. We are not connected with the Regimen. Their ways are not our ways. We believe in the freedom of the individual."

"Here, here," Bot said, though the reply made no sense to me.

"Some of us live under the cities," she said, "keeping an eye on the government and rescuing those we can."

"How do you decide?" Bot said. "No one likes living like this. We have no voice. We have no rights. We have no power to live as we want."

"It's not easy. We want all people to live free but our numbers are few and, compared to the troops of the Regimen, we are weak. So our crews listen to the chatter of the CSS and Unity Troopers. We find out who are the rebellious citizens, especially those being considered for re-education. These are likely candidates. We watch for individuals that we believe would find fulfillment in our way of life, those we can trust, those with a moral compass, and we wait until the time is right."

"Who wouldn't find fulfillment in freedom?" I said. "Who wouldn't want to be free?"

She chuckled. "With freedom comes responsibility. Not everyone is prepared to accept that. Many prefer the handouts and conveniences the Regimen offers. Our way of life isn't easy. You will each have to work and work hard. The conveniences you enjoyed yesterday are no longer yours."

"What if we don't want your life?" Jessen said, a twinkle in her eye. Though I didn't know her, I gathered she was testing Miriam.

"We trust that you will. And we don't choose candidates lightly. But once you've tasted life in one of our free colonies, if you don't like it, you can always live with me under the city." She smiled at Jessen.

"Well, let's get to it," Dedrick said. He stuck his hand into a wide pocket of his backpack and drew out several papers. He handed one to each of us. Handwritten words and markings covered the soft, thick paper.

"Who made this?" I said.

Dedrick smiled. "Where I come from, we learn to write by hand. You may not always have access to a computer." He threw a glance at Bot.

"I can write by hand," I said but Bot drowned out my words with a desperate, "No computers?"

"Don't worry," Miriam said. "We have work that will employ your skills, should you choose to accept it."

"So where are we going?" I said.

Dedrick spread his map on the crate in the middle of the group. "Here." With his index finger, he stabbed a blank part of the map.

Bot leaned in. "What's there? That's outside the boundaries, isn't it?"

Dedrick nodded. "The electric fences and rules of the Regimen keep our colonies safe." He winked. "No one's permitted out there. The scientists and security drones don't even go out that far. They know nothing of us." He slid off the crate, squatted, and turned his attention entirely to the map. "These are the underground passages. We'll leave by this tunnel and head north to this section." He pointed to an area marked *residential.*

"So this is under a residential area?" I said.

"No, we have underground communities, too. Miriam wasn't joking when she said you could choose to live under the city. You'll see. That group likes visitors." He pointed to another passageway on the map. "We'll have to surface here. This is where it gets a little dangerous. But we have Intel on their surveillance equipment and drone fly-bys. And we can power down sections of the Boundary Fence for brief periods of time. To get through, you'll each need to pay close attention to my instructions. And you can't hesitate when it's your turn."

"Or what? What if someone loses their nerve?" Jessen said.

Dedrick locked eyes with her. "The electrical current will kill you."

No one spoke for a moment, each of us absorbing the plan and considering the risks.

I broke the silence. "Since beyond the boundaries is off limits, is it easy going on the other side?"

"That depends on how you look at it. We have miles to go before we sleep."

~~~

"Where is she?" With a racing heart and sweaty palms, Dr. Supero stood over a young man in the CSS surveillance station. He could barely think over the deafening chatter from dozens of phone conversations and covert listening devices, with the flashing images on the array of glassy monitors, and because of the messengers that rushed back and forth. Liberty's signal had appeared sporadically on the area map displayed on a large wall monitor. Smaller monitors showed live feeds from active
~~~

cameras she should have passed in her escape. Whatever disguise she wore, it worked. The recognition software could not pick up her image.

"Looks like she's headed for that mall," the young man said. His hands moved continuously over the control panel as he changed and adjusted various views from the live feeds.

"How fast can the girl move? Our well-trained Unity Troopers and your own Chief Varden cannot catch her?"

"It's not that she's fast." The boy reached to the far side of the panel. With a tap of his finger, numbers appeared on the lower corner of the map. "See? She's not even running. More like a jog. But her signal keeps jumping. They're having a hard time tracking her. Seems like she pops from one alley to another."

"What?" Supero leaned closer so that the boy had to shift in his seat. Sure enough, the signal disappeared and showed up a block away. "How is that possible?"

"That's what I'm trying to find out." He turned from his work and squinted at Dr. Supero as if, somehow, Dr. Supero impeded his progress.

Dr. Supero huffed and backed up.

The boy's hands flew over the control panel. "I think she's got a device that interferes with our ability to detect her true location, bounces the signal. I've heard about those things but never seen—" He froze for a second then glanced back and forth between the map on the monitor and the control panel over which his hands flew.

Dr. Supero noted nothing unusual on the map. The view hadn't even changed. "What is the matter?"

The boy pointed. "The signal's gone. It's just gone. She got right to the middle of that mall and it stopped."

"No. That is not possible. Even if she dies her implant sends a signal."

"Well, I don't know what to tell you. Her signal's gone."

"No. No! It is not possible!" Supero slammed his fist on the control panel. Images on the wall monitors flipped. "You cannot have lost her!" A vein behind his eyes pulsed. He saw red. With a brush of his arm, he cleared the control station of loose items: a mug, a pocket computer, other trivial items. They crashed to the floor but barely made a sound over his long, tension-filled scream.

12

Excitement raced through my blood. Every hair on my body stood at attention and hope burned within me. *My Friend,* or my imagination—I cared not which—stirred my soul with the feeling I had experienced many days ago when my shovel clanked against the underground bunker. *Cages bursting open. Walls coming down. Secrets made known.* I would uncover more secrets before the end of my journey. I no longer wore the chains of the Regimen.

Dedrick led us through a cold dark tunnel, his flashlight revealing the next several meters, darkness looming ahead and behind. I followed him. Bot and Jessen brought up the rear, Bot talking incessantly about old forms of government and images of documents he discovered online. "Yeah, and it was a photocopy of an original document on some sort of parchment or something. It was so old I didn't recognize the font. Some type of cursive. It took time, but I was actually able to read it. Even memorized some of it. The words really moved me." He cleared his throat and spoke with a formal tone. "When in the course of human events, it becomes necessary for one people to dissolve the political bands which have connected them with another . . ."

I couldn't hold down a thought. I glanced at the bandage on my hand. Was this a dream? Was I really free? Would I make it to the colony or get caught trying? What exactly was a *colony*? Would I like it there? Would the people there accept me? What would I do?

The tunnel narrowed and descended for a time, allowing us to march at a good pace. Other tunnels branched off this one, but Dedrick paid them no attention. He walked without speaking, without even so much as a glance off to the side.

Several kilometers and over an hour later, the tunnel began a gradual incline. Sweat gathered on my hairline, refreshing me in the dank air. An hour or so later, my thighs complained at the steady incline and my boots had rubbed my toes raw, but Dedrick kept up the pace. Bot had even stopped talking and now breathed through his mouth.

"How much farther?" Jessen asked. "I guess I misjudged the length of the tunnels on your little map."

Dedrick turned around, grinning, and walked backwards without slowing. "My *little* map has a scale. Did you look at it?" Light from his flashlight bounced off the dark floor and reflected on our faces.

"I guess not." Jessen glanced at Bot. Bot shrugged.

"You'll need to be attentive if you want to stay safe, at least until we reach the colony."

"Can't you just answer her question? I saw your scale and I figured we'd be there by now, especially at your pace." The words flew from my mouth. "And I don't know about them . . ." I nodded to indicate Bot and Jessen. ". . . but I'm anxious to get outdoors. These tunnels reek."

He chuckled, his eyes holding no trace of annoyance. "You never struck me as one to shy away from inconvenience." He turned around, returning us to darkness as light shined on the tunnel ahead. "The point of departure is less than an hour away, but first, we'll pass through an underground community. We'll stay there, eat, and rest up until nightfall."

My sneer faded. I regretted snapping at him, but the toes on my right foot ached and felt wet from either sweat or blood. Dedrick seemed like a nice guy, genuine, different from other guys in a way I didn't understand. And something about his eyes, his brown eyes . . . How did he get brown eyes?

Half an hour later, we turned down a narrow tunnel that ended at a low metal door. Dedrick spun a dial on the door, a lock of some sort, and something clicked.

My heart skipped a beat. Jessen sucked in air. Bot stuck his thumbs in the straps of his backpack and bounced on his feet.

The heavy door swung open to warm light and indistinct voices. A man appeared in the doorway, blocking our way, a dark-haired, bearded man with a machine gun at the ready. He gave us the once-over and then glared at Dedrick. They knew each other, right?

"Hey, Maco," Dedrick said, taking a step toward the burly man.

Maco did not step aside. He grunted, tightened his grip on the gun, and edged toward Dedrick, not stopping until they stood close enough to smell each other's breath. "What's the word?" he growled. Head tilted back, he glared down his nose at Dedrick.

Dedrick stood his ground and held Maco's hostile gaze. "Vescere bracis meis." He paused between each strange word.

The man's eyes, fixed on Dedrick, darkened. The two remained locked in a silent staring contest for five beats of my heart. Then Maco lowered the gun, threw his head back and laughed. "Vescere bracis meis! I hardly recognized you with the blue hair." He slapped Dedrick on the arm and motioned with the gun for us to come in.

Unsure as to whether I trusted him or not, I went first.

"Welcome, friends." Maco closed the door with a thud. "I suppose Dedrick has you all tired out from the hike here. He could've taken a cart."

"What?" Bot shrugged his backpack from his shoulders. "Like a golf cart?"

Maco leaned on the door and eyed Dedrick. "I don't know about Dedrick. He likes to test everyone."

"Keep it to yourself." Dedrick smirked. "You trying to turn them against me? They're stuck with me for a few days yet. I'd like to have their confidence."

A young man with a limp pulled a flatbed wagon to us and took Bot's backpack. Dedrick said something to him, slapped him on the shoulder, and put his own backpack on the wagon. Jessen and I added our loads to the pile. The man whispered to Dedrick and then, limping, rolled the wagon away.

"We could've taken a cart?" Jessen punched Dedrick's shoulder and stomped past him.

"Come on," Dedrick called after her. "I'll show you around, introduce you."

Without looking back, Jessen threw a hand up to decline his offer and marched off toward a nearby group of people. The group opened at once to her, touching her arms, smiling and greeting her.

Dedrick said to Bot and me, "So, this is one of our underground communities." We walked as he spoke.

The area resembled the other two underground areas I had seen, the one I first saw when rescued from Sid and the one from which we just hiked: a high ceiling, a rough cement floor, darkness surrounding lighted areas, and crude doorways in the walls. This place also had a section with monitors, computers, and busy people, but it had a homey feel to it. Most people lounged at tables or on cushioned furniture under light fixtures that dangled from the darkness above, rugs underfoot, and conversation and laughter everywhere.

Dedrick stopped by a canvas wall that separated a cozy sitting area from a medical-care section. There, a gray-haired woman lay in a bed surrounded by equipment. Tubes came from her arms. A woman sat on the edge of the bed, speaking to her in a low voice.

"Some of the people here received a bad diagnosis from the death panels. Their time was up, according to the Regimen, so we took them in." Dedrick looked at me. "They came the same way you did." He waved his brows. ". . . via crematory."

"What? No way. That ride would be enough to kill an old person. Shoot. I thought I'd died."

He chuckled. "The ride is smooth. Besides, we usually sedate them."

"So how do you . . ." Bot shook his head. ". . . fix them, er, keep them alive."

We resumed walking as Dedrick spoke. "Some treatments are costly or time-consuming, but life is worth it and we have the technology, so if there's something we can do, we do it. If not, we do what we can to make people comfortable, happy in their last days."

"Well, that's a different approach," Bot said, not giving away by his tone of voice whether he approved or not.

The cold look in his mottled blue eyes irritated me. "It's a respectful approach," I said. "I hate how old people are treated like— Richter!" Could Richter have been saved? I spun around, glancing from group to group, my gaze lingering on the groups of old men, searching for one with mocha-colored skin and wild gray eyebrows. I took a step, ready to dash for a rowdy group of old men on the far side of the room, when a hand landed on my arm.

"He's not here." Dedrick spun me to face him. "I know who you're looking for: Richter from the Senior Center where you worked."

"Why?" I tugged my arm from Dedrick. My body tensed with my anger. "Why isn't he here? Do you pick and choose, just like the Regimen? Are some lives more valuable—"

"He died." Dedrick grabbed my arms again, my trembling arms. "He died in the ambulance. There was nothing we could do."

Not wanting anyone to see me lose control, I twisted away from Dedrick and steeled my emotions. I thought I had shed all the tears I had for that old man. I loved him so. And what would become of Abby and the others? It wasn't fair. It wasn't fair.

"Come," Dedrick said over my shoulder. "You're probably hungry."

We ate dinner with a lively group of old folks, with much laughter and good food. Beth, a woman with stained fingers and deep smile creases, monopolized the conversation for a while. "What do you think of the salad? Grew those vegetables myself, the lettuces, tomatoes, cucumbers . . ." She chuckled. "Well, not entirely by myself. There's a group of us. Grew the carrots and green beans, too."

"How is that possible?" Bot smirked. "I mean, how do you get sunlight down to this wormhole."

Beth laughed. "Mirrors. We use mirrors to redirect the sunlight. Our gardens flourish."

Mouth hanging open, fork poised above his plate, Bot huffed.

"It's the best salad I ever had." I spoke up before Bot said something sarcastic. "I'd never given much thought to the food I'd get from the commissary, to the process of planting and growing things. I wonder who grows those vegetables."

"You mean the soggy ones in the white-label cans?" Jessen laughed. Several others laughed with her.

"As with all vocations, the Regimen has an impersonal method of selecting gardeners." Dedrick sat across from me. "They're taught horticulture from their youth, about how plants grow, the properties of soil, different types of mulch and fertilizers, the various planting and harvesting procedures, procedures that require less manual labor than our gardening. I doubt many of them appreciate their vocation." A smile spread on his face. His gaze turned to Beth. "Not like our gardeners, anyway."

Beth blushed and sat up straight.

Though others in the dining area finished before us, our dinner lasted over two hours, everyone having something to say and questions to ask of us newcomers. After clearing our table, old women brought tea, reminding me of Abby. Their smiles, the sincerity in their eyes, their obvious concern for us, and their laughter gave me warmth. I liked these people and knew I could fit in here. Would it be the same at the colony? What would life be like without the Regimen controlling every aspect? Would I be able to choose my vocation? They had something planned for Bot, Miriam had said, if he chose to accept it.

After a while, the throbbing of my toes distracted me from conversation, so I excused myself from the others. I walked without favoring the foot, not wanting anyone to know of my discomfort, although I avoided making eye contact with passersby, not wanting to get sucked into a conversation.

The lavatory was nearby. It had several stalls and sinks, like the ones in Secondary, but no electric hand dryers. Real cloth towels hung from black metal bars. Paintings and artistic light fixtures decorated the ugly cement walls. A canvas canopy, draped from steel beams, served as a ceiling, with bits of debris in the drooping sections.

After taking care of business, I sat on a wire-backed chair and unlaced the boot on my left foot. My little toe screamed as I eased the boot off. Blood stained the sock. *Great.* Hoping no one would barge into the lavatory, I peeled the sock off and stuck my raw foot in the sink. I rinsed the sock, wrapped toilet paper around my toes, and put the sock and boot back on.

No sooner had I stepped out of the lavatory than someone called my name.

"It's time." Dedrick came up behind me, my backpack hanging from his arm. "Bot and Jessen are waiting for us near the tunnel that leads to the chutes."

"The what?" I glanced about but didn't see them.

"The, uh, transporters. You'll see. Come on." He handed me my backpack and led the way.

Everyone we passed stared. Some nodded and smiled. A few offered a word to say *goodbye* or *good luck*. "Blessings," more than a few said. It reminded me of the ancient history we briefly studied in Secondary. People once believed in invisible higher powers that would do favors for or send curses upon them. *A childish belief*, they told us. Sarkin, my close friend from Secondary, said it only made sense. There had to be a higher power, an uncreated Creator. While I understood the concepts we learned of the Big Bang and evolution, I almost shared Sarkin's beliefs. *Blessings*. I was being blessed right now, even if my fate would later take a turn for the worse.

In a quiet corner of this underground shelter, next to a low metal door, Jessen and Bot leaned against the wall, talking. A man in camouflage, and with a blaster rifle slung over his shoulder, sat hunched at a table nearby. He stared with intensity at something on the table.

"What's the armed man doing?" I said to Dedrick. "What's he staring at?"

Dedrick chuckled. "He's reading. That's a book."

"A book?"

"Novels haven't always been electronic."

Jessen caught sight of us and stooped for the backpack at her feet. Bot kept talking as if unaware that we drew near.

"Bot, get your backpack on." Dedrick went to the metal door, turned a dial, and slid back a high and a low latch.

He opened the door to darkness and flicked a flashlight on. Light bounced off narrow stone walls and a low ceiling. "You'll have to watch your head in some places." He plunged into the tunnel.

Our footfalls thudded as we walked, seeming to die under us rather than echo as in the other tunnels. We plodded along for fifty or so meters then turned down a tunnel that branched off this one. A few hundred meters later, we turned again. More and more tunnels branched off to either side, some silent, others having sounds of distant drips or hums. We took one tunnel after another, as if our destination lay at the center of a maze.

"We made it." Dedrick's voice came from around a corner, from a tunnel he had turned down but that we had yet to reach.

Bot pushed past me and darted around the corner. "What is that?"

Jessen and I saw it at the same time. The tunnel ended at a dirt wall a short distance away. Wood beams framed the dirt walls and the ceiling. Something like an old-fashioned glass phone booth stood in the corner. A tube came from the top of the booth and connected to the low ceiling.

"This is the transporter?" Bot walked around the booth, examining it. He slid the door open, revealing a high-backed seat with vertical bars on the sides.

"Yup, this is it," Dedrick said. "And I'll go first just in case."

"Just in case of what?" I said.

Dedrick tapped his ear. "I'm in contact with the surveillance team. They'll let me know when to go. When I'm above ground, I'll double check that the coast is clear. You'll need these." He handed each of us a small black device with an antenna on the top.

Bot started pressing buttons right away.

"Don't mess with it." Dedrick snatched the device from Bot and pressed a button a few times. "These are two-way radios, and communication can be picked up by anyone. We'll use them only for emergencies and to get out of here. When it's safe above, I'll say, 'Go' and one of you will get in the chute."

He handed me the flashlight, stepped into the booth and slid into the seat. "Make sure the belt's tight." He demonstrated, pulling a thick belt diagonally across his chest and buckling it at his hip. "Close the door and flip this lever." He pointed to a metal lever on the side of the chair back. "And then hold on." He gripped the bars on the sides of the chair and gave a lopsided grin. "Don't worry, it's a fun ride."

"Where do we end up?" Jessen said.

"You'll be in the dark until I open the door. If it takes me a moment, just wait. I have my reasons." Dedrick's hand shot up to his ear. "Okay, it's time." He whisked the door shut and flipped the lever. The chair lifted and shot up into the tube atop the booth.

Jessen, Bot, and I stood gaping.

Bot snickered. "Well, that was cool."

"I don't know." Jessen rubbed her belly.

"I'm sure it's safe," I said.

"I don't even know how far underground we are," Jessen said. "How long is the ride? And where do we come out? What do we go through to get to this colony?"

"I'm sure it's a safe enough journey, and it's gotta be worth it. They wouldn't risk your . . . your baby." After my experience at the Breeder Facility and all that Lee had told me, it felt odd saying it was *her* baby. But the Regimen could make no claim on the baby. It hadn't begun in their laboratories or been implanted in their breeders. No. It was Jessen's baby. I couldn't imagine how strange that would feel.

"I don't know." She strolled to a wall, turned around and leaned on it, using her backpack as a buffer. "The reproductive procedures of the Regimen are so controlled, every step monitored. Fertilization takes place in a sterile lab, under a microscope. Scientists examine the genetic information of the zygote. Those suspected to be defective are terminated. Only the healthy are implanted, implanted in girls whose health, exercise and diet are closely monitored." She dropped her head into her hands, spiral curls tumbling forward. "What am I doing? What was I thinking? What can I do if something goes wrong? Will I even know?"

Still standing before the booth, Bot glanced at me and shook his head. He checked the radio dangling from his belt, folded his arms, and stared at the booth again as if anxious for Dedrick's call.

I went to Jessen, keeping the beam of the flashlight low to give her privacy. "Don't worry. This is new to all of us. And I know there are risks, but it's better than re-education or life under the Regimen. Isn't it?"

She lifted her head and met my gaze.

"You said yourself, the Regimen's way wasn't natural. You're a woman. Your body was designed for this. You'll be fine. The baby, *your* baby, will be fine."

"Thanks." She smiled and squeezed my shoulder. "You're a strong girl, full of hope. The Mosheh was wise to rescue you."

"I didn't expect it to take this long. Why isn't he calling?" Bot unfolded his arms and planted his hands on his hips. "He's got to be above ground by now." He flung a hand out in the direction of the booth. "That thing is fast."

"Maybe he's checking the area out," I said. "Give him time."

"Where's the seat? Why hasn't it returned?" Bot shook his head and walked a few meters away. He muttered something and came back. Every few minutes he walked away and came back. Jessen slid down the wall and sat on the ground, her arms resting on her raised knees.

I just stood there, trying not to show my anxiety as the minutes passed, five, ten, twenty . . . Could something have gone wrong?

"What if he's in trouble?" Bot slid the radio from his belt. "Maybe we should try contacting him."

"Don't." My hand jerked. I had to resist snatching the radio from him. "You could put him in danger."

With his whiskery jaw jutted and waving the radio, Bot came up to me. "Maybe he's already in danger and contact with us can save him."

"Use your brain. If he needed us, he'd call," I said. "And what can we do? None of us has a weapon. Put your radio away."

"Maybe one of us should go back," Jessen said. "They have a surveillance team back there. They can find out what's going on. It's not that far. Half an hour's walk, maybe less."

"No, we should stick together," I said. "I'm sure they know Dedrick's situation. I'm sure they're in contact with him now. Besides, we only have one flashlight." I shined the light at Bot's feet then at Jessen's, glancing at their expressions as I did so. Neither one seemed convinced.

"Maybe we have flashlights." Jessen wriggled out of her backpack and dragged it to her lap.

"Instead of trying to go back, we need to know who's going first." They both looked at me. "When he calls, which one of us goes first?"

Jessen shook her head. "One of you two. I'm still getting my nerve up. How far away is this colony?" She stuck her hand into the backpack and dug through the contents.

"Yeah, you know . . ." Bot, still holding the radio, paced the floor. "I'm not sure I want to live out there. They have little power, few conveniences, hard work. Isn't that what Dedrick and Miriam said?" He looked from me to Jessen. "What kind of work? Do I have to grow my own food like that old woman at the table? Do I really want colony life? Maybe I want to stay in one of these under-city communities. I should be working with the others on surveillance. I bet I can increase their capabilities, discover things they hadn't even thought of. I mean, what happened to Dedrick? Something the surveillance team couldn't have warned him about?"

"Chill, man. Just relax." I forced the scowl off my face. "They said you could choose once you got to the colony. Give it a chance. They have their ways, and we should respect them. They saved each one of us from re-education or worse. And besides, lives depend upon their methods of security. You don't want to blow that, do you?"

"How would I blow that?"

"I don't know. I know little about these under-city communities and less about the colonies. I don't understand their methods any more than you do. We all just have to wait and see. Unless you want to get caught and risk the welfare of all these people." I flung my hand toward the dark tunnel we had come through, meaning to indicate all the old and young we had just met. "I, for one, plan to trust them."

Trust them. It sounded strange hearing myself say that. I trusted no one. But now . . . I wanted to trust. I needed to trust them.

My Friend whispered in my soul, like a gentle summer breeze, and then was silent. He wanted me to trust. Even if He was my own creation, His message comforted me. Faced with the unknown and possible danger, I had hope. We may have to pass through many trials, but something wonderful lay ahead.

A clanking sound came from the tunnel above the booth.

Jessen pulled herself up. We all shot to the booth.

The chair dropped down with a hydraulic hissing sound. Static sounded on our radios and then a whispery voice said, "Go."

~~~

Well after curfew, Chief Varden strolled into the Citizen Safety Station.
~~~

Instead of having the sheepish look of a man whose confidence gravely outweighs his performance, he smiled and spoke flirtingly with the attractive girl by his side. Did he not take his job seriously?

The girl by his side? Dr. Supero jumped up and stared. Why was Ivy here? Why was she walking with Chief Varden? Was she flirting back? Certainly, she would not go for a man with such an inflated ego.

The flirting ceased as they came into hearing range. They both turned their eyes to Supero.

"So where is Liberty?" Supero spit out. "You let her get away."

Varden's jaw twitched and he averted his gaze. "I don't know where she is." He went to an unused station and hunched over the control panel.

Supero gave Ivy the once-over as she slipped past him on her way to the nearest padded chair. Their eyes met. Amusement showed brightly in hers. He tried to keep from appearing jealous, but she seemed already to know.

"Why are you here?" he said to her, his tone cold.

She crossed her legs and rested her wrist on her thigh, her attention on a game on her flexi-phone. "You told me to check with you before the end of my shift." She glanced up at him, her green eyes sparkling from the light of a monitor. Was she flirting with him? Did she want him?

No. He remembered now. He *had* told her to check with him. It was directly after Liberty escaped the Breeder Facility and Varden told him off outside. Supero had returned to his office, but he could not locate Ivy. She was on break, she had said. With his agitated frame of mind, he had not found that excuse acceptable. So he took his frustration out on her, yelling that she must be available to him at all times. Then he told her he was going to CSS and she was to check in with him before her shift ended.

"Very well," Supero said, keeping his voice and expression soft. "Do not leave just yet."

He went to the chief and stood over him until gaining his attention. "Now what do you intend to do? Should it be so easy for one girl to escape both the CSS and Unity Troopers? I am no longer surprised at the number of citizens you have simply lost."

Varden muttered a foul name under his breath and grinded his teeth. "Listen, Supero, she must've had help. There's a network, I'm convinced, of people who help others escape." Images popped up on the monitors above the station. The time display in the corners showed them to be feeds from the general time she escaped. "Right now we need to review other surveillance feeds. See what else was going on when she escaped. See what's going on now. There's got to be something. I'm going to find it." He donned in-ear headphones and began mumbling to someone while he manipulated images on the monitors.

Supero's gaze drifted to a monitor at another station. Every monitor had video images, most live feeds, some older. Despite the curfew, apparently, Aldonia never slept. One monitor held his attention. Unity Troopers moved in on what looked like one of the Warehouse zones. Jiggling images showed on two smaller monitors next to the one, probably transmissions from cameras on active Unity Troopers. "What is that? What is the disturbance there?" He pointed.

Chief Varden glanced. "That? Oh. There was a disturbance at the Fourth Zone Warehouses, probably a fray between users and dealers." He did a doubletake then squinted at the image. "Wait a minute . . ." He picked up the landline phone and shouted, "Hey, your brilliant Troopers are at the First Zone. The disturbance is at the Fourth Zone. Are you all high over there?" He slammed the phone down and muttered to himself as he returned his attention to the monitors above his own station.

Supero huffed and turned away. *Pathetic.* The incompetence of the Unity Troopers and the Citizen Safety Station disgusted him. Neither arm of the Regimen could boast superiority.

"Can I go now?"

A cool thrill went down Supero's spine at the sound of Ivy's voice coming from directly behind him. He turned, looked her over, and smiled. "You may go if you wish. Or you may stay. I will remain a bit longer, hoping they make some progress. You can stay with me." He held her gaze, taking in the shimmering gold makeup on her smooth eyelids, the thick black of her lashes, the widening of her pupils. She liked him. He could tell.

She inhaled, held it, exhaled. "I . . . have things to do." She turned to go and spoke without glancing back. "See you tomorrow at the office."

Supero watched her go. She liked him. He could tell.

~~~

"So who's going first?" I knew Jessen wouldn't want to, so I looked at Bot.

Bot took a step back and made a sweeping gesture toward the booth. "After you."

I slapped the flashlight into his hand and jumped into the booth. Maybe I should've tried to talk Jessen into going first, in case she wanted to back out, but I feared trouble might greet me above. Better me than a pregnant woman.

Bot slid the door shut as I buckled up. The backpack prevented me from leaning against the seatback and feeling secure, but I scooted as far back as possible.

Jessen gazed at me through wide eyes. Bot's mouth hung open. He nodded.

I shoved the lever into position and reached for the bars on the sides of the seat. My fingers brushed the cold metal bars. The seat lifted. I wrapped my fingers around the bars. Feet tingling, stomach sliding, I shot up through the darkness.

A few long seconds later, the ride slowed and jerked to a stop. Silence and darkness surrounded me. I peeled my fingers from the cold bars and felt around for the buckle. Where was the door?

I flung the buckle off and reached out into the blackness. The compartment had cold metal walls, all of them within my reach. Not knowing what lay beneath the footrest of the seat, I dared not stand.

Dedrick had said to be patient and that he would open the door.

My heart raced. I took a few deep breaths. I wanted to call out Dedrick's name. What had kept him from signaling us in the first place? What kept him now?

He hadn't seemed overly concerned when he had gotten into the transporter. He even had a look of humor in his brown eyes. *Relax. Any minute now—*

Something scraped the metal wall in front of me. A bang. Then another, much louder. Finally, I heard a voice.

"Dedrick?" I dared speak.
~~~

"The door's damaged. I can't . . ." Muffled words replaced understandable speech. "Try to kick it."

"Kick it?"

"Yeah, kick it. Hurry!"

I grabbed onto the sidebars and drew my legs up. With all the strength I could muster, I thrust my feet against the metal wall in front of me.

Dim light streamed in through a long crack on one edge of the door.

"Again," Dedrick said.

I slammed my feet against the metal again.

The door came loose, unhinged. Dedrick lifted and flung it to the side. The dark gray of night showed behind his shadowy figure. A wide garage door loomed a few meters behind him. Muted orange light showed in the distance to my left. Where were we?

He reached out to me. "Quick. We have to get the others."

I latched onto his hand and he yanked me to my feet. As I jumped from the compartment, he reached back inside and groped an inner wall. "Chair's not lowering." He banged his fist against something on the inside of the wall then rubbed his chin.

"Maybe it only operates when the door is closed," I said.

He glanced at the mangled door that lay on the ground near us. "Yeah."

"What happened to the door? Why couldn't you open it?" I leaned in to examine the notch for the latch in the doorjamb.

"A nasty Unity Trooper with metal legs happened to the door. He was in the wrong place at the wrong time."

"What?"

Dedrick shook his head then glanced over his shoulder as if he heard something.

"Maybe we can fudge it." The lack of light made the assembly in the doorjamb impossible to see. I stuck my finger in it and felt the end of a thin shaft. "When the door is closed it must push against this shaft. You have any tools?"

Dedrick had shuffled off a few meters away and stood peering around a corner. "Tools?"

"Something metal, something the size of the latch." I pointed to the door.

Dedrick fidgeted with his belt as he trotted back to me. He handed me a metal object the size of my thumb.

"What is it?"

"See if it'll do the trick." He reached as if to snatch it back.

I shoved the thing into the notch.

He leaned past me and pounded something on the inside of the wall. Nothing happened. He looked at me.

"Oh, I know. It's a safety, right? So the door has to be closed."

"Yeah." Dedrick jerked his hand toward the notch. "Aren't we simulating that?"

"Right, so where else does the door make contact?" I pointed to a hinge on the opposite side of the doorframe. "Put something metal against that too."

Dedrick yanked something else off his belt and slapped it against the middle hinge on the doorframe. He whacked something on the inside of the wall again. The chair made a hissing sound, dropped down, and whooshed away into the darkness.

The rush of air blew our hair.

Dedrick grinned. "Worked. You're pretty handy to have around." He brought the two-way radio to his mouth and said, "Go!"

Within a minute, the chair shot back up, bringing a wide-eyed Bot with it. The chair came to a stop but Bot didn't move, not even to release his grip on the sidebars.

"Get the buckle." Dedrick spoke with command. The instant Bot released the buckle Dedrick grabbed him by the arms and yanked him from the dark compartment.

Bot adjusted his backpack and looked around. "Where are we? And what took you so long? You know we—"

The siren of a Unity Trooper vehicle blared.

I jumped in my skin. It sounded near, but I saw no flashing lights.

"That way." Dedrick snatched the metal object from me and pointed in the direction opposite the sirens. "The sixth warehouse down has an open side door. Wait in there until we come."

"Don't count on Jessen coming." Bot stepped backwards as he spoke. "You should run with us." He turned and bolted.

Dedrick shook his head. "Go with Bot," he said to me.

"But don't you need me to help with—"

Flashing orange and blue lights reflected on warehouses a kilometer away.

Eyes bulging, Dedrick shoved me. "Run!"

I dashed after Bot, gravel slipping and crunching under my feet. First warehouse. Second warehouse. A burst of adrenaline gave me speed. Third, fourth, fifth . . .

Sirens blared behind me. A car screeched. Voices.

I skidded between the fifth and sixth warehouses. The door on the side of the sixth warehouse hung open a crack. I pushed against it and slipped inside, stepping into darkness.

Bot slammed the door shut and leaned against it.

I propped myself up with the wall just inside the door, the two of us gasping to catch our breath.

"Now what?" Bot said, still gasping for air. "Dedrick never really gave us . . . much of a plan. Has he never . . . done this before? What if he . . . gets caught? Are we on our own?"

"I wonder if Jessen came up. You knew she was getting scared. Why didn't you make her go first?"

He chuckled. "Why didn't you? She told me to go next, so I went."

"What if she needs encouragement—?"

A deep boom sounded. The walls shook. The sound of debris falling in the distance followed. More sirens.

"What was that?" Bot said.

"Sounded like an explosion."

"We gotta get out of here." Bot shuffled in the darkness.

I flung myself against the door. "Don't be a fool. We'll wait. Let's give them a chance. We've got no chance without Dedrick."

"Sure we do. We run for the Boundary Fence. Dedrick must know of an opening. We'll look for it."

I huffed. "I say we wait."

"We don't even know where we are. Let's find a light switch."

I reached to grab his arm but he had moved. "No. Light might show under the door."

More shuffling. The sound of a zipper. "Okay, how about a flashlight."

"Didn't you leave the flashlight with Jessen?"

Light from a flashlight pierced the darkness, shining on dull metal walls and beams and—-

A figure loomed nearby.

I gasped.

"Almighty Earth!" Bot shined the beam on a metallic figure. "That's armor. It's what the Unity Troopers wear." He stepped closer to the form.

Armor hung on a gray plastic model of a body. Dark stacked scales went from the neck to the groin, a few of them dented and twisted. A metallic exoskeleton with heavy boots took the place of the legs.

"Have you ever seen one up close?" He stopped in front of it and touched the scales. It towered over him.

"I saw one the day they came for you."

"Really?" Bot flashed the light on my face. "One of these was after me? Good thing I didn't know." He turned the beam away, sweeping it over the rest of the warehouse. A long table cluttered with tools and scraps of metal stood in the middle of the area. Crates and cabinets lined the walls.

"It's a workshop." I wanted to explore but this wasn't the time.

A soft rap sounded on the door. Bot redirected the beam just as it opened. Jessen came in with Dedrick following behind. Both of them had a dusting of dirt on their hair and clothes.

My spirit lifted. I pulled Jessen farther into the room and hugged her. "You made it. You're okay."

Jessen nodded.

Dedrick pushed between us, grabbing both of us by the arm. "Listen. We've got to move. I'll lead you to a hiding places in the field near the Boundary Fence. Keep your radios on low. I'll signal you one at a time and—"

"You threw my radio," Jessen said.

Dedrick's mouth hung open for a moment. "Yeah, okay. You stay with Liberty. When I signal, you go first." He said to me, "You keep the radio. The second signal is for you." His gaze went to Bot. "You're third. Run when I signal you, but don't dive under the fence until I say. Electricity surges through it at fifteen-second intervals."

"What?" Bot turned his flashlight on Dedrick's face. "Fifteen seconds! How do we know when—?"

Dedrick shoved the flashlight down. "*I* know. I'll track the seconds on my watch. Trust me. Now, shut the flashlight off and let's go." He cracked open the door, stuck his head out, and glanced to each side. Sirens sounded in the distance. Dedrick flung the door wide and motioned for us to go. Once we all got out, he took the lead.

We jogged under a dark gray sky, passed ten or so warehouses, and came to the chain-length fence that surrounded them. Without breaking his stride, Dedrick pushed the tip of his boot into the fence and hopped over. Due to my sore toe, I had to use my left foot. Less gracefully and with much rattling of the fence, we followed him.

A lumpy, unkempt field grew on the other side of the fence. The crescent moon above gave little light to guide our steps, little help for discerning whether the black spots on our path were holes or stumps or just clumps of grass. I ran a bit ahead of Jessen, hoping to notice any obstacles before she came to them. What would a tumble do to the baby inside her?

A thick trunked tree stood a stone's throw away, its branches high and leafy. We headed toward it. The few times I glanced up from the ground, I peered into the dark but couldn't see the fence of the boundaries. It couldn't be far.

Dedrick had gotten a few meters ahead, but now he stopped and waited. "Wait by the tree. Stay under its leaves. Listen for my signal." He motioned for Bot to follow and dashed up and over a low incline. They disappeared into the night.

Jessen leaned her back against the tree and stooped over, breathing hard. She laughed and straightened up. "I can't believe I'm doing this."

"Yeah, me neither." I peeked around the tree trunk, back the way we had come. The sirens had ceased. Had they given up? "I was worried you'd change your mind and not come up."

"Dedrick persuaded me."

"How'd he do that?"

She laughed again. "When I heard him say 'Go,' I just stood there, frozen and thinking when I *go,* I'll go back to that nice little underground community and not up into danger. Then he shouted, 'Get up here, now. Do it for your baby. Now!' So I did. And when I got to the top, Dedrick ripped me from the seat. Sirens blared all around us. Lights flashed everywhere. He told me to run. I don't know how they didn't catch us."

"Did you hear the explosion?"

"Yeah, that was Dedrick. Once we got around a corner, he whipped something into the air, back the way we came. He told me to cover my ears. But it didn't prepare me for that. So loud. It shook the ground. And all the dirt and pebbles raining down . . ."

"He threw it at Unity Troopers?"

"No, no. He said he had to destroy the chute. He couldn't let them find it. He said pharmaceuticals were stored in the warehouse attached to the underground entrance. Unity Troopers would think someone was after them."

"By blowing them up?"

She laughed. "No, that warehouse is tough to break into. You'd have to blow up the door."

"Oh. What about your radio? You said Dedrick threw it. Why'd he do that?"

"He whispered a message to his team then threw it over the fence. I heard voices on it as we left. Maybe the Unity Troopers would find it and think—"

"Go." The voice came through the radio.

Jessen's eyes bugged. She pushed off the tree and adjusted her pack.

I tugged her arm. "You'd better run." I pointed in the direction Dedrick had gone in. "I'll see you on the other side." I smiled to reassure her. "Go!"

Jessen ran and disappeared into the darkness.

I waited, listening, my heart thumping. It would be my turn soon. Jessen would have to get through the Boundary Fence within fifteen seconds. How big was the opening? She could do it. She seemed to have gotten her courage—

"Go!"

My heart skipped a beat. I took a breath and bolted. My feet pounded faster than my heart. I reached the incline where I last saw Dedrick, bolted up it, and had to throw my arms out to catch my balance. I stood on the edge of a steep slope, unable to see the bottom of it. Jessen had gone this way. I hadn't heard her scream or groan, so she probably hadn't fallen.

I took a step, slid a little and stepped again, reaching flat ground about four meters down.

"Over here," Dedrick whispered from somewhere off to my left, his voice revealing that the slope wasn't as steep as I had thought.

I jumped the rest of the way down and stumbled toward his voice. "Where?"

"Here." He crouched near a scraggily bush at the foot of the slope.

The Boundary Fence loomed a few meters away. Thick metal bars went from the ground to about two stories high. Sharp pieces of metal ran along the high top, angling toward Aldonia, claws warning of danger from the world beyond.

I squatted by Dedrick. Half-meter-long bars as thick as my arm lay under the bush.

"Listen. I made an opening." Dedrick pointed. "You'll have to crawl through and run for the woods. Avoid—"

A rustling sound and a grunt came from the top of the slope a few meters away.

Dedrick yanked something from his belt—a gun of some sort? He dove between the intruder and me, got to one knee, and leveled the gun.

The intruder slid down the slope, its shadowy arms flailing. It sprinted toward us and skidded to a stop. "What the—Son of the Earth, man, it's me." Bot raised his hands.

"I didn't call you." Dedrick spit the words out as he shoved the weapon into his belt.

"I'm not waiting. I kept hearing noises in the grass."

"It's the wind." Dedrick squatted, yanking Bot down with him. "Or an animal." He shoved Bot toward the scant cover of the bush. "Unity Troopers don't worry me now." He checked his watch. "It's the drones. Only one of us can hide here. You two need to get through and get to cover. We haven't much time."

Bot made a move in the direction of the fence, but Dedrick latched onto his arm and yanked him back.

"The electricity will kill you."

Bot's mouth fell open. "Right." He gulped and took a deep breath. "So tell me when to go."

Dedrick looked at me. "She's going first."

"No, he can go." I didn't trust Bot. I didn't want him behind me. "I'll go next."

"You'll have to lie flat and crawl through. Then dash for the woods. Find good cover and stay there. Oh, and try not to touch the bars as you crawl through, just in case. You have fifteen seconds from my mark." Dedrick stared at his watch.

Bot huffed. "Nice. So I might end up fried after all."

"Go!"

Bot dashed for the fence and dropped down as if he were about to do a push up. He hesitated.

Dedrick shook his head and whispered in a voice Bot couldn't have heard, "Go, Bot. What are you waiting for?" He turned to me. "You'll have to go right away. The drone is nearly upon us. Count your seconds down. No matter where you are, drop to the ground and freeze when you get to three."

I nodded. I was ready.

"I mean, if he gets moving so you can get through the next interval, you have twenty-five seconds from when I say *Go,* and there's a bit of ground to cover, and you can't let the drone spot motion. It'll zoom in on you and send a live feed to the Citizen Safety Station."

Bot crawled like a man fighting paralysis, moving a bit and pausing. Head, shoulders, chest . . . He picked up speed. Waist, thighs, knees . . . Once he made it through the opening he paused and looked back. Maybe he wasn't sure if his feet had cleared the metal.

Seconds later, Dedrick said, "Liberty, it's time. Twenty-five seconds. Drop at three."

My first impulse was to clarify that he meant I had to run *now*. He didn't say *Go*. But I ignored the impulse and dashed at once. Twenty-four, twenty-three, twenty-two . . .

I dropped down by the fence as Bot had done. The opening was smaller than I figured when I had seen the bars he removed. Cheek and gut to the ground, I used my forearms to walk myself through. Nineteen, eighteen, seventeen . . .

With my gaze locked on a tree at the edge of the woods, I sprung up and bolted. Fourteen, thirteen, twelve . . .

Would I make it to the woods? Would I hear the drone? Would I see it? Would it see me? *Run faster*. Ten, nine, eight . . .

Legs straining. Breathing through my mouth. Wind watering my eyes. Halfway there. Five, four . . . Not going to make it to the cover of the trees.

With a burst of all my strength, I lunged. My hands and knees pounded to the ground. I dropped onto my belly and froze. My lungs screamed for air. The pounding of my heart rattled my body. I heard nothing. How long would it take the drone to pass by?

I lay there motionless on the cold ground, waiting. Minutes passed. But how many? It felt like an eternity.

"To your feet." Dedrick tapped my leg with his boot and jogged into the woods.

I pushed myself up, sprung to my feet, and dashed after him into the black woods.

"Over here," someone whispered.

I moved toward the voice, deeper into the woods. The woods. I couldn't see a thing, but the cool air and the smell of dirt, leaves, and evergreens refreshed me. The knowledge that I stood in nature, among trees and free-roaming little animals—outside Aldonia—elated my spirit.

"I thought you were the second one." Jessen came up behind me, her footfalls making no sound.

"Yeah, well . . ."

"You and Dedrick took a long time. We been waiting for you." Bot's voice broke as if he stumbled on something while speaking. "What went wrong?" He came up to Jessen and me. "Seems to me the Mosheh needs some better Intel. The Unity Troopers were right on us. A few more seconds and—"

"Bot, we're safe." Dedrick stood between trees, a black silhouette against the dark gray of Aldonia. "I had to repair the fence, cover our tracks. At fifteen-second intervals, it takes time."

"Do you think the drones spotted me?" I said.

"What!" Bot sounded angry. "Drones too?"

"No, you did good. You were under the cover of the tree branches. Movement might have drawn them to you, but you were still."

"A drone flew by." Bot whispered harshly. "And what about cameras? There're cameras all over the Boundary Fence. Cameras are everywhere. What are the chances they didn't catch our escape on camera? I know the CSS watches everything. They—"

Dedrick darted in front of me, coming between Bot and me. "Chill man." It sounded like he shoved Bot. "Those cameras are down for now. That's why we came through here." He paused. "I need you to trust me."

A long silence passed then Bot said, "Okay."

I exhaled. "Now what?"

"Now we walk in the dark." Dedrick moved past us. His watch or something on his wrist glowed blue and swung with his stride.

"I hope you know where we're going," Bot muttered.

"Trust me," Dedrick said, still walking away. "Stick together. Anyone needs to stop, say so. We've got miles to go before we sleep."

13

My legs complained. My feet ached. I stumbled every few steps but I couldn't stop for rest. I had to go on. I dragged myself through a dank and narrow tunnel, on and on, occasionally passing an opening on my left or my right. I needed to go straight. Or did I? How long had I been down here? When would I see light? Perhaps I should've—

"Jessen. Liberty." The deep, rumbling voice traveled to my ears. Was it Dedrick? "It's morning. Wake up. We've got a lot of ground to cover."

Morning? My dream dissipated and my eyes popped open. I tried to throw back the covers. No, not covers. *A sleeping bag.* I had zipped it to my chin last night, or early morning, or whatever time Dedrick had finally decided to let us stop for the night. We had trudged along in utter darkness for close to a kilometer, the rest of the way by the light of one flashlight.

I unzipped the sleeping bag and sat up. The wall of the tent glowed rusty orange. The sun was up!

Last night, the walk through the woods in darkness had stimulated my senses. Leaves and clouds prevented moonlight from disclosing physical features, allowing us to make out only vague shapes of trees and plants, forcing other senses to work harder. I had never experienced crunching over a rough terrain of roots, twigs, leaves, and pine needles. We walked without speaking, stopping only when Jessen asked for breaks. New sounds had overwhelmed me—the chirping, whirring, and buzzing of the insects, the hoot of an owl somewhere overhead, and the howl of a distant wolf. The cool and woodsy-scented air refreshed me, giving me energy at first. Hours into our journey, the unceasing drone of the insects and the chill air had me staggering along in a stupor. My eyes grew heavy. For a time, I had fixed my gaze on insects fluttering in the beam of the single flashlight.

But now, daylight had come! The secrets of the off-limits Fully-Protected Nature Preserves would make themselves known.

"Come on, Jessen." I shoved her shoulder. "Let's check things out."

Jessen moaned.

I crawled out of the sleeping bag and unzipped the tent door.

The scent of a campfire hit my nose. Birds chirped overhead. A stream gurgled nearby. Dedrick and Bot sat on a log by a small fire, eating something by hand.

I stepped from the tent and into a picture Aldonians could only see from computer databases. Tall trees with high branches and smooth gray trunks surrounded our campsite. Dew glistened on knee-high, spiky green plants and clusters of yellow grass that grew between trees.

"Good morning." Dedrick smiled. His hair was wet, the blue streaks gone. "Hungry?" He reached into his backpack and tossed something to me.

I caught it: a sandwich wrapped in a big leaf. "Thanks."

"It's pretty good." Bot spoke with his mouth full. "I think that gardener woman made it."

"That gardener woman has a name." Dedrick glared at Bot. Then he jerked his face toward me. "Oh, maybe you'll want this first." He stuck his hand into the backpack, drew out a toilet paper roll, and tossed it.

I caught it. "Yeah, as a matter of fact . . ." Dedrick had given us each a flask of water last night. I drank it all and only went once.

Leaving the sandwich behind, I ventured off into the trees, toward the sound of trickling water. Several meters back, concealed by tree trunks and plants, I did my business and hung the toilet paper roll on a branch. I still couldn't see the stream, but I wanted to. I also wanted to check on my aching toe.

A dozen or so meters later, the trees opened up and I saw it. Here, the stream was narrow enough to jump over and no more than a meter at its deeper points. Clear water rippled over smooth stones and boulders, turning white and bubbly. The song of the stream and the thought of cool water lured me.

I sat down on a wide rock at the water's edge and unlaced my boot. I inhaled deeply, savoring the green scent of the woods. When I had stood on the balcony of my room at the Breeder Facility, I'd considered myself lucky to have the view and to smell the woods. But now . . .

Was this real? My heart leaped and warmth enveloped me.

Mechanically, I removed the boot and stripped off the sock. Blood-red toilet paper clung to my toe. I peeled it off, glanced at the chafed toe, and lowered my foot into the stream. The cool water both stung and refreshed my toe.

The warmth in my soul increased until I realized *My Friend* wished to speak with me. My eyes closed. The sounds of nature—birds chirping, water gurgling, a breeze rustling leaves—grew more distinct as if I analyzed each separately. Cool, soothing water rolled around my foot and between my toes. A breeze played on my cheeks and in my hair. As my senses heightened, I became intensely aware of the presence of *My Friend* in my soul. He spoke, rolling like the water, stimulating as the breeze, but I couldn't grasp the message. It had to do with the trees and plants, with the animals and waters, with the rocks and air. It had something to do with Him. It had something to do with me.

"Liberty?"

I gasped and snapped my eyes open.

"Are you okay?" Dedrick came up behind me. His hair, dry now, shone yellow under a beam of sunlight. "You were gone for so long, I started to worry." His gaze dropped. "Oh, hey . . ." He crouched by me, his attention on my foot in the water. "That looks bad. Why didn't you say something?"

I drew my foot out of the water and grabbed the sock. How long had I been gone that he had come looking for me? "It's not a big deal. I'll be fine."

"Looks like you need wider boots. You should've said something. We could've—"

"Really, I'm fine." I dried my foot with the sock, but the sock stuck on my pruned toes when I tried to put it on.

"At least let me give you a bandage and some antibiotic." He straightened up. "Leave the sock off. I'll help you walk back."

"Well, I . . ."

"Come on." He gave a little smile and offered his hand. "Let me help."

"All right." I took his hand and he tugged me up. "On the way back, maybe you can answer some of my questions."

He grabbed my boot and sock and slid his arm underneath mine, around my back. "Sure. What do you want to know?"

His manly scent and the feel of his body made me uncomfortable. I drew back. "I can walk on my own."

"Okay. I just thought . . ." He shook his head and motioned for me to go first. "So what do you want to know?"

I walked on my bare heel to avoid hurting the toe more. "Well, for starters, what was that metal thing we used last night to throw the safety, to get the seat back down the chute? That little metal thing you handed me . . ."

"You mean this?" Grinning, he pulled a little silver thing from his belt. "Haven't you ever seen a lighter before?" He flipped the lid with his thumb and flicked a flame.

"Well, sure, I guess. Not one like that." Our lighters were all the same: gray plastic.

"My dad gave it to me. It's old, really old." He stuffed it back in his belt. We came to the tree where I hung the roll of toilet paper. He grabbed it and we kept walking.

"Your dad?"

"Yeah. You'll meet him. My parents live in the colony we're going to."

"Your parents?"

He chuckled, dipping his head. "Sometimes I forget that you guys don't know a thing about families. The Regimen has utterly destroyed every concept of family. That's how they took over. It's how they survive." His smile faded as he spoke and now he turned to me, his brown eyes hard and proud. "Our families are strong and wise. We'll never allow a government to weaken them."

I didn't want the conversation to switch topic. "I found a picture, a real picture. An old photograph, I guess. I think it may have been of a family. There was a woman and a man and children, all together. I couldn't understand it. Children live together in the facilities."

He sneered. "Yeah, that's sad and unnatural. Kids need a mom and dad."

"I'd like to know more about families."

"You will."

I knew our conversation had ended when I heard Bot's voice and smelled the campfire. We reached camp, too soon for me, and rejoined the others. Jessen sat on the log with Bot, laughing about something, half a sandwich in her hands. They both looked as we stepped into the campsite.

Jessen jumped up. "Where you been, Liberty? You left me hanging." She handed her sandwich to Bot and skipped to Dedrick. "I need that." She snatched the toilet paper, gave an elfish grin, and dashed into the trees.

"Have a seat." Dedrick motioned toward the log as he went to his backpack. He returned carrying a white plastic box and squatted at my feet.

"What happened to you?" Bot leaned in, grimacing at my toe.

"Nothing."

"You guys need to ask for help when you need it." Dedrick glanced from me to Bot. He dabbed my toe with something cold and wet and then taped a thick gauze pad around it. "This should prevent more chafing." He handed me my sock. "If it hurts when you walk, let me know. We'll take it slower."

A look of utter sincerity flashed across his face. Then he popped up, shoved the white box in his backpack, and stooped by one of the tents. "We need to pack up and go." He stuck his head into the tent.

I put the sock on and grabbed the boot. The gauze buffered my sore toe but made the fit tighter. I laced up.

"I thought we were safe out here." Bot stood up and stretched. "What's the rush?"

"We are safe. I'm just a little anxious to get home, see my friends, rest between rescues."

I crawled into the other tent, zipped up the sleeping bags, and started rolling one of them.

"The Unity Troopers were on to us last night, weren't they?" Bot said. "You think they're still looking for us? Think they suspect anyone lives out here?"

"Huh? No, they weren't looking for us," Dedrick said from inside the other tent. "They were looking for someone else. They were sent to Warehouses on the east side, not the ones we were at. There was a break-in over there. Guess they got confused."

"The Unity Troopers?" Bot laughed. "No. You really think they'd mess up like that?"

"Catch," Dedrick said. Two soft thumps followed. Then a zipper and the swish of tent fabric. "Unity Troopers mess up all the time. Half of them don't care about their job. Just like the Citizen Safety workers. It's easy to throw them off. We have them believing their missing citizens have a hideout in another city."

I pushed the sleeping bags through the door of the tent and crawled out. The other tent and sleeping bags were gone. Someone had extinguished the fire and covered the area with dirt. Dedrick stood over a hole in the ground. He motioned for me to toss the bags to him.

"How do you know what they think?" Bot stood with folded arms, head cocked to one side.

Dedrick grinned. "We plant seeds and then eavesdrop on their conversations." He dropped the sleeping bags into the hole in the ground. "If they start to suspect the truth, we drop more clues to lead them away. It's like a game to some of the Mosheh."

I edged closer to the hole. Why was he putting everything in the ground?

Dedrick glanced at me. "It's a steel-lined box for storing things, camping gear or whatever." He slid a section of weedy turf over the box. It scraped, metal against metal, as he covered the hole. Straightening up, he brushed his hands together. "What d'ya think? Can't even tell it's there, huh? We've got supplies stored all over the place."

"Catch!" Jessen bounced into the campsite, the toilet paper roll leaving her fingertips and sailing through the air.

"It's about time." Dedrick caught the roll. "I don't know what takes you girls so long." He secured his backpack and worked the straps over his shoulders.

"What takes *us* so long?" Jessen stomped to her backpack. "We're always waiting on you guys. Yap, yap, yap. All you do is talk."

I shrugged on my backpack.

Bot shook his head. "Hey, I can walk and talk. It doesn't slow me down."

Dedrick turned in a circle, scanning the site. When he was satisfied, he checked his watch and strode into the woods. "Well, then talk your way down this trail. Let's go."

"Ha, ha." Bot readjusted the straps of his pack and stomped off after Dedrick. He began talking, mumbling to Dedrick, at once.

Jessen and I followed, walking side by side.

"They do talk a lot." Jessen spoke loud enough for them to hear. "Have you ever heard guys talk so much?"

I laughed. Sure, Bot had proven he could blabber on incessantly, but not Dedrick. He answered questions and gave directions. At times, his smirking expressions gave the impression he could say more but that he chose not to. What went on in his head? Did he like rescuing people? Who waited for him at home?

"And what language was Dedrick using yesterday, you remember, when he greeted that guard? Didn't sound like Universal to me. Sounded like one of those ancient languages they tell you about in Secondary. Did you hear him?"

"Yeah, I heard him." I spoke loud, too. Maybe Dedrick would explain himself. "I wondered what he said."

"You don't want to know." Dedrick didn't turn around to answer. "If you remember the words, I suggest you forget them. Not everyone would laugh at the expression."

"What expression?" Bot said.

"Eat my shorts." Dedrick spoke in a low voice, maybe only for Bot to hear.

"What?" Bot sounded insulted.

Dedrick laughed.

~~~

Dr. Supero studied the report Ivy just sent him, the report he should've written himself. He didn't have the time or concentration to do it this month. He had referred Ivy to the previous month's report for an example. She obviously reviewed it thoroughly. Her work was impeccable, her attention to detail amazing. He could not have done a better job himself. *Good. Good.* One less thing for him to worry about. He should thank her, let her know how he appreciated her.

He tapped the icon on his glossy desktop to summon her.

The door to his office slid open.

Supero's breath caught in his throat. He spun his chair to face the door.

Ivy sauntered into the room, her shimmery white dress swishing with every step, one hand clutching her pocket computer, the other swinging by her hip.

"My, but you are fast," Supero said.

A faint smile appeared on her face then faded. "I was on my way to see you."

"What timing. I think we are on the same wavelength." He stood up and stepped toward her.

She blinked as if she did not understand the idiom. "I came to tell you about a message."

"I want to compliment your work. The report you put together is—Message?" He froze. Was this the day? Had the Medical Care Evaluation Panel come to a decision? He had no reason to panic. Of course they would approve the operation. "Do you mean a personal message?"

She pushed her hair off her shoulder and nodded. "I sent it to you, but it was marked *urgent* so I thought—"

"Yes, very good." Supero stepped back, wanting to run to his desk but forcing himself to appear calm. "That will be all."

She turned, sauntered a few steps, stopped at the door, and faced him again. "I've switched as many of your patients as possible to other physicians, but you still have four appointments today."

"Four appointments," Supero said mindlessly. He took another step back and bumped his chair. *Why did she not leave already?*
~~~

"You are the only one who can see these particular patients. I scheduled them early, so you could get them out of the way. I assume you'll want to get to the Citizen—"

"Yes, yes, you are correct. That will be all."

She finally left the room and the door slid shut.

Supero dropped into his chair and smacked the message icon on the desktop. A single message remained unread, locked. Sender: The Regimen MCEP. Holding his breath, he entered his password and opened the message.

The Medical Care Evaluation Panel has reviewed the Recommendation for Care submitted for Dr. Supero. We have taken into consideration the risks and possible complications of the suggested procedures, the statistics related to the outcome of the surgery, and the contribution to society that this citizen provides. The panel has not reached the necessary agreement to approve or deny the recommendation. We request additional testing of the subject in order to provide the panel with a more complete picture of current abilities and health. Thank you, in advance, for your timely cooperation.

Supero took a breath and held it. *Control. Control. Do not lose control!*

He jumped to his feet and pounded the desktop. The overhead lights flashed. Music came on and went off, repeatedly and with increasing volume. Random images of files and patients appeared in rapid succession on the sleek, trembling monitor connected to the desktop.

Turning from his desk, trying to regain control, stifling a groan, he bumped his chair. His hands latched onto it independent of his will. He flung it. The chair landed four meters away and rolled, smacking into a wall.

The door on the other side of the room slid open.

Fists clenched, trembling, Dr. Supero took a breath and glared over his shoulder.

Ivy sauntered into a room that was now dimly lit and blaring with classical music. A semi-nude holographic image of a patient rotated above the desk. An audio of a patient file played. "You called me?" Her voice was calm, her expression placid, and her gaze did not travel from him to the wreckage that surrounded him.

"No." He sneered. "But you can cancel all my appointments. I will be at the Citizen Safety Station." They would find that girl, Liberty, if he had to do it himself. He would insist that Varden conduct a full investigation into the security personnel, the procedures of the CSS, the computer search programs, and every piece of equipment. Chief Varden assumed she had help. They will find that help.

Ivy stared for a moment. Then she nodded and left the room.

Dr. Supero thrust his hands into his hair and groaned. His previous assistant, Sage, would have drawn near. With compassion contorting her face, she would've asked him what was wrong. If she were here now, he would have her in his arms already. They would find a private room in the facility by shift's end. He would probably be too distracted to help search for Liberty. Perhaps it was a good thing that Ivy was not like Sage.

He went to a safe in the wall and removed Liberty's notebook. He should read the entire thing. He may find clues. Tucking it under his arm, he strolled from his office.

Ivy turned her glittering, green eyes to him as he passed. She was not as easy as Sage, but she would come around. She needed time. They needed to understand each other.

He opened the notebook as he walked down a long empty corridor, and he read as his footfalls echoed off the walls.

Every day, the walls close in a little more. I want to scream. And run. But there is nowhere to run. Walls are everywhere . . . They claim to have the answers to all life's questions. No one can think for himself, take his own risks, decide his future. Whether I succeed or fail, I want the freedom to choose.

He slammed the notebook shut. *The Medical Care Evaluation Panel. Who do they think they are? They cannot reach a decision, cannot decide whether I should have the surgery or not. Whether I should live or die. Who do they think they are? I decide my fate. I live. I will have the surgery and I will return to my normal life, my life that benefits society immensely. Who can deny my importance in the medical field? Who do they think they are, deciding my fate?*

~~~

Amber sunbeams streamed in angles into the woods. Leaves of trees and plants glowed gold. I thanked the Regimen for having preserved this wilderness in all its natural beauty so that I could experience it now, but I
~~~

resented that they had kept it from us as if we had no right to enjoy it. *My Friend* stirred my heart more and more each day, weaving in and out of my joy. As anxious as I was to reach the colony, I didn't want this excursion to end.

Purple mountains loomed ahead, though we could not always see them through the dense trees. My heart fluttered whenever I happened to catch a glimpse of them. Until two days ago, when we had climbed a bare hill to look out, I hadn't even realized Aldonia was close to mountains. Every day we drew nearer, our goal to reach the other side. I couldn't imagine anything less than a long, treacherous trail with lots of climbing and sliding. How would Jessen fare? Dedrick must've known a path through or around them.

Jessen walked beside me with one hand on her belly and a distant look in her eyes. She took a deep breath and exhaled through her mouth.

"Everything okay?" I said.

Her smile came quickly. I liked that about her, but if she really had a problem, it might be hard to detect. "I'm fine. Just tired of walking and walking and walking." She stuck her thumbs in the straps of her backpack and shifted her load. She chewed on something, probably one of those tablets Dedrick insisted she eat every four hours. They were for the baby, he had said.

"It's awesome to be free though, isn't it? To be out here in the forbidden wilderness?"

"Yeah." She smiled at the treetops and took another deep breath, exhaling this one slowly.

"Does that hurt?" I glanced at her belly.

She laughed. "Hurt? No."

I felt stupid, like a naive child, and wished I hadn't brought it up. "I don't know what it's like to be pregnant. They were going to teach me the stages of pregnancy, you know, as a breeder."

"Oh, that's right. So you would've known all about it, experienced it for yourself, if you hadn't been rescued."

"I don't want to know firsthand. I'm not ready for that. It seems so, so . . . invasive."

"Invasive? Yeah, the way they do it is quite invasive. But it's not this way. It's amazing. I can't explain the way I feel." She smiled, gazing at treetops as she spoke. "I'm carrying a little person, someone who is not me. I'm responsible for her, and I feel this strong protectiveness. It's just amazing."

"Her? It's a girl? You know that? They don't let the breeders know, not even after birth. You never know which one you carried."

"I found out when I was seven weeks along. I told my boyfriend. He got me pregnant, and I foolishly thought he'd be excited too, or that he'd at least want to know."

"He didn't?"

"No." She pressed her lips together and dropped her head. Curls covered her eyes. "He couldn't believe I was pregnant. He said it wasn't possible. I told him what I did: the reversal. And he . . . he looked at me as if I was a freak. Then he reported me."

My heart sank. "I'm sorry. I didn't know someone so close to you had . . ."

"Betrayed me?" She shrugged and gave me a sad smile. "Happens to people all the time. The Regimen rewards that, you know, turning people in. I don't care. I guess I can thank him for getting me started on this adventure." She sighed. "I do wish we would reach the colony already."

She put a hand beside her mouth, faced forward, and shouted, "Don't you have a cart or a wagon or something? I'm tired of walking."

Dedrick, several meters ahead, shouted over his shoulder, "Sorry, Jessen. Not yet." He stopped walking, leaving Bot to take the lead, and waited for us to catch up. "This is probably harder on you than on anyone. You'll have a ride soon." He linked arms with Jessen.

She leaned her head on his shoulder. "Really? You'll get me a ride?"

"See those hills?" He stretched out an arm and pointed to an open area between tree trunks, to low hills at the foot of the mountain. "There's a mine entrance. You can't see it. It's hidden. But we'll go through the mountains on a railcar. You'll get a rest."

"Won't we all get a rest?" I said.

"No." He gave me a playful grin. "You, Bot and I will—" He spun his face to the woods on our right. A full second later, he looked back, his expression carefree. "We'll take turns pumping the lever on the handcar."

"The what?"

"You'll see. We should get there just before dark." Dedrick jogged ahead of us, throwing glances to either side as he caught up to Bot.

~~~

The sunlight dwindled. Darkness and the chatter of bugs increased. The air chilled, so we all wore the camouflage capes. Trees stood closer together, their low branches reaching for each other, weaving a thick net. We walked within arm's reach of each other, no one speaking, all eyes on the narrow deer trail under the beam of Dedrick's flashlight. Something rustled the branches of a bush then dashed off as we drew near.

Dedrick stopped and swung the beam of light one way and then the other. "Wait here." He squinted at the woods. "Stay quiet and stay together." He strode forward a few meters and disappeared into the night.

"I'm getting my flashlight out." Bot shrugged his backpack off his shoulders and squatted. "There's no reason we shouldn't each carry . . ." His voice trailed as he dug through the pack. "Ah ha!" Light burst from his flashlight. He whipped the beam around, scanning shadows in the woods. "Do you think he heard a bear or something? Think there're bears in these woods?"

"Probably." Jessen sounded matter-of-fact. She brushed something from her arm. "But Dedrick said to stay quiet. Maybe you should turn off the light. Maybe he doesn't want us to draw attention. I don't think we need to worry. Dedrick didn't seem scared."

"I'm not scared," Bot snapped. "I'm just wondering." He continued to shine the beam at the woods around us, at tangles of tree branches and twisted roots on the ground. "Maybe we're lost. He said we'd reach the mine entrance by nightfall, didn't he? It's black as a dead monitor out here. So where's the mine?"

"We're not lost," Jessen said. "He's got that GPS on his watch."

"Is that what he looks at all the time?" I said. "Here I thought he was obsessed with checking the time." I meant to be funny, to lighten Bot's mood, but Bot only grunted.
~~~

"He's also got a gun. Have you noticed that?" Jessen said.

"I noticed." Bot shined the light on Jessen. "He waved it at me, might have shot me if I hadn't given my name right away."

Jessen laughed.

"Quiet," Bot whispered and jerked the beam of his flashlight to the woods. "There's something in the woods."

"Turn off your flashlight," I whispered. "Jessen's right: it draws attention."

Bot obeyed and we stood for a long moment without words, surrounded by the shades of night.

Minutes passed. I strained to listen, to interpret the noises.

The incessant chatter of insects rose to a mind-numbing level then fell, rising again not long after. A broken call, maybe the shout of a man, rang out in the distance and then drowned in the noise of the night creatures.

"Did you hear that?" I said.

"Hear what?" Jessen stood to my left, closer than I had realized.

"I thought I heard someone shout."

"Do you think Dedrick's in trouble?"

"He's got a gun," Bot said, a cocky edge to his tone. "He can protect himself. Anyone else wonder why he's the only one who gets a weapon? And he's got more than a GPS on his wrist. I've seen him pressing buttons. I think he communicates with people."

"Would that bother you?" I said. "Rescuing people from Aldonia is a team effort. I'm sure he's in constant communication with others."

"Why doesn't he tell us about it? Why don't we ever know the plan? He tells us things just before they happen, gives us no time to think things through. *I'll signal you and you have to go up this chute, or you have to run when I say 'go.' And you've got ten seconds to crawl under that electrically-charged fence or you'll die.*" Bot's tone grew harsher with each word. "Trust me, he says. Maybe we shouldn't trust him."

"Why shouldn't we?" I spit back. "We're out of Aldonia, thanks to him. Would you rather be in Re-Education?"

"Yeah, Bot," Jessen said. "He's just trying to keep us safe."

"Safe? He left us here in the dark without a weapon. What if a wild animal or something tries to attack? We're defenseless."

"I'm sure he knows the area." I squinted into the darkness, willing my eyes to make out shapes. Had I heard a shout? Could he be in trouble? "He's done this before. He's probably just getting something or checking something." My words did nothing to reassure me. Did I trust Dedrick? What ulterior motive could he possibly have in helping us to escape from Aldonia?

"What if he's hurt?" Jessen whispered.

"Let's give him a few more minutes," I whispered. I did trust Dedrick. Honesty and sincerity: I had perceived those virtues in his eyes.

"Then what?" Bot spoke in a loud voice. "What if he doesn't come back?" Light burst from his flashlight. He aimed the beam at the path Dedrick had taken.

"Let's make a little fire and wait for him. I'm tired." Jessen stooped for a branch, took a step, and grabbed a few more. "We can make a lean-to or something. If he doesn't come back, we'll need to get through the night."

"I'm going to find the mine entrance myself," Bot said. "Maybe it's nearby. Something could've happened to Dedrick. Are we just going to stand here and wait for something to happen to us?"

"No!" I grabbed his arm and turned him to face me. "Let's just stay quiet and stay together. No fire. No going off alone. Something might happen to you."

Bot yanked his arm free and shined light in my face. "You're not the boss, Liberty. We're free, right? I'm going to do what I want." He stomped off down the trail Dedrick had taken. The light of his flashlight faded. Then he grunted.

"Hey!" It sounded like Bot.

"Where you going?" I didn't recognize the low voice.

"Where you been?" Definitely Bot.

"We need to go." It was Dedrick! "We have a short trek to the mine entrance. Once we're through the mine, we'll camp for the night. We'll have only a little distance to cover tomorrow."

Grass rustled then Dedrick burst through the trees. He dimmed the beam of his flashlight with his hand, making a red hue shine on him. He had no backpack, no cape, and a rip on the shoulder of his shirt. "Come on, you two. We haven't far." He jogged back the way he came.

Jessen and I sprinted after him. Dedrick picked up speed, the light of his flashlight bouncing on the path. The four of us ran as though pursued. My heart pounded. I pumped my legs and arms, forcing them to seize more and more ground, ignoring the pain each pounding step caused my toe. It would mend later.

An animal howled nearby. A wolf? Didn't they move in packs? Would one gun be enough against a pack?

Another howl came from the opposite direction.

Jessen and I exchanged wild-eyed glances. I wanted to run faster, but I didn't want to pass her. We kept pace, about ten meters behind Bot, and a good twenty behind Dedrick.

Then the light went out.

I reached for Jessen, caught the edge of her cape, and slowed down. We had no choice but to stop running or risk colliding with a tree.

Jessen whispered, "Where'd they go?"

I strained to peer into the dark. "I don't know. A can't see a thing."

"Me neither."

"I'm sure they're just up ahead."

We stumbled along, keeping to the path as best we could. My boot brushed plants whenever I strayed.

"Over here." Something in the woods rustled. Dim light shone on the ground under an overgrown bush a stone's throw from the path. The branches shuddered and then convulsed. Dedrick, stooping, emerged from the bush, a cape in his hands—Bot's cape since he'd lost his own? He spread the cape over branches and wrestled to push them aside.

"What're you doing?" I went up to him.

Jessen stooped and peered under the bush to where the light came from.

"Go on through." He held branches back, using the cape to protect his arms. Then he glanced over his shoulder at Jessen. "Careful of the thorns. This bush is a killer."

Jessen dropped on all fours and crawled.

"How are you going to get through?" I said.

Dedrick peered into the darkness behind me. "Hurry, we're being tracked."

I stooped and crawled through the thorny passage. Branches scraped my cape. Something caught my hair, but I jerked it free without hesitating, ignoring the pain. What did he mean *we're being tracked*? By wolves or men?

The flashlight lay in a pile of shiny dark leaves, a vine of some sort. Its beam, muted by dense vegetation, illuminated a steep, ivy- and moss-ridden hillside a few meters away. A curtain of ivy hung over a low black opening. The doorway to the mine?

I climbed to my feet. The overgrown bush and the steep hillside formed walls around me. Where were Bot and Jessen?

Light flickered in the opening behind the ivy.

The bush rustled. Dedrick emerged, squirming and twisting one way and the other, branches scraping the cape he wore. He lunged for the flashlight and grabbed my wrist. "In there." He pushed me through the low doorway.

Bot and Jessen stood by a platform on wheels. Bot stepped onto it and hung an old-fashioned lantern—the kind I've only seen from computer images—on a post that rose out of a waist-high lever. The lever had a fulcrum in the middle and double handgrips on each end.

Dedrick leaned his shoulders against the thick metal door to the mine and scraped it shut. He turned a key in three separate locks. "Okay, let's go." His voice echoed.

"I got this thing lit." Bot bobbed his head and grinned at Dedrick. He glanced at the lantern he had hung in the middle of the platform. "Burnt my finger. Want your lighter back?" He tossed it.

Dedrick caught it while striding toward Bot. He removed the cape with one hand and tossed it to Bot. Then he stooped and examined or did something to the track that ran under the platform.

"Pretty cool lighter." Bot pulled the cape on over his head. "Never saw one like that before. What's it made of, metal?"

"Jessen." Dedrick popped up. "You have a seat. We'll do the work." He pointed to a low wooden bench that stretched across the back of the platform. "Keep your legs up." He stuffed our backpacks under the bench and hopped onto the backside of the platform where he took a wide-legged stance and grabbed one end of the lever. Light from the flickering flame in the lantern fell on him.

I gasped.

Scrapes covered his arms. Pale skin and blood showed through a long tear in his shirt. And his face—

He looked at me, so I averted my gaze, but the image of his puffy lip, bruised face, and the bleeding gash on his cheek stayed with me. What had happened to him? Who followed us? Wolves or men?

"You two can take turns," Dedrick said. "We'll let Jessen sit this one out."

"Lucky me." Jessen sounded as cheerful as ever. She brought her legs up and hugged her knees. Didn't she see his face? Didn't it bother her?

I climbed onto the front side of the platform. I wanted to ask Dedrick what had happened to him, but I couldn't find the words. Facing him but head down, I grabbed the handgrips on the opposite side of the lever.

"I got it." Bot gave me a smug grin and pushed my hands off the grips.

"Whatever." I hopped off and stepped to the back, took a seat beside Jessen and tucked my legs under me. We each had a handle on the edge of the platform to hold onto.

"I don't suppose we can sleep sitting up." Jessen smiled.

"You can rest your head on me," I said.

"You better hold on," Dedrick said over his shoulder. He stood with his back to us, about a meter away. "This thing really gets going."

"What is this thing?" Bot said.

"It's a hand car or a pump trolley, whatever you want to call it. They used it for mining. It runs on a track that winds through the mountain. It's simple to operate." He pushed his side of the lever down, bending at the waist. Bot's side lifted and the platform moved. "Your turn."

Bot pushed his side of the lever down. Dedrick's lifted. And away we went, with the two of them bending and pushing, pumping away. A breeze blew through my hair, and the wheels creaked beneath us.

After covering a bit of level ground, the tunnel descended gradually. The lever flew up and down. We rushed into darkness. The glow of the lantern lit up jagged walls and a ceiling of stone. We traveled through wider areas that stretched out on one side or the other, their farthest walls lost in the dark. We came to rows of support beams that reflected light from our lantern, flashing like strobe lights with a mesmerizing effect. Down and down the railway took us until at last we leveled and began a gradual incline.

The ride slowed. The incline must've made the lever harder to operate. Bot grunted at times so loudly I could hear it over the whir of the wheels along the tracks. His effort showed in the contortions of his face as he worked. Dedrick, who stood with his back to us, pumped the lever like a man rowing a boat, reaching and bending with smooth motions. Light from the lantern hanging before him made a glowing halo of his dyed blond hair and played on the muscles of his arms. Sweat gathered on his—

Jessen's foot cracked my shin. She laughed, nodded at Dedrick, and waved her brows, the imp in her coming out.

Heat rushed to my face. I shook my head. She had no reason to think I had desires for him. I only wondered . . . "What happened to him?" I mouthed. The rumble of the wheels over the tracks made it impossible to hear each other unless we shouted. I wasn't about to shout that question.

She gave a little headshake as if she didn't understand the question. Her eyes still held a mischievous gleam.

I pointed to my face and mouthed, "His face. Did you see?"

Her grin faded. She nodded then shrugged. She stared at me for a moment. The gleam in her eyes and the grin returned.

I shook my head again. Of course she would assume I desired him. That's how it worked. That's how a hook-up began. When you wanted someone, you leered. Not me. I had no desire for a fling with him or with anyone. It wasn't my way. I didn't want to be used or to use another for a moment of pleasure. Sure, some people stayed in a relationship for longer periods, but they were few and their relationships rarely exclusive. Even Tatum's boyfriend Finley hit on other girls behind her back. He had even hit on me. No. I had no desire for such shallowness. I liked things that made sense, things that lasted.

It felt like an hour had passed when the tunnel leveled out and we picked up speed. Bot grunted then bellowed, "How much farther?"

"All right, give it a rest." Dedrick stopped pumping and stepped on a foot break. Our ride clanked and squealed to a stop.

I jumped up before Dedrick turned to face me. "My turn?"

"Uh, yeah, if you're up to it," he said.

I shed the cape, traded places with Bot, and latched onto the lever, pushing it down before Dedrick took hold of the handgrips.

The handcar lurched. Dedrick stumbled back. His mouth dropped open. A crooked smile crept across his bruised face. "Oh yeah? You wanna play like that?" He seized the handgrips and shoved the lever down.

I shoved back. The car took off and, before long, rolled like thunder down the track. It made my stomach tingle to move backwards while standing. But the feeling faded as I threw myself into the rhythm of pumping the lever. My hair whipped against my cheeks. My arm muscles enjoyed the workout. The breeze caused by our speed refreshed me as it hit the sweat that soon covered my upper body.

We gradually climbed uphill and the workout intensified. The continuous physical exertion wearied my arms, my back. Bot's turn lasted about an hour. How long had I been at it? I wouldn't complain. Dedrick showed no signs of fatigue even with his injuries. I could handle it.

As I pushed and lifted the lever, my gaze rested on the connecting rod moving up and down. I pictured the inner workings of this simple machine. The connecting rod turned a crank that worked gears that turned the drive axel that turned the wheels. Simple. Clean. Reliable. It had been designed and originally used years ago. How many? Hundreds? Any problems would be easy to diagnose, easy to repair. A good cleaning. Replace a few parts. The handcar must have fallen out of use as technology developed, being replaced by engines of various designs. As society matured and grew in its knowledge and appreciation of nature, and the destructiveness of mining, it became all but obsolete. But here we were, traveling through an old mining tunnel, journeying to a place of freedom in an antique pump car.

"Slow her down, girl," Dedrick said. "We're here."

14

We set up camp a short distance from the mine entrance on a bed of pine needles in a clearing on the other side of the mountain through which we had traveled. Dedrick built a campfire unlike the miniscule ones he had provided every night since we started our journey in the wilderness. This one would not need to be fed often nor would it burn out in a mere fifteen minutes. This one would comfort us for at least two hours. Bot arranged logs near the campfire for something to lean against. Jessen got out dishes and opened cans to make soup for our dinner. I set up tents.

After tapping the last stake into the ground, I straightened up to look over my work.

Something in the shadows on the far side of our camp moved.

Dedrick squatted by a rectangular hole in the ground, a storage unit, I guessed, though I hadn't seen him uncover it. He lifted a dark lantern out, stuffed something into a bag, and slung the bag over his shoulder. He glanced at me as he stood up, lantern in hand.

"I'll be back," Dedrick said to Bot as he passed him. He strode off before Bot had a chance to reply.

"Where's he going?" Jessen looked up from the pan of soup she held over the fire. She watched Dedrick walk away.

"I don't know." Bot patted the log he had just moved and brushed off his hands. "He never tells me anything. Maybe he's got another boxing match." He chuckled, dropped to the ground, and leaned against the log.

"That's not very funny," I said. "What do you think happened to him?"

"The man's a mystery." Bot reached into his backpack and drew out a water bottle. He tipped his head back and took a swig, water dribbling down his scraggily, unshaven chin.

"There must be others out here besides their group, besides the colony," Jessen said.

"Or wolves. Did you hear those wolves last night?" Bot said.

"You don't fight with a wolf," I said, picturing the bruises and gash on Dedrick's face.

Bot chuckled. "Maybe he did something stupid, something clumsy. That's why he didn't explain what happened to him."

Jessen filled bowls with soup and handed them to me. I gave a bowl to Bot and sat beside him, leaning against the log.

"Minestrone again." Bot let a spoonful dribble back into the bowl. We'd eaten it, with a hunk of bread, every night of our trip.

"I'd eat it every day if it meant freedom from the Regimen." I blew on a spoonful and shoved it into my mouth.

"Me too." Jessen carried a bowl of soup and half a loaf of dry bread. She sat on my other side and waved the bread in my face. "Did you ever wonder how the Regimen Custodia Terra rose to such power?"

I ripped off a hunk of bread. Bot did, too. Then the three of us ate without speaking, lost in our separate thoughts as we watched the yellow and orange flames lapping the cool air. The musky smell of the smoke and waves of heat on my face soothed me. The steady song of the bugs increased the calming effect.

Bot wiped his bowl clean with the bread and tossed the bowl aside. He stretched his legs and propped his arms on the log behind him. "I want to know why they don't have tunnels under the Boundary Fence, the Mosheh, that is." He paused as if to let the thought sink in. "It'd be a lot easier way to go than what we went through. And safer. For that matter, why not expand them all the way out here? Pilgrims— That's what they called us, right? Pilgrims could take turns with that pump car. We'd get to the colony in no time."

"I'm sure they have their reasons." I scraped up the last of my soup, wishing for more. My stomach hadn't felt full since the dinner with the underground community. "Besides, we covered a lot of ground. Maybe they don't have the resources to build a long tunnel. And as far as building one under the Boundary Fence—"

"Impossible." Dedrick stepped from the shadows, wearing a clean short-sleeved shirt and with wet hair. The cut on his face glistened in the firelight as if it had an ointment on it. He set the lantern down and let the bag he had taken with him slide off his shoulder.

Jessen jumped up and went to the pan of soup she had set on a rock by the fire. She grabbed an empty bowl.

"There are underground sensors around the Boundary Fence. They would detect any attempt to tunnel."

"Where'd you go?" Bot looked Dedrick over.

Jessen handed Dedrick a bowl of soup and sat back down. "We were wondering how the Regimen ever got to be so powerful."

"Yeah," said Bot. "What happened to the idea that everyone should have a say in the ordering of society? Did you know that hundreds of years ago, people came to this very continent in order to live free of an oppressive government? They declared freedom and justice for all."

Dedrick seated himself on the ground, across the fire from us, and brought a spoonful of soup to his mouth.

"What happened to them?" Jessen said, ". . . to the people who wanted freedom?"

"I don't know. As far as I could gather from the documents I uncovered, they developed a government created by the people for the people. It had checks and balances and provisions to keep those in government honest. In a foundational document, they claimed the people had the right to abolish any government that failed to protect certain unalienable rights."

"Unalienable rights?" I said. "What does that mean?"

"It means our present world government is all screwed up," Bot said. "We have no rights, only responsibilities—responsibilities to the Regimen and to nature. We're the bad guys, polluting, corrupting, bringing destruction into the world. And the Regimen has found a way to help us live in harmony with nature. Only thing, we have to deny our freedom and our individuality and follow their rules. . ."

". . . whether we find them morally acceptable or not." Jessen gazed at the fire and rubbed her belly.

"Yeah," I said, "like accept whatever vocation they give you. Who are they to tell me what I am to do with my life? Shouldn't that be my choice? Whether I succeed or fail, my vocation should be my choice."

"And the bearing of children. What right do they have to rob us of our fertility, our ability to bear our own children?" Jessen wrapped both arms around her abdomen.

"The Regimen needs to be abolished." Bot clenched a fist. "The government no longer serves the people. People fear the Regimen. When the people fear their government, there is tyranny. When the government fears the people, there is freedom. People need to band together and rise up against them."

"They're too big." Jessen shook her head and a matted curl fell over one eye. Her hairdo of spikes and curls had wilted over the days, making her look as bedraggled as I felt. "Our Regimen is a part of the world government. Who are we? What can we possibly accomplish? Rebels would only end up in Re-Education."

"It can start small . . ." Bot turned toward her and spoke, gesturing with his hands. ". . . with the dissemination of ideas. They're all asleep right now, everyone seeking their own interests, their own pleasure, content with their games and narrow pursuits. We could wake them up, give them something to think about, something bigger than themselves." Bot looked at me.

I shrugged. What he said made sense, but the idea of waking people up seemed hopeless. No one had ever listened to me. They told me to watch what I said.

"When I found electronic copies of these old documents," Bot said, "I woke up from a dream. I realized I had been fooled, all these years, fooled into believing I was a part of something good and responsible. I was taught to feel proud of my contribution. I was doing my part, helping with something crucial to existence: repairing the damage the human parasites caused to the planet. I had no clear idea of what I sacrificed to do my part." He made a sweeping motion with his upturned hand, indicating all that surrounded us.

"Being out here in the wilderness . . ." The flames leaped, sending a gust of warmth to my cheeks. My heart stirred. "This feels right, natural.

How many untouched acres of land are there? We live stacked up in apartment buildings, in our crowded little cities with a single tree here and there. Why has this been kept from us? Why—" I swallowed my sentence.

My Friend came to my thoughts. He wanted to tell me something, but I didn't want to listen right now. I looked at Dedrick, wanting to know what he thought. He grew up with a different view of life. He grew up free in the wilderness.

"Creation belongs to us all." Dedrick set his empty bowl down and looked at each of us. "It was given to mankind at the beginning. You're right. No one ought to be deprived of enjoying it."

"Creation?" Bot smirked. "The word assumes a creator, a god. A primitive belief, isn't it? We've been taught to call it nature, even Mother Nature."

"You've studied science. Does it seem reasonable to you that all this came to be without a Creator?"

"I- I don't know. The Big Bang, you know . . ."

Dedrick laughed and dipped his head. His hair had dried and shined like gold in the firelight.

"If there is an all-powerful, uncreated Creator," Bot said, "where is He?"

"I imagine there is much you don't know about genetics and cells, but they exist. And there is much you don't know . . ." His eyes went to Jessen. ". . . about electronic databases and communication." He returned his gaze to Bot. "There is more to existence than you can even imagine."

Bot shook his head. "I don't know, buddy. I like for things to make sense, to have some foundation. A creator? God? I don't know what to make of that."

The conversation ended and we all stared at the flames. A breeze had stirred up the embers, sending them coasting in careless circles in the darkness.

After a while, Jessen broke the silence. "You look like you got washed up." Her eyes were on Dedrick.

"There's a pond over there . . ." Dedrick twisted and pointed. " . . . behind those pines. You've each got a towel and soaps in your packs. Go bathe if you want to."

"I'd love to." Jessen jumped to her feet. "I'm covered with sweat and dirt from head to toe."

"Me too. Let's go." I scrambled to my feet and went to my backpack. At the bottom of the pack, I found a change of clothes and a big bag labeled "Shower Supplies."

Jessen got her things and grabbed the lantern.

Bot stood up. "Yeah, a bath sounds great."

"Sit down," Dedrick said, his voice low and threatening. "You'll wait."

"Why? I'm sure the pond's big enough."

"Sit."

"Yeah, but there's no reason why . . ."

Jessen and I took off. I didn't care what Bot had to say. I had full confidence in Dedrick. He wouldn't let Bot go near the pond until we had returned. Not many in Aldonia seemed to give a shred about privacy. But I did.

Jessen and I strode to the pines, her in the lead. I quickened my pace and passed her. She laughed and sprinted past me. I bolted. We broke through the pines simultaneously, but I reached the edge of the pond first.

The moon in its first quarter hung low in the sky and created a clear reflection on the dark, tranquil waters. Tall pines surrounded the pond, appearing both protective and ominous, giving the impression of privacy. Footprints went from the grass, through a strip of fine dirt, to the water's edge. Dedrick's footprints.

"Last one in is the stinker." Jessen set the lantern down, dropped her clean clothes and shower bag, and yanked off a boot.

"You're on."

We stripped in seconds and raced into the cool water, taking big, awkward, splashy steps.

Jessen squealed and then moaned as she immersed herself to the neck. "This feels great. I've never gone so long without a shower." She tilted her head back and wet her hair.

The water came up to my chest. Not wanting to get in over my head, I slowed, creeping forward with careful steps. "I wish I knew how to swim."

"You don't?" Jessen lifted one arm to the air and stretched the other before her in the water. She took a breath and swam toward the opposite side of the pond, reaching overhead with one arm and then the other. At the other side, she popped out of the water and laughed. "I can't believe you can't swim." She moved her arms through the water at the same time, swimming back slower but keeping her head above water. "Didn't you learn in Secondary?"

Still taking careful steps, I neared the middle of the pond. Cool water lapped my chin. Perhaps I had reached the deepest point. Ready to take another step, I reached with my toes but found nothing. The ground sloped down more than I expected. I stepped back. "No, none of us did. We had a pool, but it was empty, in need of repair. I never saw anyone working on it during my four years there. We used to play with the yellow tape that was stretched across it, making it sag by throwing things on it, knocking it down and daring kids to jump down and get it. It was like a major crime to be caught down in the empty swimming pool."

She laughed and swam to me. "Want me to teach you?"

I splashed her and backed away. "No, I just want to wash my hair."

Her gaze snapped to the shore, and the light of the lantern flickered in her eyes. "Oh yeah. I hope we have shampoo in those bags. I don't know how I'm going to get my hair the way I like it without . . ." She swam off toward our things.

I tipped my head back to wet my hair. The water lifted me off my feet. Suppressing the urge to stand secure, I allowed myself to float on my back for a moment. I stretched my arms to each side and drifted.

Trust. Surrender. My Friend spoke, making Himself known in an instant and overwhelming me.

I forced my head up, flapped my arms, and searched for the ground with my feet. The ground! I couldn't reach it. I gasped for a breath. My head submerged. *I can't swim. Help!*

Darkness surrounded me. I clawed the water above, reached around me, kicked my feet—

My toe touched something. The bottom of the pond? I descended until my whole foot pressed against it. Then I pushed off, propelling myself upward. My face popped out of the water. I snatched a breath of air. The quarter moon hung before me. Pulling water with cupped hands, kicking my legs, I twisted around, searching for the light of the lantern. An instant later, my toes touched ground. On tiptoes and with hands grasping desperately, I forced myself toward the yellow light. A few steps later, I regained my footing.

My heart beat wildly. I panted to catch my breath. Unexpected peace enveloped me. I closed my eyes. *Trust. Surrender.* I was about to enter a new life. Unfamiliar. Strange. Filled with new challenges and hard work. This journey, culminated by this bath, symbolized the change that needed to take place in me. The Regimen Custodia Terra had indoctrinated me since birth with their ideas and attitudes. Though I rebelled inside, I knew of no better way. This bath and my surrender would wash away their indoctrination, like the filth and sweat that accumulated over the past few days. I would emerge clean and new. The laws of nature, the pursuit of truth, and common sense would guide me in my new life.

Would the colony live by a natural code that respected the individual?

~~~

A zipping sound brought me to consciousness. The gears in my mind stopped and reversed. My dream slipped away, leaving only a trace of the emotions I experienced in my subconscious: hope and anxiety.

I tore out of my sleeping bag, gave Jessen what had become a routine morning shove, and crawled from the tent.

Last night I had imagined things differently than what I now saw. We camped on a cheery carpet of pine needles the color of rusted metal. Rather than a surrounding of dense woods, tall pines with trunks of crinkled bark stood all around, allowing open views in every direction. On one side, the mountain we had come through rose up like a rugged gray wall, the mine entrance invisible from here. The branches of the pines, high on the trunks, stretched from one tree to the other and reached for the crystal blue sky, their needles shining golden-green where sunlight reached them.

"I'm anxious to get going." Dedrick tossed me the toilet paper roll. He stood over the hole in the ground, the storage compartment, and pushed something into it with the toe of his boot. Bot, chewing something
~~~

and holding a drink, sat on the log by the cold ashes of last night's campfire. Jessen stirred in the tent.

Dedrick and I got the camp torn down and the backpacks loaded before the toilet paper made its rounds. We all agreed to save time by eating breakfast while we walked, so Jessen distributed beef jerky, the last of our dry bread, and water bottles.

In the shadow of the mountain, we set out, walking silently over pine needles. The shadows shifted, putting the sun in our eyes as our path turned. The shade returned as the path wound between jagged walls of the mountain. Loose gravel slipped underfoot as we climbed and then raced us down the steep parts.

After a time, we veered away from the mountains and plunged into a thick woods. Trees grew close together. We followed a deer trail through undergrowth of knee-high plants and bushes, Dedrick occasionally moving fallen branches out of our way. The trees grew taller, their tops high above us, and thinned out the closer we got to our destination.

A bird called in the branches overhead. The chirps and songs of birds had accompanied us all the way, but none sounded as clear and strange as this one.

Dedrick squinted at the treetops. He raised a hand. I thought he meant to shade his eyes, though no sunlight came through the canopy of leaves, but then I noticed him waving.

"Is someone up there?" I peered but saw nothing other than branches and leaves.

Dedrick's brown eyes twinkled. "Someone, yeah."

I sharpened my senses, trying to take in every sound and sight. We had to be nearing the colony. What would it look like? I could only picture towering apartment buildings of glass and concrete, the overcrowded living accommodations of the common folk in Aldonia. Surely, their colony would look nothing like that. They wouldn't want to be noticed. Their structures would probably blend in with—

"How much longer?" Bot groaned. "My legs ache, my back aches, and my stomach is eating itself. You said we'd be near once we passed through the mountain. We've been walking all morning." He squinted at the canopy of leaves. "It's got to be close to noon. Maybe after."

"I've got a little more jerky in my pack," Jessen said.

"Patience, my friend," Dedrick said. "I guarantee you'll have a comfortable seat and a warm meal within the hour."

A few minutes later, I glimpsed movement in the distance. Something zipped from behind one tree to another. No sound accompanied the motion, and no one else noticed. Maybe my eyes played a trick on me.

I scanned the woods around us as we walked on.

A branch cracked.

"I think we're being watched." Bot slowed his pace.

Dedrick grinned. He gazed at a particular point in the distance. "Come on out," he shouted.

A pale face showed from behind a tree, the face of a girl no more than ten years old. Her stringy brown hair dangled over her shoulders.

Dedrick strode a little faster, an amused grin on his face. "Well, come on. You know it's me."

She stepped into full view but still held onto the tree trunk. Dressed in a ragged off-white dress that hung past her knees and moccasin-type shoes, she reminded me of the natives we learned about in school. Caution, not recognition, showed in her eyes.

"Come on, will ya?" Dedrick threw his arms out. "It's me."

Her eyes grew round and her mouth dropped open. She reached forward and bounded for Dedrick.

As she neared, Dedrick dropped on one knee and opened his arms. She threw her arms around his neck as he swallowed her in a hug.

Dedrick got face to face with her. "I missed you."

"You look terrible." She looked him over. "What happened to you?"

"Ah, I'm okay." He ran a hand over his blond hair and stood up. "It's my disguise."

"You look silly with yellow hair." She frowned. "Will it go back to normal?"

"Sure. I'll just cut it all off."

"You're all beat up. Does your face hurt?"

He chuckled. "Not so much. Does Mom know you're out here?"

She nodded. "Andy heard Pio's call, said you were almost here." Her questioning brown eyes turned to me now.

"Hi, I'm Liberty."

"Yeah." Dedrick glanced at me and swallowed hard, looking as if he had forgotten about us. "These are the new pilgrims: Liberty, Jessen, and Bot." He glanced at each of us in turn. "This is my little sister Paula."

Little sister? We all said "hello" and shook her little hand. What did it mean to have a mother and a sister? A family? The idea of it, while strange, appealed to me. I couldn't wait to meet the rest of his family, to see how a family interacted.

Paula tugged Dedrick's arm. "Well, come on. I bet you're all hungry. Mom made chicken casserole."

"That sounds great," Bot said. "Anything but canned minestrone soup."

~~~

We hadn't walked more than a kilometer when Paula ripped her hand from Dedrick's. "I'll tell Mom you're here," she said and sprinted away.

"Where's she—?" Bot's gaze locked onto something.

In this part of the woods, we had passed several clusters of close-growing trees, so I almost overlooked the house. Trees surrounded a two-story gray and brown structure, some almost seeming to support its walls.

We quickened our pace, Dedrick in the lead.

As we neared, I made better sense of it. The house resembled those of medieval times, with walls of stone, wood, and mud. Ivy grew all over it, helping to camouflage it in the winter when the trees lost their leaves, I supposed. The second story had a few dark windows. Open shutters flanked windows on the lower level. Uneven branches jutted from the edges of the roof.

Dedrick pushed open the door and motioned for us to go in. "Welcome to my home and to the Maxwell Colony."

We stepped inside but remained close to the door.

"Wow," Jessen said. "This place is . . ."

"Strange," Bot said.

Warm yellow light filled the house, streaming from lamps in a sitting room off to the left and from the open kitchen before us, promising comfort. Furniture and cabinets of polished wood and decorations in colors of deep red, green, and yellow abounded. Rugs covered a floor of
~~~

wooden planks. Paintings and wall lamps hung on plaster-like walls. Bowls, pitchers, and other clay items lined high shelves. *Real* books, figures carved in wood, candles, and potted plants decorated tables and a hutch. Five big copper pots holding blankets, glass jars, and various utensils sat against a wall. A savory aroma wafted in the air, making my stomach growl at once.

"I like it," I said. "Your house is beautiful."

"Go on in." Dedrick stood on the threshold. He waved us farther in, squeezing past Bot when he had the room. He shrugged his backpack off and hung it on one of many hooks just inside the door. Then he took our packs.

Paula dashed from around the kitchen counter. "Mom's not here. But we made food. Are you hungry?" She led us through a clean but cluttered kitchen to a dining room with a long wooden table with a chair on each end and two bench seats. I sat on the far bench so I could continue to take in the interesting layout and strange decorations. Jessen sat across from me. Bot took a chair at the end. Dedrick, I could see by peeking through the sitting room, still stood in the hall just inside the door. He was reaching into one of the backpacks. When he found what he wanted, he stuffed it into the back pocket of his pants and turned around.

A young woman breezed through a doorway in a little hall off the kitchen. She wore her hair in a ponytail, faded denim jeans, and a long, off-white shirt similar in fabric and design to Paula's gown. Her gaze snapped to Dedrick and she gasped. "Dedrick, you're—" She ran to him. "What happened to you?" She grabbed his arm and dragged him into the kitchen.

Twice he jerked his captive arm, as if making weak attempts to free himself from her grasp. "I'm okay. Don't worry about it."

"Who did this to you? Those boys from the Torva clan?" She sat him on a bench against the back wall in the kitchen. A shelf of jars, some empty, others with herbs, hung over him. She squatted and flipped open the lid of a box on the floor.

Paula brought glasses of a pale drink to the table. "I hope you like lemonade."

I smiled. "Love it. I can't remember the last time I had some. Maybe it was in Secondary or—"

"Put that away. I took care of it." Dedrick glared at the young woman but he didn't get up. "I'm fine."

"Do you like chicken casserole?" Paula said, smiling at Bot, Jessen, and me.

"Yeah, sounds great," Bot answered.

"Sure," Jessen and I said together. Its savory aroma made my mouth water.

"You took care of what?" The woman tending Dedrick poured something onto a piece of gauze and dabbed the cut on his face. "You haven't done anything to this wound. It'll probably get infected, definitely leave a scar."

I couldn't stop eavesdropping. Was she Dedrick's girlfriend?

Scowling, he pushed her arm away with the back of his hand. She grabbed his wrist with her other hand and continued dabbing the cut. "You need sutures."

He rolled his eyes and leaned back, his head banging the wall. "No, I don't. Can't you offer our guests some hospitality? They're tired and hungry."

Paula stuck a big spoon into a glass casserole dish on the counter and plopped the food into a bowl.

"Paula's taking care of them. Let me do this and I'll leave you alone."

"Yeah?" Dedrick gave the woman a crooked grin. "Really? No more questions?"

"I'm not making any promises." The young woman continued to treat his wound. "So, what's with the hair? You look silly as a blond."

"You said *no more questions*. And maybe I like my hair like this. Besides, you look silly as a brunette."

The woman slapped his upper arm.

Dedrick winced and shrunk away, shielding his arm.

"Oh, so you've got other wounds." She tugged the bottom of his shirt.

He tore her hand from his shirt and stood up. "You're done."

Paula carried a tray of steaming bowls to the table and placed one before each of us. Melted cheese and bits of bacon topped layers of chopped chicken, pale vegetables, and pasta.

"No, I'm not." The woman put a hand on her hip and spoke with command. "Take off your shirt."

He huffed and raised his brows. "No."

"You're hurt. I can tell."

Dedrick, shaking his head, strutted through the kitchen to the casserole dish on the counter. Paula, beaming with love, filled a bowl and handed it to him.

"So, where's Mom?" he said to Paula.

"Oh, you know." Paula hugged him and skipped back to the table. She sat beside me.

"Mrs. Orlando sent for her." The young woman spoke without looking at Dedrick, her attention on the box by the bench, arranging things. "She's having her baby."

"Already?" With a bowl in hand, Dedrick leaned his backside against the counter, bowed his head and moved his lips as if he were talking to himself. Then he took a bite.

"What do you mean already?" The woman glanced at him over her shoulder as she slid the box under the bench. She stood up and sauntered into the kitchen, coming to stand beside him. "You've been gone awhile. It's already nine months for her. Close to, anyway."

"Aren't you going to try it?" Jessen said, leaning across the table, toward me. "It's delicious."

"What?" I glanced at the spoonful I held then at Paula who sat beside me.

"It's not polite to stare," Paula said.

"What?"

"Liberty's busy watching the lovers fight." Bot chuckled. "Maybe she's jealous." He had wolfed down half the contents of his bowl already. "This stuff is great," he said to Paula.

"Lovers?" Paula's eyes went wide. "You mean Dedrick and Ann?"

My face warmed with embarrassment. Jealous? No, I wasn't jealous. Why would I—

I dropped my gaze to my food and shoved the spoon into my mouth. Smooth and savory tastes melted in my mouth. I had never tasted anything so good.

Paula put a hand to her mouth and giggled. "Ann is our big sister. She's the oldest of all. She bosses everyone."

"Are you talking about me?" Ann came to the table and sat down next to Jessen, on the bench. "I guess I didn't introduce myself. I'm Ann." She smirked at Paula. "And I'm not the oldest of all. You make me sound like one of the elders. I'm older than you, Andy, and Dedrick. I'm twenty-three. Ew." Her eyes went wide. "How old." She leaned toward Paula, smiling playfully.

"Well, you're old enough to find a husband and start your own family." Paula sounded defensive. "I don't know why you won't go with the other girls on retreats to the other colonies. It's like you don't want to get married."

Ann blushed. "Paula, where are your manners? This isn't a conversation our guests would enjoy."

"I would." Jessen pushed her empty bowl aside, leaned her arms on the table, and stared at Ann. "So how does all this work? I keep hearing about families. But that's not something we're familiar with, except animal families." Her impish grin came out and she stifled a laugh.

"You'll learn all about it," Ann said. Her blush had faded and she spoke with control. "It's really quite simple. Boy meets girl and falls in love. They commit themselves to each other and their love bears life."

"Children." Jessen dropped her hand under the table, to rub her belly, I assumed. She seemed to do that whenever something reminded her of the life she carried.

"Yes, children." Ann smiled. "But we need to talk about what happens next for you. This evening, we'll join other colonists at the Dining Hall. You'll meet your sponsor family."

"Sponsor family?" Bot scraped his empty bowl with the spoon.

"Would you like more?" Paula took his bowl. "I forgot the bread and broccoli." She skipped to the kitchen.

"Yes, your sponsor family. When the Mosheh sends us a list of candidates, we gather to discuss which family would be most suitable to sponsor a particular pilgrim in their home. Your family will provide an example of life within our colonies and can answer questions as they arise. You're welcome to stay with your sponsor family until you find your place, your calling in the Maxwell Colony. Then we all help you to achieve your goal."

A prickling sensation washed over me. "Wow," I said. "That's so different from the all-controlling ways of the Regimen."

Ann smiled at me. "We respect the individual."

"So, if one of us decides we don't like it here?" Bot's eyes held a look of challenge.

"Give us a chance, Bot. Wait until you see our Communications and Technology Center."

"Your *what*?" Bot leaned back in the chair and folded his arms. Paula brought him a plate of food but he made no notice of it. "I see everything here runs on gas. Gas lamps, gas stove, gas heat, I'm guessing." He gave a nod here and there to indicate things. "Do you even *have* electricity?"

I studied the look in his mottled blue eyes, the challenging tone of his voice, and his haughty body language. He expected he wouldn't like it here. Whatever problems he'd had with life in Aldonia did not convince him that he would like life here any better. He wanted to find fault. He had shown his doubt ever since I met him. How long had the Mosheh studied him? What made them think they could trust him? He wouldn't stay. Maybe no pilgrim had ever wanted to return to Aldonia before. He'd be the first. Would he threaten the safety of the Maxwell Colony? Of all the colonies?

"Well, no, we have no electricity in our homes, but . . ." A smile flickered on Ann's face. She glanced over her shoulder then did a double take. "Dedrick!"

In a room off the back kitchen wall, Dedrick stooped over something, his backside barely visible from where I sat.

Ann jumped up from the bench seat. "Bot, don't worry . . ." She cast a look to Bot as she stormed through the kitchen. "Trust me, you'll like it here."

"Why are these people always saying *trust me*?" Bot mumbled to me.

She stopped in the doorway and stood hands on hips and eyebrows low. "What do you think you're doing?"

Dedrick straightened, reached overhead and squatted again. "I'm doing what I have to do."

"You're taking food and supplies to *them*. Are you crazy?"

Dedrick stood and pushed past her with a backpack slung over one shoulder. "Tell Mom I'll be back tonight."

Ann followed him to the front door, anger flickering on her face. "They attacked you, and you're going to help them?"

Dedrick stopped at the door and faced her. He mumbled something I couldn't make out and then yanked open the door.

Ann remained motionless as the door swung shut. She shook her head and returned to the table, a pleasant smile forming as she neared. "If anyone wants a shower . . ."

15

"What do you mean you have not interviewed her friends?" Doctor Supero could've exploded right there in the middle of the Citizen Safety Station, in front of the twenty or so workers at monitoring stations, who each threw glances at him whenever he spoke. Some of them smirked or exchanged looks with one another. Perhaps he spoke too loudly. More likely, they liked the way he stood up to their chief. Maybe they all wanted to stand up to Chief Varden, their physically strong but mentally incompetent taskmaster.

"I mean just that. Why do I need to talk to them? Why do I want to waste my time?" Chief Varden leaned toward Supero and jerked his hands out as he spoke, a display of strength to mask his intellectual weakness. "We have surveillance video and phone taps. We've analyzed her every conversation by phone and every bit of footage for the past three months. We know everywhere she's been, everyone she's spoken with, even the gist of every conversation. Building from that information, we've analyzed every person she's had contact with — all their phone conversations and video footage. What can her friends tell me that I don't already know?" Chief Varden swung his beefy arm out in the direction of a team of CSS workers all armed with sleek headsets and happily gazing at monitors. No one dared make eye contact with the chief unless called on by name.

"Liberty is a loner," Supero said. "Do you know that?"

Chief Varden smirked down at Supero. "Sure, I know that. Wherever she goes, she goes alone, takes the long way, roads less traveled. Aren't you listening to me? We see everything."

"So, who is her *one* friend? I should at least like to interview that one."

Varden's expression went blank. His eye twitched. "Her *one* friend?"

"Yes." Supero stood taller. "Certainly you read her notebook before you gave it to me."

"Her notebook?"

With a huff, Supero snatched the book from the chair where he had left it and shook it in Varden's face. "Do not tell me you did not read this, did not analyze it for clues as to who may have helped her escape."

Varden slapped the notebook away. "Oh that. Of course, I read it. It was a bunch of nonsense, words that only someone like you could find interesting. That's why I gave it to you." He smirked, looking satisfied with his retort. "Besides, that was before she escaped. And there's nothing in there anyway." He turned away, headed toward his team. "Now, if you'll excuse me—"

Stars flashed in Supero's vision. His hands tensed. He lunged, grabbed Varden's bulging arm, and jerked the man back. "Nothing? In here?" He would let neither the ice in the chief's steely eyes nor the flaring of his wide nostrils silence him. "If you would have read this, you would know that Liberty claims to have *one friend.* She no doubt confides in this *one friend.* This *one friend* will know her plans. They have probably met in secret, making a mockery of your insufficient surveillance system. If you have been unable to identify the person she considers her *one friend,* then you need to interview her roommate and her associates."

Chief Varden flexed the arm that Supero clutched then jerked free. The squint of his eyes said he wanted to finish the conversation outside, but he took a breath and his jaw relaxed. "Listen, Supero . . ." His tone was oddly mellow, not what Supero expected. ". . . this is my operation. You're welcome to your own ideas, but don't let them interfere with our work. I know what I'm doing. You think the clue to her whereabouts is in there." A nod showed he meant the notebook. "But I think the clue is in here." He glanced to either side.

"In here? Your confidence in your surveillance equipment and computer search engines is—"

"No." Chief Varden wrapped a hand around Supero's arm and led him to a quiet corner of the room. Hands on hips and back to the monitoring stations, he spoke in a low voice. "Someone working for the Regimen is helping people escape. We have drones all over Aldonia.

We've sent drones to neighboring cities. But we haven't been able to read her implant or catch so much as a glimpse of her or any of the others who have gone missing. Too many have gone missing over the years. We never find a trace. It's just not possible without inside help."

He glanced over his shoulder then leaned closer to Supero, sharing his stale breath as he whispered, "I trust very few people. I have a select team looking into employees here and among the Unity Troopers. We think they're using the down time on cameras to slip through the boundaries. The cameras, the working ones, are supposed to go on and off randomly, but we think there's a pattern or that someone could predict, even manipulate the pattern. Someone might be able to know which cameras aren't working or which go down when."

"What?" Supero shook his head, disgusted. He wanted to add to the insults he had already uttered about the incompetency of the CSS, but since Varden had confided in him, he refrained. "You are telling me that your surveillance equipment is not always in operation?"

"Hey, don't blame us. Some committee for saving money and energy . . ." He sneered down his nose at Supero. ". . . that you probably belong to, gave us that directive. We only implemented it."

"That makes no sense. How can we have any assurance of protection from our Citizen Safety Station when—"

Varden tapped a knuckle to Supero's chin. "Don't worry my funny little friend." He grinned and rubbed a bent finger back and forth on Supero's star-shaped beard. "We're going to uncover this operation. It's just a matter of time." He turned away.

Supero wiped the disturbing feel of Varden's touch from his chin and stepped out of the corner. "What about the interviews?"

Chief Varden stopped but didn't turn around. He shook his head then glanced over his shoulder. "Fine, you can have your interviews, but I'll conduct them."

One of Liberty's entries came to Supero's mind. *Would I see Dedrick again? Was he for real? Or was he only a kid who had never grown up and who found a way to live out the video games of his youth. Maybe the Mosheh was nothing more than a group of people doing the same thing. It was only a game, a risky game — a game the Regimen wouldn't like. People lied and manipulated others every day.*

Why should I think these people were any different? If he did come for me, should I trust him?

"Make sure Dedrick is on the list," Supero shouted to Varden, who was now across the room and standing over a young, male worker at a monitoring station.

"Dedrick?" He shouted back. "I don't recall any Dedrick." He mumbled something to the worker about pulling up the list of contacts.

Supero bit back an insult as to the efficiency of the CSS as he strolled to Varden's side. "Dedrick must be on the list of acquaintances. She mentioned him in the notebook."

Varden squinted at the list of names that popped onto a monitor. The young male worker's hands danced over the control console. The list grew, shrunk, and then disappeared. The boy shook his head. Varden turned to Supero. "There is no *Dedrick* on the list of people she's had any sort of contact with in the past six months. Maybe it's a nickname."

"Or maybe it's the unknown man in the reflection of the Unity Trooper area car's window. He seems able to avoid your surveillance."

"Maybe." A distant look came to Varden's eyes. "Incidentally, we were analyzing the emergencies and disturbances that occurred the night she disappeared. Unity Troopers saw a lone man they couldn't identify at the warehouses."

"What? Tell me about this."

"You were here when Unity Troopers went to the First Zone Warehouses to investigate a disturbance. They were supposed to be at the Fourth Zone but went to the First by mistake. Well, at the First Zone, they glimpsed a man in the shadows. Couldn't get near him, couldn't get a read on his implant, tried to call to him. Of course, he didn't reply. They recorded his image with their body cameras, but our recognition software can't identify him."

"Bring up the image." Supero approached the workstation. The young worker did not seem to hear him but continued to observe whatever lists and images Varden had previously told him to work on. "Is he the same one, same as the man in the reflection?"

"Hard to say. He wore the shades and cape of that little group of anarchists I told you about, so he could be." Chief Varden flicked the worker's shoulder with the back of his hand. "Pull up the feeds from the Unity Troopers' body cameras, from the First Zone Warehouses, night Liberty disappeared."

"Where are the First Zone Warehouses?" Supero said.

"Uh, they're up here . . ." He leaned over the boy and tapped the control panel until a map of Aldonia appeared on a high wall monitor. He pointed to a spot on the map. "The ones closest the west Boundary Fence."

Supero squinted at the map. "The Unity Troopers could not catch him?"

"They were told to ignore him and get to the warehouses they were originally called to. I guess they didn't obey the command, still followed him because of his suspicious behavior, followed him to another warehouse zone where he disappeared. They were again commanded to get to the Fourth Zone, but then there was an explosion in the First Zone. So they went back. They found a two-way radio which he probably dropped in his rush."

Supero glared. Varden had commanded them to get to the Fourth Warehouse Zone. He remembered that distinctly. "What was blown up?"

"A wall to a warehouse full of pharmaceuticals."

He was after drugs? Supero shook his head. Chief Varden was wasting his time. This would not be the man. Why was Varden even telling him of this? There was no relation. Liberty had nothing to do with drugs. Her tests came back clean every time. He had never found a trace of illegal substances in her anatomically perfect body.

Supero turned to leave. He'd had enough. "Call me for the interviews. I want to be present." He had questions about several items in the notebook, about a bomb shelter and a boy named Dedrick, about her *one friend* and a group called Mosheh. Yes, he had many questions.

~~~

Under dwindling sunlight, Jessen, Bot, and I followed Ann across a grassy plain, a thin strip of woods to our left, rolling hills to our right, strangers all around us. People strolled in pairs and in groups that I found hard to take my eyes off, especially the groups of adults that had several children of various ages. The *families* greeted one another by name or with strange
~~~

phrases. "Peace and blessings." "The Lord be with you." The children who neared us stared, but the adults smiled and most said, "Welcome, friends."

Everyone headed in the same direction, toward a long and steeply-sloped hill, everyone except for two men in long black robes. One wore a straw hat, the other glasses. They strolled across our path, heading to some destination to our left. They drew more glances and greetings than the other passersby did, though their lively discussion caused them to miss half the attention thrown their way.

Ann stared at them, too.

"Who are they?" I asked, assuming they had some significance in the community and that we would meet them soon.

"Those are our priests," she said. "Well, the one with the hat is. The other is visiting from a neighboring colony. They won't be joining us for dinner. They fast on certain days."

"Priests?" The term sounded familiar. *What is a priest?* I almost said, but the history lessons from Secondary came to me and I shuddered. Images flashed in my mind, images from the historical re-enactment videos we had watched. Priests served as mediators between the people and their invisible, silent god or gods. They offered sacrifices on behalf of themselves and the people. I found myself wincing as I gazed at the figures of the black-clad men now entering the thin strip of woods. Images of priests slaying cows and lambs flashed in my mind in graphic, bloody detail.

I couldn't imagine people offering bloody sacrifices in this day and age. Nor could I imagine a people putting credence in things they couldn't detect with either their senses or technology. Most of all, I couldn't believe people would tolerate a man telling them what they could and couldn't do, making them feel guilty over personal choices. That was the main point that remained with me from our lesson on priests and religions of the past generations. They controlled people by making them feel guilty about personal choices. Our generation didn't need them, we were told. We could decide matters for ourselves.

I laughed to myself. No, we couldn't decide matters for ourselves. The Regimen did that for us. If a person did not properly respect nature, accept his vocation, or agree with the ideology of the Regimen, he wasn't just made to feel guilty. He was sent to Re-Education.

In a sense, we did have priests. The Regimen. And they sacrificed our freedom at the altar of the world. Nature became our god, a god we could see and touch, as permitted by our priests — a fragile god that needed the enormous, powerful Regimen to keep it safe.

"There it is." Ann swung her arm out to indicate the long stone structure built into the side of the steeply-sloped hill. "Our Dining Hall." The wall facing us had a few narrow, unadorned windows. The wall sticking out of the hill had a door painted grass green. As she led us to the door, she pointed to the roof where vines with yellow flowers hung over the edge. "We have a vegetable garden on top."

"Are all your buildings hidden?" Jessen said.

We had passed at least ten homes on our long walk to the Dining Hall, each one blending in with nature in its own unique way. A few houses, Ann pointed out, were underground, accessible through doorways hidden in hillsides or amidst tangles of bushes.

"We try. Sometimes drones fly by. Rarely, but it's been known to happen." Ann put her hand on the doorknob and looked each of us in the eye. "Ready?"

We were ready. After our lunch of chicken casserole back at Dedrick's house, we'd each showered and dressed in clean clothes. Jessen had taken a long nap in Ann's bedroom. I fell asleep on a couch. I didn't know if Bot had rested. He was reading a book in the sitting room when I awoke. But he had a cleanshaven face and pleasant smile now.

Ann opened the door to a long, loud room lit by lanterns. Rich aromas filled the air. Men and women, old and young, sat at two rows of tables that stretched across the room. The talking and laughter lessoned a few seconds after we came in. Smiling faces turned to us. A white-haired man stood up. Two boys zoomed past and ran to the far side of the room, to a low square table of children. "No running," a woman called.

The white-haired man pushed his chair out and hobbled in our direction using a cane.

"The kitchen is in there." Ann pointed to a wide doorway. The doors swung open and a woman wearing a bandana backed out of the kitchen with a tray of food.

"The bathrooms are that way." She pointed to a short hallway in front of the kitchen. "Come. I'll introduce you."

The white-haired man came around the end of the table and stopped. "Greetings, friends."

"You shouldn't have gotten up," Ann said to him. "We were coming to you."

"Nonsense," the old man said, "I can walk just fine." He lifted his cane, thrust it to the floor and caught it as it bounced up. Then he winked at me and rubbed his thick white mustache.

I liked him at once. "I'm Liberty." I stuck out my hand.

"I'll shake your hand this time," he said as he put his stiff and boney hand into mine. "But next time I'll expect a hug."

"You got it," I said.

"This is George Bauer. But most people call him Grampa Bauer."

"Grampa?" I said.

"Sure." He stood a little taller and put his shoulders back. "We have seven children, fifteen grandchildren and one great-granddaughter. We even have one consecrated."

"Grampa Bauer is one of the elders on the ruling council," Ann said. She took the old man by the arm and led us to specific seats, all toward the middle of the long table. Jessen sat next to her sponsor family; Abila Cruz, a black-haired woman with the roundest belly I had ever seen—even considering my brief time in the Breeder Facility—and her husband Manolo. Bot got the seat between Grampa Bauer and a man in his late thirties, the father of Bot's sponsor family. I sat across the table from them, between Ann and Patty Shenoy, the mother of my sponsor family. I scanned the others in the room. Dedrick was not with us.

"I'd like to know all about your form of government," Bot said to Grampa Bauer. "I'm very interested in that."

"Are you, now?" Grampa Bauer chuckled. "I guess I'll have to tell you everything I know. With my memory, that might not be enough for you." He chuckled again, harder.

Bot looked at me. I shrugged.

"But first . . ." He tapped his glass and cleared his throat. Everyone stopped talking and bowed their heads. "This will be new to you, I imagine." He folded his hands and closed his eyes for a moment. When he opened his eyes, his gaze went directly to the ceiling.

Bot, Jessen, and I looked, too. Metal beams, steel I guessed, formed the support for the ceiling. It only made sense. It had to be strong enough to keep the garden and the hill from caving in on top of—

"Dear Lord . . ." Grampa Bauer said in a loud voice, eyes still on the ceiling. "We thank you for bringing these pilgrims safely to our humble community . . ."

Bot's brows drew together and his upper lip curled. He glanced from the ceiling to the old man, to Jessen and then to me.

Wide-eyed with confusion, I mouthed, "I don't know."

The old man continued. ". . . for giving them Your grace despite the evils of the society in which they were raised, for inspiring them to yearn for lives of freedom and virtue where none are forgotten or dismissed . . ."

Jessen's impish expression suddenly melted, and she bowed her head like the others. Bot and I were left staring at each other, sharing confusion. The old man's words made no sense. To whom did he speak? He rambled on for a minute or two, his last words concerning the meal we were about to share. When he stopped talking, everyone said, "Amen," and lifted their heads.

The chatter and laughter began at once. People brought dishes of food to the table: sliced meats, steamed vegetables, little loaves of bread, and potatoes in sauce. Ann handed me dish after dish, taking little for herself and encouraging me to try everything. Girls filled our glasses with water or wine.

Manolo Cruz couldn't take his eyes off his wife Abila, the black-haired woman with the round belly. He scooped food onto her plate, allowed the servers to give her water only for her drink, whispered to her, gazed at her . . . He seemed incapable of taking more than one bite of food a minute. She held his complete attention, like a kid on a new video game.

Jessen watched Abila, too, probably curious about her stage of pregnancy. She caught me staring and widened her eyes as if to communicate something to me.

I didn't know what she meant, so I smiled and looked at Bot.

While managing to eat faster than those around him, Bot had started an intense conversation with Grampa Bauer. I caught the phrases *each person ought to have a say*, *the government should fear the people*, and *if the people of Aldonia were educated, informed, maybe they'd wake up*. Grampa Bauer said something about God, which silenced Bot for a moment.

"What are you thinking?" Ann said.

I had a bite of savory green beans with almond slivers in my mouth. "Well, I . . ." I snatched the closest glass and took a swig of wine. The sweet, burning taste shocked me. I coughed, grabbed the water, and gulped it while Ann smiled at me.

"You don't like the wine?" she said.

"No, it's good. It's just. I don't think I've had wine before. I've never felt it right to waste my credits on unnecessary things. Water suits me fine."

She nodded, still smiling, maybe amused. I couldn't tell. She looked different, though. Maybe she wanted to impress someone. Rather than the ponytail, she wore her hair in curls that fell past her shoulders. Her cheeks and lips were pink, and a hint of brown colored her eyelids. It was nothing compared to the dark makeup guys and girls wore in Aldonia. I couldn't imagine anyone here ever getting made up like that. Simplicity, cleanliness, and natural purity characterized their faces, every one of them. Their eyes . . . so many of them had brown eyes like Dedrick.

"You still haven't told me what you're thinking about," Ann said. "You've been so quiet."

"Just taking it all in. This is all so strange to me. We ate in groups in Primary and Secondary, but never as adults. And here you all are, people of all ages, together. It's . . ."

"Weird?" She smiled and took a bite of bread.

"No. It's nice. I guess it feels natural. Families together. Speaking of which . . ." I made a few random glances at the people around us. "Where's Dedrick? I thought he'd be back."

Ann averted her gaze and gritted her teeth. After a little headshake, she looked at me again, her smile back. "Dedrick thinks he's responsible for everyone. He's taking food and supplies to . . ." She frowned. "Did you see the guys who attacked him?"

"No. He left us for a long time and came back wounded." His dirty, bruised, and bleeding face popped into my mind. "No one asked, but I doubt he would've told us what happened to him."

"Yeah, that sounds like him. The people who attacked him are wild men, the Torva. They wander from place to place, going south as winter nears, so we only need worry about them for a few more months. But they always come back."

"Why aren't they part of the colonies?"

She gave me a blank stare.

"They don't share the same ideals as you, so they aren't welcome in the colonies?" Irritation tugged at my jaw. I wanted this place to be different.

She laughed into her glass of wine. "No. You need to clear the Regimen's ways from your mind. All are welcome here, all who are willing to work and who respect the freedom and conscience of others. True, they don't share our faith, but we pray one day they will." She set her cup down and stared into my eyes. "God loves us all, so all are welcome. They don't live here because they don't want to. They don't like to stay in one place, I suppose, so they have little set aside when hunting fails. And they're quite comfortable taking from others. The sooner winter comes, the better." She scowled. "I don't know why Dedrick goes out of his way for them."

"Do they attack the colonies often?"

"No. They wait for groups that go out: a hunting team or members of the Mosheh. No, they don't bother our colonies. But if they did, we could protect against them."

"How would you do that? Do you have people like our Unity Troopers?"

She laughed. "No, we protect ourselves."

"Mommy, can I sit with you?"

I turned at the sound of the little girl's voice. She sounded like Paula, but this girl had blonde hair. She climbed onto the lap of my sponsor mother and peeked at me.

"Hi," I said.

All shyness left her as she smiled. "Hi, I'm Nadie. I know your name. You're Liberty."

"That's me."

"I like that name. It means freedom. Did you pick your name?"

"Pick it? Uh, no." It amused me that she thought it possible that we could pick *anything* in Aldonia.

"Who gave you that name?"

"I, uh, I don't know. I guess it was the next name on the list when I was born."

"Well, it's perfect for you. 'Cuz you're almost free."

"Almost?"

~~~

Darin 476-111364-21 of Woodrow sat alone in the interrogation room, a shadow of a man, a suicidal drain on society. Had he not failed to accept his vocation in his youth, he would've been actively raising and slaughtering cattle, an appreciated vocation, providing the rare treat of beef products to a largely vegetarian society.

His beady eyes had swiveled to every miniature camera in the room, several times. Sweat gathered on his brow. He wiped his palms on his jeans and changed his position in the hard-backed chair, yet again.

Darin was the weakest of Liberty's associates, so Chief Varden chose to interview him first. Probably a good call. While he'd had a series of casual relationships with men, they were all short lived. No one cared about him, and he cared for no one. He had friendships of convenience, most relating to recreational drugs. He met Silver during a short stint in rehab. She had been his physical instructor, but she let him off easy. Data compiled from phone conversations and videos did not indicate how Darin met Tatum, but it showed that she once introduced him to a dealer. He only knew Liberty because she was Tatum's roommate. Darin had no other recorded connection to Liberty.
~~~

Supero slumped back in the padded chair provided him in the observation room and folded his arms behind his head. Darin wouldn't hesitate to divulge Liberty's secrets, if he knew any.

Chief Varden slipped into the room and came up behind Darin. "You must be—" Darin cussed and jumped in the chair, startled. "—Darin."

"Uh, yeah. Yes, sir." He took a breath and settled back in the chair. His experiences in rehab and Re-Ed probably made him jumpier than most would be in the situation. He was no doubt wondering what they had caught him doing. Probably contemplating which of his "friends" would've ratted him out. He had yet to learn the purpose of this interrogation. He would find it easy, a relief. He wouldn't have to admit anything about his own wasted life.

"Relax, Darin." Chief Varden sauntered across the room in a way that emphasized his muscular physique. "I just want to ask you a few questions."

Head down, gazing up at the chief, Darin nodded and gulped. "Sure." He sounded pathetically cooperative.

"We have reason to believe that a friend of yours is in danger. We need you to tell us everything you can."

"A friend of mine?" The tone seemed to indicate he thought there had been a mistake already.

"Yes. Liberty. Before she left for the Breeder Facility, did you notice anything strange about her behavior? Did she have any new contacts? Share any secrets with you?"

Distrust flashed in his eyes. He shifted in the chair. "Liberty? No."

"Well, you know she didn't particularly like her vocation, didn't you?"

"Uh . . ." Darin shook his head. "I don't know. Every girl wants to be a breeder. I hear the facility is . . ."

"Liar!" Supero pounded his fist on the table in the observation room, wishing the boy could hear him.

Chief Varden jerked his face to a camera and glared. He could hear Supero. He had a wireless earpiece for communication.

"The boy is covering for her?" Dr. Supero said. What reason would he have for protecting her? He knew something.

Varden nodded and returned his gaze to the boy. "Don't lie to me, Darin." He spoke in a calm tone. "Everyone who knew her knew she detested the vocation of breeder. She may have done something foolish to escape her vocation. Liberty may be in danger."

"Why would she be in danger? She's in the Breeder Facility."

"Tell me about the night Liberty, you, and your friends went out." While reviewing video feeds of Liberty's acquaintances, Chief Varden had discovered a strange event that took place a couple weeks before her disappearance. He had shown it to Supero. They could only find a few video images of that particular night, but they both agreed the event warranted further investigation.

"We went out?" Darin shook his head and something like fear flashed in his eyes. "Liberty never went out with us. She really in danger? You saying she's not in the Breeder Facility?"

"Well, she went out *that* night. I'm sure you remember. She and Finley carried shovels."

Darin opened his mouth but had no reply. He lowered his head and fixed his gaze on the table.

Dr. Supero stood and leaned his palms on the table. If he wasn't going to confess easily, the boy needed motivation. "Certainly, Chief," Supero said through gritted teeth, "you have some way of threatening him into talking."

Chief Varden grinned at the camera. He folded his arms across his muscular chest and leaned against the wall. "So, what is it you use?"

Darin lifted his head. "What?" He brushed the hair from his eyes and blinked.

Varden pushed off the wall and sauntered toward the boy. "Drugs. I can get you anything you want."

Darin's mouth fell open.

Varden sat down opposite the boy. "I know you're a user. We watch you all the time. Someone should probably send you back to rehab. But we've got priorities."

Darin glanced to either side. "I dunno what you're talking about. I'm clean." He wrapped his arms around his torso.

Varden snickered and nodded to a different camera, giving permission to proceed to whoever operated the video. A video appeared on the glassy wall used to display computer images needed for interrogations. Pictures flashed in rapid succession, dark and dirty images. Men watched over their shoulders as they made illicit trades in abandoned alleys. Crude words filled the air, anger and betrayal in the tone. Knives flashed. Wicked laughter and curses rang out. One man shoved another. A fight began. A siren sounded in the distance, and the group dispersed like rats. All but one lanky man.

Darin's face drained of all color.

The image zoomed in on the man who remained behind. *Darin.* He slunk into the shadow of a dumpster and, with trembling hands, pressed a needle to his arm.

"Stop!" Darin shrieked. He flung himself at the wall, his chair crashing to the floor. "Shut it off. You can't do this to me." With a tight fist, he pounded the huge image of his face as all the muscles appeared to go limp and his eyes rolled back. "Leave me alone."

"Listen to me." Varden spoke with command, no trace of pity in his tone. "We can make a trade. Any drugs you want, within reason, for everything you know about Liberty."

Darin slid to the floor. "I don't know anything about her. Ask her friends. I'm nobody."

"He is right," Supero said. "He is nobody. You should be interviewing her roommate."

~~~

The second interview: Liberty's roommate, Tatum 722-011667-85 of Aldonia, a mediocre clerk at the local exchange. She had a pattern of arriving late to work, leaving early, and living for the newest 3D video games and for her boyfriend Finley.

The thin girl hugged herself, looking cold, as she sat in the interrogation room. She followed Varden with her heavily made-up, cat-like eyes. Varden paced the floor, staring at a pocket computer. He stopped and directed his gaze to her.

She shrunk back. "I told you everything I know. Didn't I report that strange book of hers as soon as I found it? If I knew something more, I'd
~~~

tell you. Even if Liberty is, I'm no traitor. Sure, I'm late to work sometimes, but I follow all the rules."

"There's something you aren't telling me," Varden spit. "Where'd you go that night? What did you do with the shovels?" A frozen image of the five friends from *that night* showed on the wall as a backdrop.

She dropped her gaze. The yellow and black makeup on her eyelids made a perfect teardrop shape. "I told you I don't remember that night. I partied too hard." She met his gaze, a look of pleading in her eyes. "The shovels aren't missing, are they? I'm sure Finley brought them back to work. He doesn't steal. Silver steals. Sid steals. Maybe even Darin. But not Finley. He doesn't do anything wrong."

Supero shook his head and resumed reading Liberty's notebook. Tatum was useless. She was a coward, afraid of getting herself or her boyfriend in trouble. She knew nothing or she would've divulged it already.

"Who would you say Liberty's best friend was?"

Tatum shrugged. "She liked the old people where she worked."

"What can you tell me about Liberty's friend Dedrick?" Chief Varden said.

Supero's gaze snapped to the monitor. Maybe . . .

"Dedrick? Never met him. Never heard her mention the name. I didn't think Liberty had many friends our age, besides us. I mean everyone likes her, everyone in the apartment building. They all go to her when something needs fixing. That's all she does: work and repair things."

Varden's eyes narrowed. "How'd she get the tools?"

Tatum shrugged. "You know, trading. She did work for the tools."

Supero dropped the notebook and stood up. Trading? Why did the CSS know nothing of her trades?

"What became of her tools?" Varden said.

"Silver's got them."

~~~

Third interview: A woman—he was sure of it now, though the bulging muscles and the aggressive way she carried herself had thrown him at first—sat opposite Chief Varden at the solitary table in the interrogation room. Silver 798-060662-91 of Aldonia, the community physical
~~~

instructor who spent more time working on her own body than instructing the men and women sent to her for therapy.

Her wild hair, the color of silver ore dug straight from the earth, stood in tufts and hung down past her bare shoulders. She had a raw, animal quality that appealed to Supero. No, she was much too masculine for him. He would never get involved with a woman like her. A girl should have strength and confidence but without losing her air of femininity, of vulnerability. This woman would probably bring Chief Varden to his knees before he finished questioning her.

"I understand Liberty gave you a considerable amount of tools." Chief Varden leaned his arms on the table, his biceps bulging from his short-sleeved shirt. "What did you give her in trade?"

Silver gave a sly grin. "Is that what this is about? The tools? Can't a person own a few tools without the Regimen coveting them? Do I owe a tax? A fee?"

"No, this isn't about the tools. Answer my questions and no one will care about the tools. I understand that Liberty had collected an impressive set. What'd you give her in return?"

With raised brows and a smirk on her face, Silver shook her head.

Supero did not envy the chief's job. The woman was coy, cocky, intolerable.

"Nothing, huh?" Chief Varden said. "I find that hard to believe. Did you perhaps introduce her to Dedrick?"

Silver's brows twitched. "Dedrick? Who's Dedrick?"

Chief Varden stared for a long moment. Then he nodded to a camera, giving the signal to start a video.

"We know Liberty doesn't usually hang with your group, usually keeps to herself. So, Silver, what happened the night the six of you went out? You got back just before curfew."

The video played on the glassy wall. Silver, Finley, Tatum, Darin, Sid, and Liberty walked as a group from Liberty and Tatum's apartment building. Darin lugged a cooler. Tatum clutched a flashlight. Finley and Liberty each rested a shovel on their shoulders.

Silver cast a disinterested glance through heavy-lidded eyes at the video and returned an unflinching gaze to the chief. "I'm sure we were just having a good time."

Chief Varden smirked. "You managed to avoid cameras for much of the night. Where'd you go?"

She shrugged. "The usual, I guess. Can't say I remember."

"What's the usual?"

She rubbed her prominent jaw in a most manly way. "Stop at clubs. Hang out. Get drunk." She imitated his smirk, her full lips inviting, despite her masculine jaw line. "Use your imagination."

Varden leaned forward and narrowed his eyes, but his tone remained calm. "A shovel seems like an odd thing to take to a bar."

"I didn't have a shovel."

"Your friends did. Why? What'd they use them for?" Varden's upper lip twitched. He wasn't losing control, was he? Surely, he had an ace to play, an offer to supply steroids or something. She had to get them from somewhere. A woman just did not develop muscles like those naturally.

"Can't remember." She yawned and glanced at the flexi-phone on her wrist.

"Where is the bomb shelter?" Chief Varden said.

"Good," Supero said aloud though he hadn't meant to praise Chief Varden for his line of questioning. Liberty had mentioned the bomb shelter in her writing. It was about time Varden asked someone about it.

She jerked her face to Varden. "The bomb—" Her expression relaxed. "Oh, is that a bar? I think I've heard of it. It's one of those places you can stay at past curfew, right?"

Anger flashed on Varden's face. "What did you use the shovels for?"

A flame flickered in Silver's eyes, her expression mirroring Varden's. "Why don't you ask Finley? He's the Environmental Stewardship guy. He was probably borrowing them, or returning them, or who the hell knows. Got any questions for me?" She jerked her hands up and out. "That I can answer?"

Varden cracked his neck and stood up. He leaned his palms on the table. "Okay, what did Liberty trade you for all those tools? You sent her to Dedrick, didn't you?"

"Yes," Supero said aloud. No one just gives things away. Liberty got a connection, at the least. "Ask about the Mosheh, too." Liberty's writings seemed to indicate Dedrick had a connection to a group called the Mosheh.

Silver pushed her chair out and leaned her palms on the table, bringing her face right up to his. "I told you. Nothing. I got them free. She couldn't take them with her, so I asked for them. And I can be a hard one to deny."

"I don't believe you." Varden straightened and took slow steps, circling around the table to her side of it. "I know you're heavily involved in trade and you're quite capable of hiding things from the Regimen."

Silver straightened and faced him. With a grimace she said, "Believe me or don't."

Varden stepped closer, so close that he may have made contact, but she didn't flinch. "I think you helped her escape. And you got the tools in return. And I want to know how you did it and where she is."

"If that's all you want to know, I guess I can go. I don't have those answers." She turned and headed for the door.

Varden's nostrils flared. He grabbed her upper arms and interrupted her stride, yanking her back.

A strange, cold look swept over her face. She swung her arms outward, breaking Varden's grip, and turned for the door again.

He snatched her wrist. "I'm not done with you."

Eyes blazing, Silver spun, breaking his grip, and came around behind him. He made an effort to turn, but she had two meaty arms around one of his in an arm lock.

Varden grunted, twisted, kicked, and broke free.

At the same instant, the door flung open and two Citizen Safety Officers tore into the room.

Silver raised her hands and stepped back. "Easy, boys. I don't want to hurt you." She wore a self-confident grin.

Chief Varden snarled at the officers. "Get out. I don't need your help."

"Apparently, you do," Dr. Supero muttered, indifferent as to whether Varden heard him or not.

~~~

Fourth interview: Tatum's boyfriend, Finley 444-123164-136 of Aldonia, one of the most reliable employees in Aldonia's Environmental Stewardship Units and another three-dimensional video game addict.

"You work for the Environmental Stewardship Units, don't you?" Chief Varden sat on the edge of the table in the interrogation room, swinging one leg.

"Sure, yeah." Finley straightened in the chair and nodded, probably thankful for such an easy question. He wore a dark green uniform with the Environmental Stewardship logo, a tree and a shovel with the letters ESU.

"So, I imagine you have a pretty good idea which surveillance cameras are in operation and which aren't."

"Uh . . ." He turned from Varden's cold gaze and swallowed hard. "Well, you know we repair the ones that are down. And we get a list at the beginning of each day. Can't say we get to them all. You know the list is pretty long." He cast a troubled glance at Varden. "We work as fast as we can. Sometimes we need to order parts. Or the damage is more extensive—"

"My question is: Do you know which ones are working and which aren't?"

Finley shrunk back, face muscles twitching, worry in his eyes. "Well, no, I mean, yes. I guess, I know about some of them. I don't remember specifically. I mean we get a list of assignments at the beginning of the day. Is there one in particular you're talking about? I could look into it and—"

"You're lying. You know exactly which cameras are working and which aren't. I've reviewed footage of you. Compared to the ordinary citizen, there isn't much of it."

"Footage of me?" Finley's eyes snapped open wide. "Why do you have footage of me?"

Varden grinned. "Are you going to play the fool? Who do you think gets the feeds from the surveillance cameras throughout Aldonia? Why do you think the cameras are there? The Citizen Safety Station sees everyone, sees it all. It's how we keep you safe." He stood and slammed
~~~

his fist on the table, making Finley jerk back. "Unless the cameras aren't in operation!"

"We work as fast as we can. Are that many down?"

"Where did you go the night you and your five friends took some shovels for a walk?" He glanced directly at a camera and snapped his fingers. An image appeared on the glassy wall, Finley walking with one arm around Tatum and a shovel on his shoulder. "What were you up to that night?"

Finley took a deep breath. "I, um, I . . ." He leaned forward, clasped his hands and dropped them onto his thighs. "Let's see, I think I-I borrowed the shovels from work so I could lend them to a friend."

"Give me the name of your friend."

"Well, I didn't actually find him. So I brought the shovels back, brought them back to work the next day." He took a breath.

"What did your friend want them for?"

"I don't know. I didn't ask."

"Give me the name of your friend."

Finley bit his lip. "Okay. That would be . . ." Head down, he glanced up at Varden. "I guess I don't know his name. He goes by Wolf Man."

Varden snickered and shook his head. "Okay, right. Wolf Man." He kicked Finley's chair, sending it squeaking back. "Who do you tell about the down surveillance cameras?"

"What? Nobody. Why would I tell anyone? We're supposed to repair—"

Varden leaned in his face. "Where is Liberty? What do you know about her escape? Who is Dedrick?"

"Wow, man." Finley's hands shot up. His body trembled. "I wish I could help you. I-I don't know. I don't keep track of her like that. We're not that close. Maybe you should talk to Sid. I mean, he likes her, follows her sometimes. Maybe he can help."

~~~

Fifth interview: Sid 236-110164-101 of Jensenville, one of Aldonia's team of roofers. He works long hours when the weather is good and finds various, often reckless, ways of entertaining himself when the weather is foul.
~~~

He stared through squinted eyes for a long moment as if Varden's question set off a series of personal thoughts. "Why would you need help finding Liberty? She's in the Breeder Facility. Has been for weeks."

"No, Sid, she's not. She escaped and we want to know how."

Sid gave a little headshake. "I, uh, I thought she was in the Breeder Facility. When did she escape?"

"I'll ask the questions. You need to tell me everything you know that might help us find her."

A coy smile crept onto his tan face. "And why would I do that?"

"We know you want her, that you've been after her for a long time. If we find her, you'll be rewarded."

"In what way?" He tugged at his shirt, a tight shirt that showed off the muscles he had developed as a roofer. The way he styled his wavy black hair and the hint of facial hair gave him a conceited appearance. No doubt, girls found him attractive, but not the one girl he wanted. Not Liberty.

"Liberty. She'll be sent to Re-Ed, but there's no reason you can't be rewarded first."

Sid sat silently with lips parted and eyes darting from Chief Varden to distant points in his mind, obviously contemplating the offer. Then a storm brewed in his blue eyes—he wanted that reward. His lip curled up on one side. "Okay. What do you want to know?"

A smile flickered on Chief Varden's lips as if he had to force back a triumphant grin. "Did she have a boyfriend?"

"No. She always said she didn't want—" He froze. "Hold on. Maybe she did. There was this guy once. I was with her and he showed up. Never saw him before or since, but I'll never forget him. He beat me up."

"Do you know his name?"

"No."

"Have you heard her use the name *Dedrick*?"

"No."

Chief Varden gazed into one of the cameras, as if he saw right through it to Dr. Supero in the observation room.

Supero nodded and said, "Yes, Chief Varden, we can use him."

"We're going to need your help for a few days," Chief Varden said to Sid.

16

In the weeks that followed, I learned what Nadie meant by "almost free." I attended morning classes with Bot, Jessen, and teenagers from the colony. A gray-haired man with an easy smile taught us about life in the colony, about responsibility, virtue, selfless love, and family. A person wasn't considered free until they could master themselves. I devoured all I heard in these classes. I longed to learn more. My inner being stirred continuously with the presence of *My Friend,* giving me certainty that all I heard was true. I began to wonder if others had an inner friend that guided them.

After morning class, we went with one or another of the teens. We saw firsthand where they lived and what work their parents did. We practiced the skill ourselves most of the time. Bot hated this part or our orientation and made no effort to hide his feelings. Would he find dissatisfaction with this physically more demanding, technologically less advanced way of life? Would he want to return to Aldonia?

Most people pursued occupations that concerned the necessities of life: food, clothing, health, safety, and shelter. We learned the basics of making cloth, sewing, farming, canning, cooking, nursing, carpentry, forging, hunting, and more. These visits and instructions were meant to broaden our understanding of life in the colony and the roles individuals played. They were also meant to help us determine where we fit in, where we felt "called." I appreciated each experience and could picture myself making a living at several things, finding metalwork and construction among my favorites. I also enjoyed meeting people. Every one of them, even the grumpy ones, had an honest look about them and a unique, free personality. The overpowering government of Aldonia that told you what to think, where to go, and what to do tended to make us all alike. We cared about ourselves and little else.

Bot had that Aldonia selfishness. He knew what he wanted to do and hated the waste of time. The oldest boy of his sponsor family worked where Bot planned to work, in the CAT Cave— the Communications and Advanced Technology Cave. I hadn't seen the place yet, but I had a pretty good picture of it because Bot spoke of it daily.

Deep in the heart of the mountain, a cave several stories high housed a power generator, a hospital, and advanced communications equipment. Closer to the hidden entrance was a housing complex, apartments of a sort, for those who needed more medical care, those who wanted to live near their work (CAT employees), or those who preferred the safety of living in complete hiding.

"You've got to see the caves," Bot said. We stood under an oak tree with our class, watching one teen's father drive toward us on a tractor.

"Someday." I shifted my position to move into the sunlight. I enjoyed living in nature and had no great desire to see inside the caves. I'd see them in time. My sponsor father said they wanted to enlarge the entrance and make an inconspicuous door for it. Right now, the entrance was hidden but natural, a low opening in a hillside of boulders and trees. I could help design a good door. Ideas had already begun to form in my mind.

"Granted," Bot said, "they don't have the resources of the Regimen, but they've got some smart kids in there and methods I've never seen used before. Still, once I get in there, I'm certain I'll be able to teach them a thing or two. I don't see why I have to go around with you guys. Who cares how they grow crops?"

"Don't you think it's interesting that they've learned to plant and harvest in a sporadic pattern that isn't obvious from above?"

"Not really. How often do you think the Regimen flies out here? They'd send drones anyway. I'm just wasting my time with all this, this orientation. And so is she." He nodded at Jessen.

Jessen, all smiles and curls, spoke with one of the teenage girls. Her belly had grown quite a bit over these past two months. I couldn't believe she only had about three more months to go. She seemed different to me now, more sullen or maybe just serious. I wanted to talk to her but we were never alone. She seemed to have changed after having assisted in the delivery of her sponsor mother's baby. She offered to help, saying she wanted to be a midwife. Everyone already referred to her as the new midwife. I hoped she liked it here. I couldn't imagine anyone wanting to leave.

I loved being here, in the Maxwell Colony. And I loved my sponsor family, the Shenoys. There was Patty and her husband, and then Nadie and three other children, two older ones and a baby. It reminded me of the family in the picture that I took from the bunker. It didn't take long for me to understand and appreciate the functionality of a family. Mr. Shenoy built and repaired houses throughout the colony, taking special pride in his family's house. When he came home in the evening, he delighted the children by reading to them—from actual books—and listening to them read. Mrs. Shenoy cared for the children, prepared amazing meals, washed clothes in the oddest machine I ever saw, and kept the house clean and organized. She and the children also tended a small herb garden and sold the surplus herbs. The older children, Nadie and James, attended school a few hours a day and helped with chores in the afternoon. Grandma Shenny, as the children called her, even did her part. She knitted between naps, snapped the ends off green beans, and shucked corn. She also watched the baby and the four-year-old for short periods.

Miriam had said colony life wouldn't be easy. These people worked, every one of them, yet I hadn't heard anyone complain. I think they each felt useful, needed. Life within a family gave so much more to an individual than a life of transitioning through group residences in Aldonia.

A family lived together, each member caring about the others, putting up with each other, and enjoying each other. Parents made little sacrifices all the time, unbeknownst to the children, in order to provide for a family need or for that of a particular child, or just to make someone happy. The older people, the grandparents, often lived with the younger families.

Grandma Shenny was healing from a broken hip. She needed help dressing, caring for herself, and even with moving from room to room. She repeated herself and forgot names. Yet no one ever shied from or complained about assisting her. Rather they smiled more and tended to linger by her side. I had never seen an old person in Aldonia who needed so much help, nor had I seen one so loved.

Was this the way of life in Aldonia before the Regimen took over? How had we allowed our lives, our freedom, and our families to be taken over and destroyed? How long ago had the family in the picture from the bunker lived? This devastating transformation of society must have taken place over hundreds of years. I couldn't imagine people letting go of the family so easily.

~~~

I returned home late in the afternoon to the Shenoys' three-story tree house and wanted to clean up. Jessen and I arranged to meet outside the Dining Hall an hour before dinner.

The rough, untreated wooden front door opened to a silent house and the aroma of freshly baked bread. Dusty sunbeams streamed through an upper window and created a geometric pattern of shadows and light on the spiral staircase across from the door. A big table, with a tree growing though the center of it, had pride of place in the open floor plan. Mr. Shenoy had carved it himself. Natural light bounced off the table, counters, and polished wood floor. A yellow glow came from a back corner of the house, Grandma Shenny's area.

I went toward the light to check on her and say *hello*. I usually came home to a quiet house and wouldn't see the rest of the family for close to an hour. Rainy days were the exception.

"Patty, dear . . ." Grandma Shenny sat on a wooden rocking chair under a lamp in a little sitting area, now her bedroom, her latest knitting project on her lap. She held out a wrinkled hand to me.

I stepped into the room, to where sunlight shone on my face. "It's me, Liberty."

"Oh, my." Grandma dropped her hand to her lap and chuckled. "That's right. Patty's gathering herbs. But I knew it was you, Liberty. The wrong name came out. That's all. Happens a lot. Can't keep the names straight. Even when I do in my mind, the wrong name comes out my mouth." She chuckled and rocked the chair.

I stepped closer. "Can I get you something?" Seeing her kind and wrinkled face and offering to get her something, my mind turned to the
~~~

Senior Center and to Abby. I was glad to have Grandma Shenny in my life right now. My heart found comfort in her while it ached for Abby.

"That pan over there." She pointed a crooked finger at a cluttered hutch.

I went to the hutch and scanned the decorations, looking for anything one might call a pan.

"Oh, not a pan. A, uh, a pot. One of those canning pots." She waved her finger.

A large metal pot filled with things sat on the floor next to the hutch. I squatted by it. "What am I looking for?"

"A little bag of knitting needles. Marked 'Emily.' Has my name on it."

In the pot with glass canning jars, stuffed in one of the jars, I found a flowered bag of soft material with the name Emily crocheted on it. "Your name is Emily?" I took it to her.

She nodded. "That's me. Third of four siblings." Rocking a bit and smiling, she examined the knitting needles by pulling them one at a time from the bag. "Had an older sister and brother, and a younger brother, the baby of the family." Her eyes set in a glassy stare, and she stopped moving. "He didn't make it."

Emily. The name on the notebook I had found— "Do you know about the bunkers?"

"Bunkers?"

I sat on the edge of the coffee table. "Before I came here, a group of us, we found an underground bunker in the outskirts of Aldonia. It had food and supplies and six bunks. I found a picture there, a picture of a family. I think it was their bunker. And I found a notebook. Someone had written a name on it: Emily."

Grandma Shenny stared at me. Maybe she was tired. Maybe the bunker had nothing to do with her. Or maybe it brought back a memory she'd rather forget. The baby didn't make it, she had said. What did that mean?

She rested her hands on the knitting on her lap, leaned back, and sighed. "I remember the bunker. They started taking land, taking houses, making people move to crowded residential areas. Took over family businesses. We had a restaurant. That's why Patty's so good at cooking." She snapped from her distant gaze and smiled at me. "Gets that from my side of the family."

Her attention went to the knitting bag. She slid two needles out and tugged the drawstring, but it slipped from her grasp.

"Here, let me." I took the bag, closed it, and set it on the round end table near her. I watched her work the needles, count loops, wrap yarn, make knots, hoping she would say more but unwilling to prod her.

A few minutes later, I took a deep breath and placed my hands on my thighs, ready to get up.

"Closed so many places," she said. "Signs everywhere. Closed for business. They adopted a new name at that time, the government, a name that would tell everyone they were doing the right thing. All the countries took the name. A single world government. I can't remember. Something about the earth." She shook her head. "Then they took all the guns. My parents were afraid. Everyone was. I didn't know we had the underground shelter . . ." She smiled at me. ". . . the bunker, until we went to it one day. My father and his friends held meetings there. They stockpiled guns, made plans. He had said one day that it wasn't far enough out. Then we started on the long journey. We came out here. Many of us came."

"Your brother didn't make it?"

"No. His body rejected the vaccine." She dropped the needles and rubbed her hand as if beset by a sudden pain. "No, not a vaccine."

~~~

"So, this is the man? You are sure?" Dr. Supero sat next to Sid at a corner workstation in the central surveillance control room of the CSS. The image of the dark-haired man on the roof, from the reflection on the window of the Unity Troopers' area car, appeared on the glassy monitor before them. The man mouthed something and thrust his index finger to one side, obviously pointing the way he wanted Liberty to go.

Sid sneered at the image. "Yeah, that's him. I've got his face burned in my mind. If he ever crosses my path again—"

"Curb your jealousy for now. You may have a chance to unleash it yet." Supero leaned over the control panel and tapped the image controller to scroll to the next image. "I have a few more figures I want
~~~

you to look at." The CSS team had found several images of individuals the recognition software could not identify, individuals who wore the mottled capes and shades. Supero searched for the video taken from the body cameras of the Unity Troopers who were at the Zone One Warehouses. "Are you sure you did not hear his name? Did Liberty say nothing when she saw him?"

Sid folded his arms across his chest and leaned back in the chair. "She didn't seem to recognize him. In fact, I'd say she was as shocked as we were."

"We? I thought you and Liberty were alone."

"Well, no. But that's not important. We were *going* to be alone." Sid kept his gaze on the monitor.

"Perhaps it is important to me." Dr. Supero turned Sid's chair to make the boy face him. "Why don't you tell me who was with you?"

Sid glanced at him and looked away, face to the monitor. "It's not important."

"There is no record of this incident in the database. Where were you that no surveillance cameras picked you up?"

"Really, it's not important."

"It is to me." Supero began to dislike the young man, his alluring air and the smooth sound of his voice.

"I think we found them!" The rough voice came from across the room. Chief Varden strode into the central surveillance control room, a confident grin on his face and a steaming mug in his hand. He was late this morning. A dozen or so surveillance specialists, sitting dutifully at their stations, eyes glazed from their labors, swiveled their faces to him then back to their monitors. Chief Varden spoke only to Supero.

Dr. Supero's heart skipped a beat. He wanted to leap from his chair and beg for details, but he forced himself to remain seated, to merely turn his head. He would not give way to the unprofessional impulse. Could they have found her? What did Varden mean by *them*?

With parted lips and sleepy eyes, Sid gawked openly as the chief approached.

"Them?" Supero said. "Who are *they*?" He cared only about finding Liberty. For too many days now, he had shirked his own responsibilities in order to teach himself to operate various CSS search programs and in order to work with Sid. Liberty had become a festering boil in his mind, a reminder that weeds still grew in Aldonia, that an occasional fetus still warranted termination, that cancer still found a way to infect the healthy.

Varden took an empty chair and rolled it to Supero and Sid, the chair Ivy had just vacated. Her seductive perfume still lingered. While sipping his drink, he squinted at the wall monitors that displayed live feeds. Faces caught on security cameras throughout Aldonia flashed one after another. The computer identified most in less than a second. Every human eye was different. Hooded figures, partial figures, and those with tinted glasses took longer. The software tagged the unidentifiable ones and reduced them to the size of an icon. Sid would need to examine them and try to match them to the image in his mind, the one of the boy who beat him up for Liberty.

"What're you doing here?" Varden pushed Supero's hand aside and tapped the smooth control panel. Two more screens popped up, one of a map of Aldonia. It had flashing dots indicating which cameras sent the individual images. "Learn how to optimize your time, Doctor? Who taught you on this?" He meant the question as an insult; he knew full well that Supero had trained himself.

Dr Supero bit back a rude reply and gave up trying to find the video from the warehouses, for now. He could easily criticize the chief and any one of the sloppy methods used at the Citizen Safety Station, but he needed the man's help. The criticism could wait. He needed answers and Varden was slow to give them. "You said *them*? What do you mean *them*? Do you mean the dark-haired man, the anarchist who spoke to Liberty from the roof?" He considered trying to locate that video.

Sid looked at him. "Want me to bring it up?"

Supero glared. Had Sid, the roofer, really picked up how to operate the computer console and use the search commands in such a short time?

The chief leaned back and bounced in the ergonomic chair. "What're you talking about?" His upper lip curled on one side.

"I am talking about the image you showed me during Liberty's psychiatric evaluation, the reflection in the window of the Unity Trooper's area car."

"Oh." His expression evened out and he turned away. "No, our recognition software still can't find a match for that kid. It's strange. Like he doesn't live anywhere, work anywhere, go anywhere. His face hasn't turned up on video from any other security camera. And we couldn't get a composite of his body structure, the way he was crouched like that. Sometimes you don't need the face, just the body structure. It's not as reliable but . . . No, he's too careful."

"If you are not referring to him, please, Chief Varden, explain." Supero found his jaw tightening. "You said *them*. You found them."

"The *them* I'm talking about are the anarchists. Your girl is not the only one who's gone missing. For years now, these, these insurgents have slipped from our grasp, disappeared one by one. The same week your girl ran so did two more that I know of. At first, I blamed the inefficiency of the Unity Troopers." He grinned and nodded as if he thought Supero would agree with that assessment. Supero only flinched. "But I've always suspected these guys meet up somewhere, that they live in a secret community, somehow remaining undetected by the Regimen."

Sid leaned toward Varden and spoke low, almost whispered, "You think Liberty's living in a secret community? Where? Why?" Desperation seeped out in his tone. If given the location, he would probably steal a scooter and fetch her himself.

Supero shook his head at Sid then said to Varden, "How is that possible? They need things. They need food, clean water, medicine. Are they animals and thieves?"

Mug to his mouth, Varden shrugged. He leaned between Sid and Supero and set the mug on the glassy control panel, directly over a search control icon. "Maybe. I'm sure they have many methods. Trading, stealing, growing their own. A few have surfaced, trying to use their ID implants to make purchases."

"How foolish. Is that how you caught them?"

"Caught them? We haven't caught them yet," he said.

Supero's temper spiked. "You said—"

"I said I *think* we found them. We've found clues that have led us some distance from Aldonia. Can't figure how they get across boundaries, yet. They can't go under. We'd detect it with the underground sensors. So maybe they go over. But that seems unlikely. It'd be too obvious. Maybe they have connections we don't know about. In fact, I'm certain they have connections within the Regimen. A person would need inside help to get so far."

Supero turned his chair to face Chief Varden and leaned in. He did nothing to hide the irritation in his tone or on his face. "You are telling me everything but what I want to know. You say you *think* you have found them. Where do you *think* they are?"

Varden's eyes held a distant look. "Too far to run. We believe they obtain transportation from someone. Has to be someone within the Regimen." He leaned forward and rested his chin on templed fingers. "We need to maximize the investigation of our own people, of Regimen workers." He made a sideways glance in either direction.

Supero shoved the mug from the control panel, coffee sloshing out, Varden and Sid jumping to their feet. "You have not answered me." He shouted, "Where. Are they?"

Chief Varden glared, wiping his pants. Then he exchanged a look with Sid and snickered. Did he take nothing seriously? "Clues lead us to Jensenville. They keep to their disguises when mobile, but we've customized our software to identify other characteristics. Takes a little more time but . . . We've found a larger concentration of unidentifiables in Jensenville."

"Jensenville? How far is Jensenville?" He turned to the map on the monitor but couldn't make sense of it. Hadn't he heard things about the inefficiency of the Jensenville Unity Troopers? They let weapons slip into the hands of citizens. It took months to reacquire them and more time to catch the offenders. According to rumor, they failed to find more than a few weapons. "I hope you are not relying on their people, the Jensenville Unity Troopers, to make the bust."

"Fear not, my purple-eyed doctor. I have two teams on their way, Unity Troopers and Citizen Safety. I'll keep you updated." Chief Varden dropped his gaze to the spilled liquid. "You'd better get this mess cleaned up. We run a tight ship."

~~~
~~~

Jessen lay on her back with her lanky limbs outstretched, gazing at the clear blue sky. The grass under and all around her grew in soft round clumps, round like her belly. She sat up as I neared, smiled in a way that made me feel special, and motioned for me to join her on the grassy slope beside the Dining Hall. "I'm glad you agreed to meet me," she said. "We never have a chance to talk." She drew her knees up and hugged them.

I sat cross-legged in the cool grass. "Yeah, every time I see you, I wonder how you're doing. How do you like your sponsor family?" I figured Jessen was placed with the pregnant couple so she could help but also so she could know what to expect when her time came.

"Oh, the Cruzes? I love them. They're so nice to me and so sweet to each other." Her gaze shifted in a way that spoke of trouble.

"Is something wrong?"

Her expression lightened. She laughed. "No, I'm fine. How have you been? I've seen you at the CAT cave. Though, never on a Sunday."

Everyone called the cave the CAT cave, though it housed much more than just the Communication and Advanced Technology center. The natural "doorway" opened to a narrow passageway which led to a dark, quiet room with a polished stone floor, a small table flanked with tall candlesticks, and a single candle perpetually burning on the far wall. They called the room a chapel. Anyone who came into the cave had to pass through it.

"I like going," she said. "Somewhere deep inside me, I understand. I believe."

My sponsor family always invited me, but I wasn't ready to join them in "worship." The whole concept was foreign to me, even scared me a bit. What did their priests do, exactly? How could these people so readily believe in an invisible God? What proof did they have? How could Jessen believe? Her newfound faith made her seem weaker to me now.

"I'm helping with the new cave door," I said. "We've widened the doorway and plan to make a door that blends in with the surroundings and gives security."

Her eyes twinkled, maybe at the abrupt change of subject. "Oh, that's a good idea. So you're good at that stuff, huh?"

I shrugged, but I felt proud of my skills. The door was my design, and the guys I worked with respected that. I had repaired everything from doors to engines, often designing little replacement parts, but I had never designed something so big. It would work. I was sure of it. And if the stonecutters were as good as they boasted, it would be imperceptible from the outside.

Jessen gazed into the distance. I did too. We sat in silence. Three women strolled toward the Dining Hall. A warm breeze rustled the leaves of the nearby trees. A sprinkling of leaves had turned yellow and orange. Fall had begun.

I sighed. I had loved walking aimlessly in the fall, down streets and alleys I had never taken before. Sadness hung in the air, on the breezes, but hope, too.

"I don't know," Jessen said and shut her mouth.

"You don't know what?"

"I can't stop thinking about what I've done." She slipped her hand into her sweater and rubbed her belly, an act of habit by now. "Was I just being selfish in getting pregnant? What if something goes wrong? It's so primitive out here. So much dirt and chance. Nothing feels predictable or sterile."

"You'll be fine." She had probably heard, as I had, about a woman in one of the colonies who had died giving birth. Of course, she was worried. I would be, too.

"It's not me I'm worried about, exactly." Her eyes went wide as if a thought just occurred to her. "Have you seen that strange, shaggy man who wanders from place to place? Is he thirty-something? Forty? I don't know what's wrong with him, but he's off." She tapped her temple. "If his odd speech and strange behavior doesn't tip you off, you can see it in his eyes. And people don't seem to notice." Her voice rose and her arm flew out in a sweeping gesture. "They let him in their homes, eat lunch with him, give him things. I don't know where he sleeps."

I knew of the man. I saw him last week, the day Dedrick returned from another rescue mission in Aldonia. Dedrick had been gone for a month and a half. I strolled alone by the fishing stream, trying to keep anxious thoughts from my mind. When I came to a tree with a particularly wide trunk, I sat down to think and rest in its shade. Something rustled above me. Before I could tilt my head, Dedrick dropped to the ground, landing a few meters away.

I jumped up and wanted to throw my arms around him but caught myself halfway to him. "You're back." I folded my arms behind me, then in front of me, and then dropped them to my sides.

He smiled and strolled toward the river. "How you doing? You liking it here in the free world?" He stooped for a rock.

"Sure. I love it here. I was starting to wonder, though, if you were coming back. You've been gone for weeks. I can't imagine a rescue taking that long. Thought maybe you decided to stay in Aldonia."

He whipped the rock, and it skipped a few times on the surface of the water. I imagined he taught himself to do that in his carefree childhood. "Still don't trust me, huh?"

"Trust you? I don't know. I was just concerned. You're not invincible, are you?"

"Sometimes I wonder. I've been in a lot of tight places, but I always come out unscathed." He gave me a subtle glance. The arrogance of the comment didn't fit his humble personality.

"I think you're just trying to get my goat."

He turned to face me and put a hand on his hip. "Get your goat? Now that's the second time I've heard you say that. Do you know where the saying comes from? Do you even know what a goat is?"

"Of course I do." I didn't know where the saying came from, but everyone knew what a goat was.

"Of course?" He skipped two more rocks. "There aren't any farms in Aldonia. Woodrow, yes. Lierreland, sure. But not Aldonia. They don't even have a zoo. I bet you've never seen a goat in your life."

I picked up a rock and tried to throw it the way he did. It plunked down to the bottom of the stream. "I've seen a goat. I've seen every known animal. Our databases are enormous." I folded my arms.

He laughed. "I'll show you a goat one day. I know who—"

A twig snapped. We both looked. A lean man in an oversized jacket staggered toward us. He had a grizzly beard and a tangle of greasy hair.

My body tensed, and I glanced around for a thick stick.

Dedrick strode toward the man and opened his arms. "Hey, Buddy." The two of them hugged and then spoke to each other, Dedrick's voice a low rumble, Buddy's voice loud but slurred so that I couldn't understand him. Dedrick took something from his back pocket and stuffed it into the man's hand. After a few more words, Buddy backed away, saying, "Thanks, Dedrick, thanks, man."

"If we're talking about the same man," I said to Jessen, "they call him Buddy. And people must not consider him a danger. He's just different."

Jessen shook her head. "But what's wrong with him? You know? And I met this girl, a young woman, really. Everyone calls her Sissy. She has the mind of a child. And she can't always control her body, her arms and legs. She can't even hold her head right sometimes. I think she has cerebral palsy. Do you know what that is?"

I shook my head. The scientists and doctors of Aldonia eradicated such conditions by gene alterations or embryo destruction. We learned about them in Secondary, but we sped through the subject. The only point they wanted us to retain was the good the Regimen had done for humanity.

"Well, I can't imagine someone having to live like that," Jessen said. "She sees what everyone else can do. How can she be happy?"

"But people care about her, don't they?"

"Well, yes."

"We need to stop thinking life has to be perfect to be worth living. We can be imperfect and still be happy, still be able to love and be loved. Especially by your family."

A crooked grinned grew on her face. "Are *you* in love?"

"What?" A wave of heat washed over me as if she had just exposed my secret. "I just meant, it's okay if your baby isn't perfect. Will you love her any less?"

"But what about my baby's happiness?"

"Does Sissy seem unhappy?"

Jessen shrugged. "I guess not, but—"

"But nothing." I took her hand. "I've learned from these people that no one is unwanted. We can be happy even with our imperfections." I wanted so much to convince her, but I had the distinct and growing impression that one from our group would give up on life in the colony.

"*Happy with our imperfections,* says the girl chosen to be a breeder."

We both laughed. The Regimen had a stringent procedure for selecting breeders.

Jessen's gaze drifted and then locked onto a particular point in the distance. Her laughter ceased and her eyes held a curious gleam. "Is he coming for you?"

A group of women stood in a circle outside the Dining Hall. Five teens hung out under a tree. A man walked alone, apparently headed for us. The casual, self-possessed way he carried himself gave his identity away. Dedrick.

"Coming for me? You mean, for us. He's your friend, too. Maybe he wants to see how we're doing." But maybe he was coming for me. I had seen him every day since he got back, never planned visits, just bumping into each other. I thought.

"I think he likes you. It's different here when a guy or a girl likes someone. They don't leer and make advances. You have to pay attention to nuances."

I laughed. "What? No, Dedrick's just a friend. He's coming to see both of us."

"Maybe we should find out." Jessen grabbed my shoulder and awkwardly got to her feet, an impish grin on her face. "You stay here. I'm going inside."

"No. Wait until he gets here. He'll think you're rude if you—"

Jessen bounced across the clumpy grass, toward the Dining Hall. She waved at Dedrick.

He nodded. He lifted a hand. But he didn't change direction. He walked toward me.

My heart thumped madly as he approached. Had our meetings been random or intentional?

He stopped an arm's length away and looked down at me through sullen brown eyes. "Hey."

"Hi."

"You two having a secret meeting?"

My mouth fell open. He didn't trust me? "A secret—"

He smiled.

~~~

Dedrick and I stood side by side, leaning our arms on a rough wooden fence. I peered into the narrow, rectangular pupils of the goat that stood just inside the fence on a tree stump directly in front of me. Three goats stared at us from the open doorway of a rugged barn. Twenty or so more goats stood around or wandered through the grass inside the fenced area, some seeming to prefer the shade, others the sunny spots.

Although I had seen them on monitors at school, I never realized how very strange, even disturbing, a goat's eyes were. This goat had yellowish eyes with brown around the outer edges. It gazed at me without blinking as if it thought we could communicate telepathically. What did the world look like to them, peering through their odd little pupils?

What did Dedrick think about them?

Dedrick had the hint of a smile as he watched a goat in the distance. The sunlight on his face made his thick eyelashes glow and played on his brown irises, drawing my attention. Eyes had always interested me. There were so many shades of blue, gray, gold, and green. But brown . . .

Dedrick caught me staring. "You aren't comparing my eyes to his." He squinted. "Are you?"

A laugh escaped me. I dropped my head and my hair fell in my face. It took a second to regain control. I lifted my head with a straight expression and tucked my hair behind my ear. "I'm sorry. It's your eyes. They're brown."

He cracked a smile. "Yeah. Everyone in my family has brown eyes. Or didn't you notice? " He squinted again. "Most people naturally have brown eyes."

"No, they don't. I'd never seen brown eyes until I met you."

His jaw twitched. I couldn't tell if he was amused or insulted. "Well, not in Aldonia. They do strange things with DNA, I guess, keep people from having brown eyes and other things."
~~~

"Oh. I never thought about that. I mean, I know they've done things to improve the quality of life, but eliminating brown eyes?"

"I wonder what they have against brown eyes." He leaned toward me with his brown eyes glittering in the sunlight and locked on mine.

An electrical current flowed from him to me, drawing me like a magnet. I couldn't resist. I dove and planted a kiss on his lips.

He pulled away and opened his mouth, shock written on his face.

I shrunk back, mortified. "I-I'm sorry." My face burned. I glanced at the ground, the fence, the yellow-eyed goat, the barn. What had possessed me to do that?

"No, I'm sorry." Dedrick brushed his fingertips against my arm and turned away as if looking to see who saw. No one else was out here. He faced me again. "I shouldn't spend so much time with you, alone." He stuck his thumbs in the front pockets of his camouflage pants and tapped the ground with the toe of his dusty black boot. "I don't mean to lead you on. You know, I . . ."

Not able to face him, I leaned against the fence and stared at the goat. "I know. You probably have a girlfriend. I should've expected—"

"No, I don't have a girlfriend. It's not that."

I glanced at him. He liked guys? I couldn't picture it. His deep voice, masculine mannerisms, manly walk . . . No. He had all the characteristics of a straight guy. "You . . . have a . . . boyfriend?"

He cracked a smile. "No. We're not like that here. We stick to natural ways."

"Oh." The reason for his rejection hit me, and I felt stupid. He just wasn't attracted to me. "Well, I have to go." I jabbed my thumb over my shoulder, spun around, and took a step. Was I even headed in the right direction? "I've got things I—"

"No, wait." He grabbed my arm and tugged.

I turned to face him.

He slid his hand down my arm and into my hand. "Let me explain something." Sunlight bounced off his brown irises as he glanced at the sky. "I made a vow."

"A vow?"

"When we near adulthood . . ." He squeezed my hand in an absentminded fashion. ". . . we're given the chance to see the world of the Regimen. We go in groups, sneak into the cities and explore. Some of us, after experiencing this, feel called to help."

"Help?"

"Yeah, help extract those who reject the ways of the Regimen, those who can't fit in, those the Regimen rejects. Some of us make commitments. We take vows. We are the Mosheh." He locked his sparkling eyes on mine. "I won't seek a wife until my service ends."

"A wife?" My face warmed. He still hadn't let go of my hand. "Husband and wife, like the parents in all these families?"

He smiled as if my naivety amused him. "Exactly like that." He swung our clasped hands. "I want to start a family someday, be a husband, a father."

The concept appealed to me deeply. It stirred my innermost being in a way similar to the stirrings of *My Friend*. I wanted a family. I wanted that exclusive love. One man, one woman, and children as the fruit of their love. Could I have that?

"Do you think that one day, even though I'm not like you guys, even though I'm from Aldonia . . ." I couldn't word my question. I felt, somehow, like damaged goods. I hadn't grown up learning about virtue and faithfulness. I hadn't grown up with parents to show me right from wrong, parents to love and guide me. I still had much to learn.

Dedrick released my hand and leaned in. He pressed his warm lips to my forehead, kissed me, and looked me in the eye. "Yeah. You'll make some man a great wife. But you'll need to learn to trust him."

17

An early fall wind stirred the leaves, making a white noise that reminded me of evening traffic as it had sounded from inside my apartment in Aldonia. Nadie's wind chime tinkled sweet musical notes. Her brother had made the wind chime and couldn't wait until her birthday to give it to her, though it was only one day away.

I felt like him tonight. I couldn't wait to get to work tomorrow, to finish what we had started.

Moonlight streamed in between half-drawn curtains and illuminated Nadie, asleep in her bed. She lay flat on her back, her mouth hanging open. She breathed loudly, almost snored, reminding me of Finley when he stayed the night with Tatum after indulging in a late dinner of rich illegally-obtained foods. The awful noise had always traveled right through my door. Granted, the doors in our apartment in Aldonia were thin, but it sure made it hard to fall asleep.

I rolled over, yawned, and closed my eyes. The mattress had no give. My shoulder and hipbone complained, so I shifted a bit, but I could have found more comfort in a sleeping bag on the hard ground. I rolled onto my back and took a deep breath. I needed rest for tomorrow. We planned to finish the door to the CAT cave, and I wanted it to be perfect.

An image of the boulder we selected for the door came to mind. Little hardy plants grew in crevices on one side of it. *Please, don't let the stonecutters destroy them.* They would add to the natural appearance, keep a stranger from looking at the rock twice. We couldn't have found a more suitably sized and shaped chunk of rock. The stonecutters needed only to slice off the face of it for us. It seemed like an impossible feat to me, but they said, "No problem. We'll have it for you in a week."

Tomorrow. I couldn't wait. If only my eyes would stay shut and my thoughts would cease.

We had chiseled grooves in the floor and in the stone above the doorway. After a few hours of making adjustments, we fitted steel tracks into the grooves. I had designed the guides for the door. Rick, a forty-year-old machinist, made them a reality. The stonecutters needed to make slots in the rock once they got it cut to size. We'd given them detailed drawings. We went over the measurements at least twenty times. Everything should work just fine.

It wouldn't be the easiest door to slide shut. But in an emergency, it would shut, lock, and be both immovable and invisible from the outside. It would be enough.

The room had grown silent except for the tinkling of the wind chime. No heavy breathing?

I lifted my head to check on Nadie. She hadn't moved. I threw back the blankets and sat up. Was she breathing? I tiptoed across the room. Her little body could've been made of stone; she lay so still. I reached for her shoulder.

Nadie inhaled.

I jumped back with a chuckle. Why was I worried? I just needed sleep. Maybe a drink of water would help.

I tiptoed from the room and down the steps. Halfway down the steps, I stopped.

Whispers came to my ears. Quiet voices in the dark. People in Aldonia often spoke in whispers. Things a person wanted to keep private, he kept to himself or spoke of in whispers. Drug deals, illegal trades, even ideas. Silver and Sid scheming. I had often whispered to arrange a trade, to get payment for my repair services. You never knew how or when the Regimen listened.

I crept down the steps and toward the kitchen, my ears straining to pick up the words. Why the paranoia? My sponsor family, everyone in the Maxwell Colony, had been kind, open, and worthy of trust.

"Sometimes I lose track of where I am." Grandma Shenny's tired voice came from her little corner of the house.

"It's okay." Mrs. Shenoy had a cheerful ring to her voice. "No one can knit cables like you. Take a rest. Let me work on it for a while."

"I do hope we get done in time."

"We will. It's turning out beautifully. Nadie will love it."

Tomorrow was Nadie's birthday. Mrs. Shenoy was helping Grandma finish her gift. My heart warmed at her act of kindness.

I slipped into the kitchen and poured a glass of water. As I brought the glass to my mouth, my eyes welled with tears. My heart ached. I set the glass down and let the tears escape. The sacrifices family members made for one another moved me deeply. I wanted that. How could I ever have it? I had no mother, no father, no brothers or sisters. These people treated me like one of them, but I wasn't one of them. I was a foreigner from a different world. I would never have what they had, someone to call my own.

I wiped my cheeks, downed the water, and slipped back upstairs. Nadie's breathing had quieted and my eyes had grown heavy. Tomorrow was Nadie's birthday. I intended to give her a placemat I had made out of dyed straw. One of the teens in morning class taught me the basics of weaving. Nadie would like it. Anything anyone did for her seemed to make her immeasurably happy.

I took a deep breath and closed my eyes. An image of Abby flashed in my mind. I clasped the coin I wore around my neck, the parting gift she had given me. Abby meant something to me. She was my friend. Maybe we had something more than friendship; maybe we had been more like family.

"Oh, Abby," I whispered through fresh tears, my heart breaking in my chest. "How could I have left you behind?"

~~~

"We'll finish tomorrow, Liberty. We're not in that big of a rush, are we? Besides, it's Sunday. We can't work today." Mark, who I had only ever seen in jeans and a t-shirt, wore a button-front shirt and dark pants. His wavy hair was greased back, out of his face for a change, and he had a clean shave. He reminded me of a high-ranking Regimen employee.
~~~

I wore the camouflage pants I had traveled here in. I wore them often, even though they had given me other clothes, including a few skirts and a dress.

We stood outside the cave entrance. More and more people walked past us, perhaps everyone in the colony, filing into the cave. Women and girls wore dresses. Men and boys wore dark jackets, or at least clean shirts.

The new cave door leaned against a boulder. I couldn't take my eyes off it. It was perfect: one side smooth and clean, the other rough and natural with the hardy, little plants intact. We really had to wait until tomorrow?

"You could always join us." Mark gave me a weak smile, probably certain I'd say "no" like I had every other Sunday.

I didn't bother answering. Disappointment held my tongue. I leaned back against the clean doorframe we had made and gazed at the new stone door. How many people would it take to move it into place? What had the stonecutters used to haul it here? It wouldn't be easy maneuvering it over the stony path outside the cave entrance.

Long ago, a waterfall cascaded over the entrance and the path was a riverbed. The original colonists had redirected the falls to gain easy access to the cave. In an emergency, everyone would seek refuge in the cave and they would return the river to its normal route, the waterfall hiding the entrance. With the cave door in place, the hideout would be undetectable. I was glad to be a part of this safety measure. If only I didn't have to wait—

Melodic voices resonated in the cave and carried through the passageway. The beautiful and strange sound spoke to me. Part of me wanted to believe in a power outside myself, in something greater than any man-made government. But I couldn't focus on that now. This new way of life overwhelmed me.

My thoughts rose to the treetops, to leaves golden and orange, to the sky so wide and pure, to memories of laughter and of serving at the Senior Center. And to Abby.

The song ceased and a man spoke, one of the priests, I assumed—probably the one with the hat—but I couldn't make out the words. His deep, strong voice rose and fell with its own melody. Light from the oil lamps and candles inside bounced on the walls of the narrow passageway.

I did not intend to join them, but I stepped into the passageway to hear the message, to see if the priest would speak words meant to control, words to make people feel guilty about personal choices.

". . . some have made nature their god. They do all they can to protect it, even to the point of cornering mankind into small, miserable pockets of existence. Mankind is the enemy to them. So creation has been kept from mankind. They use unnatural techniques to keep the population low and as a result have destroyed the family. Through the destruction of the family, they have been robbed of a natural understanding of God as Father."

"But God made man in His image. And this, all this he has given to us. He commanded us to subdue the earth, to be fruitful and multiply. Our Lord loves life. He does not want it stifled . . ."

His words struck a chord in me. My heart burned. *My Friend* made His presence known with a wave so strong I shuddered. I turned all my attention to Him. He had tried to tell me this at the river. This was the message He had for me. The earth belonged to all of us, a gift. But we had the greater value.

~~~

"Liberty, are you alright?"

Dedrick squatted before me, gazing at me through worried eyes. Voices surrounded us. People strolled from the cave. Children chanted and raced each other down the rocky trail. A woman shouted, "Reggie, watch out! You'll split your knee open again." Her voice reminded me of Abby's.

I sat on the hard ground, my back against granite. My neck hurt. How long had I been out?

Dedrick grabbed my arm and helped me up. He looked me over, his brown eyes troubled with concern.

"I'm fine." I brushed the seat of my pants. "I guess I dozed off while you guys were . . ."
~~~

"Praying." Dedrick looked good in slate gray and black, all clean and pressed with his hair combed down—still blond but with deep brown roots.

I hadn't seen him dressed up before. I preferred his rugged image, but I couldn't stop taking him in. "Yeah, praying."

"You should've joined us." He gave the hint of a smile and nodded for me to walk with him.

"Maybe someday." We strolled away from the cave entrance, down the rocky path that once was a riverbed. How could I word the question I had for him? Would he take it as me giving up on colony life?

We reached the bottom of the slope. People stood in clusters, talking. Others headed for the Dining Hall. They prepared a big breakfast on Sundays. Everyone spoke of it, but I had yet to partake. I usually spent the morning at home, enjoying the emptiness of the house.

"You wanna get breakfast?"

My cheeks warmed as if he had just asked me out, though I knew he was only being polite. "I need to ask you something."

"Okay."

"I left a friend behind, an old woman. I feel guilty. I mean . . . is there any way she can be rescued?"

Dedrick's eye twitched. He glanced at a family strolling past us. "Well, no, or I don't know." He inhaled through his mouth and glanced at his boots, his worn black hiking boots that didn't match his outfit at all. His eyes met mine. "The Mosheh decides who they can trust. I've never asked for a particular person—"

"You're one of them." My temperature spiked. I worked to keep a level tone. "You're part of the Mosheh."

"Yeah, but . . ." He pressed his lips together and glanced away. Returning his gaze, he said, "The Mosheh help as many as they can, but they can't save just anyone one wants, not without jeopardizing others. Besides, an old woman wouldn't make it safely through the Boundary Fence. She'd have to live in the underground communities."

"I can't leave her there. I think I'd rather suffer with her than abandon her like this."

His expression changed to pity or admiration, I couldn't tell. He reached for my arm but I pulled away. I wanted neither pity nor admiration — I wanted his help. How could I save her alone? "You said we should ask for help when we need it. Well, I need it now."

He frowned. "She may be under consideration for rescue. I don't know. I don't get that information. But there's nothing I can do about it anyway." He clenched his jaw and glanced in the direction of the Dining Hall. Done. That's all he had to say about it. *Nothing he can do about it. Let's go eat breakfast.*

"We can talk to the rest of the Mosheh. She's like family to me. I've seen how you people help each other. How you sacrifice for one another. I've seen you, Dedrick, risk yourself for enemies."

He shook his head. "It's one thing to put yourself in danger. I can't put the colonies in danger. I can't put the Mosheh's entire operation in danger for one person. If she's on the list, she'll be rescued." He turned away. "I'm going to eat."

I watched him stride away then sprinted after him. "That's not fair. Who gets to decide? Can't you get her on the list?"

He stopped and faced me. "It doesn't work that way. Are you coming to eat or not?"

"I'm not hungry."

He nodded and walked away.

"Wow." The voice came from behind a tree. Bot slid into view, a coy grin on his face. He was also dressed up. Was I the only one who didn't join in the worship?

Bot sauntered to me. "What're you so fired up about? I thought you and Dedrick were, uh, friends." He gave me the once-over through his mottled blue eyes, showing he thought my relationship with Dedrick was other than platonic.

I shook my head, not interested in talking to him, of all people. You could take Bot out of Aldonia, but you couldn't get Aldonia's influence out of Bot. "It's not like that between us. People are different here. Or haven't you noticed?" I stomped past him, into a line of trees, and leaned against a smooth tree trunk.

"Yeah, I've noticed. Takes some getting used to. Hard to get a girlfriend." He sighed. "So what's the matter? You want to talk?" He grabbed an overhead branch. His face held a peaceful look that I hadn't seen on him before. Nothing remained of the anxious flitting glances and twitches of the night we busted through the Boundary Fence.

"Don't you have anyone you care about in Aldonia? Anyone you left behind?"

He shrugged. "I had friends."

"You're satisfied living without them, leaving them there?" Even as I asked, I understood his lack of connection to them. The Regimen designed it so that we transitioned through stages of life with our peers rather than with a family. Any bonds we developed were ripped apart with each transition. We learned to survive as individuals, dependent on no one except the Regimen.

He stared into the distance, squinting thoughtfully. "Things need to change in Aldonia. The government needs to be overthrown. The people need a voice. The power should be in the hands of the people. But, you know, I can't think of anyone who would jump at the chance to leave that place and forfeit the handouts they get. I can't think of anyone who would want to trade Aldonia for colony life. Can you?"

Speechless, I huffed. Did he really feel that way?

He took a long deep breath, his eyes closing briefly. "No. People need to know what they're missing first. They're so wrapped up in themselves that they don't get it. They can't imagine what it could be like, what it *should* be like. They ache inside. They're miserable and lonely. But if you let them choose, I think they'd take the easy way the Regimen offers. Freedom doesn't matter to them."

"But it should."

"Yeah. A seed needs planted. They need to know there's something more. They need a taste. They need to long for it the way you and I did. They need a reason to fight for freedom. If members of the Unity Troopers or even the Citizen Safety Station could be reached . . ." He said nothing for a while. Then he looked at me. "So, who'd you leave behind?"

"Her name is Abby, and she's like family to me. I'm going back for her."

"You're what!"

"I don't know how, yet. But I know I am." I made the commitment to myself, right then. Come what may, I was going back for her.

He stared at me, the colors in his mottled blue eyes seeming to shift and intensify. "If you're looking for me to go with you, I won't. I guess I'm beginning to put something together, an idea that makes sense somewhere in here." He pointed to his chest. "But I can help you. You want to help someone else? You're willing to risk your safety and happiness to do it? I'm not there yet. But I respect that. I see that a lot of that, uh, love, in the colony. I want to have that."

~~~

"Hey, Supero." Across the central surveillance control room, a wiry boy in his twenties—was Kess his name?—waved a hand in the air. He seemed to think it acceptable to address a doctor without using his title. He was wrong.

Dr. Supero returned his gaze to the images he and Sid had isolated earlier in the day. While filtering live feeds from Aldonia and surrounding cities, they had discovered a number of figures wearing the mottled cape and shades, near the border of Aldonia and Jensenville. The wiry boy had manipulated the search engine to pick up the particular pattern of the cape. It was Supero's idea and it worked. After seeing high numbers of these caped figures, he decided they were the Mosheh Liberty had written about. And Dedrick was one of them.

"Supero, hey, Supero."

"Kess is calling you," Sid said, taking his eyes off his job. "Maybe he found something."

"I do not answer to Supero. I am *Doctor* Supero." Dr. Supero set his jaw. "The younger generation has no respect for their wiser, more experienced, highly-educated elders. They need to strengthen the curriculum at Secondary, find ways to develop the students' respect for wise and influential citizens before they are released into the world."

Sid snickered under his breath then hollered at Kess, "What'd you find?"

"I'll send the image to your station. It's that kid, I think. What do you call him? Dedrick?"
~~~

A new image popped onto one of the monitors. Against the backdrop of an old brick building, Liberty stood by a tall bush, looking at something. She seemed to be talking.

"So, what is this? She's alone." Supero glanced as Kess weaved past workstations and came to theirs.

"She's not alone. Watch," Kess said, leaning an arm on Sid's shoulder.

A hooded figure stepped out of the bushes, directly in front of Liberty. He had something or took something from her. She grabbed his wrist, and they struggled over the object. Then he spoke and darted around the corner of the building. After glancing around, she followed him. The video ended.

"That is it? There is nothing to it. His face is not even visible."

"Sure it is." Kess hunched over Sid's work area and moved his hands over the control panel. The video replayed and zoomed in to the hooded figure's face. Kess froze the image. The hood hid the eyes, but the nose and mouth showed clearly.

Sid jerked back in his chair. "Yeah, that's him." As Kess straightened, Sid took over the control panel. The image Kess gave them shifted to one side of the screen and a second image came up beside it, the image of Dedrick on the rooftop.

Dr. Supero leaned forward to examine the two. The mouth, the nose, the shape of the jaw . . . it was him. "Where is this? When did this happen?"

"Date and location is on the bottom of the image," Kess said. He returned to his station.

"Now that we are certain of Dedrick's face," Supero hollered to the wiry boy, irritated that he had left so soon, "get your software to isolate him from the other unidentifiable figures."

Kess nodded. "On it."

"I don't know why you think his name is Dedrick," Sid said. "The name isn't on the list of people she's communicated with in the past six months."

"The list Chief Varden compiled?" Supero snorted. "Chief Varden does not hold my confidence. The Chief of CSS successfully uncovers a community of miscreants in Jensenville. Hooray for him. They are the rejects of society, not content with the base pursuits the Regimen permits—or those they overlook—but who desire to go lower. And though they are lowlifes, they found a way to block the reading of their implants and have remained untouched for years by Regimen security."

"Wonder how they did that?" The look in Sid's eye showed more than mild curiosity. The idea of being off the Regimen's radar must have appealed to him.

"Something about the material of the roof of their hideout and the material of their gloves, I suppose. The point is: our chief cannot keep track of one girl here in Aldonia."

"Who's to say Liberty isn't in Jensenville?" Varden shouted from his huddle with two workers on the far side of the room, the dark-eyed girl and a redheaded boy. "That's where the clues led."

"That is where you were *mis*led."

Varden strutted across the room, toward Dr. Supero, a cocky grin on his strong-jawed, freckled face. "What do you know, Supero? What're you even doing here? Don't you have patients to see? Studies to conduct? Genes or DNA, or whatever, to manipulate in some unnatural way?"

Supero stood as Varden neared him. "After observing your team at work, I see that I am more needed here." Fortunately, he had been able to get away with working two days at the medical facility by passing his duties off to others. For the sake of Aldonia, he would spend his time and energy here until Liberty came to justice.

Ivy had been most helpful. She had even started to worry about him. "Are you breaking for meals?" she'd asked him earlier, looking him over. Dr. Supero could not identify the look in her eyes. It could've been attraction, but it may have been disgust. Perhaps she knew about the tumor and pitied him. Would she have pried into his locked, personal messages?

"You could have dinner with me," he had told her, taking in her gaudy outfit—a loose black and white dress with slits in the sides that revealed a pink top—as if it pleased him, "and make sure I am eating right. We could review the daily duties together. You could tell me if I am slacking at any of mine."

She had laughed, her green eyes sparkling. "You're slacking at all of them."

"I am, but I have a reason."

She'd sighed and dipped her head, blonde and green-streaked strands falling over her face. "I know. You're obsessed with that girl." She spoke through her hair and crossed her legs, drawing attention to her shapely leg and . . . her shoes!

Dr. Supero's heart had nearly stopped. She wore sleek black heels. They were nothing like the hideous styles she typically wore. He'd never seen her in such attractive shoes. She must have worn them for him. She liked him.

He reached for her hair, wanting to brush it from her face, but hesitated. "I am not obsessed with—"

She touched him, placed her hand on his arm for a split second, looked into his eyes. "You are. But I don't care. We can have dinner. You can tell me when you want your appointments set, the ones for you, the ones with the specialists. Remember?"

Supero's mouth fell open. She agreed to dinner?

"Physicians' lounge, then?"

"Physicians' . . . Yes." If Ivy had had reservations about him because of rumors concerning his past assistant, she had them no more. He had her now.

"What time?" she wanted to know.

"Hey." Varden's vulgar voice ripped through the air and snapped Supero back to the moment. "When you're done daydreaming about me . . ."

Supero's face heated. A cuss word slipped from his mouth. "Do you have an update for me? Or are you still wasting your time on security cameras?"

"Wasting time? Ha! We've discovered a pattern, a very complicated pattern that appears random." He bounced on his toes, lifted his chin, and stood hands on hips.

"You have discovered a pattern. Now what? What does that do for us? Liberty is gone, living somewhere else. You will not see her image again on your security cameras."

"Oh yeah? You think you'll find her by finding that, that Dedrick. You won't find him. Those anarchists know how to avoid surveillance. And that's how we're going to find them. We need to break the pattern of the surveillance cameras, when they go off, when they go on. That's when we'll see them, bring those rats to the light."

"You believe there is a pattern. Who is responsible for that? Perhaps your efforts would be better spent searching neighboring cities. Have you no one tracking suspects on the ground? Or have you no suspects?"

Chief Varden grimaced. "Supero, we have more going on than you could possibly understand. I don't tell you every detail. You don't need to know. But we're going to get them. And it'll be through the surveillance cameras."

"Perhaps you should question Finley again. He seems to have a way of avoiding working cameras. Maybe he knows more than he let on. Maybe he can lead you to someone else."

"Did that. We interviewed him again. Got us nowhere. The kid acts like we're on him about not working hard enough. Doesn't seem to understand we're accusing him of trading information, of working for the anarchists." Varden glanced over his shoulder, grabbed Supero by the arm and whispered, "Listen, too many people are in this operation. We can't trust everyone."

"I thought you investigated the CSS staff already," Supero whispered and then glanced around to see who watched them. No one did.

"We have and we're not done. But . . ." In a lower voice he said, "We need to go dark."

~~~

To My Dear Family,

This letter is hard to write. I don't want you to misunderstand my actions. I appreciate the sacrifices you have made in making me a part of your family. Your kindness and generosity to me, to each other, has taught me so much. Your way of life, here in the colony, feels so natural and good. Everyone is appreciated. No one is a burden. I want that. I want it for everyone in the world.
~~~

Because of your example and my experience here, I am a different person than when we first met. I have come to realize there is something I must do, a sacrifice I must make. As you gather on Sunday to worship your Creator, remember me. I hope that what I do does not hurt anyone. Thank you for everything.

Your newest daughter,

Liberty

I placed the letter on the dinner table, near the tree trunk that grew through the center, under the light from the sole candle that burned in the dark house. Mrs. Shenoy called it a nightlight and made sure to light it before she went to bed. "In case one of you children should need a sip of water at night."

Light from the flame reflected on a shiny pot on the stove and on the polished woodwork of the chairs and cabinets handcrafted with love by Mr. Shenoy. The rest of the house remained in darkness, but I pictured every cozy detail in my mind, the pictures of family members and paintings on the walls, the decorations on every shelf and in every corner, the neat rows of glass jars in the pantry.

Nadie's wind chime tinkled for an instant, though the wind hardly blew tonight.

I took a deep breath, my heart warming at the savory scents still lingering from the dinner I helped Mrs. Shenoy prepare. Then I tiptoed to the door.

The night air chilled my neck as I stepped outside, though it was warm for September. The nights would grow colder soon, maybe even on my trip back to Aldonia. I tugged the door shut and stepped to the bush where I had hidden my backpack. Squatting, I unzipped the bag and made a quick check: tent, pillow, blanket, flashlight, voltage tester, lighter, bread, fruit, dried meat, and a few other necessary supplies. My map and a water bottle I had put in outer pockets. I hoped I hadn't forgotten anything, but I could always make do.

I stuffed an arm into a strap, hefted the heavy pack onto my back and headed out. My steps made a swishing sound as I strode through fall leaves on the grass. The only other sound came from a few distant bugs, so I hoped no one was up and listening to the noises outside.

A big yellow moon hung low in the sky, providing enough light so that I wouldn't need a flashlight until deep in the woods. The moon had never looked so big in Aldonia. The tall buildings may have hidden it, but the curfew would've had me inside anyway. I remembered the moon more from images viewed at Secondary. It hadn't impressed me much. Just a flat white circle in the sky. The reality was far different. The moon seemed alive and wise.

The Shenoys' house soon blended in with surrounding trees. Though I knew where other colonists' houses stood and which ones I passed, I saw none of them. I felt like I walked alone, far out in the wilderness.

Familiar surroundings soon gave way. The wilderness would grow louder and darker before I stopped to rest.

I had waited three days from the day I made the commitment to return for Abby. Each day I planned in my mind and on paper what I would need to bring and to know for this trip. Using my memory and a scrap of paper, I made a map of the route we had taken from Aldonia to the Maxwell Colony. My first goal was to return to the mining tunnel. I figured I could get through the mountain before stopping to rest. I would walk as far as I could each day, pushing myself. The hard part would be getting through the fence of the boundary. Bot had given me a—

A rustling sounded behind me.

An animal? Without slowing my pace, I glanced over my shoulder. An animal would not come so close to a—

A hand grabbed my arm and spun me around.

Dedrick whispered harshly, "Would you risk us all?" Moonlight illuminated the blond tips of his tousled hair and cast enough light to show the anger in his eyes.

I shook my head. My heart beat hard. I hadn't wanted anyone to catch me leaving, especially not him. "I can be careful. And if I get caught—"

"If you get caught! Do you even remember the way? Do you know the storage points? How to open them?" He released my arm and stepped back, frowning, holding my gaze.

"I have a map and a compass. And I don't need a lot of supplies. Everything I need is in here." I looped a thumb in the strap of my pack.

"That's nice. What will you do at the Boundary? You'll have no communication with our base. You'll be caught or electrocuted. Then the Regimen will wonder how you got over the fence, and our colony will be in—"

"No." I swung my backpack off and unzipped it as I squatted. I dug through it, saying, "Bot gave me a phone." I couldn't find it but kept looking. It had probably fallen to the bottom of the pack. "And I can always short-circuit the fence."

Dedrick laughed. "Right. And then what?" He snatched the backpack from me and zipped it up. "Come on." He started walking.

"No." I grabbed the straps of my backpack and yanked. The pack slid from his arm, but he didn't turn and look at me, so I spoke to his back. "I can't. I feel like I've abandoned my . . . my mother. Abby is like family to me."

Dedrick nodded. "Yeah, I know." He turned. "But you're going the wrong way."

"You're . . ." Was he serious? ". . .trying to trick me."

He exhaled loudly and shook his head. "Haven't I earned your trust yet?"

"You're really going to help me?"

He shrugged and walked away. "You won't make it without me."

I stood there for a moment then sprinted after him. "I might make it."

"You might not."

~~~

The night grew darker and louder. We hiked for hours, following the beam of a flashlight, until we reached our old campsite by the pond. No trace remained of our having camped there, but the memory came clearly to my mind. Something had changed in me at the pond. A new stage of life had begun.

Dedrick wanted to stop for the night, and nearly insisted, but he wouldn't give his reasons. I wanted to get through the mining tunnel before resting. I had planned to travel at a quicker pace than when we'd had Bot and Jessen with us. I didn't want to waste time.
~~~

"When we travel through the mountain, there won't be anyone to trade off with," Dedrick said. "You'll have to help me with the pump car all the way."

"If you can do it, I can do it." I set my jaw. "Besides, I had planned on doing it alone."

He grinned.

Every muscle in my body ached, my heart raced, and sweat drenched my shirt by the time we made it through the mountain. I stepped through the mine entrance on wobbly legs, into the cool night. A slight breeze blew, at first refreshing me. Soon my body trembled, and all I wanted was to curl up in a blanket by a campfire.

Dedrick gathered dead branches and led the way. "I know a good spot to rest. We won't have supplies, but it's concealed by rocks and bushes."

Concealed from whom? And where would he sleep? I carried a single tent, blanket, and pillow in my backpack. And what about food? Having no idea as to the locations of the buried supplies, I hadn't expected to use anything but what I brought with me. After our conversation last Sunday, I never imagined we would be making this journey together.

After a short jaunt down a narrow deer trail, Dedrick pushed through a wall of bushes. The light from his flashlight disappeared, and his firewood clattered to the ground.

Anxious for rest, I ducked my head and pushed through, after him. Cold leaves brushed my face and the arms of my jacket. I stepped into a small, flat clearing with a few scattered plants, jagged boulders at one edge, bushes behind me, and thin-trunked trees forming the other walls.

Dedrick stood motionless by the pile of branches, his flashlight off. "Turn your light off," he whispered.

I did. Then I held my breath and listened.

Nothing. No wind rustled the leaves. No animal scurried through underbrush. Nothing howled or hooted. No footfalls or voices. A few bugs sang night songs, but even that was nothing compared to the noise they made on our journey to the colony.

Dedrick's light came back on. He squatted and arranged the firewood.

"Did you hear something?" I wriggled out of the backpack and sat, half fell, onto the cold, hard ground. I opened the pack to get the blanket.

"I don't know." He arranged a last branch on the pile and went to the edge of the campsite, to where the trees grew. He gathered a handful of dead leaves and came back. "I guess not."

I wrapped the blanket around my shoulders. Once my heart settled and I warmed, I would put up the tent.

Dedrick put his lighter to the leaves and a little flame began. It grew quickly, spreading through the leaves, catching on twigs and then on bigger branches. Dedrick crept back to the edge of the woods.

My mind quieted as I watched the little fire grow. A moment later, my soul stirred with the presence of *My Friend*. I closed my eyes. I didn't like to attend Him with others around, but I couldn't resist this call.

Deep, inner silence. Another stirring. No message or image. A stronger stirring. Was it a warning of some sort?

"You sit quiet sometimes."

I opened my eyes and took a breath.

A good campfire burned. I hadn't heard Dedrick return yet he sat nearby, hunched over with arms resting on raised knees. He stared intently at the stick in his hand, peeling its bark with a pocketknife. "You close your eyes for a long time. It seems like you're asleep." He glanced at me.

A branch in the campfire fell and a spark flew. I watched the spark swirl up, up into the dark sky. The fire warmed my cheeks and probably colored my skin. I let my hair fall in my face and pretended to be interested in a twig on the ground. "I wasn't sleeping. I was . . ." My heartbeat quickened. I wanted to tell him. He might think I was strange and that I'd created *My Friend* as a coping mechanism. Why shouldn't he think that? I had thought the same thing for a while. "Do you ever hear a voice from inside you?"

His head turned toward me, but I didn't look up. A long moment passed and then he said, "Sure."

Now I met his steady gaze. Was he humoring me? "Maybe it's not really a voice but a communication. A strange feeling often comes with the message, peaceful and yet . . . electrifying. I can't ignore it. Sometimes it takes me away from the present. I guess that's what you see."

"What is the message?" His gaze remained fixed on me.

My trust wavered. "Did you mean it when you said you hear a voice, too?"

He gave a shy smile and returned his attention to the peeled stick. "Well, yeah. I think we all do. Unless we get comfortable ignoring it. The inner voice guides us to live a freer life, a life not guided by unruly passions and selfish desires, but by goodness and truth."

A smile grew uncontrollably on my face. He understood me. He heard a voice, too. "Does the voice you hear—"

Dedrick jumped to his feet and peered into the woods through the dark gaps between tree trunks. He snatched a flashlight from the ground and strode to the trees. "I'll be back."

Not again. I straightened up and listened. We were near this spot when Dedrick had disappeared last time, when he had disappeared and returned bruised. I threw the blanket off my shoulders and leaned forward to get up.

"It was nothing." Dedrick stepped back into our little clearing. "Just a raccoon."

"Are you sure?"

"We made eye contact, me and the raccoon." Dedrick grinned and sat down beside me, snatching up the stick he had dropped.

"So, does He ever leave you?"

"He? The inner voice? Yeah, He's silent sometimes. I think He wants me to grow in trust."

I laughed. "What is it with you and trust?"

"Sometimes He asks me to do things, to believe things that I don't necessarily want to, things that put me in danger or make others doubt me. But I try to trust and eventually I come to see His reasons."

"Do you hear Him very often?"

He nodded. "I turn to Him at crossroads."

"Did you ask Him about coming with me? Did He want you to do this?"

He smiled and tossed the whittled stick into the flames. His smile faded as he turned to me. "I think so. But I felt a warning."

"A warning? About what?"

He shrugged. "Does He want you to do this?"

"I-I don't know. He doesn't always make Himself known. He comes when He pleases."

"You didn't consult Him first?" His expression hardened.

I looked away and gazed into the white of the flames. No, I hadn't asked Him. Were there rules to this relationship with *My Friend*? I had asked Him things in the past, but He often remained silent. "Should I ask Him now?"

"Only if you're willing to do as He wants. Sometimes He asks a person to give up what they have their heart set on."

Give up rescuing Abby? Why would *My Friend* want that? Maybe He spoke with her, too. Maybe He inspired the rescue. "Is He always right?"

"I think we don't always interpret Him correctly. Selfishness can get in the way. But if you let go, He guides you to greater virtue."

Yes, I believed that. He also comforted me in sorrow, grieved with me, rejoiced with me. He was *My Friend.* But could I trust Him completely? What if He said to turn back? Could I do it? Did I want to know His will? What of Dedrick's warning?

Dedrick took a drink and let the canteen dangle from his hand. Dancing flames reflected in his calm, brown eyes. His breaths came slow and even.

Was I bringing Dedrick to danger?

~~~

A strange sound woke me. I pushed myself up on my elbows and listened for it again. Dim light came in through the thin fabric of the tent. *Morning already.* My body ached from pushing it last night, but I wanted to get started early. I sat up and began to fold the blanket.

The sound came again: a snort and a loud exhale. Then Dedrick spoke in a soothing tone. I couldn't make out what he said.

I crawled out of the tent. Cool, damp air, a dark morning sky, and a little campfire greeted me. A pile of grass and leaves lay nearby. Dedrick's pillow. He had slept under the stars, by the campfire. He probably couldn't wait to get moving so he could work the cold and kinks out of his body.
~~~

“Good morning.” Dedrick stood by a thick-trunked tree, just inside the woods. “Come and see our transportation.”

“What?” I pulled my jacket tight on my way over to him. Then I saw what he referred to, and I gasped.

Two huge animals—real live horses—stood among the trees. Dedrick rubbed the neck of one and smiled at me. “You ever ride a horse?”

“What?” I hesitated but then stepped closer. “No. When would I have ridden a horse? Can you imagine horses in Aldonia?”

Dedrick took my hand, dragged me even closer, and placed my hand on the neck of the horse.

The brown fur felt warm and soft as silk under my rough hands. The horse snorted and bobbed its head.

I jumped back.

Dedrick laughed. “I think he likes you. You can ride this one. We’ll get to Aldonia in no time now.”

“Where’d they come from?”

“Friends, I guess.”

“Friends?” I eased back to the horse and stroked its neck again. “You mean the wild men you brought supplies to?”

Dedrick jerked his face to me. “Ann told you about that?”

“She thought you were foolish, that it was dangerous.”

He shrugged then adjusted the thick blanket on the horse’s back. “When you know someone has a need, and you know you can help . . .”

I understood. It was how I felt about Abby.

~~~

A hawk soared through the distant sky, making an amazing use of air pressure and the tilt of its wings. No human machine could ever match the gracefulness of a bird in flight. How would it feel to have so much freedom that even gravity could not hold you down? The hawk glided in a relatively straight line, not displaying the carefree dips I enjoyed seeing. I watched it until the canopy of leaves blocked the view.

“A drone.” Dedrick gazed toward the same area of the sky. “We’re almost there.”
~~~

"A drone?" I tried to catch another glimpse of the gliding black not-really-a-bird thing. "We're that close already?" We had ridden our horses at a casual trot to make the ride more comfortable and to avoid wearing them out, but we still cut days off our trip.

"Yup." Dedrick looked at home on a horse, sitting tall but relaxed, the reigns resting in one hand.

I kept shifting in the saddle, my thighs and seat begging for a break.

"We'll get a little closer and make camp. We won't go in until after curfew. I'll use your phone and arrange things while we wait."

Before long, we reached the campsite. We had caught glimpses of the Boundary Fence as we neared, but we had no view of it here. Dedrick seemed familiar with the area. To me, the campsite looked no different from the rest of the woods.

After we dismounted and I unloaded my backpack, Dedrick whispered to his horse and stroked its neck. Then he hollered and smacked the horse's hind end with a stick. The horse snorted and reared up. Both horses took off, galloping into the woods.

He stretched, breathed deep, and leaned against a tree. "Mind if I have the phone?"

I dug it from my backpack and tossed it to him. As I straightened up, my thighs felt tight and sore. "I'll go take a walk."

"Don't get too close to the Boundary. Remember, they've got surveillance."

I nodded and strolled into the woods. My legs wobbled a bit at first, but a few minutes into my walk they relaxed. The quiet noises of nature and the sunlight shining through colorful leaves lifted my heart.

The coin Abby had given me shifted under my shirt. I reached for the chain at my neck and pulled it out, smiling when I saw the coin. I couldn't wait to see Abby, to tell her about this other way of life. She wouldn't have to worry about going to a doctor and never coming back. A few more hours and I would see her.

We made the trip in less time than I had planned, but we still had to sneak through the Boundary Fence unnoticed. Dedrick had come with me. I wouldn't need to search for the exact area we had gone through. I wouldn't have to remove the bars myself and get the timing right, risking electrocution. I hadn't looked forward to contacting the Mosheh either. They might have resented my return and not have wanted to help me. Dedrick would take care of things. Everything would work out. Somehow.

A half hour later, I returned to our campsite. I didn't want Dedrick worrying about me. And I wanted to know if he'd successfully contacted the Mosheh with the phone Bot had given me.

Dedrick sat on the ground with his back against a tree. The remainder of our bread, dried beef, and fruit lay out on my half-folded blanket near him. He looked up from his wristwatch as I approached. "Hungry?"

"Sort of." I sat cross-legged on the ground, on the other side of the blanket, and grabbed an apple. As anxious as I was to get into Aldonia and see Abby, I was glad for some time to rest and talk. "Did you contact them?"

"The Mosheh? Yeah." He answered without looking at me then bit into a stick of dried beef.

"Are they going to help?" His distant attitude made me fear the answer.

He shrugged. "I don't know yet." His eyes locked onto mine. "You had to know they wouldn't be happy."

"I guess. But we're here now. They'll help us, won't they?" I hadn't considered the possibility that we would get all the way out here and the Mosheh would not help us get in.

He didn't answer.

"Well, maybe we should make a plan." I considered meeting Abby outside the Senior Center, since cameras were unavoidable on the inside. I wanted her to know about this other way of life. I wanted her to choose it for herself before I asked the Mosheh to arrange it. But we wouldn't be inside Aldonia until after curfew, so I'd have to wait until tomorrow to try to speak with her.

"We'll wait until we hear back from them." Dedrick still had not looked at me.

I struggled to think of something to say, something to change his mood. "You seem very familiar with these woods. How long have you been doing this, rescuing people from Aldonia?"

"I don't know." He smiled, glancing at me shyly, as if my question reminded him of something.

I blushed. I hoped he wasn't thinking of the day he took me to see the goats, the day I kissed him. He had told me of the vows he took when he joined the Mosheh, how he wouldn't seek a wife until his service ended. I wouldn't dare ask the other question that came to my mind: When did his service end?

"I've been with the Mosheh for over three years, I guess. We've rescued a lot of people in that time." He ripped a hunk of bread off the half-eaten loaf and handed the rest to me.

"I expected to see new people in the Maxwell Colony when you returned from your last mission. You were gone for a long time."

"I took them to a different colony. We had farther to go."

"How many colonies are there?"

"Hundreds. They're all over, on every continent."

I couldn't wrap my mind around that. There were hundreds of colonies, unbeknownst to the Regimen? "How many have you been to?"

"Oh, five, I guess. If you want to know about other colonies, talk to the Merchants. They have routes that stretch across the country. Bot could tell you a few things, being in CAT. He's probably communicated with a few." He pushed himself up and brushed off his black jeans. "I'll be back. Don't go anywhere." He slipped into the woods and disappeared.

I picked at the food for a long time. It took effort to control my anxiety. I wanted to trust. We had gotten this far, and with the help of the wild men, making better time than I had expected. Abby's rescue would work out. The Mosheh just needed time to formulate a plan. Maybe Dedrick had gone off to call them, to speak with them privately.

18

The anarchists would most likely avoid the daylight hours, skulk through alleys and the dark places of Aldonia under the cover of night. Therefore, Dr. Supero, Chief Varden, Sid, and a team of three of the CSS's most trusted met just prior to sundown in a fully-functioning, private surveillance room.

"You don't need to whisper," Chief Varden said to the wiry boy, Kess, who had been whispering to the kid at an adjoining station. "I had the room checked for bugs."

"Do not mention that the rest of CSS knows we are here." Supero folded his arms across his chest and directed a glare to Varden. The chief had gaps in his reasoning skills. What he did with one hand, he undid with the other. Logic evaded him as easily as rats and anarchists. "Do you not have off-site surveillance stations?"

"We do, but they're not fully functioning. Don't worry. The others don't know what we're doing in here. I told them we're watching new suspects. And, uh, that I got told by higher-ups that I'm spending too much time on this project. Which I am!"

"Keep your voice down," Supero said.

Chief Varden threw his arms up and walked away, to the opposite corner of the dimly lit little room. "No one can hear us. The room is soundproof, designed for clandestine operations." He stopped by the dark-eyed girl, Rowen. A wall of black glassy monitors hung above her. "Got the feeds ready?" She nodded but the monitors remained dark.

"How we coming on your stealth program?" Varden shouted to Kess.

"Good to go. Should be able to jump in there, interject my pattern into the apparently random pattern, activate all the down cameras for a window of time." Kess, Varden had boasted, was their best programmer. He could do anything.

"Good. Let's test her out." Chief Varden stood, hands on his hips and face to the monitors.

Sid shuffled to Dr. Supero's side. "Think we'll see anyone?"

Supero smirked. "You know what confidence I have in the chief."

Kess operated a control panel, and all eyes went to the dark monitors. Live images popped onto them one at a time, images of alleys and quiet streets, of apartment buildings and schools, of warehouses and the grassy boundaries near the Boundary Fence.

"There are too many images to display on these few monitors," Rowan said, turning her pretty face and dark eyes to Varden.

"Drop the feeds of the main streets and apartment buildings—" Varden began.

"Use the surveillance cameras that have picked up Mosheh before," Supero commanded.

Rowan turned her sultry eyes to him. "Mosheh? I don't know—"

"Don't listen to him." Varden stomped over and situated his large body between Dr. Supero and the dark-eyed girl. "The doctor is here only to observe. I want feeds from border surveillance and from cameras that have picked up unidentifiables in mottled capes."

Supero huffed, satisfied that Chief Varden used his idea but annoyed at the chief's pride. He hated having to work with the man. The two of them would never be friends outside a work situation. The man had much pride and vanity, but little to show for it.

Rowan's hands flew, graceful as butterflies and quick as snakes over the control panel. New images flashed onto the monitors in rapid succession. Sid rolled a chair over to observe. Kess and the kid beside him continued to monitor data at their stations: numbers, text, and colorful patterns on smaller screens. The kid beside Kess did not seem suited for this work. He had a shock of white hair with black roots and his body jerked oddly, twitched like a bird with a worm, as he worked. If his appearance did not disturb one, his incessant mumbling would.

"What happened!" Varden shouted. "Where'd they go?"

The monitors had all gone dark.

Kess hunched over the control panel, his hands flashing from one control to another. The odd kid beside Kess straightened up, shook his head, and mumbled. He reached to a higher control panel.

"The computer detected our interception as an error. It's working to correct itself." Kess turned to Varden. "The original pattern has resumed."

Varden shot to his side.

"Wow. Impressive." Supero sneered. He was wasting his time. "I am so glad you invited me to this midnight rendezvous. Your team is highly efficient."

"Shut it, Supero," Varden snapped. "I know what your problem is."

"Do you?"

"You had plans with your hot assistant, and I ruined them by calling you here."

"Plans with my . . ." Dr. Supero felt the gaze of everyone in the room. "I am a professional. You know interoffice relationships are not permitted. Do not insinuate that a man of my stature—"

A knock sounded on the door.

The room fell silent except for the hum of computers. Varden and Supero exchanged glances. Varden shrugged then tapped the remote controller built into his wrist phone.

The door clicked and slid open.

Ivy stood there in a slinky black dress and gorgeous black pumps, her green-streaked blonde hair falling loose over one shoulder—just the way he liked it. She clutched a canvas bag. Had she come to see him? She could not have picked a more inopportune time.

She sauntered into the room under the scrutinizing gaze of the chief. "Hi, Dr. Supero, Chief Varden." She reached out to Supero with the canvas bag. "I knew you were working late. You didn't respond to the messages I sent you from work."

Chief Varden threw his head back and laughed. "You're a professional all right." He returned his attention to Kess and the problem with their software. "See if you can get back in and . . ."

Supero shook his head, trying to soften his angry expression before he spoke to Ivy. "This is not a good time. How did you find me here?"

"Well, the guys in the central surveillance room—"

"Never mind." Supero wrapped a hand around her bare, slender arm and led her to the door. "Is there an emergency?"

"I don't know. You had an urgent message. I sent it to you, but I see that you haven't checked your messages yet. And you don't answer my calls."

He stopped at the door. "Urgent?" The decision concerning his surgery? No, he only submitted to the tests earlier this week.

"It was from your previous assistant." Ivy pursed her lips and narrowed her eyes.

"My previous assistant?"

"Sage." Ivy spoke the name with disgust.

Supero's heart skipped a beat. What had Sage said to Ivy? "I do not have time for trivial matters. Does this concern a psychological evaluation at the center where she works? That does not seem like an emergency." He pressed the control to open the door.

"No, it's personal." Ivy yanked her arm from Supero's grasp. She would not step outside the room. "The girl didn't give me details. She left three messages. Then she showed up at work."

Supero's eyes popped. "She. What?" He was glad he had not been there.

"Sage insisted she speak with you today."

"That will not be happening." He grabbed her arm again, led her from the room and stood in the hall, wishing the door would slide shut for privacy. "In fact, disregard all messages from her. You need not pass them on to me. You are aware, I am sure, that she left our office on disagreeable terms. It was not my fault. She will probably make things up." Sage must have said something to Ivy. It showed in Ivy's eyes.

"Here." Head down and uncharacteristically meek, Ivy shoved the canvas bag into his hands. "I thought you might be hungry, probably skipped dinner to work late."

"How considerate." He gave her a pleasant smile, not wanting this incident to ruin things between them. Their relationship had just begun, had not even blossomed yet. If only his business with Liberty were through. How much of his life would he waste pursuing that wretched girl? He had better things to do. No, for the sake of Aldonia, for the sake of the next generation, he could not give up.

"I suppose I should've brought more. I didn't know you were working with a team." She tucked her hair behind her ear and dropped her hand to her waist.

He caught her hand in his own but, since the door remained open, let it slide from his grasp before anyone noticed. "More? Yes. We will probably be here for some time. I am sure everyone is hungry."

As Supero returned to the surveillance room, Chief Varden threw him a cocky glance and laughed. The dark-eyed girl even gave him a judgmental glare.

Dr. Supero pulled a chair up beside Sid and took a deep breath as he sunk into it.

"What was that about?" Sid had a crooked grin and a knowing look.

"Women," Supero said in a quiet voice.

~~~

The sky turned darker and darker shades of blue. Stars appeared, one here, one there, until they filled the entire sky with flecks of light. Shadows deepened. The air grew chill. Night shrouded more and more of the woods around me.

When would Dedrick return? I assumed he knew his way through this part of the woods, but he could have taken a wrong turn. With the failing light, one could easily get lost.

I had gathered branches, twigs, and a few dried leaves into a little pile and now carried the lighter in my back pocket. It took great effort to keep from starting a campfire. I had to keep reminding myself that Aldonia lay just beyond the trees. Someone might see the light. Dedrick wouldn't need the light to guide him. He knew his way. He would return soon enough.

I sighed. Where had he gone? Why hadn't he said more than, "I'll be back. Don't go anywhere." Waves of anger undulated through me. I wanted to trust. But what if something was wrong? How long should I wait here? I didn't even have the phone Bot had given me. With the voltage tester to show when electrical currents ran through the fence, I shouldn't have a problem getting through. But avoiding surveillance without the Mosheh's guidance wouldn't be easy. I wouldn't be able to
~~~

time it. I would have to guess. If I got on camera, my mission would end in failure.

I took a deep breath, sat on the ground, and leaned against Dedrick's tree. *My Friend* let me know He still kept me company. He had made His presence known earlier in the day, but without the inner stirring or the overwhelming sensation that often signaled His coming. He had made Himself known in a unique way, a simple, matter-of-fact sort of way that did not require me to stop and discern His message. He didn't seem to have a message today.

In fact, I had spent the whole hour before the sunlight faded circling the campsite, walking in an ever-growing circle in order to see farther into the woods. I had even lost sight of the campsite, at one point, and had started back in the wrong direction. *My Friend* had walked with me the entire time, saying nothing, wanting nothing, not even pointing me in the correct direction. He was simply there. He almost seemed to be outside of me, by my side, waiting with me. His presence gave me comfort and reminded me that anxiety accomplished nothing.

A voice came from the darkness, from somewhere off to one side of the camp.

I jumped up and peered into the dark. "Dedrick?"

Fallen leaves rustled and the voice grew louder, Dedrick's voice. "Got it. So call me back when you know more." A pause. Still no visible sign of him. "No, we'll wait. We'll play it safe." He strutted into view and stopped in the middle of our campsite where dim light from the night sky gave him visible form. He stuffed something into a back pocket, probably the phone.

"Sorry I took so long," he said, reaching into his jacket.

"Where'd you go? I thought you got lost."

"Lost? Me? Here, take this." He handed me a blanket or something. "Put it on. And keep this safe." He handed me glasses.

As I unfolded the item, I realized he had given me a camouflage cape and night-vision glasses.

He pulled a cape on, too. "We've got a bit of a problem." He did something to his watch that made it glow.

"A problem? What kind of a problem?"

"Well, maybe it's more of a concern than a problem. They aren't sure yet." He squatted, turned the flashlight on, and search inside my backpack.

"Tell me."

"Miriam says there's something odd about the active and down cycle of Aldonia's surveillance cameras."

"Okay. What does that mean for us?"

He stood and flashed the light toward me before shutting it off. "The Mosheh developed a program that makes the cycle appear random to the Regimen, but it's predictable to us. It's been tampered with—they aren't sure if it's an intentional interception or not. If it is, we could be caught on camera. The Regimen might see us, if anyone happens to be looking."

"Do you think they're always watching?"

"Yeah, they're supposed to be. They have people whose entire vocation is to sit and watch monitors. We still slip by them all the time, but they do catch some things. If they're intentionally intercepting the surveillance camera operations system, they're watching."

"So Miriam's going to call back?"

"Yeah, when she knows more." Dedrick paced the width of the campsite, glancing at the sky when he got under a gap in the canopy of leaves. Was he watching for drones? Was he praying? Maybe he had become anxious, too, because our situation was more dangerous than the ones he typically faced.

He stopped pacing. "We'll go closer. Come on."

~~~

Half an hour later, the cotton-head kid let out a holler. Varden flew to his side. They mumbled to each other for over one minute. Then Varden stepped back and jerked his face to the monitors on the wall. Live video popped onto one, two, three monitors . . . then all went black and everyone groaned.

"I got it," Kess said. "I know what's wrong." His hands flew wildly over the control panel. He seemed like the smarter of the two programmers. If anyone could find a solution, he would be the one. But what good would it do? What chance did they have of catching anyone?

A knock sounded at the door. No one seemed to notice. They probably all assumed it was Ivy again, returning with their dinner. The girl
~~~

was extremely efficient. How could she possibly have reached the physicians' dining room, obtained meals for everyone, and returned in so short a time? Maybe she went somewhere closer.

With a stretch and a yawn, Dr. Supero got up and strolled to the door. He pressed the control and smoothed his hair as the door slid open. Then his breath caught in his throat.

Sage stood before him.

"Hello, Dr. Supero." Sage wore a long dark jacket and the balmy perfume that used to drive him mad with desire. Red lips on a pale face and short copper hair to frame it. Revenge showed in her eyes but, otherwise, she was gorgeous.

Dr. Supero tried blocking the door, but Sage slipped past and gained the attention of everyone in the room without as much as a word.

"What is it you want?" Supero followed her, keeping close so he could speak low. "You should not be here. How did you find me?"

She stopped in the middle of the room and turned in a slow circle, as if taking in every detail of the small surveillance room. Then she faced him and smiled, looking like a woman who dominated the moment. "I followed your assistant. Wasn't that clever of me?"

"Doctor Supero, this is a private operation," Chief Varden said then hunched over a control station.

"You must go." Supero gestured toward the door. "Call me at my office."

"I tried that. You're never there. But I need something from you, and I need it now."

She needed something from him? His hands had once caressed every curve of her smooth skin. He could lose himself in her scent. Her kiss could send every other thought from his mind.

"I, uh . . ." Supero cleared his throat, averted his gaze, and took a breath through his mouth. He could not let his imagination wander. They were not alone.

Chief Varden and his team paid no attention, but Sid gawked openly.

"Shouldn't you be watching monitors," Dr. Supero said to Sid. Sid gave him a crooked grin and shrugged. The monitors were still dark.

"I want to live in the Breeder Facility," Sage said.

Everyone in the room cheered and shouted.

"We got it!"

"You did it!"

"It's up!" Rowan jumped from her station, bounced over to Kess, and hugged him. The white-haired kid threw his hands in the air. Every monitor had a live feed, some in alleys, several apparently near border fences, and others in warehouse zones. Figures moved in several of the images.

Chief Varden slapped each crewmember on the back. "Good work. Let's see what we can see, team."

Dr. Supero returned his gaze to Sage. "The Breeder Facility? No, I cannot grant your request. I have nothing to do with that. Besides, you are too old."

She opened her mouth and narrowed her eyes. But it was true. She was over thirty.

"Now, you will please go." He needed to focus on the matter at hand, to identify the people in the images. What time was it? Was it past curfew? No, it couldn't be that late.

"I will not go." Anger shot through her eyes. "I have something of yours." She unbuttoned her jacket and flung it from her shoulders, revealing a slinky black dress . . . and a distended belly.

He had always found her irresistible in that particular dress, but not today. What could have caused the distension? "What is the matter with you?" He shook his head and stepped back. "No. I am not your physician. Get yourself looked at by your own physician." If she did not soon leave, he would call security. He folded his arms and turned to study the monitors. *My*, but many people wandered the streets at night.

"There's nothing wrong with me. I'm pregnant."

The room fell silent. Supero's heartbeat sounded in his ears. He turned slowly to face her. "What did you say? That is not possible." Every girl who reached childbearing age underwent sterilization. Breeders alone remained fertile. Occasionally, a girl slipped by or the sterilization failed. Rarely though.

"It is possible and you're responsible. I'm over four months, I would guess." She rubbed her belly, emphasizing the roundness of it. "It's yours."

Over four months? Yes, she was his assistant then, had been for over a year. Once they recognized mutual attraction, they had satisfied their urges at least three times a week, most of the time at work in vacant offices and dark rooms. The risk added to the enjoyment. Had she known of her fertility? All those times in his arms, knowing . . . A wave of heat washed through him from head to toe. His head throbbed. He staggered back.

Sid jumped up and put a hand on his back. "You okay, Doctor?"

"Son of the Earth, I'm losing it," Kess shouted. "The computer is correcting itself."

~~~

"Tell me about Miriam," I said as we walked through the darkness. We headed for the border of Aldonia and the seven-meter-high fence through which deadly currents of electricity pulsed and to surveillance cameras on the other side, cameras that may or may not catch our images. I wanted Dedrick to relax. Seeing him anxious doubled my anxiety. How would I ever rescue Abby if I couldn't keep my calm?

"What do you want to know?" he said.

"I don't know. You said people make commitments to the Mosheh when they reach adulthood. She's older. How long has she been with the Mosheh?"

Dedrick chuckled. "Don't let her hear you call her *older*. She's tougher than most of us young ones." He paused. "Miriam's been doing this for years. She made a permanent commitment to the Mosheh, to rescuing others."

"Did she make vows?"

"Yeah, permanent vows."

"What if she meets someone, falls in love? That could change things for someone, couldn't it?" Aldonians used the word *love* so casually, so superficially, but I knew it meant more to my new friends in the colony. Love meant something real and permanent. A person gave more than he or she expected to receive in the love I had witnessed in the colony.
~~~

"Nah, Miriam already met him, already fell in love. That part of her life is over, she once said."

"What do you mean?"

Dedrick didn't answer right away. "A long time ago, I guess about fifteen years ago, she was seventeen, and she made her temporary commitment, promised four years like we all do."

That answered a question I had: *How long does a commitment last?* I was glad I didn't have to ask the question directly. Dedrick told me he had been rescuing people for over three years. He had only months, then, until his service ended.

"She worked with a team," he said. "Over time, she fell in love with another member of the team. His name was Matthias. They agreed to work apart for the remainder of their commitment so they could stick to their vows and avoid compromising rescue missions. At the end of their service, they intended to live in a free colony and enter courtship."

"Courtship?"

"Preparation for marriage, a time to discern God's will."

"Something went wrong?"

"Shortly before the end of his service . . ." He paused. "Unity Troopers got him. Everyone looks up to Miriam, admires her faithfulness to promises and her dedication to saving others, and for the way she handled that sacrifice."

I gasped. "He died?"

"Yeah." He picked up his pace. "We're here."

The trees thinned, partially revealing the posts of the Boundary Fence. *Aldonia.*

My stomach flipped. Could I do this? I felt like a prisoner who had gained freedom and now, foolishly, returned to her cage. If I failed at this mission, I would be caught, never to escape again.

Abby. I did this for her. Steeling my resolve, I quickened my pace.

Dedrick took my hand and tugged me back. My heart skipped a beat at his touch. "Not yet," he said, nodding upward.

A drone, silent as an owl after its prey, glided overhead at a low altitude.

"We're close enough here, anyway," he said, bringing the phone to his ear though I hadn't heard it ring.

"Yeah, whaddya got?" He checked his watch. "You're certain? Okay, I understand. Two minutes, thirty-five seconds. Got it." He stuffed the phone into his back pocket and said to me, "In two minutes I'll go ready the fence. You stay here. I'll signal for you to come. You'll climb under and run to the nearest tree."

"How will I know—"

"There's only one tree in that field. There're plenty of little shrubs though, so watch your step. We don't need any accidents. I'll get the fence back together and meet you under the tree. We'll use an underground route to get close to the Senior Living and Recreation Center. The Mosheh will call Abby and have her go outside." He squatted and drew in the dirt but the darkness hid his picture from me. "The Mosheh will manipulate the surveillance cameras of a particular area outside." He yanked the flashlight from my backpack and shined it on the ground.

He had drawn a map in the dirt. It showed the Senior Center and the strip of grass behind it. While I watched, he drew an "x" between one of the benches and the back wall of the center. "You'll come up this way and stand here to talk to her. You'll have roughly five minutes, no more. Then you'll have to leave the way you came."

"With her?"

He shook his head and shut off the flashlight. "No, you'll give her this." He took my hand, turned it palm up, and placed a small box into it. "If she wants to be rescued, tell her to take the pill in this box and press the emergency button on her wristband at once. The pill will make her appear to have had a heart attack. Rescue workers will take her to the hospital. We take it from there. You can assure her: she'll be free."

His watch beeped. He tapped it, silencing the alarm. "Wear the night-vision lenses when you come. Watch for my signal."

"What is your signal?"

He waved the dark flashlight, slid the night-vision lenses over his eyes, and bolted for the fence. Within seconds, he covered the ground between the woods' edge and the slope by the Boundary Fence. When he stooped over, he disappeared from my view.

~~~

"What is *she* doing here?" Ivy's voice came from behind Dr. Supero.

Supero sat slumped in an ergonomic chair and held a damp cloth to his forehead. He had heard the knock and the door slide open, but he didn't want to see Ivy's face when she saw Sage in the room.

The monitors came to life again as Ivy walked into his peripheral vision. She held two canvas bags and scowled. Odd how both girls decided to wear skimpy black dresses tonight. Sage would've looked better in hers, shapelier, if not for the bulbous belly.

"Why is she here?" Ivy dropped the bags onto Rowan's monitoring station without regard for the work Rowan did. Rowan peeked into one of the bags and handed the other to Sid.

"I do not know." Dr. Supero shook his head. He still had not felt the return of blood to his face. Perhaps he needed to eat something. "She wants to live in the Breeder Facility. She assumes I can arrange that."

Through green eyes narrowed to slits, Ivy gave Sage the once-over. "She's fat. Why would they want her? Only the physically superior go there."

"I am not fat. I'm pregnant," Sage snarled. "He did this to me." She thrust out her arm and pointed directly at the doctor. One could make no mistake. She meant him. He got her pregnant. Yes, the rumors were true.

Dr. Supero's eyes rolled back in his head. He placed the cloth over them. As soon as his strength returned, he would find that wretched girl Liberty. She was probably spreading her corrupt ideology to secret groups in Aldonia, planting seeds in the dark, paving the way for an insurrection. She could not see herself living in peace and doing her part for the good of all. She had to have things her way, had to be the designer of her own life, make her own choices regardless of the impact it had on the collective.

Dr. Supero found himself rubbing his head in the area of the cancerous tumor, but he didn't stop once he realized it. His assistant and his previous assistant carried on a heated discussion that he preferred to know nothing about.
~~~

"Look there!" Rowan shrieked.

Supero opened his eyes. He had dozed. What time was it? Past curfew? He glanced at his watch. Yes, it was past curfew.

"Where is that?" Varden said. "Switch that feed to the main monitor."

"Boundary Fence," Kess said.

"What're they doing?" cotton head mumbled. "Where'd they come from?"

"I think they were outside the fence!" Varden thundered. "Zoom in on the figures."

Supero sat bolt upright and jumped to his feet. The largest of the monitors showed a live video of the high, electric fence of the boundaries with its towering poles and closely-spaced horizontal beams. Two tiny figures moved near the fence. The image zoomed in on the figures. Mottled capes, hoods, and shades. It was them. It was the Mosheh.

"Where is this?" Supero shouted. "Get to them. Arrest them!"

Varden held the landline to his ear and barked into his wrist phone. He threw Supero a look of warning and turned his back to him. Different images appeared on smaller monitors, close-ups of the two caped figures, views of the surrounding area.

Sid clutched the back of Rowan's chair and squinted at the monitors. "That's her. I can tell by the way she moves. And that's him. I recognize that mouth and nose."

"Her body's covered with a cape. How can you tell anything about her walk? And you can barely see . . ." Rowan questioned Sid, but he defended his assessment.

"I'm losing it!" Kess shouted. "The computer's correcting itself. We have seconds. It almost seems like another programmer, somewhere, is working on this, working against me."

"No!" Varden slammed the landline down and leaned over Kess. "I've got Unity Troopers on their way. We need to keep the visual, keep the live feed. Can't let them disappear. Get the feed from the drones I sent out . . ."

"The reason I came up here was to tell you something." Ivy whispered over Dr. Supero's shoulder.

He shivered and glanced. “I have heard enough today. Can it wait?”

“You decide. You received the message you’ve been waiting for.”

As she spoke, the monitors went down and everyone let out a collective groan. Curses, theories, and commands filled the air.

Dr. Supero turned to Ivy. Was she playing a game with him? Irritated because of Sage? How much did she know about his condition? He’d had her set his personal appointments, the ones requested by the Medical Care Evaluation Panel, but he never explained the reason for them. She couldn’t have read his locked messages, could she have?

Ivy had no smile for him now, no flirty expression on her flawless face. Secrets hid behind her glittering green eyes. She knew.

“Tell me.” Dr. Supero grabbed her shoulders and pulled her close. With a threat in his tone, he said, “You have already invaded my privacy, read my personal messages. So you know. Tell me the verdict.” He paused. “Do I live or die?”

She tried to pull back but he wouldn’t let her, kept her close enough to kiss. She swallowed hard but held his gaze. “The Regimen recently cut the budget for risky, major procedures. The panel had no choice but to deny—”

“The risks are minimal! It is not a risky procedure.” He shoved the girl away from him. It could not be true. They would not abandon a doctor of his importance because of a single operation. “You lie! You speak out of jealousy.”

“Supero!” Chief Varden shouted from across the room. “Get your play things out of here! This is a covert operation. If you can’t control the situation, I’ll make you leave, too.”

Sage sat on a dark desktop control panel, legs crossed, arms folded, and bright red lips pursed to display her annoyance.

“You, Sage . . .” Dr. Supero stomped to her. “You will see your physician tomorrow and explain your unwonted situation. He will see that you have your pregnancy terminated and that you are properly sterilized.”

Her brows creased. “Terminated?”

“Yes, you will have an abortion. You are in no way qualified to be a breeder.” He stepped back and pointed at the door. “Now go. We are done here. I have nothing more to say to you.”

Fists raised, she lunged at him and shrieked, "But you did this to me."

Dr. Supero threw an arm up to block her blows and tried, with the other hand, to grab her arm.

Sid came up behind her. "Settle down, girl." He pinned her flailing arms to her sides with a bear hug. Then he wrestled the shrieking girl to the door.

Ivy didn't wait for her dismissal. She threw a scalding glance at Supero, flipped her hair off her shoulder, and strutted from the room.

"What do you mean you can't find them?" Varden shouted into the communication device on a control panel.

Supero spun to face him. "Do not tell me you have lost her already?"

"Do I have to be out there myself? Find them." Varden turned to the white-haired kid. "I want surveillance on every one of her friends' flexi-phones, old co-workers, too. I want to hear every conversation." And to Kess he shouted, "Get my cameras back."

~~~

Dedrick bolted toward me and slammed into the trunk of the tree. "They caught us," he said, breathing hard. "Miriam called to warn. We've gotta run fast." He squeezed my hand and we took off racing through the grassy plain between the outskirts of Aldonia and the Boundary Fence.

The world, turned yellow from the night-vision glasses, jiggled as I ran. We bolted toward a group of warehouses. Bright city lights in the distance drew my gaze. Everything nearby—a landscape of pits, weeds, and bushes—appeared strange. I couldn't get used to the night-vision lenses or make good sense of my surroundings.

Maybe we ran for no reason. I clung to the hope that no one had seen us, that whoever had the job of monitoring live surveillance feeds had dozed off or had been more interested in a new 3D game on his wrist phone.

Dedrick jerked my hand, tugging it to himself.

Trying to keep balance, I moved closer to him and scraped my leg on something waist-high. A glance back told me I would've ran into a huge spiky weed if not for Dedrick's redirection.

"Look out!" Dedrick pushed my hand away this time. He let go.
~~~

I glimpsed a big black pit in my path. Grass rimmed the edges, preventing us from seeing it sooner. My foot pounded the ground before the pit and I leaped. Good, flat ground greeted my foot on the other side but my next step brought me down.

My toe slid into a hollow. My ankle twisted. I threw my hands out as I sailed to the ground. Pain shot through my leg.

"You okay?" Dedrick was at my side, grabbing my arms. "We can't stop. If they saw us, they'll be here—"

A siren broke the silence. Pulsing orange and blue lights appeared on the far side of the warehouses. *Unity Troopers.*

Dedrick yanked me up. Squeezing my hand, he jerked his face to either side. We couldn't go to the warehouses now.

I scanned the area, too. Where could we go? I knew nothing of the secret entrances to the underground world of the Mosheh, but the scraggily landscape reminded me of the place where we had found the bomb shelter. Some distance away, to one side of the warehouses, I thought I saw a damaged chain-length fence with orange barrier tape weaved though and dangling from it.

The sirens grew louder. The flashing lights moved, heading our way. The gate surrounding the warehouse had probably stopped them, but not now. They were coming.

"This way." I clutched his hand, and we ran as one. My ankle screamed with every step but I would not yield to the pain. We had to get to safety.

"Where to?"

"There's an underground bunker. Regimen doesn't know of it." I hoped no one with the Regimen knew of it, but a lot could've happened in my absence.

More sirens. More flashing lights. Coming from a different direction than the first troopers. Soon Unity Troopers and Citizen Safety Officers would swarm over this stretch of land.

World jiggling around me, pain numbing my mind, I scanned the area for the dead branches and old boards we had dragged over the hole around the bunker door. Clumps of tall grass and wild bushes dotted the landscape. Nothing stood out. Then I spotted it, the pile of dead branches, not too far away.

I let go of his hand and slowed as we neared, trying to remember how we had arranged everything. It didn't look the same. Someone had moved it. I limped closer and gasped, feeling a glimmer of hope.

Dedrick and I stared down into the hole, down at the bunker. Nothing covered it. And the bunker door hung open.

"This it?" He looked at me. Orange pulsing light framed his face. Sirens blared, coming from every direction.

I nodded. "Yes, but—"

A head appeared in the bunker doorway. A figure climbed out, a figure with wild silver hair, grim eyes locked on us, a black jacket over a bulky body, and a big black duffle bag last. Silver—one of the last people I would want to come across—climbed out of the hole. She swaggered right up to us and stared at me as she dragged the strap of the bag over her shoulder. The bag bulged and the strap cut into the shoulder of her jacket. Pulsing blue and orange lights reflected on her hair.

A black Unity Trooper's area car screeched to a halt on the other side of the chain-length fence. They would see us soon. We had no time. I wanted to dive into the hole and climb into the bomb shelter. Would Silver let us hide? Would she report us? Citizens weren't allowed out here, in this stretch of land that ran up to the Boundary Fence. She could avoid trouble for herself by reporting us.

Silver looked us over, her gaze resting on me. She nodded in the direction of the Unity Troopers. "Déjà vu." She gave a crooked grin.

"Yeah," I said. The Unity Troopers had been crawling through the neighborhood last time we were here. My eyes went to the bunker door. *Please* . . . My thoughts went to *My Friend. . . . help me.*

"Better go on." Silver nodded toward the bunker door. "They're coming."

Unity Troopers, at least a dozen of them, jumped the fence. Flashlights swept the land. Lights approached the tree we had just left. There would be no escape.

"Come on." Dedrick jumped into the hole and reached for me.

I grabbed his hands and, favoring my injured leg, jumped down with him. Silver bent over the pile of dead branches and straightened up with a board in her hands. She was going to cover the hole! She was going to help us!

"You go first." Dedrick crouched by the bunker door.

I wished he would go first since he could move faster, but I didn't waste time arguing. I descended the ladder into the dark bunker, taking every other step gingerly and wincing at the pain.

Dedrick followed close behind. "It's gonna get dark," he said as he closed the bunker door.

I groped the outer pockets of my backpack, desperate for the flashlight.

"They're going to find us," Dedrick said, his voice in my ear.

"No, we can hide." I found the flashlight and shined it on the far side of the bunker, on the carpet where Finley had found a panel. "Pull back the carpet."

"What's there?" Dedrick jumped at my command, dashed to the back of the bunker, and peeled the carpet up. He lifted the panel and stuck a hand out to me.

I hobbled to him and gave him the flashlight. "It's a storage area. We can hide—"

Something thumped against the bunker door.

My breath caught in my throat. I jerked my face to the ladder.

"Let's go." Dedrick scooted into the storage area.

Ignoring the throbbing pain in my ankle, I crouched at the edge and jumped in beside him. We had little room between drums of water, the power generator, and cold steel walls. Stooping to avoid bonking my head on the low ceiling, I limped to an area two meters away, the only space big enough for both of us to sit.

Dedrick closed us in and shut off the flashlight. We huddled together in the cold and the dark, listening to the beating of our hearts and our labored breaths.

The bunker door opened with a bang.

I gasped.

Dedrick took my hand and squeezed it.

Voices. Hard boots on a metal ladder. They were coming.

"So I took a few guns. Big deal." Silver spoke with an attitude. "Who's to say I wasn't going to turn them in?" She laughed.

"How did you find this place?" a man said. Boots still pounded on the ladder. How many were coming down?

"Here they are." Another man's voice.

I drew in a breath. Had they noticed the panel in the floor? Maybe the carpet didn't fall back over it right.

Dedrick rubbed his thumb on my hand.

"I couldn't fit them all in one bag," Silver said.

"Wow. Check this out. Looks like people lived here. Beds, bedding . . . What's in here?" A door to one of the metal cabinets creaked open.

"Are you sure you didn't see two people out here while you were, uh, about your business?" the first man said. "Answer wisely because you're about to be arrested for possession, concealing, and trading weapons."

My heart pounded in my chest. I held my breath and gazed wide-eyed into the dark. What chance did we stand? Silver had no loyalty to me. She had been willing to help Sid, willing to betray me into his hands.

"If you're really looking for someone, you're wasting your time with me. All I care about is the guns."

Silence.

"Silver 798-060662-91 of Aldonia, you're under arrest for possession, concealing and—"

Something or someone thudded to the floor above our heads.

I jumped. Dedrick squeezed my hand.

More thuds and crashes followed. An officer shouted curses. Grunting, shouts, and more crashes sounded. Then laughter, Silver's laughter.

"Fine, you got me." She sounded amused. "Take me in. It's been awhile since I've had a ride in one of your radically-designed cars."

"Let's go," one of them said. "We'll get a work order for this underground place, get it destroyed."

Boots clanked on the ladder. More and more boots. The bunker door slammed shut.

I took a deep breath and exhaled slowly. We were safe.

~~~

Dawn crept into the sky, pushing back the night and all reasonable hope they had of finding Liberty.

Dr. Supero stormed through the Citizen Safety Station and headed for the private, joke of a surveillance room. Apparently, surveillance meant just that to the CSS. They could watch anarchists all day and night, but they could effectively do nothing to capture them.

Heads turned as he strutted thought the central surveillance room. He met their gazes, irritation in his eyes, until every one of them got back to work. The entire CSS had joined in observing live feeds, listening in on phone conversations, and analyzing data concerning Liberty and Dedrick. It was probably a mistake to include everyone. They had not yet identified the moles. The extra help had accomplished nothing, anyway.

They'd had one glimpse of Liberty and Dedrick, mere seconds of live feed from surveillance at the Boundary Fence. And that was it. The two could be anywhere. Had they really been outside the fence? Or were they trying to get out?

Supero took the hall that led to the private surveillance room. Sage and Ivy would not be there, he had to remind himself. He had thrown them out. The two had lingered in the lobby of the CSS, he had been told, deep in conversation, and not with the malicious tones they had first used with each other. Maybe they had become friends. *How nice.* At least he would not have to bother with them at this early hour of the morning.

He approached the implant reader but hadn't even lifted his hand when the door slid open.

"Oh, hey, you're back." The cotton-headed kid sauntered from the room, a green bag hanging from his shoulder. Was he on his way home? "We thought you called it quits for the night, uh, day."

"Called it quits?" Supero snapped. "Is there no one here of our special team? You are CSS's most trusted."

"Oh, well, uh . . . Everybody left an hour or two or, uh, three ago."

"The girl has not been found."

The boy gave Supero the once-over. "Were you out there searching for her yourself?"
~~~

Dr. Supero ran a hand through his sweaty hair and stepped into the room. The door slid shut behind him, leaving him alone in the small surveillance room. Images of Warehouse Zone One, of the Boundary Fence, and of other nearby places showed on wall monitors. Text and numbers scrolled on smaller screens. Indistinct sounds, voices maybe, came through an abandoned headset.

Supero slumped into a chair and closed his eyes.

When he had received word that the two had escaped—despite the numerous Unity Troopers and Citizen Safety Officers—he had gone to look for her himself. He went directly to the location where they had been sighted and found a myriad of footprints— all from Unity Troopers. The fools had trampled underfoot any trace of Liberty and Dedrick's footprints. It would've been nice to know which direction the two had taken when they fled. When he had mentioned that to the officers still present, the logic evaded them.

With a flashlight and binoculars, Dr. Supero had scoured the nearby warehouses and neighborhoods. He continued searching long after the Unity Troopers and Citizen Safety Officers had given up.

Supero sat up and glanced to see where he had placed the girl's notebook. Where could she have gone?

As Dr. Supero stood, his wrist phone played his personal ringtone. *Ivy?* He glanced at the caller ID and frowned. *Chief Varden.*

He tapped the control to answer the call. "Tell me you have found her. Otherwise, I am not interested in hearing your voice." The notebook lay on a desktop on the far side of the room. He headed for it.

"No, we haven't found them. But troopers arrested one of her friends. Silver. Remember her? Brute of a girl. Found her in the same area as our search, in the field by the Boundary Fence."

Supero picked up the notebook. This could have nothing to do with Liberty. They spotted Liberty hours ago. Certainly, she would not have comrades wandering the field, drawing attention. Unless maybe they dropped something important. "When was this?"

"Earlier. Last night. Same time our search began."

"Same time—" Supero's eyes bulged as anger welled up inside him. His head throbbed. "Your incompetency! Why have you waited so long to tell me?"

Shouting, Chief Varden addressed him with a foul name. "I just found out myself. U.T. just decided I ought to know." His voice dropped a decibel. "They have her in custody. Apparently, she was out at some underground bunker or bomb shelter, mining a secret stash of guns."

"Bomb shelter? Where is this bomb shelter?" Supero opened the notebook to the page where Liberty had written about a bomb shelter. Silver knew about it, too. They must've discovered it the night they went out with shovels.

"It's in the field off Warehouse Zone One, between Aldonia and the Boundary Fence."

"Get out there! Search the bomb shelter, and we will find them!"

"U.T. searched it already. Found nothing. Just the guns she was talking about."

Dozens of glowing gnats swirled in Dr. Supero's vision. He pounded his fists on the desktop, and the images on several monitors flipped to new images. "Search it yourself. Or do I have to do everything! There must be a secret compartment in the bunker that the inept troopers overlooked."

"Yeah, I see your point. I'm on it."

19

I had never given much thought to the sewer tunnels that ran under Aldonia. The dank air felt good on my cheeks but reeked of things spoiled and dead. Unseen water dripped before and behind me, usually in the distance but sometimes so close I shuddered. Occasionally, something somewhere clanked. My crutches clomped on the hard brick floor of the dark sewer tunnel. The beam of my flashlight swayed at my feet and illuminated the lower parts of the curved, brick walls. A thread of water trailed down the middle of the passageway, glimmering under the moving beam. Dedrick had attached the flashlight to one of the crutches, but I bumped it on my way down here. I had tried securing it again, but it kept slipping, so I gave up. I didn't want to waste time.

Dedrick had said it would take half an hour on this underground route to reach Abby's neighborhood. A blue ladder would mark my exit point. It would take another ten minutes to hobble to the Senior Center. Once above ground, I would have to use caution and stick to the exact route he had drawn for me last night.

Last night. We hadn't remained long in the storage compartment after hearing the hatch door slam shut. Dedrick had helped me out and over to one of the bunk beds.

I wouldn't have found better care for my ankle at any Regimen hospital. He tore open every cabinet and all the plastic bags on the bunk beds until he found everything he needed for treatment. Soon I had pillows behind my back and folded blankets propping up my foot. He held a chemical cold pack to my ankle for twenty minutes and later wrapped it with elastic wrap bandages, his gentleness making him all that more masculine to me.

I expected to see anger in his eyes, or at least irritation. Either he masked it well or he didn't blame me for any of this.

I blamed myself. My impatience to rescue Abby brought this trouble. The Mosheh did nothing in haste. They planned everything, down to the smallest detail. That was the reason he couldn't rescue me sooner, the reason I had to wait so unbearably long. They didn't just rescue a person. They considered everything, including the Regimen's response. They created diversions and planted clues for the Regimen to follow, clues that led them away from the colonies.

My crutches came down with a splash and one of them slipped.

I lost balance, jerked to one side, and dropped my foot to the ground. Pain shot through my leg. I groaned but the way the tunnel carried it, it didn't sound like my voice. It didn't sound human. I shifted my weight to my good side and twisted the flashlight.

The trail of water had widened to a dark puddle, stretching across two-thirds the width of the tunnel floor. A few meters farther, black water covered the entire width. How deep would it get before I reached the blue ladder?

I let go of the flashlight, letting it dangle again. My foot throbbed. After reaching Abby, I would get to safety, lie down, and elevate my leg, maybe even get something for the pain. Dedrick had given me a different route for my retreat. He had everything planned.

While I had lain helpless in a bunk bed, he had left the bunker several times to contact the Mosheh. The phone wouldn't pick up a signal in the bunker. "Get some rest," he had told me whenever I asked what they said. "We'll go over the plan in the morning."

Sleep came in fits and starts. I dreamed of tools slipping from my greasy hands, gears too worn to make contact, liquid dripping from a gasket too brittle to seal. At least twice, I woke to a sound I couldn't make sense of, the sound of a handsaw slicing through wood. It wasn't until morning that I understood.

Dedrick woke me before dawn. "How's your ankle?" He sat on the edge of the bed, crude crutches made from the bunk bed railing on his lap.

I pushed myself up and touched the wrappings on my ankle. My ankle felt numb and a little sore. "What are those?" I stared at the crutches.

"Can't you tell?" He stood and stuffed the ends of the crutches under his arms. Bending one leg, he took a few steps. "See?"

"Wow. They're nice. Did you get any sleep at all?" I glanced at my wrist, though I hadn't had a flexi-phone or even a watch in months. "What time is it?"

He sat on the edge of the bed again. "It's early. But we need to get an early start. Abby goes outside in the morning, and you need to be there. You'll need to wear this." He handed me a long black jacket. "They're on the lookout for our capes. Keep the hood up."

Next, he had given me the details of the plan, saying *you* and not *we* with every step. "The Regimen has their eyes on your roommate and everyone they consider to be your friend, but they aren't watching Abby or the Senior Center. Yet. When they can't find you, they'll widen their search. So you need to get to her quickly."

"What about you? You're not coming with me?"

He averted his gaze. Worry showed in the wrinkle between his brows. "I need to get back to the Mosheh. We need to close certain points and secure others. And we have to send a signal to the nearest colonies so they can prepare in case . . . And now that the Regimen discovered our counter surveillance, we have to generate another plan for moving around unnoticed."

My eyes welled with tears. This was my fault. "I'm sorry—"

"Don't worry. You need to get Abby." He stood and handed me the crutches. "Still got the pill she'll need to take?"

"Yes, I—"

Water sloshed into my boot, cool and murky, forcing me back to the present moment. *How much farther?*

I grabbed the flashlight and directed the beam to the darkness before me.

Either the tunnel got lower ahead, or the water deepened. Plastic bottles and other garbage floated against the brick walls. A long section of wall appeared darker than the rest. The ladder! The blue ladder!

I dropped the flashlight, letting it swing down to its useless position, and waded to the ladder. I would've passed it if not for the water splashing into my boot. With the crutches in one hand and gripping a cold bar of the ladder with the other, I hoisted myself up. I used the crutches and my good foot to climb, simply resting on the sprained foot, taking a step at a time.

The rungs went up higher than I could see. Light from the flashlight danced on the water below me but darkness loomed above.

Another step— My boot slipped. I tightened my grip and leaned into the ladder. Heart pounding and with greater caution, I stepped again and again and again.

Soon darkness surrounded me. I reached the last rung. I must've climbed over ten meters. Dedrick had told me, once reaching the top, to look for the wall that had a few yellow bricks. I had to push two bricks, the one in the third row from the top, fifth from the left, and the other, seven bricks diagonal from that. He said a secret door would open.

I didn't want to look down, but I needed the flashlight.

Standing on one foot and clinging to a rail, I stuffed the crutches safely between my body and the ladder. I reached down to where the dangling flashlight tapped against my knee. My finger brushed it. I wrapped my fingers around the handle and tugged.

The flashlight was stuck. While still tied to one crutch, it had fallen behind a rung of the ladder. I had grabbed it from the wrong side of the ladder. Without the rope attaching it to the crutches, I'd have it. I gave it one last yank, hoping to get it loose from the rope. When that didn't work, I let go. It banged against the wall, gave a jerk, and slipped . . . down.

"No!" I reached in vain. Clinging to the ladder, I peered down just as it splashed into the black water far below. A greenish glow showed where it now rested under the water.

My muscles tensed. Pitch-blackness surrounded me. Now what? Which wall did I want? How would I find the yellow bricks?

I touched the wall in front of me: brick. Maybe the others weren't made of brick. I stretched my arm out and touched the wall to my left: brick. The wall to my right: brick. Even the wall behind me was brick.

Filled with frustration, I sighed. Here I stood, one-legged on a ladder in the dark, ten meters above filthy sewer water, surrounded by brick walls.

The idea of groping around blindly, counting bricks and rows under the watchful eyes of the creatures that lived in dark places, made me shudder. I had to it. I couldn't waste any more time. I couldn't miss Abby's morning stroll.

I put my hand to the bricks at eyelevel and traced a path upward and to my left, searching for the corner. I would try every wall.

My fingertips brushed rough brick. The brick crumbled in places. I reached higher and higher. I stretched, reaching and groping, and then pushed my fingers into something soft and cottony. If felt like a—

A spider's web! Gagging, I jerked my hand back and wiped it on my jacket.

Something the size of a small stone fell . . . dropped . . . leaped . . . onto my head.

I yelped. Whisked my hand through my hair. Was it alive? A spider? A crumb of brick?

My body trembled. The trembling spread from head to toe. I swooned. With a gasp, I leaned into the ladder and gripped the rung.

Eyes wide, peering into darkness, clinging to the ladder, I tried to regulate my breathing. *I had to do this.* I took a deep breath and let it out slowly. *I could do this.*

I reached again, sunk my fingers into the cottony web and found the top corner of the wall. Running my finger along the bricks, feeling for their edges, I counted: third row, fifth from the left. I pushed the brick.

Nothing. It wouldn't budge.

I pushed the bricks above and below it, then the bricks on each side.

Nothing. This was not the wall. I had to try another one.

~~~

"Well, you must've found something there." Dr. Supero sat alone in the private surveillance room, feet propped on a desktop, Liberty's notebook on his lap. He could not be wrong about this. They had to have gone to the underground bunker.
~~~

Videos of Liberty showed on every monitor on the wall, old videos that might give some clue as to where she had gone: Liberty at home, showing the brief moments she strolled through the living room and past the hidden camera in the standard-issue wall television. . . . Liberty at the Senior Center, crouched under the kitchen sink in one image, helping old people in others images. Liberty had spent a considerable amount of time with an old man who had recently died. Who was he? Could he have been connected to the anarchists? . . . Liberty sitting at a table with a grumpy old woman. Most of the video in the database showed Liberty strolling alone down back alleys and less-traveled streets. What of the alleys with no surveillance? Much of her time had not been captured with surveillance cameras.

Chief Varden's voice bellowed over a speaker on the desk. "The place has been ransacked, every cabinet and storage container opened and rooted through. Expired canned goods, bedding, seeds, even a gun cartridge. There's sawdust or something all over the floor. The place is a wreck."

"What about a secret storage or a clue as to where they could've gone?"

"You're assuming they came here to this underground bunker. We don't know that. We have nothing proving they did."

Supero slammed his feet to the floor, sitting upright. "We have her notebook," he shouted, leaning toward the speaker. "She discovered that bomb shelter. She and her friends. They uncovered it the day they went out with shovels. You could get no one to say a word about the place in your interrogations. But the place has some significance. I am certain that, as soon as the Unity Troopers blared their sirens, she would've fled to it. She and that man, that Dedrick."

"I don't know what to tell you, Doctor. She's not here. We found a secret storage, if you want to call it that. Has a power generator and a water purifier. Supplies. No girl. And no Dedrick. But if you want, we can—"

Supero tapped the control panel, ending the conversation. He glared at one and then another monitor on the wall. "Where have you gone, my little anarchist?" He sneered, his gaze moving from one image to another.

"You were outside the boundaries. You were free. Why have you come back? Out of supplies? Did you find that living free without the aid of the Regimen was a bit more than you bargained for?" Chief Varden had ordered security details to the unsavory markets that had previously operated without working surveillance cameras. If Liberty and Dedrick had gone for supplies, perhaps they would catch them.

Still studying the images, he grimaced, shook his head and huffed. "Your ideas are poison. They have poisoned you, and you will not find the cure unless you return to Aldonia repentant. You want to choose the direction of your own life. You will meet with failure. The smartest minds have built our society. You need the Regimen."

His gaze lingered on a video of the Senior Center. Liberty sat across the table from the grumpy old woman she often sat with. A bag lay on the table. Liberty pulled something from the bag and slid it to the old woman.

Supero leaned and squinted to get a better look. *What is that she is giving to the old woman?* He glanced at the control panel, tapped the number of the monitor to control the image, and brushed his hand over the zoom control. *Who is that woman?*

Supero sat back, his mind turning on a thought. He reached for the landline, the direct line to the Unity Troopers.

~~~

The brick sunk into the wall.

My eyes watered. I laughed. I did it! This was the third wall I had tried. Something had bitten me as I groped the second wall, and I did not want to try the wall behind me. I would've had to really stretch to reach the top corner. And how would I get through the door once it opened, me with my sprained ankle?

I rubbed my fingertips diagonally along the rough wall, from the sunken brick, down and to the right, counting for the seventh brick. Finding it, I pushed the heel of my hand against it. The brick sunk in a wee bit. I shoved harder. It sunk in further. Something within the wall clicked and then creaked.

My heart pounded with delight.

The wall, a square meter just above the top rung of the ladder, moved back, slowly at first. Then it began scraping to the side with the sound of
~~~

grumbling gears. Dim light streamed in through the widening doorway. Dedrick had said the door would open completely, pause two seconds and close.

The opening grew wide enough for me, about half way, so I lifted the crutches and shoved them through. Then, favoring my sore leg and clinging to the threshold, I climbed the last few rungs of the ladder and crawled through the doorway and into a dimly lit shed. The wall stopped moving. I could almost picture the gears and levers at work. Two seconds later, gears groaned and the door began to close.

I got to my knees, grabbed the crutches and heaved myself up. I had wasted too much time in the sewer and then more time trying to get out. I needed to hurry.

Dedrick had said I'd end up in a Regimen storage unit. The place smelled of grass and petrol, which struck me as odd since they claimed to use only clean energy. Light crept in under a narrow garage door and shone on a disorganized arrangement of utility and lawn equipment, including a riding lawnmower, a narrow street cleaner, and a scooter.

I went to a panel on the wall by the garage door, ready to enter the code Dedrick had given me. I had a ten-minute walk to the Senior Center. If I stuck to the route he had given me, I would avoid working cameras—he hoped. A ten-minute walk . . . I had probably wasted more than ten minutes trying to find the hidden door. Would Abby still be outside? What if she wasn't?

I punched the code and glanced over my shoulder . . . at the scooter.

As the garage door rolled up, I donned the shades Dedrick had given me, dumped the crutches, and jumped onto the scooter.

~~~

I stuck to the route Dedrick had mapped for me. Within minutes, the tall backside of the Senior Living and Recreation Center came into view. My return trip would not take me this way, so I abandoned the scooter in an alley and hobbled across the street. I would have to do without crutches and without the scooter. I would have to limp for the rest of my journey and find rest only at its end.

The leaves of the solitary tree in the strip of grass behind the center had turned orange and brown. A high brown composite fence wrapped
~~~

around the side and back of the center, preventing me from seeing Abby—if she was there.

As I limped closer, my gaze rested on the leaves and a nostalgic feeling overcame me. Abby and I had sat on a bench near that tree before I left Aldonia. My hand went to my chest, to the tarnished silver medal under my shirt. Abby had given it to me. "I'll wear it always," I'd told her. I pulled it out of the shirt so that she would see that I had kept my promise, so she would know I had not forgotten her. Abby's blue-green eyes, sparkling in the sunlight, came to mind . . . the hint of a smile she had given me . . .

Reaching the service gate, I yanked it open and slipped onto the property of the Senior Center. A driveway sloped from the gate to a wide garage door on the side of the building. I hobbled along the edge of the driveway, toward the building. From there, I had to keep close to the building, to avoid the cameras. Pressing a hand to the wall, to lessen the weight on my sprain, I edged to the back corner, to the spot Dedrick had instructed me to take when I spoke with Abby. I peeked around the corner.

A sprinkling of brown and orange leaves lay on the strip of grass and on the empty sidewalks and benches. Abby wasn't here. An outdoor clock hung on the back wall, over one of the doors.

My heart sank. I was too late.

Now what? *Do I abandon my mission and make my retreat?* It wouldn't take long to get to the underground entry point Dedrick had wanted me to use. But, then, I did have the hand phone. Dedrick had warned against using it. If I called Abby and she said my name, traffic analysis programs would tag our conversation. The Regimen would find me. What else could I do? She wasn't here. I couldn't just give up.

I pulled the phone from my pocket and made the call. I had called her flexi-phone many times in the past, so I tapped out her number without a second thought.

The moment's wait felt like minutes. Then her voice sounded through the phone, and I almost cried.

"Don't say my name, Abby." I spoke without pausing to keep her from giving the natural response of saying my name. "I know you recognize my voice, but you can't say my name. Just listen. I have to see you."

"Okay, then. Is everything all right? Where are you?"

"I'm here. I'm outside, out back where you walk in the morning. I need to talk to you."

"Okay, then." She paused. "Did you want me to come out back?"

"Yes, yes, and hurry!"

"Okay, my dear Li—"

"Don't say it! Just come." I stuffed the phone into my pocket and leaned against the building.

The next moment felt longer than any I had experienced on this journey. A camera hung over my head, swiveling from side to side, taking in every falling leaf and silent bench, unaware of me. Sirens sounded in the distance. Could they be for me? No. The Regimen would not know of my visit here. Unless a surveillance camera had caught me. Unless someone had figured out my friendship with Abby. No, I couldn't believe that. I would succeed. Abby would live free.

My foot throbbed with pain. The boot cut into my skin. Oh, how I wanted to slide to the ground, peel the boot off my swollen foot and let it rest. "Hurry, Abby."

Finally, a sliding sound came from around the corner.

I leaned and peeked. *Abby!*

The door slid shut behind her. Her eyes made a quick sweep of the area and then found me.

Standing with the weight on my good leg, I yanked the shades from my face and motioned her over. What would I say to her? How could I convince her with so little time?

Abby gazed upward at the leaves of the tree as she strolled to me. Her behavior would appear natural to anyone who watched the live feed from the camera: just an old woman outside, enjoying nature in the little patch of freedom permitted her. She came to the corner, out of camera range, and her gaze swiveled to me. "Liberty?"

I smiled but resisted the urge to hug her. "It's me. I don't have much time."

"I miss you, dear girl. None of the other aids care." A smile flickered on her lips and faded. "Something's wrong. You shouldn't be here. You should be at that Breeder—"

"Listen, Abby. You have to listen. I want to rescue you from this place. Life doesn't have to be like this, with every detail under the Regimen's control. You can live free, live with people who love you, make your own choices, and . . . and . . ." What could I say to convince her? "You can get medical care without having to worry about never coming back from the hospital."

Her blue-green eyes shifted, her thoughts probably going to Richter as mine just did.

I dug into my pocket and withdrew the box. "I can't explain everything now, but I've experienced this other way of life. People live in families. They believe in God." My heart stirred. I don't know when or how it happened, and I had much to learn, but I almost believed in God.

Her eyes snapped back to mine. "Families? God?"

"I came back for you, Abby. I risked everything to do it." I took her hand and pressed the box into her palm. "Go to your room. Take the pill in this box and press your emergency button. If you can talk, tell them you think you've had a heart attack. You'll fall asleep. And when you wake . . ." I could hardly get the next words out. ". . . you'll be with me. You'll be safe."

She stared at the box in her hand. "I don't know what you're saying. What do you mean? What will this pill do to me? How can I—"

Sirens shattered the silence. Orange and blue lights flashed on the other side of the high fence.

My breath caught in my throat. They found me. The Regimen Unity Troopers.

I turned to Abby. "I have to go. Go inside now. And do what I said." I stepped away from her, taking a few steps along the wall.

She glanced from me to the fence and back to me. "I can't take this." She held out the box. "I don't know what it will do to me."

I dashed back to her and closed her fingers over the box. My eyes welled with tears as I spoke. "Please, please take it. Trust me. It'll be okay."

I wouldn't be with her, now that they had found me, but she could still be safe and live in freedom.

The service gate and a second gate, one closer to us, flung open. Unity Troopers poured onto the grounds, three at each door, their sleek black tasers leveled at me.

"Don't move!"

"Put your hands up."

"Return to the facility, old woman." A trooper motioned with his weapon.

I looked at Abby, begging her with my eyes.

Abby shook her head, sorrow and confusion in her expression. She backed away.

Grief overtook me. And failure. I slid down the wall and stretched out my throbbing leg. I wanted to take the boot off, alleviate some of the pain. Would they shoot me if I did? I reached for the buckle on the side.

The troopers fanned out. Two of them bolted to me. One spoke into his wrist phone. "Retina scans positive. We have her."

20

Gray helicopters flew in formation over the high electric Boundary Fence. More than half of the helicopters continued over the treetops, shrinking until they disappeared. The others hovered over the thin strip of ground between the tree line and the electric fence. Their bellies opened and ropes dropped down. Troopers armed with rifles slid down the ropes. They descended upon the Fully-Protected Nature Preserves.

I sat alone at a small table in a gray interrogation room, my back to the door, my face to an array of video images on a glassy wall. My ankle ached and my face stung. The smell of dirt, sweat, and blood filled my nostrils. Earlier, in this same room, I had endured hours of interrogation.

The video images flipped to views of treetops and cloudy sky, live feeds from the Unity Trooper transport helicopters. Within minutes, they covered land that had taken us hours, even days to cross. How long before they reached the Maxwell Colony? Had the Mosheh succeeded in warning them?

Something small moved in one of the images, drawing my attention. A figure ran from the cover of trees through a field, heading for more trees. The image zoomed in on the figure, the girl. Her stringy brown hair and pale skirt fluttered she ran. An instant later, the breeze from the helicopter sent her hair and skirt flapping wildly. With a hand shielding her eyes, she turned her face to the sky. She peered directly into the camera.

My hand shot to my mouth. Tears blurred my vision. *Paula! Dedrick's little sister.*

The camera view zeroed in on her face. Numbers scrolled in the corner of the screen as the Regimen's computer tried to identify her. Paula's brown eyes had not the look of a timid child. They held courage and anger, courage for her present mission, anger that the Regimen dared to threaten life as she knew it. Paula kept running.

"Run, Paula." I steeled myself for her.

Paula crossed the field and reached the cover of trees. A woman dashed onto the field, coming from the direction Paula had come from. *Paula's mother. Dedrick's mother.* She tore off after Paula but then stopped and looked back. Their father emerged from the woods, arms waving, shouting. He glanced from the helicopter to his family.

My heart burst. Why hadn't they made it to the cave? Hadn't Dedrick sent a warning?

A helicopter landed and four Unity Troopers, weapons at the ready, disembarked. The family huddled together at the edge of the woods. Their father kept motioning to someone in the woods, then Dedrick's younger brother Andy stomped into view. He had a rifle in his hands but turned it over at his father's request. His father tossed it to the ground and wrapped his arms around Andy, pulling him into the family huddle. The Unity Troopers surrounded them.

Another figure appeared on a different video image, too far away for me to identify. More and more people appeared in the videos until the entire wall showed images of colonists. The views zoomed in on individual faces. Numbers scrolled in the corners. The computer database would find no record of them. I knew them. Some I knew well. Others I had at least met or had seen across the Dining Hall or around the colony.

A group of teenage boys and grown men stood surrounded by Unity Troopers. They had guns. They had been hunting. They hadn't heard the alarm, hadn't known of the emergency, hadn't fled to safety. The Unity Troopers wore armor like nothing these men had ever seen before, but they could tell that shooting them would avail nothing. All of them laid their guns on the ground and raised their hands, all but one boy. He lifted his rifle and leveled it at a Unity Trooper. Three troopers turned their guns on him.

"Don't do it," I said. I knew the boy. *Rick*. He had attended morning classes with me. His father led hunting expeditions.

Another man emerged from the woods and dashed to the colonists, the priest with the straw hat. Why hadn't he made it to the shelter? Hands up, palms out, he positioned himself between the boy and the troopers.

My heart melted. He was there to offer sacrifice, to sacrifice himself for his people, for the boy.

He shouted something to the troopers then spoke to the boy over his shoulder. The boy shook his head, still clinging to his gun. The priest turned to face him, turned his back to the troopers. As he spoke, the breeze from the helicopter stole his hat, sent it sailing, swirling in the air, but the priest made no effort to retrieve it. He pushed the barrel of the gun down and hugged the boy. The boy collapsed in his arms.

The yellow hat twisted and turned in the air until it landed at a trooper's feet.

Unity Troopers swarmed in, banded the colonists' hands behind their backs and rushed them to gray helicopters, the men and boys, the priest, Dedrick's family, those I'd known well, those that I'd only met. All of them.

Fires began, one here, one there. Houses burned. *Dedrick's house, hidden in a cluster of trees.* We had sat at his table, eating chicken casserole and drinking lemonade, Dedrick's two sisters, Bot, Jessen, and I. It was there that I had begun to learn about families. I saw the concern they each had for the other.

Families. The Regimen would separate the families. They would not let them stay together. Would they? Could they be so cruel?

A fire blazed in the side of a hill. *The Dining Hall.* They found it. Houses and buildings, safe and hidden for so long, now burned to the ground. Black smoke rose in the air, through branches, through leaves of red and gold. Black smoke now hid everything. Had the colonists the time to take needed possessions or irreplaceable mementos? How many had reached the cave? Would the cave be safe?

"Did you really live out there?"

Dr. Supero's arrogant voice came from behind, making my skin crawl. I didn't bother to face him. The video images ripped through me like knives to my heart, but I couldn't look away. I loved these people. Why did this have to happen?

"What kind of life could you have out there, living without technology and resources?" Dr. Supero edged closer. His smirking face came into my peripheral vision. "Did you return for supplies often?"

I had no intention of answering. The Unity Troopers' interrogator and the chief of CSS had already questioned me at length. No matter the technique they used—the bribes, the stern voices, the lies, the physical violence—I said nothing that could get my friends in more trouble. They knew I had gone to see Abby, so I only said I missed her and needed to see her.

With eyes glued to me, Dr. Supero pulled out a nearby chair, turned it around and straddled it. "Your friends must have lived out there for years, scavenging off of nature, living like animals, inbreeding." He paused as if to gauge my response. I was, after all, selected for my superior makeup to be a breeder. Aldonia would produce only the best. Every generation would surpass the next in health, intelligence, and every other desirable quality. One would find no intellectual or physical deficits here. In contrast, the colonists treasured every life, without exception and welcomed the imperfect.

"I do not know how we will integrate all these backwards-thinking individuals into society. Even with re-education . . ."

My gaze snapped to him, fire in my eyes.

". . . it will be difficult."

"You can't. Please. It's not right."

"What is not right?" He shook his head. "Was it right for you, for these people to live in the Fully-Protected Nature Preserves? Those areas are off-limits for a reason. If not for the Regimen stepping in, taking us in a new direction, we would have no forests and natural resources. You people have no respect for the earth. If we had not found you and your rebellious friends, who knows what damage you might've caused."

"What will you do with them?"

He shrugged. It seemed a matter of little importance to him. "I suppose, the youngest will be sent to breeder facilities, the older children to Primary or Secondary, according to their ages. I do not suppose we will place them based on aptitude. We would lack the room in breeder facilities." He smirked. "The adults, after re-education, will be assigned vocations according to their abilities. I understand we've had higher suicide rates these past few years. There should be jobs to fill. They will be given identifications, sterilized, and inserted into society in various locations and communities where they can contribute to the common good. The ill members need suffer no more. They will be taken care of humanely . . . like your friend from the senior center. What was her name? Abby?"

"Abby? What about her? Did something happen to her?"

"The old woman is no longer with us."

"What? What happened to her?" Had she believed me? Had she taken the pill? Or had something else happened? The Regimen had probably questioned her because of . . . my visit. I brought ruin to her. *Oh, Abby, no.*

He continued to speak, but my ears closed to his wicked words. My eyes overflowed with tears that I could not keep at bay. Abby had died. More people I loved would die. Anger flashed inside me. "Those people are innocent! They're hard working. They don't want to hurt anyone. Please, don't separate them. Don't make them go through Re-Ed. Do anything you want to me. Just leave them alone."

"They will not be returned to their homes." Amusement showed in his expression. He flung a hand out in the direction of the wall of videos. "Their homes are burning."

"At least let them live together. Let them live as families. Don't take that away from them. What does the Regimen fear about letting people live in families?"

"Families are an invention of the capitalists of old, a means for mass production, like machines in a factory, the machines you wish to build and repair, machines that nearly devastated the earth. The Regimen has ended that exploitation of women and children through equal opportunity and education. The Regimen has ended the exploitation of the earth."

"Please don't separate them." I grabbed his arm. His violet eyes swiveled at once to my hand, but I did not let go. "Help them."

"I have little say in the matter. The adults will need re-education, just as you do. There is no way around it. But I will see what can be done about the children. If you cooperate with us fully, I will see."

"I will cooperate." If I could save the children from the trauma of Re-Ed, I would cooperate. I dropped my head to the table and let the tears come. So many families separated, forced to live in a society of individualism, a society without sacrifice, without love.

I hoped the Regimen only knew of the Maxwell Colony. Each colony took measures to leave no trail between the others. I had seen no video, heard nothing about any discovery of the underground communities. I hoped nothing would lead the Regimen to them. The Mosheh was careful. Dedrick and the Mosheh had probably destroyed and sealed up any risky entry points. They would be safe. Perhaps, somehow, they could rescue the colonists. It wouldn't happen at once. But some day. Maybe. *Please.*

"Your hopes, your ideas, Liberty . . ." Dr. Supero folded his arms on the back of his chair and leaned down to my level. ". . . they are selfish. You have only yourself in mind. You want the freedom to choose your own path, but you do not consider what it does to the collective, to the world. Have you learned nothing from the sins of our past?"

I shook my head. "You don't know what you're talking about. You want us to be re-educated, but it's you who are brainwashed."

"Brainwashed?" He chuckled and stood up. "Your ways, my dear, lead to failure, utter failure. Ruin has come upon you and your new friends." He walked to the door, tapped the control, and the door slid open.

After a moment of silence, he spoke again. "Do you know what my name means?"

I turned to face him.

"Supero." The corner of his mouth curled up. His violet eyes gleamed. "It means *I conquer.*" He gave a nod and left the room. The door slid shut behind him.

My tears blurred the images on the wall, the images of flame and destruction. My mind grew numb. This could not be happening. It just could not. I closed my eyes and inhaled deeply. "Why," I said to *My Friend.*

I had felt His presence almost continuously since we had neared the fence of the boundaries. He had been with me as I crawled back into Aldonia, as I ran across the pitted field, as I twisted my ankle and continued onward in pain. He had been there in the bunker, not with words, warnings, or ideas, but with His presence. It had comforted me. As I had stumbled through the tunnels in the dark, I knew He was there. He witnessed the agony in my soul when Abby rejected my help, rejected her own freedom, rejected my sacrifice. As I had collapsed to the ground in misery and defeat, as the Unity Troopers laid hands on me and brought me here, He was with me. His presence remained even now. He knew all this would happen. Why?

There is a reason. These words alone He spoke to me. I accepted them. I trusted.

21

Dr. Supero sat in his office, reviewing the file of the last rebel he had examined. He had personally examined every one of the thirty-seven people they had captured. Every one of them was relatively healthy. Some suffered from allergies or headaches, but he had found no diseases or debilitating conditions. One middle-aged man had a long scar on his chest, though he wouldn't reveal the name of his doctor or the reason for the surgery. It probably had something to do with his heart. Did they really perform advanced surgeries out there in the woods?

Dr. Supero rubbed his head on the spot over the cancerous tumor.

The Unity Troopers had utterly destroyed all they found of the rebels' housing and facilities. *Fools.* They should've investigated first.

Supero leaned back and let his gaze travel to an overhead monitor. He'd had his computer system updated so that he could observe several video feeds at once. He wanted to monitor the rebels to see how they adjusted to life under the Regimen. Some would undoubtedly need counseling. Perhaps re-education.

Video from Aldonia's North Primary Residence showed one of the pitiable little girls from the rebel community, Paula 911-051176-21, now, of Aldonia. The Regimen had assigned the warning numbers 911 to every rebel, the easier to keep track of them.

Paula lay face down on a pillow, her stringy brown hair sprawled out around her. A girl sat on the foot of her bed, watching as Paula wept into her pillow. Other girls had gathered to watch the spectacle. Children transitioned into Primary on their fifth birthday. Paula was eight.

"Why don't you stop crying?" the girl on the foot of the bed said, with neither rudeness nor compassion. She merely sounded curious. Every girl cried when she transitioned. But no one cried for days.

Paula sat up and wiped her cheeks. She gave the girl a weak smile and wrapped her arms around her knees. "I miss my family."

"What's a family?" the girl said.

The room grew silent, all eyes on the ideologically-warped little girl.

"I know things are different here, but I have a mom and a dad, a sister and brothers. We lived together. I miss them."

A girl in the growing crowd of spectators giggled, but the others simply stared. "What does that mean," one of them said, "a mom and a dad?"

"Well . . ." Paula looked thoughtful for a moment, and then she began to spread her poison.

Did you enjoy this book? If so, help others enjoy it, too! Please recommend it to friends and leave a review when possible. Thank you!

Every month I send out a newsletter so that you can keep up with my newest releases and enjoy updates, contests, and more. Visit my website www.theresalinden.com to sign up. And while you're there, check out my book trailers and extras!

Facebook: www.facebook.com/theresalindenauthor/
Twitter: @LindenTheresa

ABOUT THE AUTHOR

Theresa Linden is the author of award-winning *Battle for His Soul* and *Roland West, Loner* (Catholic Press Association Book Awards, 2016 & 2017). Raised in a military family, she developed a strong patriotism and a sense of adventure. Her Catholic faith inspires the belief that there is no greater adventure than the reality we can't see, the spiritual side of life. She has eight published novels, including a fast-paced dystopian trilogy that tackles tough moral questions of our day, and two short stories in *Image and Likeness: Literary Reflections on the Theology of the Body* (Full Quiver Publishing). She holds a Catechetical Diploma from Catholic Distance University and is a member of the Catholic Writers Guild and the International Writers Society. A wife, homeschooling mom, and Secular Franciscan, she resides in northeast Ohio with her husband and three teenage boys.

Made in the USA
Monee, IL
17 April 2021